Myths for the Modern Age

MYTHS for the Modern Age

PHILIP JOSÉ FARMER'S

☆ WOLD NEWTON UNIVERSE ☆

Edited by Win Scott Eckert

MYTHS FOR THE MODERN AGE: PHILIP JOSÉ FARMER'S WOLD NEWTON UNIVERSE

A MonkeyBrain Books Publication
www.monkeybrainbooks.com

MonkeyBrain Books
11204 Crossland Drive
Austin, TX 78726
info@monkeybrainbooks.com

ISBN: 1-932265-14-7

Printed in the United States of America
10 9 8 7 6 5 4 3 2 1

Acknowledgements

Special thanks to Michael Croteau of the Official Philip José Farmer Home Page for encouragement, keeping me in touch with Phil and Bette Farmer, and contributing Phil's bio; and to Rick Beaulieu of the Official Philip José Farmer Home Page for his continued support.

Thanks to Chris Roberson of MonkeyBrain Books for his unflagging belief in this book and helping to make it a reality. And for getting John Picacio to knock me out with the drop-dead-gorgeous cover. Thanks John, it brought a tear to my eye.

For years of scholarship, camaraderie, moral support, and friendship, and for many invigorating discussions and gracious debates, which have helped me to solidify and form the direction of the Wold Newton Universe over the years, my deepest appreciation to Dennis Power, Chuck "The Savage Chuck" Loridans, Matthew Baugh, Jess Nevins, Mark Brown, Brad Mengel, John Small, Loki Carbis, Pete Coogan, Jean-Marc Lofficier, Rick Lai, and Art Bollmann.

Special thanks also to the rest of the unusual suspects over at the New Wold Newton Meteoritics Society (NWNMS): Chris Carey, Andrew Henry, Tom Kane, Greg Gick, Vincent Mollet, Cheryl Huttner, Steven Costa, Mike Winkle, I. Ronald Schablotski, Patrick Lozito, Lou Mougin, Jay Lindsey, Andrew McLean, Josh Sager, and George Henry Smathers, Jr., aka "Henry Covert."

To the original Wold Newton Meteoritics Society: Timothy J. Rutt, Todd R. Rutt, Arn McConnell, Kirk McConnell, Clay Powers, and Scott Koeller. Although I did not know it until I was well into my own Wold Newton studies, these gentlemen put out five issues of The Wold Atlas fanzine in 1977 and 1978. They were based in Colorado—as am I—and in one issue expressed their thanks to the folks at Mile High Comics for their support—as do I, almost thirty years later.

To my family: Lisa, Andrew, and my father, Hank, for their love and extraordinary patience.

I cannot exaggerate the enormous debt I—and we all—owe to the NWNMS's Honorary President, Philip José Farmer, without whom *Myths for the Modern Age* would not exist, both literally and figuratively. He is a true scholar and gentleman.

Dedication

In memory of my mother, Joan "Jorie" Scott and my grandmother, Juantia "Benny" Dyer

For Lisa, whose secret identity in the Wold Newton Universe is "The Book Widow"… Always, my rock—or in this case, Meteor—in this, and all possible universes

And for Philip José Farmer

Contents

Frontispiece

Wold Newton is a small village in the East Riding of Yorkshire County, England. It is chiefly famous for a meteorite which struck near it in 1795, the exact location of impact being marked by a monument which tourists, or anybody else, may see now. At the moment it struck, two large coaches with fourteen passengers and four coachmen were within a few yards of it. All were exposed to the ionization accompanying meteorites. The descendants of all those in or on the coaches include an extraordinary number of great crime fighters, scientists, and explorers. So many, in fact, that the only reasonable explanation is that the meteorite caused a beneficial mutation of genes in those exposed.

The mutated genes were reinforced, kept from being lost, by the inbreeding of the descendants of those present at Wold Newton… Some of their descendants were more than extraordinary; they bordered on, and in some cases attained, the status of superman.
—“The Fabulous Family Tree of Doc Savage (Another Excursion into Creative Mythography)”
Doc Savage: His Apocalyptic Life, Philip José Farmer

[The meteor strike was] the single cause of this nova of genetic splendor, this outburst of great detectives, scientists, and explorers of exotic worlds, this last efflorescence of true heroes in an otherwise degenerate age.
—“A Case of a Case of Identity Recased, or, The Grey Eyes Have It”
Tarzan Alive: A Definitive Biography of Lord Greystoke, Philip José Farmer

Myths for the Modern Age

Farmer's Wold Newton Family and Shared Universe

By Win Scott Eckert

The Wold Newton Concept

The Wold Newton Family is a group of heroic and villainous literary figures that science fiction author Philip José Farmer postulated belonged to the same genetic family. Some of these characters are adventurers, some are detectives, some explorers and scientists, some espionage agents, and some are evil geniuses.

According to Mr. Farmer, the Wold Newton Family originated when a radioactive meteor landed in Wold Newton, England, a village in the Yorkshire Wolds, on December 13, 1795. (The meteor landing is a real historical event.) The meteor's ionized radiation caused a genetic mutation in those present, which endowed many of their descendants with extremely high intelligence and strength, as well as an exceptional capacity and drive to perform good, or, as the case may be, evil deeds. Additionally, some of the ancestors of those present at the 1795 meteor strike were extraordinary individuals, and so their genetic stock was excellent to begin with.

Popular characters who Philip José Farmer concluded were members of the Wold Newton Family (both pre- and post-meteor strike) include: Solomon Kane; Captain Blood; The Scarlet Pimpernel; Harry Flashman; C. Auguste Dupin; Sherlock Holmes and his nemesis Professor Moriarty (aka Captain Nemo); Phileas Fogg; The Time Traveler; Allan Quatermain; Tarzan and his son Korak; A.J. Raffles; Arsène Lupin; Professor Challenger; Richard Hannay; Bulldog Drummond; the evil Doctor Fu Manchu and his adversary, Sir Denis Nayland Smith; G-8; Lord Peter Wimsey; The Shadow; Sam Spade; Doc Savage, his cousin Pat Savage, and one of his five assistants, Monk Mayfair; The Spider; Nero Wolfe; Mr. Moto; The Avenger; Philip Marlowe; James Bond; Lew Archer; and Travis McGee.

The roots of some of Farmer's ideas can be traced to Professor H.W. Starr's articles "A Submersible Subterfuge, or, Proof Impositive" (included as an addendum to Farmer's *The Other Log of Phileas Fogg*) and "A Case of Identity, or, The Adventure of the Seven Claytons" (included as an addendum to Farmer's *Tarzan Alive*).

It should also be noted that, although Farmer incorporated the theory that Sherlock Holmes and Nero Wolfe are father and son in his Wold Newton mythology, he was not the first to advance this hypothesis. For a more expansive treatment of Holmes and Wolfe, the reader is referred to William S. Baring-Gould's *Sherlock Holmes of Baker Street* and *Nero Wolfe of West Thirty-Fifth Street.*

Further Ruminations on the Nature of an Expanded Wold Newton Universe

(with Dennis E. Power)

Canon vs. Pastiche

Myths for the Modern Age: Philip José Farmer's Wold Newton Universe Universe is a work of fiction (or metafiction) which uses as a foundation the works of Philip José Farmer: *Tarzan Alive, Doc Savage: His Apocalyptic Life, The Other Log of Phileas Fogg, The Adventure of the Peerless Peer*, and many others. Farmer's works, in turn, are an extension of the type of scholarship propounded by W.S. Baring-Gould, H.W. Starr, and other Holmesians. These works by Mr. Farmer are certainly non-canonical, in that they are not accepted, approved, or endorsed by any of the original authors (Doyle, Dent, Burroughs, Verne, and so on). They are pastiche.

Since Farmer wrote pastiches in the course of his Wold Newton works, one is unquestionably free to continue using pastiche to expand the WNU. Each work added to the *Crossover Chronology*, pastiche or not, is carefully evaluated on a case-by-case basis. Many works fit into continuity; those that do not will be listed in Addendum 2 to the *Chronology*: *Alternate Universe Crossovers, Parodies, and Farces*.

The same holds true regarding integrating ideas or characters from the efflorescence of Wold Newton articles which came in the wake of the posting of the first Wold Newton website, Win Eckert's *An Expansion of Philip José Farmer's Wold Newton Universe*. They are evaluated and added to the *Crossover Chronology* on a case-by-case basis. As long as any additions made to the *Chronology*, and to an expanded Wold Newton Universe in general, are logical in the context of the work and the WNU, then the "canon vs. pastiche" question is secondary.

The "Real" World

One question that garners periodic discussion among Wold Newton game-players is that of whether Mr. Farmer's works (and by extension, an expanded WNU) take place in the "real world" or not. The answer, as with so many ultimately unanswerable questions, is "Yes and no."

Anyone who has read Farmer's seminal Wold Newton fictional biography, *Tarzan Alive*, understands that he followed in the Holmesian tradition of treating his subject as a real person who actually lived. That premise works very well in *Tarzan Alive*; so well, in fact, that the book is sometimes shelved in the non-fiction section. However, those who have carefully and scrupulously reviewed the remainder of Mr. Farmer's Wold Newton works, including his follow-up fictional biography, *Doc Savage: His Apocalyptic Life*, understand that he moved rapidly away from this confining literary pretense. Even *Tarzan Alive* departs from reality with its contention that Tarzan is immortal, as well as the inclusion of Doyle's Professor Challenger stories. Arguments that his other Wold Newton-related writings, such as *The Other Log of Phileas Fogg*, "After King Kong Fell," "The Freshman" (a Cthulhu Mythos tale) and "The Problem of the Sore Bridge—Among Others," take place in the "real world," are utterly unconvincing.[1]

Of course Mr. Farmer's original intention was to take his favorite literature and relate it to the world in which we live, and he did it so convincingly that many enthusiastic readers of *Tarzan Alive* actually searched for the Greystokes in Burke's *Peerage*. Farmer is ever the trickster, and there is much to admire in his audacity. Yet, in the end, when one tries to force the fantastic into the real world, it undergoes a transformation from gold into base matter. In doing so, the original material can suffer for it. In *Tarzan Alive,* for example, several of the lost civilizations that Tarzan visits are said to be mostly fictionalized by Edgar Rice Burroughs, in that they were never quite as large or grand as depicted. Several canonical Tarzan novels were rendered "fictional" primarily because they could not have happened in the real world. *Tarzan and the Ant Men* and *Tarzan at the Earth's Core* are prime examples of this.[2]

Yet Mr. Farmer did not use this literary tactic to a great extent in *Doc Savage: His Apocalyptic Life.* He did not analyze the Lost Cities or supervillains to make them fit better into the real world, as he had done in *Tarzan Alive,* but rather reported adventures as they happened. In his genealogy for Doc, he also added fantasy elements through Manuel of Poictesme and horror aspects through Lovecraft's Robert Blake. He did not bother to force these elements into the real world. Perhaps he intended to do so eventually, but he never did.[3] Even his inclusion of the pulp hero The Spider (Richard Wentworth) in the Wold Newton Family tree begs the question whether the Wold Newton Universe can be the real world.[4] And his narrative Wold Newton fiction, such as *The*

Other Log of Phileas Fogg, and "After King Kong Fell" doesn't even touch on the real world approach.

Farmer's movement away from the confining non-fiction real world literary premise has lead many WNU game-players, who have chosen to work together to reach consensus on many Wold Newton issues, to treat the WNU as a parallel universe. Farmer's genealogies, as he established and modified them in *Tarzan Alive, Doc Savage: His Apocalyptic Life, The Other Log of Phileas Fogg* and *The Lavalite World,* are used without attempting to shoehorn the characters into the "real" world, thus allowing some fantastical elements to be added if they make sense in conjunction with the rest of the Universe's continuity. This approach allows one to work with Mr. Farmer's genealogies and still allows Tarzan and Doc to have all the adventures ascribed to them by their creators and later writers. In homage to Farmer's *Tarzan Alive*, the WNU is a parallel universe that mirrors and emulates the real world as much as reasonably possible, without being compulsively, obsessively strict about it. Strictness would, after all, take all the fun and joy out of the Wold Newton speculative game.

The history of the Wold Newton Universe is oddly parallel, but often different, to that of the real world. It is a place where the laws of physics, as stated in our universe, do not necessarily apply, so that the laws of thermodynamics and the cube square law are sometimes suspended, perhaps by an Act of Congress. It is a place where costumed vigilantes are often seen, but not too many superheroes. Magic sometimes works, but it worked much better in ancient and unknown prehistory, before the advent of the scientific era. The undead live, New York and Tokyo are just not fun places to live, there are lots of immortals, time travel is possible, men have malleable flesh, and some canines have the power of human speech… And we would not have it any other way.

Bibliography of Philip José Farmer's Wold Newton Works

Normally the bibliography comes at the end of the book. However, before diving into *Myths for the Modern Age*, one might find it helpful to know exactly what books and stories comprise Philip José Farmer's original Wold Newton mythology, and so I have placed it here. There is no better place to start than with Farmer's two pseudo-biographies:

- *Tarzan Alive: A Definitive Biography of Lord Greystoke*. Garden City, NY: Doubleday & Co., 1972. New York: Popular Library, 1976. New

York: Playboy Paperbacks, 1981. Lincoln, NE: University of Nebraska Press Bison Books, 2006.
- *Doc Savage: His Apocalyptic Life*. Garden City, NY: Doubleday & Co., 1973. New York: Bantam Books, 1975. New York: Playboy Paperbacks, 1981.

Beyond *Tarzan Alive* and *Doc Savage*, Mr. Farmer further expanded on his Wold Newton mythology in several novels, short stories and articles (many written under pseudonyms, as though authored by fictional characters who are themselves writers):

- *The Adventure of the Peerless Peer, by John H. Watson, M.D.* Boulder, CO: The Aspen Press, 1974; New York: Dell Books, 1976. Due to copyright issues, Farmer was forced to remove Tarzan from this novel when it was republished as *The Adventure of the Three Madmen* in the anthology *The Grand Adventure*, Berkley Books, 1984.
- "After King Kong Fell." *The Grand Adventure*. New York:Berkley Books, 1984. Reprinted in *The Best of Philip José Farmer*. Burton, MI: Subterranean Press, 2005.
- "Doc Savage and the Cult of the Blue God." *Pearls from Peoria*. Middlesex: The Rose Press, 2005. A screenplay by Farmer for the second, and unmade, Doc Savage feature film. The screenplay was originally titled "Doc Savage: Archenemyof Evil."
- "The Doge Whose Barque Was Worse Than His Bight." *Fantasy & Science Fiction*, November 1976. Reprinted in *Pearls from Peoria*. Middlesex: The Rose Press, 2005. The second Ralph von Wau Wau tale by Jonathan Swift Somers III. Farmer began a third Ralph von Wau Wau tale, "Who Stole Stonehenge?" which remains unfinished.
- *Escape from Loki: Doc Savage's First Adventure*. New York: Bantam Books, 1991.Young Doc Savage's first adventure.
- "Evil, Be My Good." *The Ultimate Frankenstein*. Byron Preiss, 1991. New York: iBooks, 2003. Reprinted in *Pearls from Peoria*. Middlesex: The Rose Press, 2005. Farmer refers to Frankenstein's experiments in *Doc Savage: His Apocalyptic Life*; a Frankenstein tale by Farmer likely takes place in the Wold Newton Universe.
- "An Exclusive Interview with Lord Greystoke." *The Book of Philip José Farmer*.New York: DAW Books, 1973. Revised editionNew York: Berkley Books, 1982. Reprinted in *The Best of Philip José Farmer*. Burton, MI: Subterranean Press, 2005. Reprinted in *Tarzan* Alive. Lincoln, NE: University of Nebraska Press Bison Books, 2006.
- "Extracts from the Memoirs of 'Lord Greystoke.'" *Mother Was a Lovely Beast*. New York:Pyramid Books, 1976. Reprinted in *Tarzan* Alive. Lincoln, NE: University of Nebraska Press Bison Books, 2006.
- "The Face that Launched a Thousand Eggs." *Farmerphile: The*

Magazine of Philip José Farmer n1, Michael Croteau, ed., July 2005. Tim Howller, the protagonist, is undoubtedly the same Tim Howller who appeared in "After King Kong Fell."

- *Flight to Opar*. New York: DAW Books, 1976.
- "The Freshman." *The Book of Philip José Farmer.* New York: Berkley Books, 1982. Reprinted in *Tales of the Cthulhu Mythos.* New York: Del Rey Books, 1998.
- *Hadon of Ancient Opar*. New York: DAW Books, 1974.
- *Ironcastle*. J.H. Rosny, translated and retold in English by Philip José Farmer.New York:DAW Books, 1976. Farmer added some Wold Newton connections.
- "The Last Rise of Nick Adams." *The Book of Philip José Farmer*.New York: Berkley Books, 1982.
- "Nobody's Perfect." *The Ultimate Dracula*. Byron Preiss, 1991. New York: iBooks, 2003. Reprinted in *Pearls from Peoria*. Middlesex: The Rose Press, 2005. Farmer refers to a member of the Van Helsing family in *Doc Savage: His Apocalyptic Life*; a Dracula story by Farmer likely takes place in the Wold Newton Universe.
- "The Obscure Life and Hard Times of Kilgore Trout." *The Book of Philip José Farmer*.,New York: DAW Books, 1973. Revised editionNew York: Berkley Books, 1982.
- *The Other Log of Phileas Fogg*. New York: DAW Books, 1973. New York: Tor Books, 1982.
- "The Problem of the Sore Bridge - Among Others." *Fantasy & Science Fiction*, September 1975. Reprinted in *Riverworld and Other Stories*. New York: Berkley Books, 1979. Reprinted in *Sherlock Holmes Through Time and Space*. Isaac Asimov, Martin Greenberg, and Charles Waugh, eds. New York: Bluejay Books, 1984. A Holmes—Raffles pastiche by Harry "Bunny" Manders.
- "A Scarletin Study." *Fantasy & Science Fiction*, March 1975. Reprinted in *Sherlock Holmes Through Time and Space*, Isaac Asimov, Martin Greenberg, and Charles Waugh, eds. New York: Bluejay Books, 1984. Reprinted in *Pearls from Peoria*. Middlesex: The Rose Press, 2005. The first Ralph von Wau Wau tale by Jonathan Swift Somers III.
- "Skinburn." *Fantasy & Science Fiction*, October 1972. Reprinted in*The Book of Philip José Farmer*. New York: DAW Books, 1973. Revised editionNew York: Berkley Books, 1982. An adventure of Kent Lane, the son of The Shadow and Margo Lane.
- *Stations of the Nightmare*. New York: Tor Books, 1982. Leo Queequeeg Tincrowder, a Wold Newton Family member and cousin of Kilgore Trout, is a supporting character.
- *The Dark Heart of Time: A Tarzan Novel:*. New York: Del Rey Books, 1999.
- *Time's Last Gift*. New York: Del Rey Books, 1972.Revised edition New York: Del Rey Books, 1977. Note that the abbreviation of this title,

TLG, hints at the true identity of the main character -- Tarzan, Lord Greystoke.

- *Venus on the Half-Shell.* New York: Dell Books, 1975. This book, written by Wold Newton Family member Kilgore Trout, mentions Jonathan Swift Somers III and his epic biographies of Ralph von Wau Wau, making it one possible future of the Wold Newton Universe.
- "The Volcano." *Fantasy & Science Fiction*, February 1976. Reprinted in *Riverworld and Other Stories*.New York:Berkley Books, 1979. A short story by Paul Chapin, who once met Wold Newton Family member Nero Wolfe, in Goodwin and Stout's *The League of Frightened Men*. In "The Volcano," private detective Curtius Parry works with a reporter named Edward Malone. This is likely the same Malone from Sir Arthur Conan Doyle's Professor Challenger stories.
- *The Wind Whales of Ishmael.* Ace Books, 1971. While Mr. Farmer makes no explicit Wold Newton connection in this sequel to Herman Melville's *Moby Dick*, later research has established that the events of *Moby Dick* do take place in the Wold Newton Universe. Therefore I feel justified in including Mr. Farmer's sequel in this list.
- *The World of Tiers* series, various publishers, 1965-1993. A Wold Newton Family member, Paul Janus "Kickaha" Finnegan, is one of the main characters in this series.

Additionally, there are several Wold Newton-related articles by Mr. Farmer, which appeared in various journals or fanzines over the years, and which have not been reprinted in book form until the present volume:

- "The Arms of Tarzan." *Burroughs Bulletin* No. 22, Summer 1971. Also reprinted in *Pearls from Peoria*. Middlesex: The Rose Press, 2005.
- "A Reply To 'The Red Herring.'" *ERBANIA* No. 28, December 1971. Also reprinted in *Pearls from Peoria*. Middlesex: The Rose Press, 2005.
- "The Two Lord Ruftons." *Baker Street Journal*, December 1971. Also reprinted in *Pearls from Peoria*. Middlesex: The Rose Press, 2005.
- "The Great Korak-Time Discrepancy." *ERB-dom* No. 57, April 1972. Also reprinted in *Pearls from Peoria*. Middlesex: The Rose Press, 2005.
- "The Lord Mountford Mystery." *ERB-dom* No. 65, December 1972. Also reprinted in *Pearls from Peoria*. Middlesex: The Rose Press, 2005.
- "From ERB To Ygg." *Erbivore*, August 1973. Also reprinted in *Pearls from Peoria*. Middlesex: The Rose Press, 2005.
- "A Language for Opar." *ERB-dom* No. 75, 1974. Also reprinted in *Pearls from Peoria*. Middlesex: The Rose Press, 2005.

- "Jonathan Swift Somers III, Cosmic Traveller in a Wheelchair: A Short Biography by Philip José Farmer (Honorary Chief Kennel Keeper)." *Scintillation* No. 13, June 1977. Also reprinted in *Pearls from Peoria*. Middlesex: The Rose Press, 2005.
- "The Monster on Hold." *Program to the 1983 World Fantasy Convention.* Oak Forest: Weird Tales, 1983. Also reprinted in *Pearls from Peoria*. Middlesex: The Rose Press, 2005.

Finally, there are several items about which debate continues regarding whether or not they fit into Mr. Farmer's regular Wold Newton continuity. Certainly they draw on Wold Newton mythology and thus deserve at least honorable mention here. As Mr. Farmer has said, "Let the reader decide."

- *A Feast Unknown, Lord of the Trees*, and *The Mad Goblin*[5]. Three novels featuring the battle of Lord Grandrith (a Tarzan analogue) and Doc Caliban (a Doc Savage analogue) against the Nine. Dennis Power has written three articles that reconcile these novels with Wold Newton Universe continuity: "Triple Tarzan Tangle," "Tarzan? Jane?" and "Tarzans in the Valley of Gold" (all available at Dennis Power's *Secret History of the Wold Newton Universe* website).
- *Greatheart Silver*[6]. One of the main factors against including this collection of three short stories in the Wold Newton Universe is an episode in which many of the great pulp heroes, now aged, engage in a massive gun battle and are killed off. Brad Mengel's "Fakeout at Shootout" (*Secret History of the WNU* website) resolves these events with Wold Newton continuity and also discusses the Grandrith/Caliban books. Art Bollmann also tackles Greatheart Silver in his "The Greatheart Silver Problem" (Mark Brown's *Wold Newton Chronicles* website).
- *A Barnstormer in Oz*[7]. Farmer gives Oz the reality twist. One factor that may argue against including this book in the Wold Newton Universe is that all sequels to L. Frank Baum's *The Wizard of Oz* are treated as fictional, except for this one. On the other hand, Dennis Power has written "Ozdyssey, or How the Yellow Brick Road Lead Me to the Riverworld" (*Secret History of the WNU* website) explaining how Mr. Farmer's book could fit in.

Further Selected Wold Newton Reading

Although one can certainly read *Myths for the Modern Age* without them, the Wold Newton completist will want the following volumes or articles close at hand:

Baring-Gould, William S. *Sherlock Holmes of Baker Street: The Life of the World's First Consulting Detective*. New York: Bramhall House, 1962.

---. *Nero Wolfe of West Thirty-Fifth Street: The Life and Times of America's Largest Private Detective*. New York, N.Y.: Penguin Books, 1982.

Dyar, Dafydd Neal. "Sunlight, Son Bright." *The Doc Savage Club Reader* n8.

Dunn, Patricia. "A Problem of Identity: Was Holmes a Vulcan?" *The Best of Trek 11*. New York: Signet Books, 1986.

Lai, Rick. "The Brotherhood of the Lotus." *Nemesis Incorporated* v4, n28, December 1988.

---. *The Complete Chronology of Bronze*. Aces Publications, 1999.

---. "The Dark Ancestry of John Sunlight." *The Shadow/Doc Savage Quest* n11, December 1982.

---. "Hell's Madonna and the Voodoo Priestess." *Nemesis Incorporated* v3, n24, March 1987.

---. "Iris Vaughan of the Invisible Empire." *Nemesis Incorporated* v4, n27, May 1988.

---. "Revelations of Kathulos." *The Fantastic Worlds of Robert E. Howard.* James Van Hise, ed., 2001.

---. "The Savage Reversion." *Golden Perils* v1, n4, May 1986.

---. "Sen Gat and the Belgian Sleuth." *Nemesis Incorporated* v4, n26, January 1988.

---. "Sirens of the Si-Fan." *Nemesis Incorporated* v2, n20, August 1985.

Lofficier, Jean-Marc, and Randy Lofficier. *Shadowmen: Heroes and Villains of French Pulp Fiction*. Encino, CA: Black Coat Press, 2003.

---. *Shadowmen 2: Heroes and Villains of French Comics*. Encino, CA: Black Coat Press, 2004.

Murphy, Jaclyn J. "The Star Trek Family Tree." *The Best of Trek 4*. New York: Signet Books, 1981.

Nevins, Jess. *Heroes and Monsters: The Unofficial Companion to the League of Extraordinary Gentlemen*. Austin, TX: MonkeyBrain Books, 2003.

---. *A Blazing World: The Unofficial Companion to the League of Extraordinary Gentlemen, Volume Two*. Austin, TX: MonkeyBrain Books, 2004.

Nicastro, C.J. "A Note on Spock." *The Best of Trek 8*. New York: Signet Books, 1985.

---. "'Spock Savage' or the Vulcan of Bronze."*The Best of Trek 8*. New York: Signet Books, 1985.

Rutt, Timothy J., Todd R. Rutt, Arn McConnell, Kirk McConnell, Clay Powers, and Scott Koeller. *The Wold Atlas*. Five issues, 1977-1978.

Schwartz, Paul. "A Theory of Relativity." *The Best of Trek 4*. New York: Signet Books, 1981.

Starr, Professor H.W. "A Case of Identity, or, The Adventure of the Seven

Claytons." Addendum I to *Tarzan Alive*.
---. "A Submersible Subterfuge, or, Proof Impositive." Addendum to *The Other Log of Phileas Fogg*.
Thompson, Leslie. "A Brief Look at Kirk's Career." *The Best of Trek 2*. New York: Signet Books, 1980.

Websites

Articles referenced but not reprinted in this volume may be found at the following websites:

Brown, Mark K.. *The Wold Newton Chronicles*. <http://www.pjfarmer.com/chronicles/index.htm>
Eckert, Win Scott. *An Expansion of Philip José Farmer's Wold Newton Universe*, aka *The Wold Newton Universe*.<http://www.pjfarmer.com/woldnewton/Pulp2.htm>
Loridans, Chuck. *MONSTAAH: Maximum Observation and / or Nullification of Supernatural Terrors Autonomous Agents Headquarters*. <http://monstaah.org>
Lofficier, Jean-Marc. *French Wold Newton Universe*. <http://www.coolfrenchcomics.com/wnu1.htm>
Nevins, Jess. *Some Unknown Members of the Wold Newton Family*. <http://ratmmjess.tripod.com/wold.html>
Power, Dennis E.. *The Secret History of the Wold Newton Universe*. <http://www.pjfarmer.com/secret/secret.htm>

The Crossover Premise

The *Crossover Chronology* is built upon the base of the genealogical and historical speculations in the fiction of Philip José Farmer, William S. Baring-Gould, Prof. H.W. Starr, and Rick Lai. Elements of the Cthulhu Mythos are also incorporated. Taken together, these stories constitute the foundation of the Wold Newton Universe.

Using this foundational framework, crossover stories are then analyzed to establish if there are other characters who coexist with the original characters included in Farmer's Wold Newton genealogy. Film, television, or comicbook sources are quite acceptable, as long as they do not explicitly contradict a literary source. If a seemingly contradictory source can be shown to fit in after all, through a scholarly article or piece of research, so much the better.

The *Crossover Chronology* is a timeline of crossover stories in which two or more literary characters, situations, universes, or, in some rare cases, actual historical personages, are linked together.[8] A very good example is *The Rainbow Affair*, which brings together Sherlock Holmes, Fu Manchu, Nayland Smith, and James Bond (all already in the Wold Newton Universe, based on Farmer's Wold Newton family trees), with The Men From U.N.C.L.E, The Avengers, The Saint, Inspector West, Department Z, and Miss Marple (all added to the Wold Newton Universe per this crossover). The crossover stories establish that there are other characters in the Wold Newton Universe, although the newly-added characters are not necessarily a part of the Wold Newton genealogy (either Farmer's original tree or a post-Farmerian expansion).

Again, when evaluating crossovers,[9] I am looking for stories that involve two or more fictional characters and that do not introduce contradictions that are too difficult to resolve. Examples of the latter would be the otherwise enjoyable *Sherlock Holmes and the Hentzau Affair*, and *Superman: War of the Worlds*. These stories are mentioned instead in Addendum 2 to the *Crossover Chronology*: *Alternate Universe Crossovers, Parodies, and Farces*.[10]

On Historical Figures

When I first began to catalog crossovers, I often used a fictional character meeting a historical character as a way of linking different fictional characters to the universe. In time, it became obvious that certain historical characters made this problematic, Adolph Hitler or Jack the Ripper being two prime examples. Who has not met them in some fictional tale? This was too easy. Therefore, I concluded that no more fictional characters should be added on that basis, although I would not retroactively exclude characters previously brought in that way. A side rule to this is that fictional descendants and/or relatives of fictionalized versions of real people can be used to make additions to the Wold Newton Universe, because this type of crossover plot is not as overused as the fictional-character-meets-real-person scenario. An example of the fictional relative crossover is a character on the television program *Alias* stating that he is the great-nephew of Harry Houdini. Since a strongly fictionalized version of Houdini exists in the WNU, this brings in *Alias*.

Furthermore, if a historical person becomes a *bona fide* character in a fictional series, then we are dealing with the Wold Newton version of that person. Therefore, Peter Heck's "Mark Twain-as-a-sleuth" series of mystery books come in through Twain's meeting with

Inspector Lestrade, because this is not the real Mark Twain, it is the Wold Newton version of Twain. The same goes for Harry Houdini's numerous appearances in the WNU.

On Superheroes and Comic Book Universes

The Wold Newton Universe is not a mirror of any superhero universe. It is essentially a pulp/explorer/detective/non-powered hero universe. Pulp heroes, Victorian detectives, jungle explorers, hard-boiled private eyes, secret agents, and, in the distant past, sword and sorcery heroes, are the mainstays of the Wold Newton Universe. In keeping with Mr. Farmer's primary source material, *Tarzan Alive* and *Doc Savage: His Apocalyptic Life*, there are also some Lovecraftian horror, mainstream horror, science-fictional, and classical literature aspects thrown in. Powered heroes whose adventures were documented by comic book publishers are welcome, but they should be imported into the WNU in a way that does not overpower continuity or the other WNU characters. Therefore, they must meet certain guidelines for inclusion, which will be described below.

Any discussion of superhero crossovers in the WNU starts with Mr. Farmer's throwaway line in *Doc Savage: His Apocalyptic Life*, mentioning Lois Lane, Clark Kent's *objet d'amour*, as a possible sister to The Shadow's Margo Lane. There is no doubt that Farmer, with this offhand comment, did not intend to open the floodgates and consolidate the entire DC Comics Universe with his Wold Newton stories and biographies[11]. Nevertheless, perhaps a very limited inclusion of superheroes might be warranted, if handled with care. Lois Lane in the WNU could imply the presence of a low-powered Superman himself, or perhaps just a non-powered Clark Kent.

In handling the topic carefully, the main concern to keep in mind is that too many superheroes in the WNU would overshadow the personality of the expanded WNU, which is after all derived from Mr. Farmer's works. Some of Farmer's works are grounded in the literary trick that everything being discussed is real and takes place in our world. In other words, it is non-fiction. Farmer's real world premise, and its impact on an expanded WNU, is discussed in more detail below.

But accept, for the moment, that the expanded WNU at least emulates the real world, if it is not actually the real world. If one is being cautious and thorough, one should not include too many superheroes in a universe that emulates the real world. The premise of a supposedly real universe filled with superheroes stumbling over each other, even though they purportedly all operate in secret, would wear thin rather quickly. A universe containing only a few superheroes operating in secret (or not operating in secret, but nevertheless regarded as urban legends) is much more believable if one wishes to maintain the premise that, to the general observer, the Wold Newton Universe emulates the real world.

Furthermore, a limited inclusion of comic-book superheroes is more appropriate because too many super-powered beings in the WNU tend to diminish and water down the incredible and remarkable accomplishments of their less-powered pulp/secret agent/explorer/detective counterparts. Finally, the less-powered characters in non-superhero stories (such as The Shadow, Tarzan, the Destroyer and James Bond) do not behave as if they live in a universe overflowing with superheroes. It is difficult to believe that Ian Fleming's James Bond novels could really take place in the Marvel Universe, because all sorts of things would be different if he lived in that universe. But Colonel Nick Fury could still have Bond-style adventures in the Marvel Universe—or, more importantly for our purposes, the Wold Newton Universe.

Handling the superhero question with care and respect for Farmer's original vision means not only limiting the number of superheroes or "mystery men," but that these characters must be alternate-universe (AU) versions of their comic-universe selves. This is important in order to avoid importing the whole history, continuity, and character-set of the comic universe (this mainly applies to the overly "ret-conned" and continuity-laden DC Comics and Marvel Comics Universes). Additionally, when the WNU versions of these heroes have extra powers, which set them apart even from the most powerful Wold Newton Family heroes such as Doc Savage and Tarzan, articles can be written or theories proposed which provide Wold-Newtonian explanations for those powers. In general, these explanations would tend to explain that the WNU versions of heroes operated for less time than as portrayed by comic book publishers, that they were much less powerful than as described in the exaggerated comics, and that their adventures were considerably less flamboyant, cosmic, and earth-shaking (both literally and socio-politically).

While superhero characters can play an entertaining part in an expanded Wold Newton Universe, they are, after all, only one small aspect of a much larger tapestry that includes pulp heroes, detectives, secret agents, Victorian heroes, explorers of hidden lands, prehistoric barbarians, Lovecraftian and other horrors, science-fiction adventurers, and classical literature characters.

Having thus established the necessity for limiting the inclusion of superheroes (if one is to include them at all), following are some general Rules, Guidelines and Exceptions:

The basic rule of my version of the Wold Newton Universe is: *Very few superheroes*. This is not because I find some of the powers unbelievable (although some are), but because large numbers of high-powered superheroes would change the nature and outcome of events in this continuity. The goal of the Wold Newton Universe is to emulate the real world, although it cannot be said to be the real world. This is clearly not the goal of superhero universes such as the DC and Marvel Universes. Too many superheroes make the Wold Newton Universe less and less similar to the real world. And too many super-powered heroes also overshadow the other heroes like Philip Marlowe and Travis McGee.

> **Exception:** *Superheroes will be admitted if they appear in a crossover with a character already in the Wold Newton Universe.* For example: Batman appears through Tarzan and Sherlock Holmes crossovers. Captain America is in through appearance in a Green Hornet story. Elongated Man appears through a meeting with Sherlock Holmes, and Plastic Man appears though a connection with The Spirit. Spider-Man comes in because he shared adventures with Red Sonja, King Kull, and Doc Savage.

Rule: *Superheroes do not automatically bring in other superheroes through crossovers that take place within their own regular universes, especially the highly continuity-burdened DC and Marvel Universes which are overflowing with superheroes. Instead, these are taken on a case-by-case basis. This rule also applies to non-superheroes from superhero universes.* For example, the Elongated Man does not imply the existence of the Silver Age Flash in the Wold Newton Universe. The X-Men cannot be added just because they met Captain America. The presence of "Hop" Harrigan does not mean that all the members of the Justice Society of America are in the Wold Newton Universe. Red Sonja's battle with Kulan Gath, an evil wizard in Marvel Comics, does not mean that other Marvel superheroes who battled Kulan Gath are incorporated into the Wold Newton Universe. Shang Chi does not bring in the other Marvel heroes. The Prowler (who is not technically a superhero) can bring Airboy (also not a superhero) into the WNU, but these characters will not necessarily bring the Eclipse Comics Universe's superheroes into the WNU. The Shadow's meeting with the Ghost does not necessarily bring in the rest of Dark Horse Comics' superheroes.

> Exception: *I allowed in a Superman/Wonder Woman 1940s crossover because the Wold Newton Universe needed more female characters.*

Rule: *Appearances or cameos of a superhero's alter ego are enough to place that alter ego in the WNU, but are not enough to substantiate the presence of the actual superhero.* For example, the mention of Billy Batson in "The New York Review of Bird" is not enough to bring in Captain Marvel. The appearance of Freddy Freeman in Lin Carter's *The Earth-Shaker* does not bring in Captain Marvel Jr. The mention of Donald Blake in the Doc Savage/Thing crossover does not bring in Thor. The mention of Carol Danvers in the Red Sonja/Spider-Man crossover is not sufficient to bring in Ms. Marvel. The appearance of Bruce Wayne in the Prince Zarkon novels is not enough to bring in Batman (but Batman comes in through his meetings with Tarzan and Sherlock Holmes).

> Exception: *A special exception is made for Superman, even though only Clark Kent appears in a Green Hornet story. The exception is made due to a mention of Lois Lane in Philip José Farmer's* Doc Savage: His Apocalyptic Life. *And even though technically only Steve Rogers appears in the Green Hornet crossover, he is definitely Captain America; otherwise, he would be portrayed as quite scrawny and emaciated.*

Rule: *Once a superhero is already validly included, that superhero can bring in other characters, as long as the other characters are not from an overly continuity-laden universe like the DC and Marvel Universes.* For example, a reference to the *Daily Star* newspaper from Superman is sufficient to bring in a pulp-like African-American hero from an independent publisher, Captain Gravity. Likewise, the appearance of the *Daily Planet* newspaper in a Jon Sable comic serves to substantiate Sable's presence in the WNU.

Rule: *Characters such as Dracula and the Frankenstein Monster are not automatically valid crossover links; many different comic publishers have used conflicting versions of these characters and so they must be evaluated on a case-by-case basis.* For example, although Dracula is a character in the Wold Newton Universe, the Marvel Comics Universe version of Dracula does not automatically bring in every Marvel superhero that Dracula ever met.

Rule: *Inter-company crossovers that are based on marketing strategies will be evaluated on a case-by-case basis to determine if they mesh with or violate continuity.* For example, Vampirella's promotional crossovers with characters from other publishers, such as Shadowhawk, Lady Death, Purgatori, and Shi, are taken on a case-by-case basis to ensure that they fit into continuity. The same goes for the many Tomb Raider, Shi, Witchblade, Spawn, Darkness, etc., crossovers.

Rule: *Superhero teams from the DC and Marvel Universes are generally excluded.* There is not enough time in a realistic chronology of a hero's life to have all of his or her own adventures and have regular adventures with a formally organized super-team. Additionally, the menaces which super-teams face are almost always cosmic or at least earth-shaking in scope. One cannot theorize the concealment of all these events from the public in the hopes of maintaining the facade of a real world—the sheer numbers are too great.

> Exception: *"Family" superhero teams like the Fantastic Four are more likely. Besides the family connections and going through the origin of their superhero powers together, they tend to have most of their adventures together, not individually.*
>
> Cameos of superhero teams in individual hero's comic books can be excluded as cross-promotional ploys designed to encourage readers to try other comics. This leaves out the following examples:

- The brief appearance of Marvel Comics' Avengers in an *Iron Man* comic book which features Fu Manchu; the Iron Man-Fu Manchu connection remains intact; and

- The appearance of Scott Summers and Jean Grey (from the X-Men) in an *Iron Fist* comic which features Del Floria's Tailor Shop (from the television show *The Man From U.N.C.L.E.*); the Iron Fist-U.N.C.L.E. connection remains intact.

Rule: *There are so many Cthulhu Mythos references throughout Marvel and DC comics that they cannot be treated as an automatically valid connector, or else the combined DC/Marvel Universe would subsume the WNU. Therefore the Cthulhu Mythos will be treated as existing across multiple universes.*

Any crossover that passes these rules must still pass the bar of being non-contradictory with existing Wold Newton Universe continuity. Therefore, even if a comic book hero meets a Wold Newtonian character, it is not necessarily a genuine crossover. As with all crossovers, the settings, characters and time placement must also harmonize with whole of the Wold Newton Universe.

This also means that there is a preference for superhero references that are set in the particular superhero's original general time frame, such as Superman in the 1930s-40s, or Spider-Man in the 1960s-70s. In a real-world continuum like the Wold Newton Universe, it is unlikely, though not impossible, that Spider-Man would still be operating in the early 21st century, absent an *elixir vitae* like Fu Manchu's. Therefore less weight will be given to superhero crossover references that take place late in a particular hero's publishing career and particularly after superhero-universe "reboots" (in which a universe is restarted, without consideration of previous continuity) or in the context of a superhero-universe "ret-con" (short for "retroactive continuity," or instances in which changes are made retroactively to prior continuity). Obviously, viable explanations will be considered, such as interpreting the 1986 Batman/Sherlock Holmes crossover as a meeting between Batman III and Holmes.

Of course, this set of rules and guidelines and exceptions will not satisfy everyone. Each individual Wold Newton Universe fan has his or her own ideas about which novels, stories, films, comics, etc., fit into their own vision of the WNU; if someone does want to include superhero references, then the *Crossover Chronology* helps that person to understand when those adventures occurred. Those who choose not to include any superhero references are free to ignore them (or any other references) in the *Crossover Chronology*.

Ultimately, however, I have found that the crossover rules and guidelines I have proposed do generally work, and have been largely satisfactory to a substantial number of Wold Newton "researchers" who have chosen to work together to reach consensus on many Wold Newton questions. In the end, my vision of the Wold Newton Universe is that of an extraordinarily complex set of sources, circumstances, and mysteries that can never be satisfactorily buttoned down into one over-arching scheme that will always work and always satisfy everyone. Kind of like real life. And as with real life, I actually don't mind when some mysteries remain in the WNU.

New Directions

As stated above, the *Crossover Chronology*, the culmination of an exercise in universe-building for which I coined the phrase, "The Wold Newton Universe," stands upon the foundation established by Farmer, Baring-Gould, Starr, and Lai. While their genealogical work was speculative in nature, the *Crossover Chronology*, as originally conceived, was not. It was originally intended to include only stories or events that were substantiated and documented in novels, short stories, comic books and graphic novels, television programs, and films. This is still the main thrust of the *Crossover Chronology*.

However, the careful reader will note that there is a limited amount of conjecture integrated into the *Chronology*. This conjecture is being included on four bases:

1) Purely for the purpose of filling in genealogical "holes";[12]
2) For reconciling seemingly conflicting information;[13]
3) For answering "burning questions" which are raised by different elements of the Wold Newton Universe;[14] and
4) With the rise of genealogical theorizing on par with that of Baring-Gould or Farmer by such Wold Newton scholars as Mark Brown, Dennis Power, Chris Carey, or others, some of these speculative relationships may be included in the *Chronology*.[15]

Myths for the Modern Age

The further excursions into Creative Mythography in *Myths for the Modern Age* represent the cream of the crop in the latest explosive resurgence of the Wold Newton literary archaeological Game. Most have been updated and revised, sometimes extensively, to reflect the latest available research.

In them you will discover why Korak is not really Tarzan's

biological son; more information about Sherlock Holmes' progeny than you ever dreamed possible; what happened when the agents from U.N.C.L.E. met The Saint and Fu Manchu; and how the League of Extraordinary Gentlemen influenced events in the Wold Newton Universe (several League members, such as Sir Percy Blakeney and Allan Quatermain, were identified by Farmer as Wold Newton Family members long before their membership in various Leagues was brought to the world's attention).

Was Mowgli a member of the Wold Newton Family? How is Edgar Rice Burroughs' John Carter of Mars related to the Outlaw of Torn? And speaking of Burroughs, he told us about Lord Greystoke's son, but what about his daughters? What is the secret history behind the anti-heroes and super-villains of the Wold Newton Universe, Captain Nemo, Professor Moriarty, and Doctor Fu Manchu? What is Fu Manchu's relationship to mighty Cthulhu?

Did Doc Savage have children, and what became of them? What about the Asian, French, and even Turkish branches of the Wold Newton Family? What is Vampirella's relationship to Zorro? And just how many Zorros were there, anyway?

Does only The Shadow know?

Myths for the Modern Age was never intended to be the be-all and end-all of Wold Newton information, but it is a great place to start. So if you are new to the Wold Newton concept, by all means, dive in and discover the answers to these and other mythological mysteries here.

But also do yourself a favor. If you have not already done so, seek out, find, and read Philip José Farmer's other Wold Newton works. At a minimum, you owe it to yourself to read his cornerstone "An Exclusive Interview with Lord Greystoke" and his classic "biographies" *Tarzan Alive, and Doc Savage: His Apocalyptic Life.* If you have read them before, it will be like meeting an old friend again.

If you have not, you are in for quite a ride.

Win Scott Eckert
Denver, Colorado
March 2005

Wold-Newtonry
Theory and Methodology for the Literary Archaeology of the Wold Newton Universe
By Dr. Peter M. Coogan

Introduction

This article presents a taxonomy of Wold-Newtonry, the practice of literary archaeology that continues Philip José Farmer's work on the Wold Newton Universe. It is intended to be, in essence, a formal statement of the theory and methodology of the field of Wold-Newtonry.

As "literary archeologists," we map and investigate the unknown history of the literary universe as revealed in novels, pulps, films, comics, legends, myths, epics, and other literary and cultural texts. We treat these texts as archeologists treat the artifacts they dig up, as clues to a larger understanding of the world that must be guessed at and constructed from incomplete pieces.

Wold Newton scholars seek to create connections between texts in a game that supposes creative works to be merely an archipelago representation of a world more exciting and interesting than the one we live in. Creating these connections recreates the "sense of wonder," in the terminology of science-fiction fandom, that we felt when we first read the pulps and other texts we work with. As a game, Wold-Newtonry is playful and has rules. In fact, "the Game" is another term for this activity, coined to describe a literary discipline that sprung from the inaccuracies and inconsistencies of the Sherlock Holmes canon and Sir Arthur Conan Doyle's willingness to "ignore consistency and even facts for the sake of a good story."[16] The Game goes back to at least 1902. That year an "open letter" to Dr. Watson was published in the *Cambridge Review* criticizing the dates mentioned in *The Hound of the Baskervilles*, and Arthur Bartlett Maurice wrote an editorial comment in *Bookman*, "Some Inconsistencies of Sherlock Holmes." In 1911 at the Gryphon Club at Trinity College, Oxford, Monsignor Ronald Knox read "Studies in the Literature of Sherlock Holmes," which is considered the cornerstone of Sherlockian literature[17] and is credited with spawning this "highly specialized and possibly unique form of literary criticism."[18] Dorothy L. Sayers, author of the Lord Peter Wimsey series, commenting on the Game, said, "It must be played as solemnly as a county cricket match at Lord's; the slightest touch of extravagance or burlesque ruins the atmosphere."[19]

So Wold-Newtonry is a version of the Game based specifically upon Philip José Farmer's biographies, *Tarzan Alive* and *Doc Savage: His Apocalyptic Life*, and novels such as *The Adventure of the Peerless Peer* and *The Other Log of Phileas Fogg.*

Certain Kinds of Literature

In *Tarzan Alive*, Philip José Farmer drew on canonical nineteenth and twentieth-century literature such as *Pride and Prejudice*, the Leather-Stocking Tales, *Moby Dick*, and James Joyce's *Ulysses* to expand the Wold Newton Family, but his main focus, as evidenced by the subjects of his two Wold Newton biographies—Tarzan and Doc Savage—was on nineteenth-century adventure fiction and twentieth-century pulp fiction. Wold Newton scholars have followed this emphasis and tend to focus on genre fiction that falls on the formulaic side of John Cawelti's division of literature into mimetic and formulaic. Mimetic literature "confronts us with the world as we know it, while the formulaic element reflects the construction of an ideal world without the disorder, ambiguity, the uncertainty, and the limitations of the world of our experience" (p. 13). Formulaic literature tends to present *moral fantasies*, "in which the world resembles our own at almost every point, presents a protagonist of extraordinary capacities in a set of circumstances that enable him to face the most insuperable obstacles and surmount them without lasting harm to himself, either morally or physically" (p. 39).

Wold Newton texts tend to display the following characteristics:

1. Continuity: More than one book (the Destroyer novels, the Doc Savage pulps), interconnected books (Cooper's Leatherstocking Tales and his Effingham novels share a few characters), or the works of authors who set most of their novels in the same moral and social universe (Jane Austen or Jules Verne).

2. Possibility: The events of the story could have happened in the world we live in. Thus, there needs to be some limit on the fantastic goings-on to explain why awareness of the events has not reached the general public. Typically, this limitation is achieved by locating the events far away from contemporary life in some isolated time or place. Another method is to involve a circumscribed number of characters, all of who either die or have some significant motivation to keep the story secret. When the events of a story clearly would be known, such as the

invasion of the Earth by Martians in H.G. Wells' *War of the Worlds*, the text is treated as an exaggeration of a much smaller event that was covered up by the authorities. One of the great appeals of *Tarzan Alive* is that it offers readers the possibility that Tarzan is a living person, thereby opening up the possibility that the readers themselves could take part in similar adventures. Because Farmer published *Tarzan Alive* as a biography and convincingly claimed throughout the work that Tarzan was indeed a living person, many people (myself included) were taken in by his hoax when they read the book. Wold-Newtonry is, in some ways, an attempt on our part to extend that delicious belief in the romantic and adventurous possibilities of a world in which we might just live.

3. Romance/Adventure: The texts answer some need in the reader for a world that is more orderly and offers the possibility of adventure—a life of heightened meaning, risk, and action, but one in which right prevails.

Taxonomy

There are two types of Wold Newton writing: creative and scholarly.

Creative

Creative pieces are written as entertainment and are intended as fiction. They stand on their own or within the context of their series as pieces of literature (that is, the Shadow novels can each be read alone, but they gain resonance by being read together). Creative pieces break down into four categories:

1. Unconnected: Pieces written without any attempt to connect them to other characters or novels and without apparent awareness of the concept of the Wold Newton Universe or of any larger continuity.

2. Connected: Pieces written with the intention of connecting to other characters or novels. The Shadow novel *Whispering Eyes* includes a mention of Nick Carter's house; Edgar Rice Burroughs connected several of his novels by having characters from one series appear in another, as when Tarzan went to Pellucidar in *Tarzan at the Earth's Core*.

3. Creative literary archaeology: Pieces created to expose the true story behind other pieces of fiction, but unconnected to Farmer's concept of the Wold Newton Universe. The film *Shadow of the Vampire* tells the story behind the making of F.W. Murnau's *Nosferatu*.

4. Wold Newton (creative Farmerian literary archaeology):

Pieces written with the Wold Newton Universe in mind. Farmer's *The Peerless Peer* in which Tarzan meets Sherlock Holmes, and J.T. Edson's Bunduki series—which is explicitly based upon Farmer's Wold Newton work—are examples.

Scholarly

Wold Newton scholarly studies fall into three categories in terms of validity. Some, such as Farmer's *Tarzan Alive*, claim all three levels of validity.

1. Speculative or deductive articles: Scholars make speculations and deductions about characters and events from the published narratives. Other scholarly works can be given the same treatment and be extrapolated from in terms of deducing and filling in holes in a character's life. Speculative articles tend to work from the published record, but go beyond it based upon clues in the text, logical reasoning, and psychological profiling or character criticism, which assumes that the characters lead realistic lives off the page. Edwin Arnold's novel, *Phra the Phoenician*, contained contradictions and lapses in the life of Phra that could not be true on their face but seemed to represent attempts by Phra to repress or deny aspects of his life that were too painful to recall consciously. In "John Carter: Torn from Phoenician Dreams," Dennis Power and I explain how the psychological damage of the repeated loss of his reincarnated love, Blodwen, caused Phra to create the personality of John Carter and to bury his original self under deep layers of repression. This pattern of denial fit with the condition of dissociative amnesia and fugue, which led us to the discovery of other historical and fictional characters alive during the time Phra's periods of amnesia who matched his physical description such as King Arthur, Robin Hood, and Burroughs' Norman of Torn.

2. Researched articles: Suggest historical cognates for characters and events related in seemingly fictional adventures, or research is used to flesh out and back up the details presented in the texts. Rick Lai's *Chronology of Shadows* presents evidence showing that Walter Gibson based mobster Nick Savoli in *Gangdom's Doom* on Al Capone and the events of the novel on the 1931 mayoral election in Chicago, and Lai uses this evidence to place the events of *Gangdom's Doom* in the chronology of the Shadow's adventures.

3. Sourced works: Purported to be interviews with or based upon actual documents written by Wold Newton personalities. Edgar Rice Burroughs' Tarzan and John Carter novels are based on this premise because Burroughs claims to have John Clayton's diary and John

Carter's manuscript. Wold Newton scholars sometimes establish sources for their articles, as with Philip José Farmer's "An Exclusive Interview with Lord Greystoke," in which he claims to have met Tarzan at an undisclosed location in Africa for a fifteen minute interview.

Categories of Creative and Scholarly Pieces

Creative and scholarly efforts fall into several categories. Any category can be represented by creative or scholarly pieces, such as *Hadon of Ancient Opar* (creative) or *Tarzan Alive* (scholarly). It does not seem possible for a piece to be both creative (in the sense of being literary) and scholarly at the same time.

Reference: (Dictionaries, encyclopedias, atlases, and annotations) I have written a Mangani/English dictionary based upon the Tarzan books and other glossaries that have been published, as well as adding definitions through analysis and deduction. Jess Nevins' encyclopedias, such as *The Encyclopedia of Pulp Fiction* (forthcoming, 2007); *The Encyclopedia of Fantastic Victoriana* (2005); and his website *Golden Age Heroes Directory* provide brief descriptions of characters and information on their publishing histories and authors.

Annotation articles: Identify and explain characters, plot elements, settings, objects, and so forth. Jess Nevins' *Heroes & Monsters: The Unofficial Companion to the League of Extraordinary Gentlemen* provides a panel-by-panel breakdown of the graphic novel, an essay on the Yellow Peril archetype, and biographies of the main characters of the book.

Cosmology: Cosmological pieces depict large events, such as the formation of the universe or the emergence of cosmic powers. Generally they feature long time frames. In "Aliens Among Us: The Ancients," Dennis Power traces the four-billion year history of a group of races known variously as the Ancients, the Founders, the Old Ones, or the Long-Gones and their attempts to oversee and shape the development of the universe, particularly the development of humanity on Earth.

Biography: The first well-known Wold Newton pieces were biographical, such as William S. Baring-Gould's *Sherlock Holmes of Baker Street* and Farmer's *Tarzan Alive*.

History: A history details the history of a group, a place, or an idea. In "Kiss of the Vampire" John Small presents a brief overview of vampirism by focusing on the lives of three key figures and their contributions to the legacy of the vampire: Lilith, the founder of vampirism; Dracula, the most famous vampire; and Anita Santiago (aka. Lady Rawhide and Vampirella), a key figure in the emergence of heroic vampires.

Genealogy: A genealogy traces a family lineage through either a family tree or a narrative history. Mark Brown's "From Pygmalion to Casablanca: The Genealogy of Henry Higgins" traces the family history of Henry Higgins, making connections with Leopold Bloom of *Ulysses* and Rick Blaine of *Casablanca.*

Chronology: Details the exact timeframe of a character's adventures and is based upon a close reading of the texts. In his impressive *Chronology of Shadows*, Rick Lai creates a coherent chronology of the published exploits of the Shadow, taking in all of the novels as they appeared in the pulps and accounting for the contradictions caused by Walter Gibson's hectic writing schedule and the inconsistencies resulting from the use of multiple authors on the series.

Establishment: An establishment piece sets a character or series in the Wold Newton Universe. Typically this establishment is confirmed by a linkage to an existing version of the universe, a published crossover story, or through a genealogy. Win Eckert's *Crossover Chronology* builds upon the foundation of the genealogical and historical speculations of William S. Baring-Gould, Philip José Farmer, H.W. Starr, and Rick Lai. The *Crossover Chronology* traces a history of the WNU from 6,000,000 BCE to the 802,071 CE by noting those stories in which characters cross over with established Wold Newton personages. Eckert uses these crossovers to establish the presence of new characters in the WNU. As an example, Eckert cites "*The Rainbow Affair*, which brings together Sherlock Holmes, Fu Manchu, Nayland Smith, and James Bond (all already in the Wold Newton Universe, based on Farmer's family tree), with The Men From U.N.C.L.E, The Avengers, The Saint, Inspector West, Department Z, and Miss Marple (all added to the Wold Newton Universe per this crossover)."

Hole-filling: A piece fills in a lacuna in the record in a literary or scholarly fashion. A literary example is Phillip José Farmer's *Escape from Loki,* which details the adventure during which Doc Savage met his five aides and fills in a hole from the original series, which did not detail precisely how the six men met during the Great War.

Concentric Circles of Wold

Scholars approach the Wold Newton Universe from a number of positions, or Woldviews, typically depending on which characters they include in their individual WNUs. Most of these positions can be represented as a series of concentric circles, with each "larger" version subsuming the "smaller" ones inside it, although there are also Woldviews outside the concentric circles.

The concentric Wold circles are: Wold-RW (Real World), Wold-FRW (Fictionalized Real World), Wold-P (Prime), Wold-PSF (Pulp Science Fiction), Wold-GW/C (Great War/Cabal), and Wold-S (Superhero).

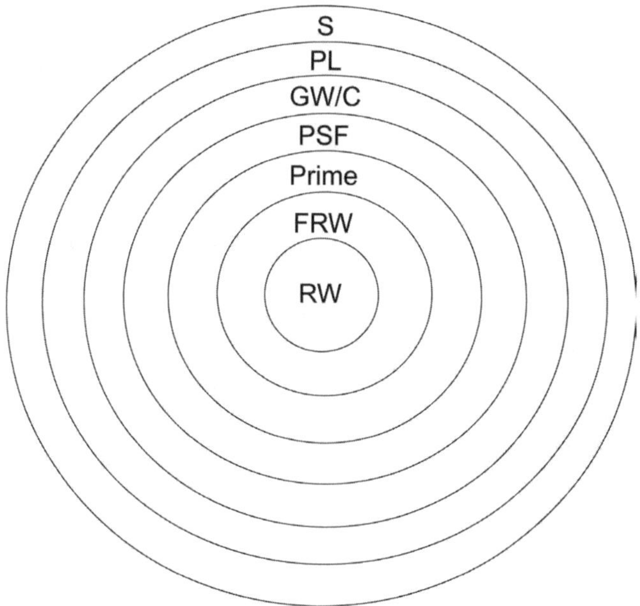

These circles are descriptive—they describe the basic position of a writer—not proscriptive—the circles are not intended to constrain a scholar's approach to the WNU. These concentric circles are representative of broad positions; any individual scholar's work can usually be placed within one of the circles, although some of their articles may fall into another circle or may overlap into the next largest circle along the lines of a Venn diagram.[20] Each scholar's position within these circles determines what is included in or excluded from a particular version of the WNU. A scholar writing from the Wold-Superhero position could accept the theory that Spenser from Robert B. Parker's Spenser novels is the nephew of Philip Marlowe, whereas a scholar writing from "smaller" Wold-Pulp Science Fiction circle most likely would not accept a theory that Hank McCoy, the Beast from the X-Men, is the son or grandson of Monk Mayfair from the Doc Savage pulps because the X-Men does not fit into the Wold-PSF view.

1. Wold-Real World (Wold-RW)

This Woldview consists of biographies and histories of the real people who served as models for Wold Newton figures, as well as biographies and histories generally. Examples include: Dr. Joseph Bell/Sherlock Holmes; Richard Henry Savage/Doc Savage and the Avenger; Sidney Reilly/James Bond, Salomon Pico/Zorro.[21] These can be written without reference to the WNU character or to the fictional version of the person; e.g. Sir John Fielding, the eighteenth century London justice and brother of novelist Henry Fielding, is a fascinating figure and could have been the subject of biographies for his role in establishing the Bow Street Runners, a precursor of the London police force before he became the subject of a series of detective novels by Bruce Alexander.

Articles for this Woldview must follow the generally accepted principles of history and biography. No fiction is permitted, although speculation within the normally accepted methods of history and biography is. This position also includes all biographies, including of people seemingly unrelated to the WNU because of the way Wold Newton researches continually expand to bring in more and more historical characters.

Examples:

Ely M. Liebow, *Dr. Joe Bell: Model for Sherlock Holmes*.

Richard Spence, *Trust No One: The Secret World of Sidney Reilly*.

2. Wold-Fictionalized Real World (Wold-FRW)

This Wold position consists of writing new fictional adventures for the real-world models of the Wold Newton characters; that is, writing stories in which Joseph Bell solves a murder or Richard Henry Savage has an adventure in India. Real-world laws of physics apply because an adventure that bends these laws probably fits in better with the Wold-PSF view.

Fiction written from this position operates at two levels. The first being fiction featuring historical characters, like Sir John Fielding, who are interesting in their own right, and the second being fiction that deals with historical persons primarily because they are the models for WNU characters, like Joseph Bell.

Examples:

Murder Rooms: The Dark Beginnings of Sherlock Holmes, a BBC production with Ian Richardson as Bell and Robin Laing as Arthur Conan Doyle.

Blind Justice, *An Experiment in Treason*, and *Smuggler's Moon*, all by Bruce Alexander, tell of cases solved by Sir John Fielding and the Bow Street Runners.

3. Wold-P (Wold-Prime)
This version of the Wold Newton Universe was proposed in *Tarzan Alive*, Farmer's fictional biography of Tarzan, which he claimed was non-fiction and which is the prime model for all other versions of the WNU. Farmer's original construction leaves out nearly all science fiction and fantasy elements of the Tarzan novels because he intended readers to accept the book as a non-fiction biography. Thus he excludes stories like *Tarzan at the Earth's Core* and *Tarzan and the Ant Men* because these novels depict events that clearly violate the laws of physics. Included in Wold-Prime are similar fictional biographies that claim to be non-fiction, such as those of Sherlock Holmes, Nero Wolfe, and the Scarlet Pimpernel. Some elements of Farmer's other fictional biography, *Doc Savage: His Apocalyptic Life*, can be included, but most of it has to be placed into Wold-PSF due to the genealogical connections and the science fiction elements present in the Doc Savage stories that Farmer includes in his chronology.

4. Wold-Pulp-Science Fiction (Wold-PSF)[22]
This Woldview is basically Wold-Prime plus elements of the pulps and pulp-style science fiction, as well as dime novels, adventure stories, and other fiction that preceded the pulps. It is very much the default Woldview of most Wold Newton scholars. Much of Farmer's work is set in this Woldview, such as *Doc Savage: His Apocalyptic Life*, *Time's Last Gift*, and the Hadon of Opar series, and much of post-Farmer Wold-Newtonry is written from this Wold position.

5. Wold-Great War/Cabal (Wold-GW/C)
The central feature of this Woldview is the twilight struggle—the Great War—between two powers that occurs behind the scenes or the unknown cabal that secretly runs the world. Great powers, either singly in cabals or antagonistically, manipulate mankind, the world, and the universe through agents, breeding programs, and other forms of power politics. This Woldview clearly includes Wold-PSF, but it goes beyond that vision to reveal what lies behind much of the straightforward adventure that is the basis of Wold-PSF. This Woldview includes the cabal of the Nine—ancient immortals who secretly control the world—from Farmer's *A Feast Unknown* and the great war between the alien civilizations of the Eridaneans and the Capelleans in his *The Other Log of Phileas Fogg*, which explains the secret events and motives that drove Fogg's adventure.

6. Wold-Superhero (Wold-S)
Wold-S is the trickiest Woldview of all. The introduction of superheroes into the Wold Newton Universe is probably the most controversial aspect of Wold-Newtonry. Wold-S typically encompasses the characters of both the Marvel and DC Universes but can also include the superheroes of other companies. The problems scholars have with the inclusion of superheroes can be summed up in the principle of universe integrity.

The number of superheroes included in the WNU should be limited, as should their powers, because using too many superheroes tends to cause the WNU's integrity or independence to be overwhelmed by the continuities of the DC and Marvel Universes. That is, once a certain threshold is crossed, the continuities of the DC and Marvel Universes tend to drive Wold Newton scholarship and the more pulpy and science-fictional elements get overwhelmed or decentered.

There are two basic approaches to superheroes in the WNU, limited inclusion and full inclusion. The limited approach puts limits on superheroes, their numbers, and their powers. One version of the limited approach is the pulpy superhero position. In this view, the acceptable superheroes are those who would fit easily into a pulp magazine, like Batman, Daredevil, or Captain America; that is, heroes with some enhanced capabilities but no significant superpowers. The full-inclusion approach accepts them largely as they appear in the comics.

Principles

Each writer comes to Wold-Newtonry with certain principles.[23] These may be formal or informal, stated or unstated, strict or loose. No set of principles seems inherently superior to any other set of principles and a preference for one set over another seems to be just that, a preference. But for obvious reasons, formally stated principles have inherent advantages in convincing people of their utility.

Foundation Principles

These principles form the foundation of Wold-Newtonry. They are generally agreed upon by Wold Newton scholars and are in a sense necessary for the game to be played.

1. Principle of Fun[24]
Wold-Newtonry is a hobby, so when it ceases to be fun, it ceases.

2. Principle of Writer's Fiat or Stewart's Principle[25]
Writer's fiat is the idea that Wold Newton scholars each do whatever they want, an extension of the principle of fun. If a writer wants to include or exclude a character or proceed in a certain way, arguing against their decision from a principle will generally not change a writer's mind, nor do writers feel absolutely bound by any principles, even the ones they devise themselves.

Justice Potter Stewart, in an attempt to define pornography, wrote "I shall not today attempt further to define the kinds of material… but I know it when I see it" (*Jacobellis v. Ohio*, June 22, 1964). This principle underlies all our Wold-Newtonry, especially when scholars work without stated principles or formal methodologies; that is, we each know what seems right when we see it even if we cannot articulate the criteria for judging something right or wrong.

3. Principle of Adherence to Farmer[26]
Farmer's works, especially *Tarzan Alive* and *Doc Savage: His Apocalyptic Life*, stand as the basic background for our work, along with the biographies by others that prompted him to formalize the Wold Newton Universe, such as Baring-Gould's Holmes fictional biography. Part of Farmer's authority in the game of Wold-Newtonry is based upon the interview he conducted with Lord Greystoke (Tarzan).

Discourse Community Principles[27]

These principles establish a writer's vision of the discourse community within which they work.

1. Principle of Compatibility[28]
Articles should agree with the published narratives and the major articles; that is, WNU articles should generally be compatible with each other.

2. Principle of Scholarly Validity
Scholarly works are somewhat privileged over the published narratives because they exhibit a greater degree of internal validity and consistency. For instance, Rick Lai's *Chronology of Shadows* is much more internally consistent than are the published Shadow novels by Walter Gibson, which contain continuity errors and multiple explanations for items such as The Shadow's girasol ring. The same is true of Lai's *Comple Chronology of Bronze*, Farmer's *Doc Savage: His Apocalyptic Life* and *Tarzan Alive*, and Baring-Gould's *Sherlock*

Holmes of Baker Street as compared to the treatments of these heroes by, respectively, Lester Dent, Edgar Rice Burroughs, and Arthur Conan Doyle. Each of these biographies reconciles the contradictions created by the original authors.

Source Principles

These principles establish the relationships between the scholar and the texts, the authors and the texts, and the authors and their sources.

1. Events Precede Publication Principle

Events depicted in the published texts have to occur before those texts were written, typically within the normal time frame of an industry's production schedule. There needs to be enough time for an adventure to occur, the notes to be given to the biographer, and the published story to be written. This process has to occur in a time frame that fits with the production methods a particular industry uses. While an individual issue could be rushed, the generally accepted minimum time between event and the cover date of a comic book is seven months, and a year is customary. Pulps might be rushed more, films and television generally less, although the turn-around time in television can be very short, as is shown by the broadcast of docudramas drawn from current events.

2. Principles of Fictionality

A. Retelling

This principle views the source texts as straightforward retellings of events, without any conscious attempt to change or shape the tale, outside of the ways all tellers influence their tales. *Scar of the Bat*, by Max Allan Collins and Eduardo Barreto, is an Elseworlds tale of Elliot Ness adopting a Bat-Man identity in his fight against Al Capone. The story is told by Oscar Fraley, the real-life journalist who interviewed Ness and wrote *The Untouchables* (1957), the source of much of the Ness legend. In *Scar of the Bat*, Fraley interviews Ness the night before Ness's fatal heart attack, and the story seems a straightforward retelling of the events of Ness's Bat-Man identity from his perspective.

B. Fictionalization

This principle views the source texts as reasonably accurate but fictionalized versions of events. Thus the names of the characters and events portrayed are treated as occurring pretty much as they did in the texts, with caveats to explain contradictions and to make new events fit into a scholar's established framework. Stories can be viewed as lightly, moderately, heavily, or completely fictionalized.

i. Lightly Fictionalized

A lightly fictionalized account presents the events almost as they happened with only small changes to hide an identity or to smooth the telling of the tale. Farmer's article "A Language for Opar" exemplifies this approach. Farmer explains how Tarzan and La, high priestess of Opar, could have understood each other in their conversation in *The Return of Tarzan.* Primarily in the mangani tongue but using Oparian loanwords, La tells Tarzan the history of Opar, and the two use many abstract words—such as *civilization*, *religion*, *creed,* and *sacrilegious*—that the mangani language does not possess. Farmer proposes that Tarzan must have interrupted La many times to ask for clarification and that Burroughs, for the benefit of his readers and to speed the story, elided these linguistic difficulties and portrayed the conversation as proceeding smoothly.

ii. Moderately Fictionalized

A moderately fictionalized account presents the core events of a story as having really happened and involving the core characters, but the rest of the story and some core elements are fictionalized. Dennis Power follows this principle in "Jungle Brothers, Or Secrets of the Jungle Lords," which reconciles Farmer's *The Adventure of the Peerless Peer*, which features Tarzan rescuing Holmes and Watson, and *The Adventure of Three Madmen*, in which Mowgli plays the same role.

iii. Heavily Fictionalized

Farmer follows the principle of heavy fictionalization in *Tarzan Alive* by showing how Burroughs greatly modified and exaggerated the life of John Clayton in order to make readers think Tarzan was a purely fictional character and so as to disguise the real, living person behind the Tarzan stories.

iv. Completely Fictionalized

Farmer follows the principle of complete fictionalization in discarding Pellucidar, the Ant Men, and other science-fiction elements in the Tarzan stories because they contradict real-world physics and thus conflict with his central conceit of *Tarzan Alive* that Tarzan is an actual living person.

C. Distortion

This principle views the published stories as great distortions of the events of the Wold-Newtonites' lives. Names, events, and characterizations can—and even should—be seen as being greatly altered by writers. The idea here is to get as far below the published texts into the hidden histories and lives of the real people on whose adventures the published narratives are based. This approach offers less in terms of material because only certain texts are privileged, typically those that fulfill a scholar's particular needs for a character or that fit into an overarching back story. The results here can go much farther afield than in the fictionalized approach. Dennis Power's treatment of Green Lantern in the piece "Marvelous, Fantastic Heroes: Green Arrow" is an excellent example of this approach. In Power's view Hal Jordan is not a heroic superhero, but an addled former pilot without any superpowers who believes that he has a power ring.

D. Germ Theory

This principle views the texts as gross exaggerations of real events that only serve as the germs for the stories. In this view, the biographers take mere ideas and blow them up into adventures. This position offers the least material to deal with as most of the texts are simply discarded once the germ is explained.

Jess Nevins' treatment of superheroes follows this approach. In his view, Captain America was the code name for an extraordinarily effective commando who never wore a costume, carried a shield, or had super powers. Speedster heroes like the Whizzer and the Flash were based upon soldiers who were exposed to H.G. Wells' human accelerator and died after a single use of their power.

E. Transformation

In the principle of transformation, the characters are transformed in significant ways and an alternative WNU is presented. Farmer in *A Feast Unknown* presents Lord Grandrith and Doc Caliban, sons of Jack the Ripper, in a struggle against the Nine, an ancient cabal. Grandrith and Caliban are recognizable as Tarzan and Doc Savage but have different personalities, biographies, and genealogies from the two pulp heroes. With this novel Farmer has transformed the characters so that they cannot be reconciled with the accepted WNU versions of the characters and so tend to be regarded by Wold Newton scholars as separate people from Tarzan and Doc Savage or dismissed entirely.

3. Objective Correlative Principle

There are two opposing versions of this principle. The first is that an objective correlative need not be found for every version of a character. That is, the movie featuring Alec Baldwin as the Shadow need not be reconciled with the pulp or radio versions of the character and may be dismissed. Texts such as this can be viewed as the products of ordinary creative activity; that is, they are fiction.

The second is the unstated assumption of Wold-Newtonry that writers are not imaginative; that is they do not come up with characters and stories through their imaginations but rely primarily upon source material and notes such as the Shadow's files or Watson's records of Sherlock Holmes' cases. Essentially, some real event or person can be found behind nearly every published story, although many of the details of a story may have been created by its credited author.

Conclusion

Despite some surface similarities, Wold-Newtonry is not a form of fan fiction. Rather, it is parascholarship. It lacks the institutional networks and hierarchies of status, prestige, and power that characterize academic scholarship, but the two share the spirit of inquiry and collegial respect that characterize (or should) the refinement, extension, and transmission of knowledge that is the purpose of both. The difference between them is that in academic scholarship truthfulness is both an ethical norm and the basis for rules of academic professionalism, whereas Wold-Newtonry is based upon a fiction—the idea that fictional characters live real lives that can be documented and traced.

In the end, Wold-Newtonry is a game, and as with any game the pleasure of playing it comes from performing well within its rules. In the case of Wold-Newtonry, scholars choose their own rules; but there does exist a group of scholars—whose work is represented herein—who generally work with the same basic assumptions and through their articles have created a kind of consensus version of the WNU that is essentially consistent with Farmer's (occasionally contradictory) vision of the Wold Newton Universe and Family. The theories and methodologies I have presented in this article should help place the rest of the articles in this book into a context that makes them more enjoyable. And—this is one of the hopes of the contributors to this book—they might prompt readers to take up the pen and propose their own versions of the WNU or further expand on the work we have done here.29

Bibliography

Brady, Laura. "Discourse Community Analysis Assignment Sheet." Center for Writing Excellence. West Virginia University. 2001. <www.as.wvu.edu/~lbrady/202discourse.html>.

Cawelti, John G. *Adventure, Mystery, and Romance: Formula Stories as Art and Popular Culture*. Chicago: University of Chicago Press, 1976.

Diogenes Club. "The Sherlock Holmes Library, Volume I." The Diogenes Club. 1999. <www.diogenes-club.com/shlibrary1.htm>.

Straight Dope Advisory Board. "Did Sherlock Holmes Really Exist?" The Straight Dope. 8 Apr. 2003. < www.straightdope.com/mailbag/msherlock.html>.

The Arms of Tarzan

The English Nobleman whom Edgar Rice Burroughs called John Clayton, Lord Greystoke

By Philip José Farmer

Burroughs Bulletin No. 22, Summer 1971

NOTE: The speech published here is not quite that given during the Dum-Dum Banquet on Burroughs' Day, September 5, 1970, in Detroit, Michigan. Some changes have been made and insertions and additions worked in due to corrections of errors on my part and a failure to resist the temptation to gild the lily. It is, however, in the main, the same speech.

Ladies and gentlemen, mangani, tarmangani, gomangani, and bolgani.

I'm happy to be here. Whether or not you will be happy remains to be seen. I warn you that what I am going to say has little "relevance." I'm all for relevancy to the problems of our time. I belong to the ZPG (Zero Population Growth), have worked in the "Write For Your Life" campaign, and have consistently tried to combat prejudice and inhumane thinking in my writings. I've been working for some time on a book concerning the need for an Economy of Abundance. I've just finished two short stories about pollution in our times. I'm writing a novel, *Death's Dumb Trumpet*, about the effects of pollution twenty years from now.

But you won't be getting any of that today. Men must have hobbies, otherwise they go mad. The works of Edgar Rice Burroughs (ERB) are, to me, a gate into parallel worlds where there are problems, but none that my hero, and, therefore, me as the hero, can't handle. There I can relax and forget, for the time being, the noisy, stinking, dusty, and hostile world that exists outside my window. And, too often, inside the window.

It's not my purpose today to justify my love for ERB's worlds. You know why I love them, otherwise you wouldn't be here.

I propose today to inspect a very small segment of the world of Tarzan, one that has been left entirely unexplored, as far as I know. For that purpose, I've had some transparencies of the subject for today, the Greystoke coat-of-arms, prepared. You can observe it in widescreen color on this wall while I lecture.

(Please show the first transparency.)

I furnished the original research for these arms, the first rough sketches, and the blazoning. But Bjo Trimble did the actual execution, which I consider to be superb. She took a keen interest in the project and put in much time she could ill afford in research on her own and in the actual calculations and drawings. The result exceeded my expectations; her visualizations surpassed my own.

NOTE: This illustration is at present, September, 1971, scheduled to be part of the jacket illustration of my *The Private Life of Tarzan*. This is a biography of Lord Greystoke along the lines of W.S. Baring-Gould's *Sherlock Holmes of Baker Street* and *Nero Wolfe of West Thirty-Fifth Street*, and also of C. Northcote Parkinson's *The Life and Times of Horatio Hornblower*. The latter was issued after the Ms for the Tarzan Life had been turned in to the publisher, Doubleday.

The Tarzan books describe, or hint at, many things. But in none is there any reference to the coat-of-arms of the "Greystoke" family. There is a reference in *Tarzan of the Apes* to the family crest on the great ring which Tarzan's father wore. But the crest is not described. Greystoke, as you know, is not the actual title of the noble family that engendered the immortal ape-man. Greystoke is a pseudonym used by ERB to cover the real identity of a line of English peers. I intend to speculate about the real title. But Greystoke has been associated too long with Tarzan for any of us to be at ease in using any other title. This is the way it should be, and this is why I have placed the legend, GREYSTOKE, under the arms.

However, though Greystoke is not Tarzan's real title, he is descended from the de Greystocks, the ancient and distinguished barons of Greystoke, Cumberland, England. I refer you to Burke's *Extinct Peerage*, Nicolas' *A Synopsis of the Peerage*, Cokayne's *The Complete Peerage* for their history. This descent of Tarzan through several lines of this family is one of the reasons ERB chose Greystoke for a pseudonym.

Now—the blazoning, I'll give it to you as it would be in Burke's *Genealogical and Heraldic History of the Peerage, Baronetage, And Knightage*. Burke's *Peerage* (to use its short title) has over 2475 pages of very small, closely set print devoted to genealogy.

After the blazoning, I'll explain the technical terms I used. Then I'll go into the history of each family represented here. I'll demonstrate that Tarzan, king of the tribe of Kerchak, chief of the Waziri, a member of the English peerage, lord of the jungle, demigod of the forest, has a noble genealogy indeed. In fact, no one in Europe, not even Queen Elizabeth of Great Britain, can boast of a more ancient and varied lineage.

The Blazoning:

ARMS—Quarterly of six: 1st, GREBSON OF GREBSON, *argent*, on a *saltire* azure drinking horns in triskele gules; 2nd. DRUMMOND, *or*, three bars wavy *gules*; 3rd,O'BRIEN, *gules*, three lions passant guardant in pale, per pale *or* and *argent*; 4th, CALDWELL, *sable*, a torn *or*; 5th, RUTHERFORD, *gules*, a wild bull's head cabossed, eyes of the first, otherwise of its own kind, between the horns a wildman's head affrontée, eyes of the first; 6th, GREYSTOCK, barry of six, *argent* and *azure*, over all three chaplets of roses gules. CRESTS—A sleuth-hound argent, collared and leashed *gules*, for DRUMMOND; issuing from a cloud *azure* an arm embowed brandishing a sword *gules*, pommel and hilt *sable*, for GREBSON; a spear *or* transfixing a Saracen's head *gules*, for GREBSON. SUPPORTERS—Dexter, a savage wreathed about the middle with oak leaves, in the dexter hand a bow, with a quiver of arrows over his shoulder, all vert, and a lion's skin or hanging behind his back; sinister, a female great ape guardant, all proper. MOTTOES—"Je Suys Encore Vyvant"; "Kreeg-ah!"

The explanation of the technical terms:

Quarterly of six. Quarterly originally meant the four equal parts into which the shield was divided for showing four arms. But some people added even more, and the family of Dent, the Baronage of Furnivall, has a quarterly of ten. The Greystokes could add a hundred, if they wished, since they are descended from that many different noble families. But the shields generally are restricted to a reasonable number.

Argent is a heraldic term for silver or white. Azure is blue. A saltire, or St. Andrew's cross, is a cross in the form of an X. The St. Andrew's cross is usually found in the field of a Scots family but not always. Gules is red. In triskele indicates a figure composed of three usually curved or bent branches radiating from a center. Triskele, or triskelion, is from a Greek word meaning three-legged.

Or is gold. A bar is a horizontal division of the shield occupying one-fifth thereof. Wavy means undulating. Passant is a term for beasts in a walking position with the right forepaw raised, although I've seen the left front paw raised, for instance, in the lion passant of the crest of a branch of the English family of Farmer.

Guardant is front or full-faced. In pale indicates that the charges, in this case, the lions, are arranged beneath one another. Per pale indicates the particular manner in which a shield or field or a charge is divided by a partition line. Thus, the lions, in pale, per pale *or* and *argent* are arranged in a vertical column and each is half-gold and half-silver, as you see.

Sable is black. A torn is a heraldic spinning wheel. Torn was an archaic English word for the early type of spinning wheel used in the late 13th century.

A wild bull's head cabossed. Cabossed, or caboshed, indicates the head of any beast looking full-faced with nothing of the neck visible. "Of the first" means that the color is the first one mentioned in the blazoning. In this case, of the first means gules. The eyes of the bull and the wild man are bright red, giving the Rutherford charges a fierce and sinister look. Making the eyes red was Bjo's idea, a stroke of genius on her part, as far as I'm concerned. Of its own kind, or proper, are terms applicable to animals, trees, vegetables, etc., when they are their natural color.

A wild man's head affrontée. Affrontée is a term applied to full-faced human heads.

Barry describes the field or charge divided by horizontal lines. Thus, GREYSTOCK, barry of six, argent and azure, means six horizontal bars alternately silver and blue.

Crests over coat-of-arms were originally derived from the actual crests of helmets worn by the nobles. The only term used for the crests so far not explained is *embowed.* (Pointing to the center crest.) An arm embowed. Embowed means bent or bowed.

The Saracen's head originally indicated an ancestor who went to the Holy Land on one of the crusades. The head is *gules*, instead of a proper or natural color, because of a story associated with Tarzan's crusader ancestor. The story will be told in the genealogy of Tarzan in *The Private Life of Tarzan.*[30]

Regard the two supporters, the figures holding the shield up. One is dexter; the other, sinister. Dexter means the right-hand supporter. Right and left, in heraldry, are as seen by the man behind the shield. Sinister, of course, has no evil meaning in heraldry; it merely indicates the left-hand position.

The savage, or woodman, or wildman, is all *vert*, that is, green.

The upper motto is French in archaic spelling. *Je Suys Encore Vyvant*. Translation: *I Still Live*. Or *I am Still Living*. Or *I Yet Live*.

Tarzan, as you no doubt recall, said these words more than once in seemingly hopeless situations. In *Tarzan the Untamed*, Bertha Kircher, the supposed German spy, and Tarzan are about to be caught by the insane Xujans and their hunting lions. She says to Tarzan, "You think there is some hope, then?"

"We are still alive," was his only answer.

And in *Tarzan the Terrible*, when Jane and Tarzan are soon to be sacrificed, Jane asks, "You still have hope?"

"I am still alive," he said as though that were sufficient answer.

Thus Tarzan echoed the motto of his ancient family, the old war cry his fighting ancestors used to rally their men around them when the battle seemed to have turned against them.

I probably don't need to point out that *"I still live"* is also the motto of another great fighter, John Carter of Mars.

The lower motto, "Kreeg-ah!" is, of course, the warning cry of the great ape. (As an aside, I'd like to suggest that it's long past time for the great ape to be given a scientific classification. And since Tarzan's father was the European to describe the great ape—in his diary, of course—I propose that we honor him by terming this new genus *Megapithecus greystoki*. This would also honor his son, who knows more of the great ape than anyone in the world, civilized or uncivilized.

The lower motto, "Kreeg-ah!", was added by Tarzan to the family arms when he assumed the title in late 1910 (according to my reckoning). The great ape supporter is also Tarzan's idea. The original supporter was a heraldic Sagittarius, a centaur with a bow. But Tarzan wanted to honor his foster mother, Kala, and so he replaced the Sagittarius with a female mangani. This changing of supporters in a coat-of-arms for personal reasons is not unprecedented. The 10th Duke of Marlborough, for instance, replaced both supporters on his family's arms. However, this type of arms is usually regarded as a personal coat-of-arms, a variation on the family's, and other members of the family may use the older type if they desire. I would imagine that Korak would keep his father's arms, inasmuch as he was also closely associated with the mangani.

While I'm at it, I might as well say that these arms are not complete or even accurate from the strict viewpoint of the College of Heraldry. All of the quarters except the first and fourth should have little symbols, such as a crescent or mullet (a five-pointed star) or others to indicate that these are different branches from the main Drummond, O'Brien, Rutherford, and Greystock lines. However, the symbols for difference are not always used, and Tarzan's noble forebears never got around to conforming to strict usage.

Also, the Drummond crest, the sleuth-hound (that must be Sherlock Holmes' crest, too) should be on the sinister side. The crests of the primary family, the Grebsons, should occupy the dexter place of honor and the center. But these crests entered the Greystoke arms a long time before heraldry became regulated by a college of heralds or by royal authority. The crests should be somewhat smaller and all placed above the shield, but, again, they were drawn thus in the distant old days, and the Greystoke family has never seen fit to change them.

The headpiece you see on top of the shield is the coronet of a duke, not to be confused with the ducal or crest coronet. It has a circle, or coronet, of gold surmounted by eight golden strawberry leaves, of which only five are visible, and by the red golden-tasseled cap with the ermine under-rim you see. I know that some of you are thinking: Why the coronet of a duke? Tarzan, according to his own statement in *Tarzan, Lord of the Jungle*, is a viscount. And several other Tarzan books assert that he is viscount.

Is he? My own theory is that he may have been a duke, a marquess, earl, baron, or baronet (a baronet is not a noble but a sort of hereditary knight), or any combination of these. But he would not be a viscount. Or, if he were, it would be only one of his titles. ERB took great pains to conceal the true identity of "Lord Greystoke." He would have altered the reply Tarzan really made when asked (by Sir Bertram of the city of Nimmr) what his rank was. ERB knew that Tarzanic scholars would search through the some 120-plus viscounts listed in Burke's *Peerage* for evidence that one was Tarzan. So he directed them down a blind alley.

I don't want to go into this theory in detail at this time. But the feudal society Tarzan found in a lost valley in Ethiopia was supposed to be descended from two shiploads of Englishmen who had set out with Richard I on the First Crusade. This was in 1191, but viscount, as an English title, was not used until 1440. If Tarzan had "truly" said he was a viscount, Sir Bertram wouldn't have known what he meant. Obviously, Tarzan did not say that. Or, if he did, seeing that Sir Bertram did not understand him, he went on to his other titles. Sir Bertram would have heard of "earl" and "baron", since these were the only English titles of nobility extant in Richard's time.

From the above argument, we can assume, with a good amount of reasonableness, that Tarzan is an earl or baron. Given the ancientness and honourableness of his line (stressed by ERB in the first Tarzan book), the chances are that he is both.

On the other hand, very few Englishmen, that is, men of Old English descent, actually accompanied Richard. Most of his crusaders were Normans, and it is doubtful that Richard had enough Englishmen to fill one ship, let alone two. (Accounting at least 60 knights per ship as a shipload.) This would mean that the people of the valley were descended from Normans and so spoke an evolved Norman. This leads to developments that I don't have time for here but will lay out for the interested reader in *The Private Life of Tarzan*.

It is, however, incredible that the man we know as Lord Greystoke would not be a duke. If Peter Wimsey's father was Duke of Denver and Lord John Roxton's father was Duke of Pomfret, then surely Tarzan must be a duke, regardless of how many other titles he holds. Don't forget that Tarzan is referred to as a "dook" twice, once in *Tarzan and the Foreign Legion*. I do have more solid reasons than this for placing him in the highest rank of nobility. But I have to expound these elsewhere, due to lack of time here.

(Please put in the second slide.)

(This was a close-up of the shield.)

To arms. The first, first. GREBSON OF GREBSON. Am I revealing, for the first time by anyone anywhere, the true name and title of Tarzan's family?

Not exactly.

The present Lord Greystoke wishes to have his identity stay hidden, and I respect his reasons. (Besides, I would not think of offending the

Lord of the Jungle.) So I have picked a title and a coat-of-arms which reveal certain facts about him, or come close to the facts, without disclosing his genuine identity. The title and the arms are analogs. They are not the real title and arms. But they are near enough to give an idea of what the genuine items are.

Some of you know that ERB, in the original Ms of *Tarzan of the Apes*, used Bloomstoke as Tarzan's title. Then he changed it. Why? For one thing, Greystoke sounds more aristocratic than Bloomstoke. Also, Tarzan *is* descended from the Greystokes. (So is half of the peerage of England as you may ascertain if you care to take the trouble to trace them through Burke.) But the *Grey* in Greystoke was also provided by ERB as a clue for some scholar who might want to tackle the formidable hunt for the real Tarzan. (We know that ERB was fond of codes and sometimes used them in making up names or disguising real names for his characters and places.)

Following this coded lead (among many others), I hunted down and identified the real-world Tarzan. The project took me two and a half years and involved reading every word of the lineages in 2457 pages of Burke's *Peerage*. However, all the work I put in would not have led me to the real Tarzan if I had not stumbled across a certain clue through sheer good fortune. Only a highly improbable sequence of events could permit another to follow the trail I followed. I am sorry, but I cannot supply the necessary clue, since "Lord Greystoke" himself has asked me not to. Therefore, I am compelled to suppress everything I know for sure and behave as if I were as ignorant as everybody else in the matter. I have to proceed by analogy, and if you choose to dispute my theses, you have a perfect right to do so.

I will tell you one thing. Tarzan's real title does not start with GR (as in Greystoke or Grebson). That initial letter cluster will, however, lead you to some of his ancestors and relatives in Burke's *Peerage*. Nor does his title contain the word *grey*. It does contain an archaic word implying grey. I won't tell you if the word is of Germanic, Latin, Pictish, or Celtic origin, however.

Grebson, our analog family name and title, comes from the Old English Graegbeardssunu. This means The Son of the Grey-Bearded One. And who was the Grey-Bearded One? He was Woden, the chief god of the Anglo-Saxons or Old English, the same as the Othinn of the Old Norse or the Wuotan of the Old High Germans or Othinus of the continental Saxons. According to the Norse *Edda*, the great god had many epithets. To read off all his titles would take several minutes, so I resist the temptation.

Tarzan's real title contains an epithet for Woden, though not the one I give here, which is an analogous epithet.

Note the argent field and azure saltire of Grebson's arms. Argent and azure are Woden's colors. Note the three drinking horns with interlocking tips. This ancient sign for Woden (or Odin) is found carved on rocks in many places in Scandinavia and a number of places in the British Isles. In Old English it would be called the *waelcnotta* and in Old Norse is the *valknutr*. It means the "knot of the slain" and stands for Woden (or Odin) in his aspect of the god of the warriors who've died in battle. Hence the gules, or red, color of the drinking horns.

You won't find this symbol on Tarzan's real shield. But you will find something analogous, if you are persistent enough and wildly lucky.

Apparently, the founder of Tarzan's family, the original Grebson, claimed to be descended from the god Woden. The Queen of England makes exactly the same claim, as you can find out by reading *The Royal Lineage* section of Burke's *Peerage*. She is descended from Egbert, King of Wessex (died 839 A.D.). Egbert, like the other kings of English states at that time, Mercia, Deira, Kent, Eastanglia, etc., had a traditional genealogy which went unbroken back to Denmark of circa 300 A.D. and to the great god Woden.

Those interested can refer to page 165, Vol. 1, of Jacob Grimm's *Teutonic Mythology*, Dover Books.

I submit that a human being can't have a more highly placed or illustrious ancestor.

That Tarzan's arms bear the ancient symbol of Woden indicates that his ancestors clung to the old religion long after their neighbors were Christianized. Originally, their shields bore only the drinking horns gules in triskele on an argent and azure field. Then the saltire was added to convince others that the family was truly of the new faith. History tells us of the tenacity with which parts of rural England held on to the ancient faiths. And ERB, in *The Outlaw of Torn*, says of the peasants' love for the outlaw, "Few…had seen his face and fewer still had spoken with him, but they loved his name and his prowess and in secret they prayed for him to their ancient god Wodin and the lesser gods of the forest and the meadow and the chase…"

Second, DRUMMOND. Drummond comes from the Gaelic *druim monadh*, meaning *back of the mountain*. This Scots family is presently represented by the Earl of Lancaster and the Earl of Perth. The family was founded by Maurice, the son of George, a young son of Andreas,

King of Hungary. Maurice came to Scotland in 1066 and settled there. He, in turn, could trace his ancestry unbroken back to Arpad, the Magyar chief who conquered Hungary (died 907 A.D.).

Third, O'BRIEN. A prominent member of this ancient Irish family is the Baron of Inchiquin. In an unbroken line it descends from Brian Boroimhe, chief Irish monarch in 1002 A.D. and victor of the battle of Clontarf, though he himself was killed by the Danes. This line can actually trace itself back to Cormac Cas, son of Olliol Olum, King of Ireland, circa 200 A.D.

Fourth, CALDWELL, *sable* a torn *or*.

Some of you pricked up your ears when I first blazoned these arms. You remembered that Tarzan, in *The Return of Tarzan*, used the pseudonym of John Caldwell when he was a French secret agent traveling on a liner from Algiers to Cape Town.

Why would he use that pseudonym? Obviously, he picked the first name that came to mind, that of his illustrious ancestor, John Caldwell. No doubt, Tarzan had been reading in Burke's *Peerage* about the Greystoke lineage and the story of John Caldwell was fresh in his mind.

Another reason you pricked up your ears was the mention of the torn, the heraldic spinning wheel. You recalled Richard Plantagenet, son of Henry III, he who would later be called Norman of Torn or the Outlaw of Torn. You probably asked yourself, "What does Farmer mean by that? The Outlaw of Torn is Tarzan's ancestor? But Norman killed one of Tarzan's ancestors, a Greystoke!"

Did he? ERB did not say that this particular Greystoke was an ancestor of Tarzan. That's an assumption by some of his readers. Perhaps the slain Greystoke was a member of the genuine de Greystocks of Greystoke Castle, Cumberland. He may or may not have been Tarzan's forefather, but I'm inclined to believe that Norman of Torn certainly was. Tarzan would certainly have the greatest warrior of the Middle Ages in his family line.

The Outlaw was born in 1240 A.D. and was 15 years old when he slew Greystoke. This would be in 1255, the 39th year of Henry III's reign. So the Greystoke whom Norman killed was probably the son of Baron Robert de Greystock (died before 1253) and the younger brother of William de Greystock. William's son, John, was the first Greystoke summoned as a baron *by writ* to Parliament. This was in 1295 A.D. in Edward I's time. This, by the way, was the first regular parliament, recognized as such.

We know that Henry III finally became aware that the famous, or infamous, outlaw was his long-lost son, Richard. But Henry died in 1272, and his son, Edward I, called Longshanks, was, though a very good king for those days, proud, jealous, and suspicious. His younger brother Richard, too popular with the common people, would have been forced to flee on a trumped-up charge of treason (nothing rare in those days). By then Bertrade de Montfort, his wife, had died, probably in childbirth or of disease, very common causes of fatality then. Richard would have taken a pseudonym again, that of John Caldwell, landless warrior. In the North of England he met old Baron Grebson. The baron had no male issue, and so, when his daughter fell in love with the stranger knight, he adopted him. This was nothing unusual; you will find similar examples throughout Burke's *Peerage*. The family name became Caldwell-Grebson, though the Caldwell was later dropped. Similar examples of this also abound in Burke.

John Caldwell could not use the same arms as the Outlaw of Torn, of course. So, instead of *argent* a falcon's wing *sable*, he used *sable* a torn *or*. That he chose the torn showed he could not resist an example of "canting arms," a heraldic pun. One, indeed, that proved as dangerous as might be expected. Edward I heard of the appearance from nowhere of a knight who bore a torn on his shield, and he investigated. The king's men ambushed John Caldwell, and though he slew five of them, he, too, died.

How can we be sure of this?

An obscure book on medieval witchcraft, published in the middle 1600s, describes the case of a knight who was, for reasons unknown to the writer, slain by Edward I's men in a northern county. When his body was laid out to be washed, his left breast was found to bear a violet lily-shaped birthmark. This was thought to be the mark of the devil. But we readers of *The Outlaw of Torn* will recognize the true identity of the man suspected of witchcraft.

This theory could be wrong, of course. I propose an alternate to consider. You may have noticed the remarkable resemblance between the Outlaw and Tarzan. Both were tall, splendidly built, and extremely powerful men. (Anybody who can drive the point of a broadsword through chain mail into his opponent's heart is strong enough to crack the neck of a bull ape.) Both men had grey eyes. Both wore their hair in bangs across their foreheads. Neither knew the meaning of fear.

But the description of the Outlaw could also apply, except for a few minor points, to John Carter of Mars. What if the Outlaw did not die, as I first speculated, but had somehow defeated the aging process? What if, like Tarzan, he had stumbled across an elixir for immortality? During his wanderings in rural England, he came across a wizard or witch, actually a member of the old faith, who had a recipe for preventing degeneration of the body. If a witch doctor in modern Africa could have such, and give it to Tarzan, then a priest of an outlawed religion in the Middle Ages could give such to the Outlaw of Torn.

Sometime during the following six centuries, the Outlaw suffered amnesia. This was either from a blow on the head (again recalling Tarzan, who suffered amnesia many times from blows on the head) or because loss of memory of early years is an unfortunate by-product of the elixir. Thus, on March 4, 1866, the Outlaw, a long-time resident of Virginia, an admitted victim of amnesia, left a cave in Arizona for the planet Mars. ERB called this man John Carter. Notice the J.C. I suggest that he may have been Richard Plantagenet, Norman of Torn, John Caldwell, and, finally, John Carter.

It is possible that John Caldwell was not killed, that he slew all of Edward's men, who actually numbered six, mangled the face of one tall corpse, and stained a violet lily mark on the corpse's left breast. And, once again, he disappeared into pseudonymity but gained immortality as the Warlord of Mars.

It's true that the Outlaw's hair was brown and Carter's was black. But hair gets darker as one ages (until it starts to gray), and 626 years are long enough for anybody's hair to get black.

If this theory is correct, the Outlaw of Torn is not only John Carter of Mars but Tarzan's ancestor by about 600 years. But John Carter may have been the ancestor of Tarzan many times over. He may have followed the fortunes of his descendants with keen interest and, every now and then, remarried into the line and begat more powerful, quick thinking, fearless, grey-eyed men and fearless grey-eyed beautiful daughters. I wouldn't be surprised if he were not only the ancestor of Tarzan's father but of Tarzan's mother, Alice Rutherford. Perhaps this regular insertion of Carter's genes into the line is why ERB insists so strongly on the influence of heredity in Tarzan's behavior.

And I point out, as something for you to chew on, that Sherlock Holmes, Professor Challenger, Raffles, Richard Wentworth, Lord Peter Wimsey, and Denis Nayland Smith were all grey-eyed. And, though some were slim, all had very powerful muscles. Could these, together with Tarzan, be descendants of John Carter of Mars?

Their relationship, with those of Doc Savage, Kent Allard, Korak, Lord John Roxton, Nero Wolfe, and The Scarlet Pimpernel, will be described in a separate essay.

Oh, yes, I almost forgot Bulldog Drummond.

Fifth, RUTHERFORD.

As we know, Tarzan's mother was the Honourable Alice Rutherford. The *Honourable* indicates that she was the daughter of a baron or a viscount, though ERB does not tell us what the title of her father was. The Rutherfords are an ancient and once-powerful Scots border family. Its name comes from the Old English *hrythera ford*, meaning *wild cattle of the ford*. The arms you see here, the wild bull cabossed and the wildman's head between the horns, are the arms of the lords of Tennington. Internal evidence in *The Return of Tarzan* convinces me that Tarzan's mother was the aunt of the Lord Tennington who married Hazel Strong, Jane Porter's best friend. The reasons for this conclusion will be given in a separate essay.

Sixth, GREYSTOCK.

Tarzan is descended through at least half a dozen lines from the barons of Greystoke. At present, the barony is in abeyance, the last male heir having died in 1569. The Earl of Carlisle, the Baron of Petre, and the Baron of Mowbray, Segrave, and Stourton are co-heirs. The Earl of Carlisle bears the Greystoke arms on his shield, and a cousin of the Duke of Norfolk resides in Greystoke Castle. I have a letter from the cousin in which he says that he was very fond of the Tarzan books when he was young. But, he adds, "…as you know, I am not Tarzan."

What he doesn't say is that he is a relative of Tarzan's.

(Please put the first slide back on.)

About all that remains to explain in the arms is the dexter supporter. Aside from its being green, it looks like the usual savage or woodman supporter. Actually, it represents the son of John Caldwell. After his father's supposed death, the son had to flee into the wilds of northern England to escape the King's officers. There he adopted a green costume and used a green-painted bow and green arrows. Because of these, he was known as The Green Archer or, sometimes, as The Green Baron. His legend was combined with that of Robert Fitz-ooth to create the Robin Hood legend.

The golden lion skin which he wears here was added by Tarzan to honor Jad-bal-ja.

So you can see that the baby born in a little log cabin on the West African coast, raised by apes, naked until twenty and then wearing second-hand clothes, yet came from a lineage few can match and eventually inherited the golden coronet and crimson miniver-edged mantle of a peer of the realm.

Before I close, let me summarize the illustrious ancestors of

Tarzan.

First, the nonhuman founder of his line, Woden, chief god of the Old English tribes.

Henry III and through him William the Conqueror and Rolf the Ganger (the Viking who conquered Normandy). Through Henry III's wife, Alfred the Great, Egbert, and Charlemagne, Charlemagne could trace his ancestry back to Pepin the Short, died 768 A.D.

Also, through Henry III, the Outlaw of Torn and his son, The Green Archer, one of the two men whose exploits contributed to the Robin Hood legend.

And possibly, many times over, the genes of the Outlaw of Torn, later known as John Carter of Barsoom. [27*]

Through the Scots Drummond family, Tarzan is descended from Arpad, the Magyar conqueror of Hungary.

Through the O'Briens, from Olliol Olum, Irish King, early 200s.

I don't have time to go into the many other famous ancestors of Tarzan, such as Sir Nigel Loring (whose story is told in Doyle's *The White Company* and *Sir Nigel*). Or such as William Marshal, the Earl of Pembroke, who served Richard I and King John and was undoubtedly the greatest warrior of his time and probably of the entire Middle Ages (outside of the Outlaw of Torn). These will be described in detail in the lineage of Tarzan, which will be in my book, *The Private Life of Tarzan*.

I hope you have enjoyed this visitation into Tarzan ancestry via his coat-of-arms.

I thank you.

The Secret History of Captain Nemo

By Rick Lai

I. A Study in Identity

In *Tarzan Alive* and *Doc Savage: His Apocalyptic Life*, Philip José Farmer did much more than just fashion biographies of two popular fictional characters. He formulated a genealogy linking scores of heroes and villains from literature. Mr. Farmer dubbed this exercise "creative mythography." In linking all these characters, some loose ends were left dangling. One such case was a comprehensive history of Captain Nemo.

As most people are aware, Captain Nemo was the enigmatic commander of the submarine *Nautilus* in Jules Verne's *Twenty Thousand Leagues under the Sea* (1869). Most people today visualize Captain Nemo bearded due to James Mason's portrayal of the seaman in the 1954 film adaptation of Verne's classic novel. In reality, Nemo did not have a beard in his first appearance in Verne's works. Nemo was initially described as follows:[31] "He was tall, with a broad forehead, straight nose, mouth clearly defined, beautiful teeth, fine tapered hand..." He also possessed black eyes set wide apart.

Nemo is Latin for "no one." The real name of the mysterious individual was not disclosed in *Twenty Thousand Leagues under the Sea*. The impression was given that Nemo was a left-wing philosopher rebelling against the repressive governments of the world. He supplied gold to people on the island of Crete. Anyone reading this novel in 1869 would be aware that the natives of Crete were fighting for independence from Turkey. The contemporary reader assumed that Nemo was funding the rebels.

One of the most memorable scenes of the novel had Nemo risking his life to rescue an Indian pearl diver from a shark. After the incident, Nemo made this intriguing remark: "That Indian, professor, lives in the land of the oppressed, and I am to this day, and will be until my last breath, a native of the same land." If Nemo was not an Indian himself, then he saw himself as a member of an oppressed people. At the very least, Nemo identified with the inhabitants of the subcontinent as fellow individuals suffering imperialist oppression.

The *Nautilus* caused many ships to sink by ramming them. Some of these incidents were accidental, but others were definitely intentional. The deliberate acts of destruction were aimed against vessels of an unnamed nation that had persecuted Nemo. While Jules Verne did not name the country that was the object of Nemo's wrath, most readers assumed it was Great Britain. During an attack on a warship of the "accursed country," Nemo made these revealing comments about his past life:

"I am the law, and I am the tribunal! I am the oppressed, and there are my oppressors! Thanks to them, everything I loved was destroyed—everything I loved and venerated—homeland, wife, children, my father and mother. There is everything I hate! So you be quiet!"

Displayed in Nemo's cabin aboard the *Nautilus* was a photo of a woman and two children. One would assume they were the wife and progeny Nemo lost.

Twenty Thousand Leagues Under the Sea concluded with Nemo and the *Nautilus* seemingly destined for oblivion in the Maelstrom, a large whirlpool off the coast of Norway. Captain Nemo and his underwater craft reappeared in *The Mysterious Island* (1874). This novel concerned a group of American Civil War refugees who found themselves marooned on an uncharted island in the Pacific. The castaways would christen their new home Lincoln Island after the then President of the United States. The plot remained a Robinson Crusoe story until the castaways concluded that they had an unknown benefactor assisting them against the island's perils. This ally revealed himself to be Captain Nemo. The leader of the Americans, Captain Cyrus Smith,[32] knew all about Nemo from having read *Twenty Thousand Leagues under the Sea.*

Having escaped the Maelstrom, the *Nautilus* sailed the oceans of the world until all its crew but Nemo had died. Presumably the other crewmen perished from natural causes. Now an old man with a beard, Nemo returned the *Nautilus* to the island where the submarine had originally been built. This was the same island where the Americans had found themselves stranded. Nemo revealed himself to be Dakkar, an Indian prince who had lost his family and kingdom in the Sepoy Mutiny of 1857-58. In fact, Dakkar was supposed to be the secret leader of the rebellion.[33] Leaving the castaways treasure chests of Indian jewels, Nemo died from old age. Smith buried him in the *Nautilus*. When the island sank due to a volcanic eruption, Smith and his comrades were rescued by a British yacht.

To the casual reader, the mystery of Captain Nemo had been solved. To the more discerning reader, Verne's solution raised even more questions about the skipper of the *Nautilus*. The inconsistencies between Captain Nemo's two appearances were noted in H.W. Starr's "A Submersible Subterfuge or Proof Impositive" in *Leaves from the Copper Beeches* (Livingston Publishing Company, 1959).

A few of Mr. Starr's sharp observations will be noted. *Twenty Thousand Leagues under the Sea* has Nemo commanding the *Nautilus* during 1866-68, but *The Mysterious Island* has the Captain aiding Smith and company since 1865. Nemo was judged by Professor Aronnax, the narrator of *Twenty Thousand Leagues under the Sea*, to be somewhere between thirty-five and fifty years of age, but Nemo was sixty years old in *The Mysterious Island.* Aronnax noticed only Europeans among Nemo's followers, but *The Mysterious Island* suggested that the sailors aboard the *Nautilus* were Indians. How could Smith have read *Twenty Thousand Leagues under the Sea* by 1865 when it was not published until 1869?

There are other discrepancies in Dakkar's statements to Smith. Initially, Dakkar asserted that he had lived underwater for "thirty years." This statement would imply that Dakkar had been sailing aboard the *Nautilus* since the 1830s. This would be impossible if the submarine was constructed after the Sepoy Revolt of the late 1850s. Another contradiction occurred when Dakkar professed that he first met Arronax "sixteen years" previously. Dakkar's meeting with Arronax would have happened in 1852, years before the *Nautilus* was created. At another point, Dakkar then shifted his adventures with Arronax to 1866-67 (as opposed to 1867-1868 as stated in *Twenty Thousand Leagues under the Sea*). Even 1866-67 still contradicts the events of *The Mysterious Island* that depicted Captain Nemo as assisting Smith and his fellow castaways during those years.

Another chronological discrepancy involve yet another of Verne's novels, *The Children of Captain Grant* (1869, also known as *In Search of the Castaways).* This novel was set in 1864-1865. In the conclusion, the villain of the novel, a criminal named Aryton, found himself marooned on another island in the Pacific. Smith and his comrades received an anonymous message in 1866 from Dakkar about Aryton's plight. Since Lincoln Island was close to Aryton's island, Smith and his followers constructed a boat to travel there. Finding a now repentant Aryton, Smith and his crew transported him back to Lincoln Island. Although there is a sufficient gap between Aryton's marooning and his subsequent rescue, Verne stated that Aryton had been a solitary castaway for a period of ten years. A footnote presented as "A Publisher's Note" recognized this discrepancy, and argued that the dates of the earlier *The Children of Captain Grant* were altered for reasons that would later become evident to the reader. Unfortunately, the reasons never became apparent. When Dakkar created a contradictory chronology for *Twenty Thousand Leagues under the Sea*, another footnote referred readers back to the earlier footnote about *The Children of Captain Grant* if they wanted any explanation for these chronological contradictions. Unfortunately, both footnotes are equally enigmatic.

Mr. Starr is not totally correct in arguing that Aronnax only observed Europeans among Nemo's followers. When first meeting Nemo, Aronnax saw him conversing in a strange language with one of his crew. The sailor is described thusly:

"The first was short, strongly muscled, broad-shouldered, with robust limbs, sturdy head, an abundance of black hair and a thick mustache, and a gaze sharp and penetrating. His whole personality was stamped with that southern vivacity we usually associate with the people of Provence."

Aronnax concluded that Nemo and his henchman were members of the same nationality:

"…But I'm inclined to think that the commander and his first mate were born in the low latitudes. There must be southern blood in their veins. But I cannot decide from their looks whether they are Spaniards, Turks, Arabians or Indians. As to their language, it is beyond any comprehension."

Though the idea that Nemo may be an Indian crossed Aronnax's mind, such a possibility seems remote because the Captain's skin was described as "rather pale."[34]

Another difficulty with Nemo being Dakkar concerned the heroes of the commander of the *Nautilus* in *Twenty Thousand Leagues under the Sea.* On the walls of Nemo's cabin were various western leaders who fought for independence and freedom. They included:

- Thaddeus Kosciusko (1746-1817), who fought for both American and Polish independence
- Markos Botzaris (1788-1823). a leader of the Greek War of Independence. His surname was also transliterated from Greek as Botsaris, and his first name was sometimes rendered as Marcos.
- Daniel O'Connell (1775-1847), the champion of Irish Home Rule in the British Parliament.
- George Washington (1732-99) from the American War of Independence.
- Daniele Manin (1804-1857), the leader of an 1848 Venetian insurrection against the Austrians.
- Abraham Lincoln (1809-65), viewed as a martyr in the war against slavery
- John Brown (1800-1859), who led the anti-slavery raid in Harper's Ferry, Virginia during 1859.

Why are there no Indian faces among Nemo's heroes? According to *The Mysterious Island*, Dakkar was the nephew of Tippu Sahib (1749-99), the Sultan of Mysore who died fighting against the British. Tippu was supposed to be the man who inspired Dakkar to launch the Sepoy Mutiny. Why wasn't Tippu's portrait in Nemo's cabin?

As a result of the numerous discrepancies between the two books featuring Nemo, Mr. Starr completely dismissed *The Mysterious Island* as a totally impossible sequel. Seeking to clear up the question of Nemo's identity, Mr. Starr propounded that the Captain was Professor James Moriarty, the archenemy of Sir Arthur Conan Doyle's Sherlock Holmes.

The premise that Moriarty was Nemo can be bolstered by similarities between the two men. Both have high foreheads. Moriarty was a Professor of Mathematics, and Nemo was seen performing mathematical calculations aboard the *Nautilus*. Moriarty and Nemo shared a love of art. Moriarty owned an expensive painting by the French artist Jean-Baptise Greuze (1725-1805). Nemo had the works of several old masters such as Raphael and Da Vinci in his cabin.

Details of Professor Moriarty's life can be gleaned by examining *The Valley of Fear* (1915) and "The Final Problem" from *The Memoirs of Sherlock Holmes* (1894). After deducing Moriarty's role as ruler of the London underworld in the 1880s, Sherlock Holmes engaged in a duel of wits with the mastermind that culminated in the Professor's death in 1891. As Mr. Starr has noted, Moriarty's life before his battles with Holmes is very sketchy. At the age of twenty-one, Moriarty wrote an acclaimed treatise on Newton's Binomial Theorem. The fame resulting from this achievement enabled Moriarty to be appointed to a mathematical chair at a British university. Rumors at the educational institution forced him to resign his faculty position. He then became an army coach in London. An army coach was a private tutor who prepared soldiers to take entrance exams for the officer corps or for exams that officers must pass to guarantee promotion. While an army coach, Moriarty erected a criminal empire. Since Conan Doyle did not provide any dates about Moriarty's career, Mr. Starr reasoned that the Professor could have disappeared for a few years to pursue his activities as Nemo.

Philip José Farmer adapted Mr. Starr's theory for a novel, *The Other Log of Phileas Fogg* (DAW Books, 1973). In fact, Mr. Starr's article was reprinted as an afterword to Mr. Farmer's novel. *The Other Log of Phileas Fogg* was supposedly the "true story" of the 1872 trip undertaken by the hero of Jules Verne's *Around the World in Eighty*

Days (1872). In Verne's original novel, Phileas Fogg traveled around the globe just to win a bet. Mr. Farmer's book bestowed on Fogg an ulterior motive for participating in the journey. The spaceships of two opposing alien races, the Eridaneans and the Capellans, crash-landed on Earth in the 1600s. Disguised as human beings, these two groups of aliens conducted a secret war against each other. Several humans were adopted into the ranks of their humans. These humans received blood transfusions from their alien masters. As a result of these transfusions, the humans became virtually immortal.

The Eridaneans recruited Fogg while the Capellans did likewise with Moriarty. The Capellans had funded Moriarty's construction of the *Nautilus*. Four years after the destruction of his submarine in the Maelstrom, the former Captain Nemo was seeking to retrieve a group of teleportation devices that had been lost in the battles between the Eridaneans and the Capellans. Fogg embarked on his global trip to find the devices for his superiors. The novel concluded with the Capellans utterly defeated, but Moriarty was still at large.

Mr. Farmer modified somewhat Mr. Starr's ideas. Captain Nemo had black eyes, and Moriarty's orbs were gray. Mr. Starr speculated that Verne endowed Nemo with black eyes because Byronic heroes traditionally had such a facial characteristic. Mr. Farmer had Moriarty using contact lenses to deliberately perpetuate the illusion that he was an Indian prince.

In the Sherlock Holmes stories, Moriarty had two brothers. "The Final Problem" identified one of the Professor's siblings as Colonel James Moriarty. Conan Doyle initially neglected to give the Professor a first name. When referring to the master criminal in "The Adventure of the Empty House" in *The Return of Sherlock Holmes* (1905), he was called Professor James Moriarty. Numerous theories have been generated by Sherlockian scholars as to how two brothers could have the same first name. *The Valley of Fear* reveals the existence of a "younger brother" who was a stationmaster in western England. No Christian name was given for the third Moriarty.

H.W. Starr suggested that the photo of Captain Nemo's family was really that of the Professor and the Colonel as children with their mother. Philip José Farmer argued that the photo was actually of the Professor's wife and children. Unable to abide her husband's egotism, Mrs. Moriarty allegedly left him and took their children with her.

The Other Log of Phileas Fogg contains an explanation of why the Colonel and the Professor were both named James. The Professor was the eldest of the three brothers. The Colonel and the stationmaster had a different mother than the Professor. Even though her stepson was named James, the second Mrs. Moriarty insisted on naming one of her progeny in the same manner. Her decision resulted because her father's name was James.

A completely contradictory ancestry of the Professor is given by Mr. Farmer in *Doc Savage: His Apocalyptic Life*. Instead of having different mothers, the three brothers each had a different father. The Colonel is now designated as the eldest. Their common mother was Morcar Moriarty, an Irish housemaid. Only the Professor's father was named. He was Sir William Clayton, a sort of heroic version of George MacDonald Fraser's Sir Harry Flashman. Clayton had been created in *Tarzan Alive*. Mr. Farmer fashions a daughter, Urania, for the Professor, but there is no elaboration about the other child in Nemo's family portrait. All that is mentioned about the Professor's wife was that her maiden name was Caber. Urania was also portrayed as the mother of two fictional criminal masterminds, Dr. Caber from Lord Dunsany's Joseph Jorkens stories, and Carl Peterson from H. C. "Sapper" McNeile's Bulldog Drummond novels.

A difficulty with depicting the three Moriarty brothers as illegitimate children stems from a statement made by Sherlock Holmes in "The Final Problem." Holmes said that the Professor was "a man of good birth." The sleuth never would have uttered this remark if he knew that the Professor's parents were unmarried.

The Professor's brothers were never physically described in Doyle's stories. Theories have been put forth by Sherlockian devotees about the appearance of the Colonel and the stationmaster. Nicholas Utechin's "The Tree That Wasn't" from *The Baker Street Journal* (New Series, v22, n4, December 1972) proposed that Colonel Moriarty was a tall, lean man with colored glasses from Doyle's "The Adventure of the Empty House." Mr. Utechin believed that the man with colored spectacles was helping Colonel Sebastian Moran, the Professor's chief of staff, search for Sherlock Holmes in London. I believe that Mr. Utechin was only partially right. The man with colored spectacles was actually the stationmaster, not Colonel Moriarty.

This theory about the stationmaster stemmed from three sources. The first is "The Lost Special," a short story from Sir Arthur Conan Doyle's *Round the Fire Stories* (1908). The tale involved the 1890 theft of a train by a master criminal who used the alias of Horace Moore. The purpose of this crime was actually the assassination of a Frenchman who could expose the true identities of the profiteers in the Panama Canal scandal. The crime remained unsolved until 1898 when one of Moore's associates confessed the details. Until the 1898 confession, the man who came closest to solving the crime was an "amateur reasoner of some celebrity." The motto of this sleuth was "that when the impossible has been eliminated the residuum, however improbable, must contain the truth." It is quite obvious that his unnamed detective was Sherlock Holmes. Moore had an expert knowledge of trains, and a somewhat military appearance. The possibility that Moore, still at liberty in 1898, was Colonel Sebastian Moran is ruled out by the fact that Moran was arrested in 1894. Moore must be one of the Professor's brothers. The military appearance suggests Colonel Moriarty, but the knowledge of trains points to the stationmaster.

"A Case of Identity" by Paul Zens from *The Baker Street Journal* (New Series, v25, n2, June 1975) theorizes that the stationmaster was Deputy Chief in charge of the Transportation Department in the Professor's crime syndicate. It is also postulated that the stationmaster was prompted by sibling rivalry to become "Fred Porlock," Sherlock Holmes's informant in the Moriarty gang in *The Valley of Fear*. Mr. Zens further contends that the stationmaster was deeply involved with Sinn Fein, and was arrested in a dragnet against those Irish saboteurs in 1894. If this Moriarty brother was Horace Moore, then he must have eluded the crackdown on the Fenians. Instead of spending the remainder of his days in prison as hypothesized by Mr. Zens, this Moriarty was still free to direct his deviltry on civilization.

John Buchan's *The Power House* (1916) featured the enigmatic Andrew Lumley, outwardly a prominent philanthropist but secretly the leader of the Krafthaus (German for "power-house"). The Krafthaus was an international crime syndicate that promoted political turmoil around the globe. A reference to the "the year of the Chilian Arbitration" places the events of the novel in 1910.[35] Like Professor Moriarty, Lumley was a tall man with rounded shoulders that seemed to be the result of years of study. Lumley was almost seventy, an approximate age for one of the Professor's brothers. He wore tinted glasses like the mysterious man from "The Adventure of the Empty House." Lumley also had pale eyes that could have been gray like those of the Professor. The power wielded by Lumley as leader of the Krafthaus was compared to that of Napoleon Bonaparte. This analogy recalls the depiction of Professor Moriarty as "the Napoleon of Crime" by Sherlock Holmes. Like the Professor, Lumley was also an art collector as shown by his possession of a painting by Henry Raeburn (1756-1823). The Krafthaus supposedly dissolved with Lumley's death.

It is easy to imagine Lumley as one of the Professor's brothers.

In "The Final Problem," Colonel Moriarty drew attention to himself by denying the charges against his brother in the newspapers. Andrew Lumley could never have engaged in such a stratagem because he was fairly prominent in British society. Besides belonging to the Athenaenum and the Carlton Club, he was a major contributor to the Conservative Party. For his various charitable activities, he had received awards from many governments, such as the French Legion of Honor. An obscure stationmaster could have more easily assumed the identity of Andrew Lumley. It would have been impossible for Colonel Moriarty to become Lumley due to the publicity that he had generated around himself. Therefore, I believe the stationmaster to be both Horace Moore and Andrew Lumley.

The hero of *The Power House*, Edward Leithen, made a cameo appearance in Buchan's *The Three Hostages* (1924). The chief protagonist of this novel was Richard Hannay. His adversary in *The Three Hostages* was Dominick Medina, a Member of Parliament who led a criminal organization very similar to the earlier Krafthaus. Dominick had a mysterious past, and Buchan drew on both Professor Moriarty and his own Andrew Lumley in fashioning Hannay's nemesis. Although Dominick's sightless mother appeared in *The Three Hostages* under the alias of the Blind Spinner, his father was apparently deceased. Dominick can easily be envisioned as the stationmaster's son and the Professor's nephew.

The stationmaster did not put in an appearance in *The Other Log of Phileas Fogg*. He was only briefly acknowledged by the Professor as "the other idiot" in his family. The Colonel, however, did enter the novel as an accomplice of his more infamous brother.

Philip José Farmer utilized a theory about the Colonel advanced in Jack Tracy's "Some Thoughts on the Suicide Club" from *The Baker Street Journal* (New Series, v22, n2, June 1972). "The Suicide Club" was not written by Sir Arthur Conan Doyle, but by Robert Louis Stevenson. Together with "The Rajah's Diamond," "The Suicide Club" related the adventures of Prince Florizel of Bohemia in Stevenson's *New Arabian Nights* (1882).[36]

Conan Doyle fashioned a similar character, the King of Bohemia, in "A Scandal in Bohemia" in *The Adventures of Sherlock Holmes* (1892). Edgar W. Smith's "A Scandal In Identity" in *Profile By Gaslight* (Simon and Schuster, 1944), a collection of Sherlockian articles, theorized not only that Stevenson's and Doyle's Bohemian characters were the same individual but also in "The Adventure of the Lion's Mane" that these characters were disguised portrayals of the

Prince of Wales, the future Edward VII.[37] The reference to a nameless "celebrated detective" in "The Suicide Club" was interpreted by Mr. Smith to indicate the indirect involvement of Sherlock Holmes in the story.

The Suicide Club was a murder society that the Prince of Bohemia was combating. In the story's conclusion, the Prince fought a duel with the President of the Suicide Club. The Prince recruited strangers to act as his seconds. This proposition was made to four men; only two accepted. The men who accepted were officers in the British army, but the two who declined were never identified. One of the men who rejected the Prince's request was a tall man with a heavy stoop. Jack Tracy's "Some Thoughts on the Suicide Club" wondered if this unknown person could be Colonel Moriarty. Accepting Mr. Tracy's suggestion, Philip José Farmer presented the Colonel as the tall man in *The Other Log of Phileas Fogg*.

One of the theories from "Some Thoughts on the Suicide Club" which Mr. Farmer did not avail himself of related to the parentage of Professor Moriarty. In his war on the Suicide Club, the Prince received assistance from Dr. Noel, a retired English master criminal living in France. Dr. Noel cocked his head like a bird while Moriarty's head oscillated like a snake. Noel could be Moriarty's father.

Another tall man with a heavy stoop played a prominent role in "The Pavilion on the Links" from Stevenson's *New Arabian Nights*. This tall man was Bernard Huddlestone, an embezzling banker. It is impossible for Huddlestone to be the character from "The Suicide Club" because the banker perished years before Prince Florizel's adventure.

The remainder of this article is an attempt to redefine the theory that Captain Nemo was Professor Moriarty. In *Tarzan Alive* and *Doc Savage: His Apocalyptic Life*, the great heroes and villains of fiction received their extraordinary abilities because their ancestors had been exposed to radiation unleashed by a meteorite which crashed in Wold Newton, Yorkshire, during 1795. *The Other Log of Phileas Fogg* augments the talents of Fogg and Moriarty by having them receive blood transfusions from alien races. While I greatly enjoy *The Other Log of Phileas Fogg* its concept of warring aliens is really too outlandish to fit snugly with the concepts of Verne, Doyle and Stevenson.

In order to create a more coherent picture of Moriarty's existence as Nemo, specific dates have to be assigned to the Professor's career as sketched by Doyle. Nicholas Utechin's "Professor James Moriarty, 1836-91" from *The Baker Street Journal* (v24, n1, June 1974) gives a rather exact approximation of the mastermind's probable career. I have made two slight alterations in Mr. Utechin's findings. In repeating the talented scholar's explanation of how two brothers could be both named James, I have reversed the ages and the medical condition of the two brothers. Rather than have Professor Moriarty become an army coach immediately upon his resignation from the university, I have assigned Moriarty's activities as Nemo between his resignation and his arrival in London.

The Other Log of Phileas Fogg has Prince Dakkar appearing in a totally different context as a leader of the Thuggee cult in India. Thuggee also played a role in Conan Doyle's "Uncle Jeremy's Household," a short story which can be found in these collections: *The Final Adventures of Sherlock Holmes* (Castle Books, 1981), *Masterworks of Crime and Mystery* (Doubleday, 1982) and *The Unknown Conan Doyle: Uncollected Stories* (Doubleday, 1984). Besides linking the events of "Uncle Jeremy's Household" to Professor Moriarty in the section that follows, I have utilized concepts about the Thuggee cult from the film *Indiana Jones and the Temple of Doom* (1984) and the works of Talbot Mundy.

Even though I am dismissing the events of *The Other Log of Phileas Fogg*, I do offer an explanation for the existence of a "phony" diary of Phileas Fogg.

II. Alias Captain Nemo

Due to a strange twist of fate, it could be argued that the great-grandfather of Sherlock Holmes is responsible for the criminal talents exhibited by Professor James Moriarty. Dr. Siger Holmes of Yorkshire had befriended a young medical student, Sebastian Noel, in 1795. Intending to visit relatives in Rayleigh, Dr. Holmes invited Noel to accompany him and a party of distinguished aristocrats to their destination. There was no room for Noel in the two coaches that were to transport Holmes and the others to Rayleigh, so he followed the coaches on horseback. At Wold Newton, a meteorite struck twenty yards away from the coaches and Sebastian Noel. As a result of radiation released by the meteorite, the genes of the travelers underwent mutation. Their descendants would demonstrate superhuman abilities in the future.

Sebastian Noel married Thomasina Vandeleur in 1803. Thomasina was the aunt of the Vandeleur brothers encountered by Florizel of Bohemia in Stevenson's "The Rajah's Diamond." Thomasina gave birth to a son, James Noel, in 1804. Like his father, James Noel became a doctor. He became extremely popular with certain members of the aristocracy because he was willing to discreetly handle the births of their illegitimate children. One of the clients for whom Dr. Noel performed such a service was Sir William Clayton.

Sir William had committed the folly of conducting a liaison with Morcar Moriarty, an Irish housemaid in his employ. As he wasmarried to Lorina Dacre at the time, it was extremely awkward for Sir William when Morcar became pregnant.

Morcar's mother had been Bernice Huddlestone, the sister of Bernard Huddlestone, a prominent banker. Although Bernice came from a wealthy English family, she had been disinherited for eloping with an Irishman, Robert Moriarty.[38] Because her family was financially destitute, Morcar (born in 1815) had been forced to seek work as a servant.

The illegitimate son of Sir William and Morcar was born in 1835. The child was christened James after the doctor who delivered him. Raised as James Moriarty, Sir William's son would eventually become a colonel in the British army. Despite Sir William's precautions, his wife soon learned about her husband's adultery. After divorcing her spouse in 1835, Lorina was granted custody of their two children, Phileas (b. 1832) and Roxanna (b. 1833). After their mother married Sir Heraclitus Fogg, the children were formally adopted by their stepfather.

Young James Moriarty was a sickly child in his early months of life. Both his mother and Dr. Noel feared that James would perish at an early age. Besides the emotional distress that the demise of her baby would cause, such an event would terminate the income from a trust fund that Sir William had established for Morcar and her offspring. In love with Morcar himself, Dr. Noel proposed a rather flamboyant stratagem to guarantee the child support payments from Sir William. The doctor offered to father another child by Morcar. If the child was fortuitously a boy, he could also be named James. If the elder James later died, his younger brother could take his place. Because Sir William never visited his offspring, the substitution would never be detected.

Morcar accepted Dr. Noel's proposal. Another James Moriarty was born in 1836. He would grow up to become the archenemy of Sherlock Holmes. In order to be as far as possible from Sir William, Morcar moved with her two children to Ireland.

In addition to the money supplied by Sir William, Morcar also received ample money from Dr. Noel. From simply providing his services to hide the indiscretions of wealthy patrons, Noel began to establish himself as a prominent leader among the criminal circles of London. Occasionally taking a respite from his illegal activities, Noel would visit Morcar in Ireland. Seeking to maintain the outward appearance of respectability, Morcar claimed to be the wife of an Irish sea captain. When visiting his mistress, Noel assumed the identity of this fictitious Captain Moriarty. Another son was born to James Noel and Morcar Moriarty in 1840. The youngest of the Moriarty brothers was named Noel.

Dr. Noel's illegal enterprises began to expand far beyond London. Gradually, he became intimately acquainted with all the criminal gangs of Europe. When his power reached its zenith, Dr. Noel would command the loyalties of rogues of many different nations. As he was forced to spend much of his time outside the British Isles, Dr. Noel found it necessary to end his relationship with Morcar in 1842. He bought Morcar's compliance by continuing to send money for her upkeep and that of the children. Since she hoped to eventually find a real husband, Morcar told her children and her neighbors that the nonexistent Captain Moriarty had perished in the recently concluded Opium War (1839-42) with China.

Morcar did find a husband in Robert Northmour. During 1843, Northmour had been courting Claire Huddlestone, the daughter of Bernard Huddlestone. Reckless financial speculation had not only ruined Bernard's banking business, but also revealed him to be an embezzler. Among the funds entrusted to Bernard's unscrupulous care were the sayings of the Carbonari, a secret society plotting revolution in Italy. The last significant revolutionary acts of the Carbonari were the unsuccessful 1831 uprisings in Bologna, Parma and Modena. Since the economic depression of 1837, Bernard had handled the Carbonari's English investments.[39]

As told in Robert Louis Stevenson's "The Pavilion on the Links," Bernard Huddlestone attempted to flee Britain aboard Northmour's yacht, the *Red Earl.* In exchange for his help, Northmour was promised the hand in marriage of Claire Huddlestone. Before the yacht could leave Scotland, Bernard was murdered by agents of the Carbonari. As for Claire, she married another man.

After failing to wed Claire, Northmour went to Italy where he became involved with the societies that had supplanted the Carbonari. There, he befriended the famous Guiseppe Garibaldi and participated in the Italian revolutions of 1848-49. The failure of Garibaldi's ambitions caused Northmour to return to the British Isles in 1850.

Upon meeting Morcar in Ireland, Northmour was struck by her strong resemblance to her cousin, Claire Huddlestone. Northmour quickly wooed and married Morcar. All of Morcar's children adored their new stepfather.

Northmour would be a great influence on the political thinking of the younger James Moriarty. Northmour was an admirer of various revolutionaries such as George Washington and Markos Botzaris. He personally knew many of the prominent Italian revolutionaries such as Daniele Manin. Northmour also supported the Irish Home Rule campaign that had been started by the late Daniel O'Connell.

The older James Moriarty followed a military career. Being a tall stooped man, this James Moriarty was reminiscent of his uncle, Bernard Huddlestone. The Colonel's brothers would similarly demonstrate a poor posture in their later years.

During 1853-56, the younger James Moriarty studied mathematics at Trinity College, Dublin. Moriarty then published an 1857 treatise on the Binomial Theorem that received critical acclaim in Europe. Even Sir William Clayton heard of Moriarty's achievement. Mistakenly assuming that this James Moriarty was his illegitimate progeny, Clayton would later identify the mathematician as his child by Morcar in his memoirs.

On the strength of his treatise, Moriarty was appointed to the post of Professor of Mathematics at the University of Manchester in 1858. He became infatuated with a beautiful prostitute, Emily Caber, in the following year. Since marrying a woman of such doubtful antecedents would jeopardize his academic career, Professor Moriarty set Emily up as his mistress. Three children were born to the Professor and Emily. Twin boys, James and Emile, were born in 1860. A daughter, Urania, was born in 1862. She was named after the muse of astronomy.

Whatever joy the birth of his children brought Professor Moriarty in those years, it was offset by the woe caused by the deaths of his mother and stepfather. Starting in 1859, Garibaldi launched a series of military campaigns that would result in the unification of most of Italy under the leadership of Victor Emmanuel II of Sardinia. The Sardinian government allied itself with France against the Austrian Empire. It was the intention of France's ruler, Napoleon III, to establish a weak Italian federation that he could dominate. When hostilities broke out between Austria and its enemies, Mr. and Mrs. Northmour were vacationing in Sardinia. Northmour was quickly contacted by the British embassy in Sardinia. The British government was distrustful of Napoleon III's designs in Italy. Northmour was asked to infiltrate Garibaldi's army to discover the exact extent of French ambitions. Acquiescing to the embassy's request, Northmour joined his former comrade from the insurrections of 1848-49. Because of the intense love she felt for her husband, Morcar insisted on accompanying him. Both Northmour and his wife died in the fighting along the Austrian Tyrol in May 1859.

Further tragedy lay ahead for Professor Moriarty. Events in India would eventually lead to the deaths of others whom he loved deeply. Indirectly responsible for the Professor's heartbreak would be Prince Dakkar. Born in 1808, Dakkar had left India at the age of ten to study science in Europe. Dakkar was the son of a Rajah of Bundelkhand, a territory in central India. Jules Verne would refer to Bundelkhand as "Bundelkund" in such works as *The Mysterious Island* and *Around the World in Eighty Days*.

After returning to India in 1849, Dakkar became acquainted with Achmet Genghis Khan, a resident in the city of Jubbulpore (spelled Jublepore in Doyle's "Uncle Jeremy's Household"). Achmet had been the Maharajah of Pankot, a kingdom in the Punjab. Pankot figured prominently in the film *Indiana Jones and the Temple of Doom*. The Maharajahs of Pankot historically had been the high priests of Thuggee, a cult that sacrificed human beings to the Hindu goddess Kali (also known as Bhowanee). Captain William Sleeman's campaign against Thuggee in the 1830s forced Achmet and his followers to flee the Punjab for central India.

Both Dakkar and Achmet joined the violent Sepoy Mutiny against the British in 1857. Due to the breakdown of British authority, Achmet and his Thuggee supporters were able to reoccupy the palace at Pankot. There they performed elaborate rites to Kali before joining the assault against the British. Achmet and most of his adherents were slain in a battle with the British. Pankot Palace would remain unoccupied until 1935 when it would be visited by a noted American archaeologist, Dr. Henry Jones Jr., also known as Indiana Jones. The newly installed Maharajah of 1935, Zalim Singh, was not descended from Achmet Genghis Khan but from another prominent cult member, Ramdeen Singh.

Ramdeen had been the tutor of Achmet's daughter. Achmet's wife had been an Englishwoman named Warrender. At the age of fifteen, Achmet's daughter was left destitute upon her father's death. A German merchant adopted her in Calcutta in 1858 and took the young girl to Europe.

The suppression of the Mutiny in 1858 also caused Dakkar to leave India. Dakkar was accompanied by several fellow mutineers, most of who were fellow disciples of Achmet Genghis Khan. These Thugs had certain scrolls that they entrusted to Dakkar. For centuries, the cult of Thuggee had been aware of the existence of the Nine Unknown, a secret society that preserved the scientific records of an ancient civilization. Seeking these secrets, the Thugs had even established a rival Nine to combat the genuine organization.[40] The scrolls that the Thugs gave Dakkar had been plundered from the genuine Nine Unknown.

Translating the scrolls, Dakkar discovered they were plans for a submersible vessel. Retreating to an island in the Pacific, Dakkar and his underlings planned to construct two such submarines. They would use these submarines to destroy British ships bringing supplies to the troops in India. Cut off from supplies and further reinforcements, the British soldiers would then be vulnerable to a reenactment of the Sepoy Mutiny.

The Thugs who had joined Dakkar in his flight also bestowed on him a bountiful fortune in jewels that the cult had accumulated through its murderous activities. With these jewels, Dakkar funded the construction of the various components of his submarines by companies in Europe and the United States. The engines were made by Krupp in Prussia, the iron plates of the hulls were created at Laird's of Liverpool, and so forth. Indian agents of Dakkar were present in each of the cities where the submarine parts were being fashioned.

By 1862, Dakkar's envoy in Liverpool heard a rumor that the daughter of Achmet Genghis Khan was living somewhere in Yorkshire. When this news reached Dakkar's island base, his Thuggee allies asked permission to send a representative to Britain for the purpose of arranging the return of Achmet's offspring to India. Dakkar agreed to the request of the Thugs.

As related in Doyle's "Uncle Jeremy's Household," the Thugs found Achmet's daughter working under the name of Miss Warrender as a governess in Yorkshire. Still faithful to the religion of her ancestors, Miss Warrender had strangled one of her charges as an offering to Kali. The conclusion of "Uncle Jeremy's Household" implied that Achmet's daughter returned to India, but it should not be assumed that the likewise was true about the Thug who found her.

This Thug stayed with Dakkar's agents in Liverpool until 1863. Just before he was about to leave Britain, the Thug was consumed by religious fervor. He felt the need to perform human sacrifice to Kali. Rather than jeopardize Dakkar's operation in Liverpool, the Thug decided to travel thirty-five miles in order to commit his murders in Manchester. He strangled two young children. They were the sons of

Professor Moriarty and Emily Caber.

The police official investigating the crime was a mediocrity in the tradition of Inspector Lestrade. The investigator arrested Emily for the murders. Distraught over her children's deaths, Emily hanged herself in her cell. Emily's only surviving child, Urania, was placed in an orphanage. Malicious rumors spread throughout Manchester about Professor Moriarty's relationship with the dead "child murderess." For the purpose of avoiding a public scandal, Moriarty was forced to resign from his position at the University of Manchester.

Preparing to depart from Manchester, the grief-stricken Professor received an unexpected visitor. For years, the Professor believed that his father had died in the Opium War. He was stunned to see the supposed Captain Moriarty in the identity of Dr. James Noel of London.

Through his underworld connections, Dr. Noel had heard of the Caber murders. When he learned of his son's connection with the case, Dr. Noel rushed to Manchester. He offered to assist his son to track down the true killer.

One of Dr. Noel's criminal underlings was a garrotter named Parker.[41] Born in India, Parker was the son of an English soldier and an Indian woman. Because his father had participated in Sleeman's campaign against Thuggee, Parker knew a lot about the worshippers of Kali. He had even studied their methods of strangulation. Requested by his superior to offer an opinion on the Caber child murders, Parker quickly identified the perpetrator as an expert Thug.

Dr. Noel had been aware of the unusual business transactions being conducted between Laird's and a group of mysterious Indians in Liverpool. Parker was dispatched to Liverpool to conduct inquiries. Because of his ancestry and his knowledge of Indian dialects, Parker was able to ingratiate himself with Dakkar's subordinates. He soon learned the nature of Dakkar's great scheme. Acting under the instructions of Dr. Noel, Parker suggested to Dakkar's agents the recruitment of European artisans to help in the construction of submarines.

Dr. Noel was pursuing his own complicated stratagem. The artisans recruited by Parker would be Dr. Noel's henchmen. After they had aided in the completion of Dakkar's vessels, they would stage a mutiny. The submarines would then be utilized by Dr. Noel in a campaign of piracy.

Believing that the slayer of his children would probably be on Dakkar's island, Professor Moriarty insisted on being one of the artisans. At his son's request, Dr. Noel equipped him with a set of contact lenses to make his grey eyes appear to be black. With Parker's coaching, Moriarty passed as a man of Anglo-Indian heritage. Together with the iron plates made at Laird's, the Professor, Parker and Noel's other agents arrived at Dakkar's island.

Moriarty was disappointed to discover that the Thug who killed his children was in India. However, the Professor did learn that a delegation of Thugs, including his quarry, would come to the island once the submarines were finished. Therefore, Moriarty poured all his efforts into the completion of Dakkar's project. Gaining Dakkar's favor, Moriarty did invaluable work on the construction of the ships' engines. From the records of the Nine Unknown, Dakkar and Moriarty had uncovered the secret of atomic energy.

The Professor and Parker befriended a group of Indian pearl divers whom Dakkar had brought to the island as laborers. Dakkar treated the divers as if they were slaves. Due to their harsh treatment, the pearl divers were willing to join in Moriarty's planned theft of the submarines. The pearl divers were so fond of Moriarty that they initiated him into a secret society that worshipped a divine nautilus. In a strange sort of way, Moriarty could consider himself one of the pearl divers.

Having witnessed the excesses of British rule in Ireland, Moriarty had sympathy for the average Indian native. On the other hand, he had no respect for the leaders of the Sepoy Mutiny. Moriarty viewed them as corrupt local rulers who were just as oppressive as the British.

The underwater vessels were ready to be launched in 1864. The Thuggee delegation including the object of Moriarty's vengeance landed on the island to witness the event. Moriarty then staged his revolt. The Professor personally strangled his children's murderer. The pearl divers allied with Moriarty were all slain by Dakkar's forces. Moriarty and his confederates seized control of one of the submarines to flee the island. Dakkar and his loyal subordinates launched the other submarine in pursuit. Little did Dakkar suspect that Moriarty had sabotaged the nuclear reactors in both of the crafts. Removing a key component from each nuclear reactor, Moriarty had guaranteed the development of a severe radiation leak if either ship was activated. The Professor had restored the component in the reactor of the vessel in which he had absconded.

Although Dakkar was able to stop the leak, he and his henchmen had suffered fatal radiation poisoning. Possessing enough power to return to his island, Dakkar brought the ship back to his base. By the next year, all of Dakkar's followers had perished. The Indian prince would not die from the radiation poisoning until a few years later.

Christening his new vessel the *Nautilus* after the god of the pearl divers, Moriarty now began his career as Captain Nemo. Possibly because his father's surname was Noel, Moriarty chose the Latin word for "no one" as his alias. The *Nautilus* had sustained some damage during the fighting on the island. It took about a year to adequately repair the craft. The *Nautilus* was relaunched in 1865. One year later, it began to be sighted by ships that mistook it for some form of sea monster.

Many of Nemo's crewmen were social outcasts with revolutionary convictions of an anarchist nature. Moriarty felt it expedient to maintain their loyalty by often expressing radical views himself. To a large degree, these left-wing opinions were sincere. Because he was raised in Ireland, Moriarty could assert that he was a member of "an oppressed people." As a youth, he had seen the devastation caused by British negligence during the potato famine of 1846, though his own family had been immune to the effects of the famine because of the money supplied them by Sir William Clayton and Dr. Noel. Due to the influence of his stepfather, Robert Northmour, Moriarty also possessed a great admiration for revolutionaries.

To Moriarty, the British flag represented all the recent tragic setbacks in his life. The British government had sent his mother and stepfather on a mission that cost them their lives. The British police had driven his beloved Emily to suicide. The Professor even held the British authorities indirectly to blame for his children's death because of the failure of India's administrators to apprehend Prince Dakkar and his Thuggee allies. In Moriarty's hate-filled brain, Britain had done irreparable harm to "homeland, wife, children, ...father and mother."

Still desiring to hide his true identity, Moriarty continued to wear the contact lenses with which he had been supplied by Dr. Noel. When seen next to Parker, a stocky Anglo-Indian with a mustache, the black-eyed Captain Nemo could be mistaken for a Spaniard, a Turk, an Arab or an Indian. The Professor added to this illusion by conversing with Parker in an obscure Indian dialect that the garrotter had taught him. Because of the grief he endured after the deaths of Emily and his sons, Moriarty appeared older than he actually was. Although only thirty-one in 1867, he looked somewhere between thirty-five and fifty.

Throughout his campaign of piracy, Moriarty was given information on the movement of ships by Dr. Noel and his European associates. Noel arranged regular rendezvous in Crete between his agents and the *Nautilus*. There the *Nautilus* dropped off the spoils of its piracy. Noel then converted the booty into cash that would be divided among numerous bank accounts. A percentage of the profits went to Noel's colleagues in Crete. They used some of the money to fund anti-Turkish activities, but they probably kept most of it for their own personal enrichment.

When the *Nautilus* collided with an American ship in 1867, Moriarty took prisoner Professor Aronnax, his servant Conseil, and Ned Land the harpooner. Moriarty normally would have disposed of his captives, but he desired Aronnax's intellectual companionship. When the *Nautilus* was lost in the Maelstrom in 1868, Aronnax and his companions escaped to the Norwegian coast in a dinghy. Unknown to them, Moriarty (alias Nemo), along with Parker and some other crewmen, also managed a similar escape.

The Professor and Parker made it back to England. Moriarty was reunited with his father. The British police had begun to suspect Dr. Noel's involvement in numerous crimes unrelated to the *Nautilus*. Having accumulated vast profits from their joint venture, Dr. Noel and Professor Moriarty thought it prudent to retire from crime. Dr. Noel left England for Paris and Moriarty established himself as an army coach in London during 1869.

Dr. Noel had gained custody of Urania from the orphanage in 1864. While his son was absent from England, James Noel had raised his granddaughter. Upon leaving for France, Noel left Urania in her father's care. The Professor arranged for the legal adoption of his illegitimate daughter. She could now officially use the surname of Moriarty.

Professor Aronnax's account of his travels with Moriarty was published under Jules Verne's auspices as *Twenty Thousand Leagues under the Sea* in 1869. Upon reading the manuscript, Moriarty regarded it with amusement. Another reader, Captain Cyrus Smith of the U.S. Army, viewed it with amazement and confusion.

While the siege of Richmond was transpiring in 1865, Smith and a group of Union supporters escaped from Confederate captivity in a weather balloon. Blown off course by a severe storm, they landed on an uncharted island in the Pacific. The castaways would not be rescued until 1869. Throughout their years on the island, Smith and his companions received assistance from a mysterious hermit. In 1866, based on information received from this unknown patron, Smith and the other rescued a castaway, a former criminal named Aryton, stranded on an adjacent island since the previous year. Their benefactor revealed himself in 1868 to be Prince Dakkar. When Smith conversed with Dakkar, the Prince was nearly dead from the radiation poisoning contracted in 1864. In his death throes, the Prince rambled about his life. All that Smith could discern from Dakkar's history was that the Prince had come to the island after the Sepoy Mutiny. After launching a submarine, all of Dakkar's followers perished. The submarine was currently docked in a cavern that served as a harbor. Smith discovered the submarine and buried Dakkar in it. In accordance with Dakkar's dying wishes, Smith caused the submarine to sink to the ocean floor after he left it.

After being rescued with his comrades by a British yacht, Smith stumbled across a copy of *Twenty Thousand Leagues under the Sea* in 1869. Smith concluded that Dakkar must be Captain Nemo. He assumed that Verne had altered the dates of Aronnax's narrative for some peculiar reason. Putting himself in communication with Verne, Smith offered his story as a solution to the mystery of Captain Nemo. Verne knew that the dates of *Twenty Thousand Leagues under the Sea* were correct, but he wrote a modified version of Smith's story to satisfy readers clamoring for a sequel. In penning *The Mysterious Island*, Verne severely altered the conversations between Smith and Dakkar in order to make it appear that the Prince really was Captain Nemo. Verne also made the description of the interior of the submarine inspected by Smith conform to that of the *Nautilus*. Since he was also altering the chronology of *Twenty Thousand Leagues under the Sea*, Verne felt it necessary to alter the chronology of *The Children of Captain Grant* in order to make the repentant Aryton more sympathetic. A contrite penitent was more believable if he had experienced over a decade of loneliness on a deserted island than just a single year.

Jules Verne was far more accurate in his depiction of Phileas Fogg's famous trip *Around the World in Eighty Days*. Unknown to Jules Verne, the true Captain Nemo was involved in a minor way with Fogg's travels in 1872. Like many other misguided people, Professor Moriarty was foolish enough to bet that Fogg would not accomplish his trip in eighty days. If the Professor had been as canny as Lord Albermarie (who bet five thousand pounds on Fogg), he could have made a fortune. Instead, Moriarty lost a sizable sum of money, though not enough to put a dent in his sizable wealth. Since Fogg's success did cost Moriarty a financial loss, it could be said that the world traveler was the only other man (besides Sherlock Holmes) to beat the Professor.

Professor Moriarty spent most of the 1870s writing a scientific book, *The Dynamics of an Asteroid*. Occasionally, he involved himself in criminal matters as an intellectual diversion. He played no role in the 1878 Suicide Club case that Robert Louis Stevenson immortalized. The Professor's lack of participation is rather puzzling since the scholarly research of Edgar Smith and Jack Tracy have established the involvement of the master criminal's father, older brother, and future archenemy with Stevenson's tale. Briefly, a royal prince became enmeshed in the toils of the Suicide Club, an organization where the members played games of chance that resulted in the members murdering each other. The organizer of the Suicide Club was a former partner of Dr. Noel, now retired in France. Due the efforts of allies that included an unnamed detective (generally believed to be Sherlock Holmes, then living in Montague Street) and Dr. Noel, the prince was able to destroy the Suicide Club. An unnamed military officer (Colonel James Moriarty) declined to join the prince's campaign against the Suicide Club.

The Professor was a collector of expensive art. By 1883, it became quite apparent that Moriarty could not continue to purchase additions to his art collection unless he returned full time to a life of crime. He then began to erect a gigantic crime network that would dominate the London underworld.

There was another motivation for the creation of this crime network. The mind of Moriarty was still harboring a warped left-wing political philosophy. He recognized that the revolutionary secret societies of Italy had drifted into crime. He envisioned the creation of a criminal syndicate that could then evolve into a revolutionary movement that would disrupt the European social order. He could eventually utilize such an organization to grant himself as much power as Napoleon Bonaparte.

Recognizing that a Napoleon of Crime needed capable Marshals, Moriarty recruited talented lieutenants to carry out his schemes. One such man was John Clay. The Professor recruited Clay by having Urania seduce him.[42] As a result of this liaison, Urania gave birth to a son in 1883. The Professor's grandson would later pursue an illegal career under the name of Dr. Caber.[43] Lord Dunsany would write of Caber's exploits in three tales: "The Invention of Dr. Caber" from *Jorkens Has a Large Whiskey* (1940) and "The Strange Drug of Dr. Caber" and "The Cleverness of Dr. Caber" from *The Fourth Book of Jorkens* (1948).

To act as his chief of staff, the Professor recruited Colonel Sebastian Moran, an accomplished solider who had left India under a cloud. An exceptional marksman, Moran committed murders with an airgun designed by a blind German mechanic.

Another important member of Moriarty's gang was his younger brother. Noel Moriarty was a stationmaster in the west of England. Feeling the need for an expert on railways, the Professor conscripted his brother into the growing crime syndicate. Noel was also the liaison between the Moriarty gang and Sinn Fein as part of the Professor's ultimate aim to gain control over underground political movements.

A woman just as dangerous as any of the members of Moriarty's organization came to England in 1885. She was Madame Koluchy, the head of the Brotherhood of the Seven Kings, an Italian secret society like the old Carbonari. She was also known as Katherine. I suspect that Mr. Koluchy was fictional, and her full name was Katherine Koluchy. Details of Katherine's illegal activities can be found in *The Brotherhood of the Seven Kings* (1899) by L.T. Meade and Robert Eustace. In 1884, she had failed to convince her lover, an Englishman named Norman Head, to aid her diabolical schemes. Head had fled to England, and Katherine came looking for him there in the following year. Hoping to use the Professor's organization to help in her search, she made contact with Noel Moriarty. She conducted a passionate affair with the stationmaster that made her forget totally about Head.

Professor Moriarty was extremely distrustful of Katherine Koluchy. He saw her as a threat to his own authority. Perhaps this suspicion was due to the fact that the Professor's uncle, Bernard Huddlestone, had been liquidated by an Italian secret society. by coercing Katherine to return to Italy, the Professor embittered his younger brother. Katherine gave birth to Noel Moriarty's son, Dominick, in Naples during 1886.

John Clay crossed swords with Sherlock Holmes in "The Adventure of the Red-Headed League" from *The Adventures of Sherlock Holmes*. Dr. Watson placed this story in 1890, but the chronology of William S. Baring-Gould's *The Annotated Sherlock Holmes* (1967) assigns it to 1887. After capturing Clay at the scene of an attempted bank robbery, Holmes recognized a sinister power behind him. By 1887, Holmes had deduced that most of London crime was controlled by Professor Moriarty.

The Professor engineered Clay's escape from prison in 1888. Clay went to France,[44] where he received a visit from Urania. As a result of this romantic reunion, their second son was born in 1889. Dr. Caber's sibling grew up to be Carl Peterson, the chief adversary of H.C. "Sapper" McNeile's Bulldog Drummond.

Sometime during 1887, Sherlock Holmes and Dr. Watson had their first conversation about Professor Moriarty. In his early remarks on the Professor, Holmes described the criminal as a man of "good birth." Having only traced Moriarty's family to their time in Ireland, Holmes was then unaware of the Professor's illegitimate birth. Certainly Holmes would have changed his view of Moriarty's birth by 1888, the year in which Sir William Clayton's scandalous memoirs, *Never Say Die*, were printed. Holmes would have read Sir William's claim that the Professor was his son. Even though Sir William's assertion was mistaken, it would have lead Holmes to conduct more strenuous inquiries into the origins of the Moriarty brothers.

Dr. Watson caused considerable confusion about the year of his first conversation with Holmes about Professor Moriarty. In order to quickly inform his readers about the Professor, he inserted the conversation into "The Final Problem," the story that related the Professor's final defeat. The conversation recorded in "The Final Problem" had Watson stating that he never heard of Professor Moriarty. When *The Valley of Fear*, a novel set in the late 1880s, was published, it contained a remark by Watson showing that he knew about Moriarty long before the Professor's final duel with Holmes in 1891.

Baring-Gould placed *The Valley of Fear* in January 1888. Holmes was now paying an unknown member of Moriarty's gang for information. Corresponding with the informant through coded messages sent by mail, Holmes only knew the traitor by the alias of Fred Porlock. Paul Zens's "A Case of Identity" established that Porlock was the Professor's younger brother. He chose the alias of Fred Porlock because he was a stationmaster of Minehead, a Bristol Channel port near the town of Porlock. Noel Moriarty probably engaged in this betrayal because he hoped to manipulate Holmes into removing his brother. With the Professor gone, Noel Moriarty could then seize control of the crime syndicate. Concluding that Holmes was too formidable to use as a pawn, the youngest of the Moriarty brothers terminated his communications with the sleuth.

In 1889, a French company seeking to build a canal in Panama failed financially. Investors lost 60 million pounds. The failure would lead to a series of criminal investigations involving charges of bribery that would extend into 1893. In 1890, the events of Doyle's "The Lost Special" unfolded. A French financier, Louis Caratal, arrived in Liverpool from Central America. He carried with him documents pertinent to the Panama Canal scandal. Prominent individuals implicated in the scandal secured the services of the unscrupulous Herbert de Lernac to prevent Caratal from reaching Paris. Caratal had hired a special train to transport himself to London where preparations were made for his protection. De Lernac's assignment was to intercept Caratal's train. In order to achieve this goal, de Lernac enlisted the help of "one of the acutest brains in England." This ally "knew the London and West Coast line thoroughly, and he had the command of a band of workers who were trustworthy and intelligent." The railway expert attempted to secure passage on Caratal's special train by posing as Horace Moore, "a gentlemanly man of military appearance." Despite this setback, the man known Horace Moore not only engineered Caratal's death, but made the train disappear off the face of the earth.

An "amateur reasoner of some celebrity" (clearly meant to be Sherlock Holmes) wrote a letter to the *London Times* asserting the train's disappearance to be the work of "an English *camorra*." The Camorra was an Italian secret society in Naples. The usage of that phrase by Holmes indicated that he suspected that this crime was the work of the Moriarty gang. It also implied the Holmes may have heard some rumors of the Professor's contacts with an Italian secret society, the Brotherhood of the Seven Kings, whose headquarters was also in Naples.

Horace Moore was actually Noel Moriarty. The Moriarty syndicate was known to undertake assassinations at the bequest of foreign parties. In *The Valley of Fea*r, an American criminal paid the Professor to murder a retired Pinkerton detective. Having revealed too much to Holmes about the Moriarty organization as Fred Porlock, Noel Moriarty adopted the appearance of a military man to make the sleuth suspect Sebastian Moran as the author of the crime. The details of this awesome crime did not become known until 1898 when de Lernac confessed after his arrest for the murder of a merchant in Marseilles. De Lernac refused to divulge the real identity of Horace Moore, but noted that his co-conspirator was "a man with a considerable future before him, unless some complaint of the throat carries him off before his time."

The final showdown between Holmes and Professor Moriarty came in 1891. Holmes had compiled evidence that would enable the police to smash Moriarty's organization. Eluding Moriarty's assassins, Holmes gave his evidence to the authorities. As his crime cartel crumbled, Moriarty chased Holmes to Switzerland. The Professor cornered his nemesis on the cliffs overlooking Reichenbach Falls. As told in "The Final Problem," both adversaries appeared to fall in the abyss. In actuality, only the Professor had fallen to his death.

Aware that key members of Moriarty's gang would not be arrested, Holmes thought it fortuitous to fake his death. The phony demise soon became merely an effort to hide the detective's whereabouts from the outside world because Colonel Moran witnessed the survival of the Professor's antagonist. Since the remnants of the Moriarty gang would desire his life, Holmes felt that he would be more difficult to trace if the public believed him dead.

Besides Moran, the authorities were unable to bring to trial Noel Moriarty as well as Parker, whose subservience to the Professor continued after the destruction of the *Nautilus*. Parker shifted his loyalties to Colonel Moran. Reluctantly, Noel Moriarty also acknowledged Moran as the Professor's successor.

Under Moran's leadership, the Moriarty gang remained in a state of stagnation. Moran's sole source of illegal income seemed to be derived from cheating at cards in fashionable London clubs. When one of his fellow club members, Ronald Adair, uncovered the cheating in 1894, Moran slew him with his airgun. When news of the Adair murder reached Sherlock Holmes, he returned to London for the purpose of trapping Moran. Aware of the detective's return, Moran instructed Noel Moriarty and Parker to search for Holmes. Posing as a plainclothes detective investigating Adair's death, Noel Moriarty was unable to spot a disguised Holmes. As related in "The Adventure of the Empty House," Holmes engineered Moran's arrest for Adair's murder.

Sebastian Moran's downfall paved the way for Noel Moriarty to make his bid for power. Reestablishing his alliance with the Brotherhood of the Seven Kings, Noel Moriarty summoned Katherine Koluchy to London in 1894. Whether or not she ever battled Holmes is not known, but her former lover, Norman Head, emerged as her principal enemy in England. In 1897, Head and the police cornered Katherine in her hideout. A detective leaped at her, and Katherine touched a switch releasing a sheet of white flame. A second detective and Head were briefly "blinded by a heat which seemed to sear our very eyeballs." The burnt body of the first detective was identified, but all that seemed to remain of Katherine was a pile of ashes.

Katherine did not perish in the flames. She escaped the conflagration through a secret exit. It was her intent to fake her own death. However, the detective's unexpected attack resulted in her failure to adequately protect her eyes from the fire. Consequently, she was rendered blind. Katherine now became known in criminal circles as the Blind Spinner. Under this alias, she appeared in John Buchan's *The Three Hostages*.

There are some inconsistencies in the physical descriptions of Madame Koluchy and the Blind Spinner, but these are easy to reconcile. The passage of more than two decades plus the shock of blindness would have transformed Katherine's dusky hair into the Spinner's white locks. In "The Doom" from *The Brotherhood of the Seven Kings*, a workman described Madame Koluchy's eyes as black after briefly glimpsing her at a railway station. The Blind Spinner's orbs were a bright blue like her son Dominick, but Koluchy's eyes could have been such a dark shade of blue that a chance acquaintance could have easily mistaken them as being black.

Katherine's defeat caused a serious setback in Noel's plans. He quietly assumed the identity of Andrew Lumley, a respected philanthropist. When Sherlock Holmes retired in 1903, Noel and Katherine began to build a new edifice from the ashes of the Moriarty organization and the Brotherhood of the Seven Kings. This new syndicate, the Krafthaus, revived the Professor's plan of using criminal operations to spread political chaos. The activities of Andrew Lumley were unmasked during 1910 by a British politician, Edward Leithen, in John Buchan's *The Power House.*

Leithen had learned that a friend, Charles Pitt-Heron, had become a member of the Krafthaus, but was seeking to escape its coils. Eventually, Leithen was able to accumulate evidence that implicated Lumley in a plot to kill Pitt-Heron. Lumley's agents pursued Leithen in London just as Professor Moriarty's underlings stalked Sherlock Holmes in "The Final Problem." Eluding Lumley's minions, Leithen was able to present his findings to the authorities. Yet Leithen was troubled that a public trial would blacken Pitt-Heron's name. Almost two hours before the police were ready to apprehend Lumley, Leithen confronted the master of the Krafthaus. Leithen suggested that Lumley flee the country to avoid public shame. Lumley replied that there were "other and easier ways" to obtain the result desired by Leithen. The next morning, Leithen read Lumley's obituary in The *London Times*. The coroner's verdict was heart failure, but there were suggestions of suicide.

Supposedly Lumley committed suicide in exchange for a promise not to publicly reveal his Machiavellian plots. There is a rumor that Noel Moriarty did not take his own life, but murdered someone else who was buried as Lumley. The alleged victim was Noel's surviving brother, Colonel James Moriarty. This rumor has yet to be confirmed.[45]

The activities of the Krafthaus during World War I (1914-18) remain a mystery. The organization was almost certainly allied to the German espionage apparatus during this period. Ties with German spies had existed before the war. In *The Power House*, Andrew Lumley had paid for the legal defense of a German professor arrested for espionage in Britain. One of Edward Leithen's friends was Richard Hannay, who had a series of adventures mainly involving wartime espionage. In John Buchan's *Mr. Standfast* (1919), Richard Hannay combated the Wild Birds, the German organization responsible for sabotaging the Allied war effort. The smashing of the Wild Birds in 1918 revealed one of its members to be Pavia, the editor of a pro-Ally newspaper in Argentina. In *The Power House*, Andrew Lumley secretly maintained an English residence whose registered owner was Julius Pavia. Although Leithen suspected that Pavia was merely Lumley's alias, the missing homeowner could have been a subordinate engaged in skullduggery abroad.

If Noel Moriarty did survive the events of *The Power House*, he was certainly dead by 1921. His empire was inherited by his son Dominick.[46] Noel and Katherine had schemed to make their son Prime Minister of the British Empire. To achieve this goal, they created a false ancestry for their son. Dominick posed as the scion of the Medina clan, a family of Spanish descent that had been settled in Ireland for centuries.[47] Before Dominick Medina could accomplish his treasured goal, his crime network was severely crippled due to the efforts of Richard Hannay in Buchan's *The Three Hostages*. As Professor Moriarty pursued Holmes to Reichenbach, Dominick stalked Hannay in the Scottish Highlands. Like his uncle before him, Dominick fell to his death.

Before his demise, Noel Moriarty was concerned that some investigative effort would uncover Dominick's true origins. To perpetuate Dominick's cover identity, the Krafthaus hoped to hide the true history of the Moriarty family. Because Sir William Clayton's controversial memoirs mentioned Morcar Moriarty, nearly all copies of the book were burnt by the Krafthaus. The thoroughness of this literary crime is demonstrated by the fact that only Philip José Farmer appears to own a copy of *Never Say Die*.

Like the CIA and the KGB, the Krafthaus practiced the art of spreading disinformation. False records discussing Professor Moriarty were forged by his brother and nephew. The fraudulent records were then hidden away for scholars to find. No doubt these forgeries would have been found earlier than the 1970s if Dominick had not perished in 1921.

Displaying the expertise in cryptography that he aptly utilized as Fred Porlock, Noel Moriarty fabricated the coded notebooks of the

Professor. Discovered by John Gardner, these notebooks formed the basis of two novels, *The Return of Moriarty* (1974) and *The Revenge of Moriarty* (1975). Here Noel Moriarty attributed to himself all of his more infamous brother's accomplishments. The stationmaster allegedly murdered the Professor, assumed his identity and committed amazing crimes that Holmes never checkmated. There were also sleazy charges about the Professor's sexual preferences. In depicting himself, the stationmaster not only gave himself the same first name as his two older brothers, but also changed his true physical appearance as well.

Dominick Medina also contributed to the effort to mislead the world about the Professor. Having been trained in the ancient languages of European secret societies by his mother,[48] Dominick chose one of these tongues to serve as the reputed language of an extraterrestrial race. After forging the log of Phileas Fogg, he hid his fraudulent work in the house once occupied by the world traveler. He then fabricated a child's notebook as a key to the log. This notebook was secreted in the former residence of Sir Heraclitus Fogg, Phileas's stepfather. The log was found in 1947, but the notebook would not be unearthed until 1962. In manufacturing Fogg's secret log, Dominick did make use of some true information (e.g., the relationship between the Professor and Captain Nemo, the physical description of Colonel Moriarty), but he also distorted pertinent details about the Moriarty family (e.g., the parentage of the three brothers, the intellectual prowess of the stationmaster). Dominick was fortunate indeed that an author as talented as Philip José Farmer reconstructed *The Other Log of Phileas Fogg* in 1973. While the forgery was never used to maintain the secret of Dominick's descent, it provided enthralling entertainment for numerous readers.

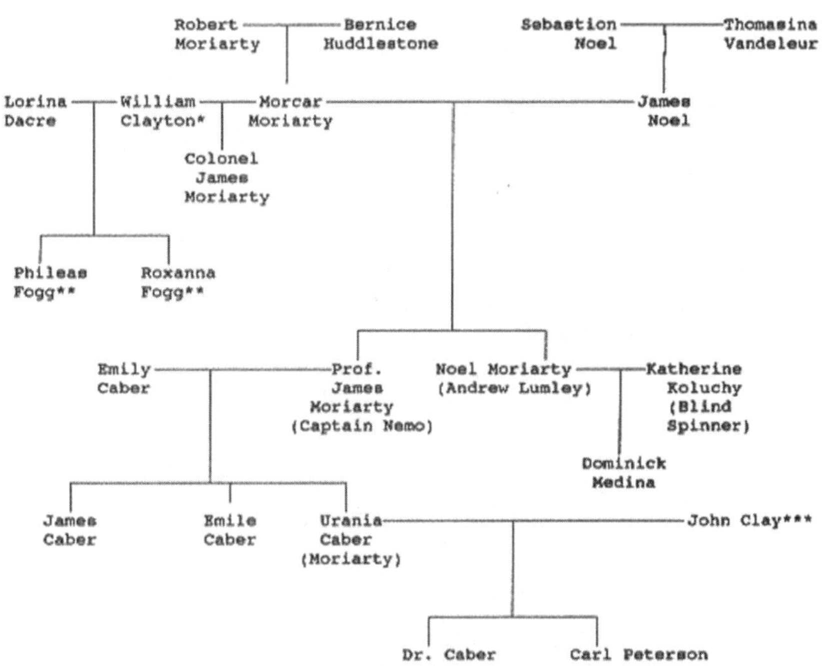

* In addition to the descendants shown here, Sir William Clayton had other children who are identified in Philip Jose Farmer's Tarzan Alive and Doc Savage: His Apocalyptic Life.

** For descendants, see Doc Savage: His Apocalyptic Life.

*** For ancestry, see Doc Savage: His Apocalyptic Life.

Probable Chronology

1795 Sebastian Noel is exposed to radiation when a meteorite crashes at Wold Newton.
1803 Sebastian Noel marries Thomasina Vandeleur.
1804 Birth of Dr. James Noel.
1808 Birth of Prince Dakkar.
1815 Birth of Morcar Moriarty.
1818 Dakkar begins to study science in Europe.
1830s Achmet Genghis Khan vacates Pankot Palace and moves to Jubblupore.
1831 The Carbonari incite unsuccessful uprisings in Italy.
1832 Birth of Phileas Fogg.
1833 Birth of Roxanna Fogg.
1835 Birth of Colonel James Moriarty. Divorce of Sir William Clayton and Lorina Dacre.
1836 Birth of Professor James Moriarty. Morcar and her two children move to Ireland.
1837 Bernard Huddlestone becomes the Carbonari's banker.

1840 Birth of Noel Moriarty.
1842 Dr. Noel discontinues his romantic relationship with Morcar Moriarty. Birth of Achmet's daughter (Miss Warrender).
1843 Death of Bernard Huddlestone.
1848-9 Robert Northmour participates with Garibaldi in Italian revolutions.
1849 Dakkar returns to India.
1850 Marriage of Robert Northmour to Morcar Moriarty.
1853-6 James Moriarty the younger attends Trinity College in Dublin.
1857 James Moriarty the younger writes a celebrated treatise on the Binomial Theorem. The Sepoy Mutiny starts in India. After reoccupying Pankot Palace, Achmet is killed while fighting the British.
1858 James Moriarty the younger becomes Professor of Mathematics at the University of Manchester. The Sepoy Mutiny is suppressed in India. Achmet's daughter leaves India. Dakkar begins to construct two submarines at a Pacific island.
1859 Death of Robert and Morcar Moriarty Northmour in the Tyrol. Professor Moriarty falls in love with Emily Caber.
1860 Birth of James and Emile Caber.
1862 Birth of Urania Caber (Moriarty). Achmet's daughter is found by a Thug in Yorkshire.
1863 Death of Emily Caber and her two sons. Professor Moriarty resigns from the University of Manchester. The Professor is reunited with Dr. Noel.
1864 Professor Moriarty steals a submarine (the *Nautilus*) from Dakkar. The other submarine is sabotaged by the Professor. Dakkar is exposed to dangerous dose of radiation.
1865 A criminal named Aryton is marooned on a Pacific island.
1865 Cyrus Smith and other Americans are marooned on Dakkar's island. After extensive repairs, the *Nautilus* is relaunched under command of Captain Nemo (Professor Moriarty).
1866 The *Nautilus* is mistakenly identified as a sea monster by ships. Cyrus Smith and his fellow castaways rescue Aryton.
1867 Captain Nemo captures Professor Aronnax and his two companions.
1868 Destruction of the *Nautilus*. Death of Dakkar.
1869 Cyrus Smith is rescued from Dakkar's island. Professor Moriarty becomes an army coach in London. Dr. Noel relocates in France.
1872 Phileas Fogg travels around the world in eighty days.
1878 Dr. Noel, Colonel Moriarty and Sherlock Holmes become involved with the Suicide Club.
1883 Professor Moriarty builds a new crime network. John Clay is seduced by Urania. Birth of Dr. Caber.
1884 Professor Moriarty recruits Sebastian Moran and Noel Moriarty. Norman Head leaves Italy after a love affair with Katherine

Koluchy.
1885 Katherine Koluchy meets Noel Moriarty in England.
1886 Birth of Dominick Medina.
1887 John Clay is arrested in connection with the Red-Headed League. Sherlock Holmes and Dr. Watson discuss Professor Moriarty's background.
1887-8 As Fred Porlock, Noel Moriarty sends coded messages to Holmes.
1888 After breaking out of prison, John Clay departs for France.
1889 Birth of Carl Peterson. The French Panama Canal Company becomes bankrupt.
1890 As Horace Moore, Noel Moriarty causes a train to disappear.
1891 Death of Professor Moriarty at Reichenbach Falls.
1894 Arrest of Colonel Moran for Ronald Adair's murder. Katherine Koluchy starts a crime wave in London.
1897 Katherine Koluchy is blinded in a fire.
1898 Noel Moriarty assumes the identity of Andrew Lumley. Herbert de Lernac, Noel Moriarty's accomplice in the 1890 train disappearance, confesses the details of the crime.
1903 Sherlock Holmes retires. Andrew Lumley and Katherine Koluchy erect the Krafthaus.
1910 Alleged death of Andrew Lumley.
1921 Death of Dominick Medina.
1935 Indiana Jones visits Pankot Palace.
1947 Discovery of Dominick's forgery of Phileas Fogg's log.
1962 Discovery of Dominick's forgery of Fogg's childhood notebook of an extraterrestrial language.

From *Pygmalion* to *Casablanca*

The Higgins Genealogy

By Mark K. Brown

Recently I have researched the background of the language expert who features in George Bernard Shaw's play *Pygmalion* and the film *My Fair Lady*. These are the results of my enquiry.

According to Philip José Farmer's *Tarzan Alive*, the father of John Jansenius and his sister, Agatha, was one Mr. Karoly, a Hungarian Jew. Farmer tells us that their third sibling was Julius Higgins, who had changed his name from Karoly after having settled in Ireland. His daughter was Ellen Higgins, who was the mother of Leopold Bloom, the protagonist of James Joyce's *Ulysses*.

Farmer was apparently unaware that Julius Higgins had two other children. Ellen was his third child. The middle child was Claudius. Claudius had at least one daughter, Meriem. Meriem had the misfortune to fall madly in love with Abraham Baline, a suitor her father could not approve. A rugged handsome man, Abraham was a bit of gambler and drank excessively. When Claudius objected to their marriage Meriem and Abraham eloped to America. Without much in the way of money, and no family to lean on, the Balines fell on hard times and ended up in one of the less affluent sections of New York. Abraham fell ill, and died shortly after the birth of their only son, Yitzik.

Young Yitzik, who went by the name of Rick, fell in with the notorious Solomon Horowitz mob, and became Horowitz's chosen heir. Eventually, his luck ran out, and when his boss was murdered by a rival gangster, Rick Baline was implicated. He fled to Europe and, under a *nom de guerre*, became a soldier of fortune. Eventually he retired to Casablanca, where he ran a successful casino and nightclub until the outbreak of World War II, when the arrival of an old flame disrupted the life he had built for himself.[49]

The oldest son of Julius Higgins was Octavius, who moved to England and made a modest fortune. I have not yet been able to ascertain the nature of his career. Octavius married Eleanor, a younger daughter of the 12th Baron Tennington (see Appendix 2 of *Tarzan Alive*). Their son was the famed linguist Henry Higgins, who won a famous wager concerning whether or not he could teach Eliza Doolittle, an uneducated street vendor, to speak like a member of the upper class.

Incidentally, Eliza might have had the proper genetics to learn a variety of dialects. Her cousin John became a well-known veterinarian, because of his ability to communicate with other species, although his ability to speak with animals was greatly, though amusingly, exaggerated by his biographer, Hugh Lofting.

A Reply to "The Red Herring"
By Philip José Farmer

ERBANIA No. 28, December 1971

I've re-read your article on Tarzan's and Korak's age (THE RED HERRING - *ERBANIA* 27) a number of times and also studied Harwood's and Starr's, which I knew fairly well before your article came to me.

It looks like a tossup, as far as validity goes. Either you accept Harwood and Starr's adopted-relative theory to explain Korak or you push the date of Tarzan's birth back to 1872. Whichever theory you choose, you do violation. You have to change a number of things in the novels and say, "No, ERB didn't present the truth here. But, of course, he had good reason. Now, here is what we believe is the truth…"

You make a good case, and if I had thought about it more, I might have used 1872 and proceeded from there. I would have satisfied very few people, the various schools of thought would all have jumped on me. Not that I mind that. But it was too late to rewrite the book[50] from the 1872 viewpoint; the work I did on the version now in Doubleday's hands was enormous and changing it to start from 1872 would have required an equal amount. Just about every page would have to be rewritten, many cast out and entirely new ones written. And I would still have felt that I was departing from the truth.

Yet—would ERB have given the true date of Tarzan's birth? Would it not have been simple then to look into the records of that year, including the sailing dates of ships from Dover in May, 1888, and locate the young nobleman and his wife who sailed out, never again to return?[51]

No, the answer is, it would not be simple. Because I wrote to the Dover Port Authority two years ago to ascertain this point, and I was told that the records are not available. I deduced that they had been destroyed in the bombings (WWII), though the Authority didn't say so. BUT —what if money and influence has been used by—guess whom?—to make sure that these records are not available? Or no longer available, I should say.

I wrote two letters to the Freetown, Sierra Leone, Port Authority, inquiring about ships that put out in the May-July 1888 period, especially those sailing ships that went southwards along the coast with the intention of setting a young English nobleman and his wife on shore on the west coast. Or, I said, I'd be satisfied with just the lists, let me do the searching. But the Freetown Authority never bothered to reply or else the mail is such that it didn't get my letters.

But it must be remembered that ERB could have shoved the true date of sailing from England a year or two ahead or behind. More probably behind, because the exploitation of the Congo by Leopold had really not begun yet. Also, from what British colony were the Belgians seducing the natives for their armies? Look at the map of Africa, 1888. I believe that the truth is that Greystoke was sent to investigate what the Germans were doing on the Kamerun-Oil Rivers. This is the only thing he could have been sent to investigate at that time. ERB knew this, of course, but deliberately misled the reader about the true destination and mission of Greystoke.

If you take 1872 as the true date, then you have to think up an entirely new reason for the Greystokes going to Africa. You would end up by theorizing that the two were really just taking a trip to South Africa, or that Greystoke was an amateur explorer and injudiciously took his wife along, or that he was sent to investigate the illegal slave trade but first meant to accompany his wife to South Africa and leave her there to visit relatives while he returned to the tropics. Or he may even have gone to Gabon, with his wife, because she wanted to find out what had happened to her uncle. (It's my contention that Trader Horn's George T— was Alice Rutherford's uncle. The reasoning for this you will read in *The Private Life of Tarzan*.)

As you know, I have gone through Burke's vast *Peerage* in an effort to find a candidate for Tarzan. I think I know who the real Tarzan was, but I can't reveal that at this moment. To make sure I'm not in error, I'm going to have to go through Burke several times more and search the records of births from 1872 on. Inasmuch as Burke contains over 1250 pages of small close-set type of genealogy, I won't be finished with my study for some time to come.

Another point. Besides the wrong date of sailing, ERB might have given the wrong port.

And perhaps Tarzan's parental ancestors weren't nobility after all but just baronets. ERB made the Greystokes even more distinguished than they were, made them viscounts. (Though, as you know from my Detroit speech, Tarzan couldn't have been a viscount, or, at least, if he were, he must also have been either an earl or a baron or both.)

The possibility that Tarzan's ancestors may have been baronets extends the search through Burke, extends it very much, since baronets take up much of the space therein. The chances are that his ancestors were of the lesser nobility or of the baronetage, since it would have been difficult to hide from the press the fact that a long-lost heir to a dukeship or marquessate or even an earlship had been found in the jungles of Africa. On the other hand, if enough money were spent in the right places, it might be done. But not very easily.

You say that the idea that Korak might be adopted, not Tarzan's real son, spoils *The Son of Tarzan* for you. This book is one of my favorites; I've read it many times and it doesn't spoil it for me to think that Korak is adopted. The way I look at it, there are two Tarzans, the real Tarzan and the fictional Tarzan. The fictional Tarzan is based on the real Tarzan that ERB knew, and, undoubtedly, ERB drew the long bow now and then in his "biography," added some things, left others out, and even wrote several Tarzan books that were total fiction, such as *Tarzan At The Earth's Core*, or only partly true, such as *Tarzan And The Ant Men*. Knowing this doesn't spoil them for me. When I read them, I read them as I would any other book of fiction and enjoy them as they are.

When I study them as biography, then I differentiate to the best of my ability and knowledge between the fact and the fiction. This is not always easy to do, but it's a lot of fun and rewarding in many ways. Thus, when I read *The Son of Tarzan*, I know that Korak is adopted (or I should say, I believe he is). My own theory is that he is the younger brother of Bulldog Drummond, reasons for which theory I give in the *Life*. I believe that Korak's career in the jungle did not last more than a year, or two years at most. A proper chronology of Tarzan's life demands this. But this doesn't bother me. In the first place, Korak was an extraordinarily strong and adaptive individual, but he wasn't Tarzan, as he was the first to admit. There is only one Tarzan, and Korak, mighty though he was, was not his equal. Undoubtedly, John Drummond was an unusually strong person, like his older brother, who, as you may remember, in his first recorded adventure, snapped the neck of a half-grown gorilla with only his fingers. (I think it was a gorilla. On the same page, the beast is called a gorilla, a baboon, and a monkey. McNeile wasn't very strong on zoology.)

Anyway, when I read *Son*, I forget the facts behind this story and read it as ERB wrote it, knowing that he had to fictionize the true story and that, as you suggest, he did want it to be regarded as fiction.

By the way, what are your thoughts regarding ERB's killing of Jane in the magazine version of *Tarzan the Untamed*? Was she really killed but ERB realized that an investigator could find out her identity and thus Tarzan's, by looking into the deaths of plantation owners' wives killed in western Kenya in 1914, and so brought her back to life in the book version to throw such investigator off the trail?

As far as I know, your idea that the person who first told ERB about Tarzan was D'Arnot is original. It seemed a likely one, but there are problems about it.

In the first place, the "I" of the first few pages of *Tarzan of the Apes* could not have been ERB. ERB was never in England. What happened, I think, is that the "I" was a man, or woman, who got the story from the "convivial host" and then told it to ERB who was, I believe, living in Chicago in 1911. ERB was inclined to give the narrator his own identity, as you will recall from *A Princess of Mars*, where the "I" could not possibly be ERB. (I mean, of course, not the "I" of John Carter but the "I" of his supposed nephew.) Besides, ERB couldn't read French and so wouldn't have been able to read the elder John Clayton's diary.

Was D'Arnot the person who told the story to the "I" of *TOTA*? If he were, he must have been in England, since he and "I" went to the Colonial Office to dig through the "musty manuscript, and dry official records." And why did he have access to British Colonial Office records? He was neither British nor a member of any secret agency which might have gotten permission to look into the records. Especially since, it seems to me, the Clayton family would have made sure that the records were not accessible to anyone except the highest authority.

But there is the matter of Clayton's diary. The last we see it is in Chapter XXVI of *TOTA*, in which the police official is reading it. Did he give it back to Tarzan or to D'Arnot? Tarzan left for America the next day, so I think it likely that D'Arnot kept it for further perusal while he waited for M. Desquerc, the fingerprint expert, to arrive. The "I" of TOTA read the diary, so he must have gotten it from D'Arnot or his "convivial host," whoever he was.

Would D'Arnot reveal to anybody, without authorization from the Claytons, the story of Tarzan? Undoubtedly not. What happened, as I reconstruct it, was that Tarzan, or a member of the Colonial Office, placed the diary with the records of Clayton's mission to West Africa. The "musty manuscript" must have been the summary of the story of the Claytons and their son. It was written by a Colonial Office clerk. The "I" was a visiting American who got loaded over a bottle with a British official who was one of the few who knew the story. The official must have been a very vain man to have insisted on "I" seeing the Greystoke material just so he could prove he wasn't lying. And he must have been unethical, too. I suspect that "I" may have used a bribe to get the official to show him the records. What the nature of the bribe was I don't have the slightest idea, of course.

Fortunately, the "I" told ERB the story and then either forgot about it or was prevailed upon not to disclose the truth after the first book about Tarzan came out and was such a hit. Perhaps, "I" died shortly after revealing to ERB what he had learned about the "Greystoke" case. ERB, of course, took care to conceal the true identities of the "principal characters," though there is evidence (as H. W. Starr has pointed out) that ERB only changed the titles of the noble persons concerned and retained the family names. Clayton and Rutherford are, after all, not unusual names in Burke's *Peerage* and *Landed Gentry*.

The reconstruction, based on the above: Tarzan never picked up the diary again, though he made sure that he could see it whenever he wished. The diary was transferred to the Colonial Office for keeping with the records pertinent to the Greystoke case. A clerk made a summary, in handwriting, of the story. (Unless "I" means that the "musty manuscript" is also the diary, since a diary is written, or was in those days, in handwriting.) The manuscript was never, for some reason, typed out. Perhaps because it was a summary for the eyes of some high authority only. (The French Naval Intelligence would also have a report, you may be sure of that. D'Arnot was Tarzan's best friend, but he would have been required, as a matter of duty, to report on the "incident." His report, plus those of other personnel of the cruiser, and the policemen's report about the fingerprints, would have been put in the secret files of the French Navy, where, no doubt, they still are.)

The "I" of *TOTA* then learned about the British records and the diary and got his egotistical and probably corrupt host to let him see whatever he wished to see concerning the Greystoke case.

AFTERWORD:

Phil is right—I shouldn't have taken the liberty of suggesting that ERB might have visited England; we should stick to the known facts. But, irregardless of whether ERB got the story of *Tarzan of the Apes* from a first or secondhand source, he did become Tarzan's biographer. In "The Red Herring," I neglected to mention one fact that we do know. If we look in ERB's notebook, we find that he transcribed the story of *The Son of Tarzan* between January and May 1915; therefore, the story must have ended before this date, which is correct if we accept the altered dates. He couldn't possibly have been transcribing a story that didn't end until 1929. —DPO[52]

The Daughters of Greystoke
By Chuck Loridans

According to Philip José Farmer, John Clayton, the eighth Duke of Greystoke, and his spouse, one Jane Porter Clayton of Baltimore, had two sons, one by birth, and one by adoption.[53]

No other offspring have been acknowledged. At least, none were mentioned by Edgar Rice Burroughs, Philip José Farmer, Fritz Leiber, or any of the writers who have chronicled the adventures of the Jungle Lord. This seems strange considering that in this particular period of time, large families were very much the norm. For a family such as the Greystokes, who possessed unlimited wealth, and according to some (including their main biographer), unlimited youth and vigor, it would be highly unusual.

It is hard to believe that the Claytons would procreate only once and then stop, but as was stated before, no other offspring have been brought to light. It is possible that the effect of radiation on the genes or some other cause might have lead to semi-sterilization, limiting the number of offspring, but a look at the family tree charted by Farmer shows a multitude of issue by the 12th Baron Tennington, and makes this theory unlikely. It is also possible that Greystoke and his mate did not do much mating, and considering the above mentioned youth and vigor, this is very doubtful.

I propose that the Greystokes did indeed have other children, but kept them secret. Understandable, considering that their known natural son was kidnapped as an infant, and that their foster son was lured into running away by old enemies.

A child of Greystoke and Jane would most likely have black hair (like their father) or blonde hair (like their mother); the eyes, probably gray.

I have found one such candidate, who is quite a remarkable adventurer in her own right, (albeit as an aide to another member of the Wold Newton Family). The woman is Nellie Gray, member of the Avenger's team, Justice Inc. She is blonde, has gray eyes, is a great fighter, and has been known to swing from tree to tree.[54]

In *The Yellow Hoard*, the second recorded adventure of Mr. Richard Henry Benson, aka "The Avenger,"[55] an archaeologist named Archer Gray is murdered, and his daughter seeks out The Avenger in order to avenge her father. Eventually Nellie Gray joins Benson and

Co., becoming a valuable friend and ally. But how can Ms. Gray be the daughter of Greystoke, when it is clearly stated that she is the daughter of Prof. Archer Gray?

First we must determine her correct birth date. Using the hints in the original source material, *The Yellow Hoard*, one might place her birth sometime between 1915-17, since it is stated in this tale that Nellie is twenty-three or so.[56]

According to Prof. Win Eckert's chronology for The Avenger,[57] *The Yellow Hoard* took place in 1938, so simple math indicates the aforementioned date, placing her birth between *Tarzan the Untamed* and *Tarzan the Terrible*. This however would make it impossible for Nellie to be the daughter of Greystoke, since he and Jane had been separated for several years at that point. I put forth that Kenneth Robeson added about three years to Ms. Gray, and her actual age was twenty, which places her birth circa 1919, not very long after Greystoke and Jane's reunion (and I dare someone to say the Claytons weren't likely to do any mating after such a long separation).

As stated before, in all likelihood, the birth of another child to Lord and Lady Greystoke would have been known to only a few. Perhaps a few close friends, such as Paul D'Arnot, Hazel Strong (Jane's best friend), Esmerelda (Jane's nanny), Muviri, Busili, and other members of the Waziri tribe, who visited the Greystoke plantation in Kenya, might have known of the existence of another child. With such a veil of secrecy, one would think that such a child would be sheltered with drastic measures, and kept out of harm's way. Jane Clayton would be a very protective parent. Greystoke the Forest God, however, would not have been able to resist teaching his daughter the ways of his kingdom. Older brother Korak and his mate Meriem (herself quite the jungle queen) were likely to have baby-sat at some point, and taken the child on outings to the green mansions. In addition to learning spoor-following and branch-swinging, the young girl would have attended the finest schools in England or America (all under an assumed name, of course).

Her father, without doubt, told her many stories of lost cities and anachronistic civilizations, and so she might well have developed an interest in archaeology and this brings us to Prof. Archer Gray, the character which tipped me off to Nellie's true identity.

> Archer Gray was a retired professor of Archaeology, Columbia University... He was a tired-looking man of sixty, stoop-shouldered but wiry, with iron-gray

> hair. He was in a faded blue robe and had spectacles pushed up on his forehead.[58]

> One was an elderly man, with white hair and large rimmed spectacles. His slightly stooped shoulders were draped in an ill-fitting, though immaculate, frock coat, and a shiny silk hat added to the incongruity of his garb in an African jungle… Professor Archimedes Q. Porter adjusted his spectacles.[59]

Now I realize this might be considered a weak conjecture, owing to the fact that these descriptions were pretty much the stereotype of the elderly professor in adventure fiction, but the similarities registered in my brain, and got me to thinking. Philip José Farmer says in *Tarzan Alive* and *Doc Savage: His Apocalyptic Life* that certain clue words and names set him on the trail, and so it was with me. The name Archer made me think of Archimedes, and the last name Gray obviously connected me to Greystoke.

I did not conclude that Profs. Porter and Gray were the same person, but were in fact brothers and that Prof. Gray's last name was actually Porter, making him Jane Porter's uncle and Nellie's great uncle, not her father.

At the age of eighteen, in order to pursue her love of archaeology, and to protect her true identity, Penelope Alice Clayton became the legal ward of her great uncle Archer S. Porter.

The two of them traveled the globe, as a father and daughter archaeology team, Nellie having taken her mother's maiden name as her own. When her adoptive father was murdered and she was accused of the crime, she sought Richard Benson's help. The murder charge was soon dropped, thanks to Justice Inc.

Though not stated in that particular adventure, Nellie, not wanting to live under the shadow of such a crime, once again changed her last name; taking one half of her family title, she became simply Nellie Gray.

But wait! There's more! I believe Greystoke sired two daughters. Jane is the mother of Nellie Gray, but the Jungle Lord's other daughter was born to a different mother. She was the most important woman in the ape-man's life after Jane, Alice Clayton, and Kala the she-ape, of course. I'm referring to La, the high priestess of Opar, and Greystoke was completely unaware of this other product of his loins.

It seems that immediately after Greystoke returned to Africa from

Maple White Land, in 1937, he made an unrecorded foray to Opar. The Lord of the Trees experienced yet another conk on the head and lost his memory (which according to Farmer was as good excuse as any to get away from Jane and have some real fun). His beast-like instincts carried him straight into the arms of La, and nature took its course.

I know a lot of people will be outraged at the thought of the virtuous ape-man breaking his sacred vows to Lady Jane (Betty, to La's Veronica), but I truly feel that it is not beyond the realm of possibility that a man in his most primitive state, with the knowledge nagging deep in his sub-conscience that he is going to be alive for a very long, long time, might give in to the passions of an extraordinary woman who has been trying to seduce him for years.

Another factor to consider is that Greystoke had a gut feeling that this would be the last time he would see La. (In *Tarzan Alive*, Farmer states that when Greystoke returned to Opar in 1946, he called for La, and she did not answer.)

So Greystoke took his leave of La and Opar, regained his memory, and returned to his beloved Jane. La's daughter was born nine months later. The name given to child from mother, we may never know. Fearful that the beast men of Opar might discover that the infant girl's father was the hated white ape, La instructed one of her handmaidens to take the child far away, perhaps to Greystoke's Kenyan plantation, or just to abandon the babe in the woods to die. Either way, neither was accomplished. Both handmaiden and child were captured by a band of cutthroat Arabs and sold into slavery. The child's early years are still shrouded in mystery, her memory erased through trauma. She does, however remember living in a prison camp in Greece, and escaping as a preteen to a displaced persons camp in Persia, where she met her mentor, an old professor who named her Modesty Blaise.

The Green Eyes Have It—Or Are They Blue?
or
Another Case of Identity Recased
By Christopher Paul Carey

The Monomyth

It is by no means necessary to use the novel *Escape from Loki* as a starting point to decode the occasionally eerie subplots of the Farmerian Monomyth. But the novel is unique in that it ties together an unusually large number of the wily tentacles of the mysterious beast which lurks behind the scenes in much of Philip José Farmer's larger works. As Farmer himself has managed to uncover the truth behind the fiction of so many other authors' work—such as that of Edgar Rice Burroughs, Lester Dent, and Jules Verne—it is only natural that the time has come to decode the hidden messages in Farmer's novels. This article is just a beginning, and, of course, only a few pieces of the Farmerian puzzle are contained herein. However, a beginning framework is offered upon which a stronger foundation may one day be built—if one keeps on his or her toes. For you see, Farmer's puzzle is three-dimensional and exists on many levels, which, like his Lavalite World, are constantly shifting.

Charles Fort, the great archivist of the unexplained, once stated, "One measures a circle beginning anywhere." And so in order to begin exploration of Farmer's labyrinthine Monomyth, we find ourselves taking a second look at *Escape from Loki*, in which a young Doc Savage—the living reality of whom Farmer has demonstrated in his biography *Doc Savage: His Apocalyptic Life*—gets his first taste of adventure and likes it. I have elsewhere examined the symbolic and often shocking levels of the book and in the course of this research was startled to see how deep this book really goes. But I was little prepared to dive twenty thousand leagues into the foreboding, murky waters of an ancient worldwide conspiracy.

To understand what forces are at work in *Escape from Loki*, the reader must understand the perceptions of an Ubermensch. Doc Savage, like Nietzsche's superman, does not see things as others do. He thinks (and acts) analogically. Thus, when he sees Baron von Hessel's cigar, he thinks, "If other cigars were small dirigibles, the one in his mouth was in the Zeppelin class." Or when he gazes at the

Countess Idivzhopu, "He was reminded of the rotary engine of his Nieuport. This image was followed by that of a pendulum, succeeded by a vision of a two-stroke-cycle engine." Without understanding the creative workings of Doc Savage's mind, we find ourselves facing a far greater task in breaking the code of the novel, for all the codes are aimed at Doc.

Loki in the Sunlight

In order to understand who is aiming the subtle codes at Doc, and why, we must take a trip down a side tunnel of the Monomyth. Farmer wrote in his biography *Doc Savage: His Apocalyptic Life* that the only villain in the Doc Savage supersagas to meet Doc in a return engagement was the infamous John Sunlight. He appeared in two books, *Fortress of Solitude* and *The Devil Genghis*. This, as we shall see, is not exactly true. Farmer, by his comment, was seeking to draw attention to the long-fingered crook. Since Farmer's comment that Sunlight was the only one of Doc's villains to appear twice, Sunlight has reappeared in DC comics, Millennium comics, numerous speculative articles, and even Will Murray has considered donning the arch-enemy's mono-colored clothes in a proposed novel. The attention that Farmer has centered on Sunlight is in itself a clue that there is more than meets the eye in this strange character.

In reality, as I shall demonstrate, John Sunlight appears in *three* of the published Doc Savage supersagas, not two. Strangely we find that *Fortress of Solitude* is not Doc's first encounter with the tenacious Sunlight. The February 1996 issue of *The Bronze Gazette* included an article of mine, on the subject of Doc's first adventure, *Escape from Loki*. In the article, I did not address the major mystery of the novel:

John Sunlight makes his *first* chronological entrance in the supersagas in Farmer's *Escape from Loki*.

At first glance one might think that Sunlight must be Baron von Hessel, the evil, experimenting genius who may hold the secret of immortality. However, this is not the case. Von Hessel is not Sunlight, but he *is* a character from *Fortress of Solitude*.

Readers will remember the monocle-wearing "smooth customer" Baron Karl, fellow conspirator of Sunlight. He is described as a ruthless man who had "personally shot to death some fifty or so political enemies" in his own castle. Apparently he is a castle lover, as he approvingly looks over Sunlight's castle, comparing it to his own. Baron Karl is something of a playboy, though apparently not with the wild abandon of the Playboy Prince. He has a deft hand with women and wears "the best of clothes." He is an eloquent speaker, obviously intelligent and well read, as indicated by his speech to John Sunlight. "'I salute again,' he said, 'the man who has inherited the qualities of the Erinyes, the Eumenides, of Titan, and of Friar Rush, with a touch of Dracula and Frankenstein.'" He could not have been more right about Sunlight, and Baron Karl knows this, as Sunlight could not have had a better teacher—Baron Karl himself. His comparison of Sunlight to Frankenstein could not have been more apt. Sunlight, who had once been a creature of the baron (as we shall see), now makes Baron Karl shake in fear. He is a monster out of his master's control. The previous master now treads lightly in the presence of his protégé. Also notice that Baron Karl says, "I salute again," in his praise of Sunlight. Again? When did he salute him before?

Apparently in Camp Loki during the Great War.

The Baron von Hessel in *Escape from Loki* is extremely intelligent and well read. "He could quote poets, dramatists, philosophers, and scientists, both ancient and modern," he has two Ph.D.s and he is an M.D. His features bear an aristocratic look and in the 1880s and 90s he inhabited his family's ancestral castle. On top of this, Doc observes that the baron was wearing a monocle, which at first appeared to him to be an affectation but later seemed to lend von Hessel a "superior air." Doc also observes the baron's "small belly bulge," which indicates that the baron enjoys the good things in life. He likes his women too, as evidenced by the company he keeps with the voluptuous Countess Idivzhopu. These are all perfect descriptions of Baron Karl as well as Baron von Hessel.

One might think, however unlikely, that this is merely coincidence, a case of literary archetypes perhaps. But this is absolutely not so, and the proof lies in the Baron von Hessel's taste for women—for his girlfriend is none other than *Miss* John Sunlight.

Here are some descriptions of John Sunlight from *Fortress of Solitude*:

> Anyway, John Sunlight didn't look the part. Not when he didn't wish, at least. He resembled a gentle poet, with his great shock of dark hair, his remarkably high forehead, his hollow burning eyes set in a starved face. His body was very long, very thin. His fingers, particularly, were so long and thin - the longest fingers almost the

> length of an ordinary man's whole hand…
>
> John Sunlight sat on a deep chair which was covered with a rich purple velvet cloth. He wore a matching set of purple velvet pajamas and purple velvet robe, and on the forefinger of his right hand was a ring with a purple jewel.
>
> John Sunlight had few changeable habits, but one of them was his fondness for one color one time, and perhaps a different one later. Just now he was experiencing, a yen for purple, particularly the regal shade of the color…

Now consider these descriptions of the Countess Idivzhopu from *Escape from Loki*:

> She wore an ankle-length white fur coat, white leather boots, and a Russian-type white fur hat…
>
> …she gave Savage a small and exceptionally long-fingered hand in a black elbow-length glove...Her large, dark blue eyes were as dazzling as her smile…
>
> Her narrow hips became an unusually small waist...
>
> Her all-white gown was the most low-cut he had ever seen…
>
> And here came the Countess Idivzhopu, Lili Bugov, taking an afternoon promenade in a beautiful pink dress and wide-brimmed sky-blue hat and holding a pink parasol...she waved a pink-gloved hand…

The descriptions of the countess in *Escape from Loki* are too similar to those of Sunlight in *Fortress* and *Genghis* to be mere coincidence, especially when the countess is juxtaposed with the Baron von Hessel, whose descriptions match exactly those given of Baron Karl. As will be demonstrated, the evidence points to the fact that Lily Bugov is John Sunlight.

The critical reader might very well point out the "sky-blue hat" which the countess is wearing while she is adorned with her pink dress, pink parasol, and pink gloves. This would seem to break Sunlight's rule of wearing only one color. There are several explanations for this inconsistency. For one, the story is occurring during the shortages and scarcities of World War I Germany. It may have been impossible for the countess to obtain all those amenities that would satisfy her fashion sense. This explanation, however, is unlikely, as her benefactor, the baron, seems able to get any supplies he needs. It may be that the countess, who was apparently a young woman at this time, was in the process of perfecting her style. She hadn't yet quite given up wearing multiple colors. The true explanation, however, probably lies in the realism with which Farmer records the adventure. The countess is not just a caricature, and certainly there were probably times when the color of her hat did not exactly match that of her dress.

Doc observes the servants of the countess the first time he sees her. One is Zad, "at least six feet eight inches tall…a kodiak bear of a man, a bearded behemoth." Two others are apparently her maids. Remember that Sunlight's servants were the Russian Civian, "a bestial black ox to look at," and the two sisters, Titania and Giantia, who were really not Russian, but American.

Von Hessel says that the countess "thinks she's another Catherine the Great, a Cleopatra, a Ninon de Lenclos." When he goes on to say that she is not as intelligent as they were, Doc becomes angry at the baron's ungentlemanly words, and a conversation arises about women's equality. The baron states that women have as much ability as men, both mentally and physically. He drives the screws through Doc's supposedly scientific armor by his comment that "Anybody not blinded by prejudice should be able to see that." Von Hessel finishes the topic with his opinion that women will not be treated as equals "until they wage a war for equality… Men won't give up their power over women until they're forced to do so, and they'll fight long and hard."

Then the baron moves on to the subject of power. The countess had power in Russia, he says, but she lost most of it in the Bolshevik Revolution, with the exception of her personal servants. She is now using her beauty to try to regain her power.

We can conjecture that when the countess was maimed at the end of the novel, her drive for power became insanely amplified. She was already insane, as her bloodthirsty practices in Russia indicate, but now she sought to dominate not just peasants, but the world. Without her beauty, she was forced to meet von Hessel's challenge to become the equal of men. When we next see the countess, she has changed or disguised her sex, and ultimately wants to be mother to the entire planet. She could not achieve a man's power being a woman, so she became a man. Perhaps this was at von Hessel's suggestion. Old habits die hard, however, and when she became a man, she still continued the odd penchant for wearing outfits of all the same color. There is also the precedent set in *The Devil Genghis* that Sunlight was fond of changing his appearance. Sunlight's hair has changed from a black shock to pure white. Doc wonders if it has been dyed to match his white clothing. Sunlight certainly is eccentric when it comes to his appearance, and any man with such odd fashion sense might certainly be suspected of effeminacy, especially in the 1930s. Remember also that he is described as having a weak appearance and the face and eyes of a poet.

Much is made in *Escape from Loki* of the countess's ability as a seductress. The baron uses her to seduce Doc and also openly discusses that she is using her charms to get back a little of the power that she has lost. Sunlight is also manipulative and seductive. He likes to use and control people rather than killing them. It is true that the countess sadistically murdered people in Russia, but by the time of *Escape from Loki* she has already changed her ways. After all, manipulation can satisfy an evil heart in a way more satisfying than outright murder.

The baron's remark about the countess's lack of intelligence does not seem to fit the character of Sunlight, until we realize that Sunlight is not really working on his own in *Fortress of Solitude*. He needs Baron Karl for his plans, and we may assume that behind the scenes Karl is coaching Sunlight. Notice that Baron Karl escapes with no punishment. Sunlight's intelligence in *Fortress* and *Genghis* may also be reflective of the years she has spent with the baron. He has taught Sunlight quite a bit since her early years in Russia and Germany. Also, the comment about the countess's low intelligence may have been a ruse by von Hessel to manipulate the emotions of the young Savage.

But is John Sunlight really that smart? He does not seem to be. His whole plan hinges on the technology he has stolen from Doc. Without it, he's just another villain with grandiose ambitions. Baron Karl is the one smart enough to get away, and Sunlight's plans fall apart quite easily in *Genghis*. Surely, he has the seductive powers to initiate a plan, but he does not seem to have the genius to hold his scheme together.

Most likely, the countess is the baron's underling in a deeper mystery about which we have few clues to go on. While the countess is not what she seems to be, the baron is even more of a mystery. *Escape from Loki* reveals that the baron certainly is a "smooth customer," with his secret experiments, strange international connections, and knowledge of an alleged elixir of immortality.

There are veiled hints in the novel that the countess was probably also privy to the immortality elixir. When von Hessel questions what the countess will do when she becomes old and ugly, she abruptly changes the subject. Also, when Doc is about to interrogate the countess at the end of the novel, she is set upon and maimed by a Russian from her past before Doc can ascertain what she knows. It seems that she may have known something about the elixir and that she was working with von Hessel in the grand scheme. The truth is, if we concur that her back was broken and she was paralyzed from the waist down, as Doc learns later in his investigations, she must have known about the elixir. The elixir must have had regenerative properties that could heal her injury, or else the baron was enough of a medical genius to cure her paralysis by some other means. Or more likely, the report of her paralyzing injury was faked. Remember that Doc got his report on the baron and the countess a long time later. The fake paralysis was probably the first step that Lily Bugov took to start a new identity as John Sunlight. This is why it is stated in *Fortress* that Sunlight is not Russian. Bugov was a Russian, but when she changed her identity to Sunlight, she became unique in the world, a nation unto herself. After all, one of Sunlight's big ambitions was to do away with nationalities.

Here I must mention Win Eckert's theory espoused in his fascinating article "Who's Going to Take Over the World When I'm Gone?" In response to an earlier draft of my article uncovering the mystery behind John Sunlight's true identity, Eckert proposes that Sunlight may be the progeny of a union between Doc Savage and Lily Bugov. I did consider this possibility when writing my original article, and hinted at this in correspondence with Mr. Farmer when I remarked:

> In *Loki*, there is a scene in which the countess gives Doc "a small and exceptionally long-fingered hand in an elbow-length glove." However, in *Fortress of Solitude* it states about John Sunlight

> that "His fingers, particularly, were so long and thin—the longest fingers being almost the length of an ordinary man's whole hand." I find it hard to reconcile the small hand of the countess in *Loki* with Sunlight's hand in *Fortress*, which seems to be freakishly large.

Such a discrepancy would certainly be cleared up by Win Eckert's assertion that John Sunlight is the son of the countess. I have dismissed this idea based on certain other evidence, some of which turns up in various facets of the Farmerian Monomyth.

For instance, if Farmer has hinted that John Sunlight is indeed a woman, there is precedence for this concept in his other work. In his science fiction novel *Dayworld*, the character Wyatt Bumppo Repp, a "great TV writer-director-producer of Westerns and historical dramas" has a predilection for writing storylines involving gender-changing. In the novel, Repp is currently writing a treatment for a movie called *Dillinger Didn't Die* in which Dillinger escapes from the F.B.I. "by magically turning into a woman." One character chides Repp, asking,

> "...why didn't you drag Robin Hood in? Though I suppose that he would have turned out to be Maid Marian!"

As *Escape from Loki* was written just after Farmer completed his three-volume Dayworld series, and as each of the split personalities of the protagonist of *Dayworld* seem to be aspects of Farmer's complex personality, it can be seen that Farmer, as Repp, has laid down an ultimate foreshadowing of his next work.

In addition, much of Farmer's other work has involved the recurring theme of the consequences for society when it loses the female element (see *Night of Light* and *Hadon of Ancient Opar*). Lily Bugov is compared to Haggard's Ayesha, which is a quintessential example of Jung's concept of the anima. In fact, Doc Savage expert Will Murray, in his article "The Genesis of John Sunlight," depicts John Sunlight as if he were Doc's anima. Sunlight is the antithesis of Doc, a mirror-self: strong, but weak-looking compared to Doc's powerful physique, pale-hued to Doc's deep bronze skin, sunken eyes to Doc's mesmerizing gold-flecked orbs. Both the countess *and* John Sunlight seem to be expressions of Doc Savage's anima.

Further, there is the question of Sunlight's age were he conceived in 1918 by Doc and the countess. This would make Sunlight perhaps twenty years old at the time of the events in *Fortress of Solitude*. If Sunlight is not Lily Bugov, but rather a relative, it would be more believable that he would be a sibling or cousin, not a son. The clues left by Farmer, however, indicate that the countess and Sunlight are one and the same.

It is interesting to note that Sunlight surrounded himself with Titania and Giantia, women whom Dent describes as "such amazons." He states in *Fortress* that, "all their lives men had been scared of them." Dent also says that they had never been afraid of any other man except Sunlight. Perhaps this is because Sunlight wasn't a man! Then Dent makes a curious statement: "But they [Titania and Giantia] did not *worry* about Sunlight" (the italics are Dent's). What does he mean by this? First Dent states that the sisters are afraid of Sunlight, but then he states that they do not worry about him. Dent must be indicating that they do not worry about Sunlight in a sexual sense. Even though they fear the terrible power he wields, they do not fear that he will make sexual advances toward them—because he is a woman! In addition, the presence of the two muscular women with Sunlight seems to fulfill the Baron von Hessel's statement that women also have the potential to match the physical ability of men. Ham would vouch for this—because of Titania, the dapper lawyer's dashing smile is now missing a front tooth. The baron's prophetic statement is also borne out in the apparent physical strength of the weak-looking Sunlight.

Intimations that Sunlight is really a woman can be seen in the fact that Doc was so intimidated by Sunlight. Doc, as we all know, cannot read women and they constantly pose a threat to his ability to solve a case. If Doc has encountered Sunlight before, as the countess, at some point he must surely have recognized him for what he was. At this point, all of Doc's defenses must have shattered. Not only had a woman made away with his one of a kind death-dealing device, but it was the very woman with whom he had had his first intimate encounter. "The Eternal Feminine," Doc reflects after sleeping with the countess, "was incomprehensible and unpredictable. More the latter than the former." How unpredictable he could not have guessed.

The final clue that the baron and the countess will return in the following supersagas is the big one at the end. Farmer writes, "But Clark Savage was not certain that he would not hear from the baron again. Nor from the countess. Both had reason to hate him." What a way to end a novel if it was not true!

Doc Savage readers had long been craving a return of John

Sunlight. Like the devious creature that he is assumed to be, Sunlight has managed to slip himself in for his last bow—right under the reader's nose.

Let us conclude this discussion of John Sunlight by pondering a line from *Fortress of Solitude*:

> *"No one knew what he was, exactly."*

The Slippery Baron

The Baron von Hessel is a mysterious character. As I have just demonstrated, the baron appears in Lester Dent's Doc Savage pulp *Fortress of Solitude* as the murderous Baron Karl. One thing is for certain, and that is that von Hessel presented himself to Doc in the role of the Norse All-father god Odin to Doc's Siegfried.

Odin is the cynical god who gave up his left eye for a look at the future. Similarly, von Hessel wears a monocle over his left eye which at first "had seemed foolish, an affectation" but which later "seemed to give him a superior air." He also knows the future, predicting the Second World War in which Germany would again rise to power, foreseeing the victories of the women's rights movement, as well as the problems of overpopulation. At the crucial first banquet scene during which the baron is manipulating Doc, he plays Wagner's *Siegfried's Funeral March*, a very dramatic score which must have played on Doc's creative mind. Further, when in his anger Doc topples the massive iron tub, a soldier remarks, "Er ist ein Siegfried." One cannot but speculate that this entire scene, as well as several others, was prearranged by the baron in order to manipulate the emotions of the youthful Doc Savage. Though inexperienced, Doc wonders if this is indeed the case.

The playing of Wagner's classic opera of Norse myth also echoes the actions of the enigmatic Baron von Hessel. In *The Ring of the Nibelungen*, the All-father god Wotan (aka. Odin, Woden, etc.) appears disguised as an old man before the hero Siegfried. (Incidentally the Old Norse word for "old man" is "Karl," thus confirming my speculation that the Baron von Hessel is one and the same as Baron Karl from *Fortress of Solitude*; another Karl will be shown to play a crucial role in Doc Savage's life by the end of this article.) Wotan proceeds to taunt Siegfried's youthful inexperience. Eventually, Siegfried penetrates Wotan's disguise and recognizes him as the murderer of his father. Wotan and Siegfried struggle, with the result that Siegfried breaks Wotan's greatest weapon, his spear *Runestaff*, in two. Wotan then disappears into the shadows. This is the perfect echoing of the events as they occur in *Escape from Loki*. Von Hessel repeatedly taunts Doc's youthful inexperience. The baron drops countless clues (as we shall see) to his own and Doc's origins, which we can only assume Doc eventually decodes. I will make a bold statement here, for which I shall momentarily present the evidence, that von Hessel is responsible, at least by association, for the death of Clark Savage, Sr., Doc's father. Doc then breaks von Hessel's greatest weapon, the Countess Idivzhopu, in two by causing the train wreck which breaks her back at the end of the novel. Finally, the slippery baron disappears into the shadows.

So the question remains: What is the baron's game? Here we need to perform some three-dimensional thinking. We see that the baron has been sending Doc a strange symbolic message by placing himself in the role of the god Wotan and Doc in the role of the hero Siegfried. Might there not be other clues, not so obvious, which the ingenious baron has managed set out for Doc without his knowing it?

Observe the name von Hessel. "Hessel" in Old Norse means "hazel." Besides being a type of shrub or tree, the word hazel is most often used to describe eye color, namely "a light brown to strong yellowish brown." "Strong yellowish brown" certainly calls forth a comparison to Doc's eyes, which "tawny and gold-speckled in a bright light, looked dark." Farmer certainly makes a point of the gold-flecked and yellow eyes in the ancestors of Doc Savage in his Addendum 2 of *Tarzan Alive*. It is by tracing the genetic trait of eye color that Farmer pieces together many of the gaps in the Wold Newton genealogy. We can only surmise that, by assuming a pseudonym meaning "hazel," the Baron von Hessel was subtly indicating something about his ancestry to the bronze man.

A further mystery is presented in *Escape from Loki* regarding eye color, and this one is blatant. Doc, however, seems to miss the clue entirely. Later, I will explain why the usually ever-vigilant Doc is apparently so befuddled. What he misses is the dramatic change in the color of von Hessel's eyes. When Doc gets his first close-up look at the baron during the first banquet scene, he observes that his eyes are "large, *green*, and seemed to shine with an inner light" (the italics are mine). Later, in the second banquet scene, when Doc slips several pieces of chocolate into his pocket, he reflects, "Von Hessel had observed this—those *blue* eyes seemed to miss nothing—but he only smiled with one side of his mouth" (again, italics mine). Certainly

Farmer, who pays such scrutinizing attention to eye color, would not make such an error. What, then, is the meaning of this drastic shift in eye color, from *green* to *blue*?

Again, the answer seems to be that von Hessel is indicating to Doc something about his ancestry. Von Hessel is smiling not at Doc's theft of chocolate, but at the trick he is pulling on him. He must know that Doc, with his photographic memory, will someday realize the symbolic message that has been sent to him and that he will decode its true significance. Utilizing clues that are provided in Farmer's biographies of Tarzan and Doc Savage, we may piece together the message that Doc probably decoded many years ago.

Only one of Doc Savage's ancestors is known to have the same color-shifting eyes as the baron. This was Wolf Larsen, Doc's maternal grandfather and the Nietzschean rouge captain who appears in Jack London's novel *The Sea-Wolf.* The narrator of this adventure, Van Weyden, describes Larsen as follows:

> The eyes themselves were of that baffling protean gray which is never twice the same; which runs through many shades and colorings like inter-shot silk in twilight; which is gray, dark and light, and greenish-gray, and sometimes the clear azure of the deep sea.

If there is any doubt but that von Hessel is referring Doc to his tough, mysterious, philosophizing grandfather, reflect on this. Wolf Larsen is referred to by his crew as "Old Man," the pseudonym of Wotan when he confronts Siegfried. Further, when Van Weyden first boards the *Sea Wolf*, he is told, "The cap'n is Wolf Larsen, or so men call him. I never heard his *other name*" (again, the italics are mine). The name Wolf Larsen, like von Hessel, is most certainly a pseudonym. The true identity of the captain of the *Sea Wolf* may be traced by another clue dropped by the slippery Baron von Hessel.

In the final climactic scene in *Escape from Loki*, in which von Hessel tempts Doc with immortality, he tells Doc, "You were *twenty thousand leagues* off the mark when you surmised that I was trying to create a disease which would be even worse than the black death of the middle ages" (italics mine). While not the final clue given to Doc, this is perhaps the most important, for indicates a connection between von Hessel and Jules Verne's classic tale *Twenty Thousand Leagues under the Sea*. Farmer, in his *The Other Log of Phileas*

Fogg and Addendum I from *Doc Savage: His Apocalyptic Life*, has recorded some of the missing details behind Verne's story, including his conclusion that Captain Nemo is really Professor Moriarty, the archenemy of Sherlock Holmes. Another look at Nemo provides some more surprising conclusions.

Captain Nemo, like von Hessel and Wolf Larsen, is a man of mystery. Even his name (also a pseudonym) literally means "Nothing." When Professor Aronnax and Ned Land are taken on board the *Nautilus*, Nemo tells them, "for you I shall merely be Captain Nemo," indicating that this is not his real name. And like von Hessel and Larsen, he lures in a young man of above-average intelligence, taunting and seducing him. While von Hessel toyed with Doc, Wolf Larsen did the same to Humphery Van Weyden, and so Nemo did to Professor Aronnax. Indeed, one cannot help but compare the banquet scene in *Twenty Thousand Leagues*, in which Nemo entices Professor Aronnax with an overabundance of exotic sea food, with the first banquet scene in *Escape from Loki*, in which von Hessel makes Doc quiver in anticipation of an unbeatable table spread (with Mozart's *Jupiter Symphony* sounding in the background, nonetheless). Nemo is also a cynic like von Hessel and Larsen. He sees humankind "fighting, destroying one another and indulging in their other earthly horrors" while "they can still exercise their iniquitous rights." Nemo, Larsen, and von Hessel also all smoke large cigars. In fact, Nemo compares his submarine to a giant cigar.

Like Farmer and Professor H. W. Starr, I can hardly conclude that Nemo is really the Indian Prince Dakkar, as Nemo claims in Verne's *The Mysterious Island*. In fact, the one shred of evidence put before Professor Aronnax while on board the *Nautilus* points to the probability that Nemo is German. Regarding a handwritten note from Nemo, Aronnax observes, "The handwriting was clear and neat, but somewhat ornate and Germanic in style."

Nemo's physical description is equally revealing. Aronnax writes:

> One strange detail, his eyes, which were rather far apart, had an almost ninety-degree range of vision. This ability—I was later able to verify—was backed by eyesight even better than Ned Land's. When this man fixed his look upon some object, he would frown and squint in such a way as to limit his range of vision; and then he would

> look. And what a look! How he could magnify objects made smaller by distance! How he could penetrate to your very soul!"

This is reminiscent of Baron von Hessel's monocle, which was like "a microscope through which von Hessel studied the smaller creatures of the world." *The Other Log of Phileas Fogg* reveals that Nemo, an agent of a secret extraterrestrial society, is utilizing a piece of alien technology to change his eye color. This is how Farmer explains how Nemo had black eyes while Moriarty had grey eyes, even though they were one and the same person. Von Hessel is apparently using a similar, perhaps perfected, means to change his eye color. That the baron's eyes "seemed to shine with an inner light" may be an indication of the artificial optical device that he uses. Remember also that Van Weyden described Wolf Larsen's eyes as being "wide apart as the true artist's are wide," just as Nemo's are described as being "rather far apart." Those still in doubt about the similarities of Nemo and Wolf Larsen can recall that both men suffer from nervous disorders resulting in severe headaches. While Farmer in his *Other Log* attributes Nemo's fits to suppression of trauma via extraterrestrial mind control techniques, the true reason for the malady may lie in the unanticipated effects of the elixir.

With von Hessel's subtle and not so subtle references to Wolf Larsen and Nemo, the pieces of a bizarre puzzle begin to fall into place. We see a remarkable resemblance among all three men, von Hessel, Larsen, and Nemo, as well as Moriarty and Baron Karl. If we look at the characters' lives chronologically, we see that they all neatly follow one another. First comes Nemo in the 1860s, then Moriarty in the early to mid-1890s, and then Larsen in the late 1890s, followed by von Hessel in 1918 and Baron Karl in the 1930s. The inference, until now shrouded in utter obscurity, becomes obvious. We are dealing with one man, who, aided by an age-slowing elixir, is living down through the ages, repeatedly changing his identity, but not his character.

The Doubtful Heritage

Here we must follow another wily tentacle which leads from *Escape from Loki* to Farmer's pastiche of Tarzan and Doc Savage, *A Feast Unknown*. In this novel we discover that a secret society known as the Nine has been manipulating and molding human society since prehistoric times. The Nine possesses an age-slowing elixir, which is used as leverage to keep its members in check. One of the leading members of the Nine is XauXaz, who Lord Grandrith (Farmer's Tarzan character) and Doc Caliban (Farmer's Doc Savage character) discover is none other than the real-life basis for Wotan, the Norse All-father god. XauXaz has secretly been planting his genes throughout Grandrith's and Caliban's lineage, and in fact was their grandfather. Grandrith and Caliban also find out that they are brothers. Their father, John Cloamby, was an agent of the Nine. Due to mysterious side effects of the elixir, Cloamby went on a violent rampage while in England and is the man known in history as Jack the Ripper. Cloamby raped Grandrith's mother, who later bore her child on the shores of Africa. Cloamby changed his name to Caliban and moved to America, where he raised his second son to be a bronze superhero devoted to righting wrong and punishing evildoers. In *A Feast Unknown* and its sequels, *The Lord of the Trees* and *The Mad Goblin*, Caliban and Grandrith learn that they were both created as an experiment by the Nine. The stranding of Grandrith's mother and uncle on the shores of equatorial Africa and his subsequent adoption by a species of semi-human anthropoids was prearranged by the Nine. Similarly, Doc Caliban's father was manipulated by the Nine into creating a scientific superman.

In *The Mad Goblin*, Doc Caliban believes that his father raised him to combat the Nine. However, before his father could reveal this to him, the Nine contacted Caliban and initiated him into the society without his father's knowledge. Later his father was killed by the Nine because he was suspected of treason. Doc Caliban hunted down and killed his father's murderers without knowing that they were agents of the Nine. This story would be consistent with what is told in Lester Dent's *The Man of Bronze*. Doc Savage's father, just before he is killed, sends a letter to his son, which is only partially complete due to sabotage by Savage, Sr.'s killers. Doc's father tells him in his letter that he is passing to his son a "doubtful heritage." He writes:

> It may be a heritage of woe. It may also be a heritage of destruction if you attempt to capitalize on it. On the other hand it may enable you to do many things for those who are not so fortunate as yourself, and will, in a way, be a boon for you in carrying on your work of doing good for all.

The reader is left thinking that this letter refers to a valley of gold which Doc Savage will inherit from his father. This is not what Doc's father is really referring to, however, and he states as much in his letter when he says, "You will find that I have nothing much to leave you in the way of tangible wealth." Certainly a valley of gold would be considered tangible wealth! Therefore, we must conclude that Doc's father was leaving him something other than a source of wealth. We may assume that Savage, Sr. was going to finally inform Doc about the Nine (certainly a heritage of woe) and that he was going to tell his son about his own experiments with the age-slowing elixir. If Doc would decide to capitalize on the elixir, he would certainly be destroyed by the Nine, who wish to keep the elixir a secret. On the other hand, if Doc could live forever, or at least a long, long time, he could do much good for the world. Of course, the same could be said of an inheritance of gold, but does Doc Savage really need to worry about resources? A man of his genius could easily find a way to make millions, billions even. Certainly he is already well on his way to this before the events of *The Man of Bronze*. A man who can rent the top floor of the Empire State Building in the midst of the Great Depression is not doing too badly for himself.

With this information as a background, we wish to reconstruct the events leading up to Doc Savage's birth, and their connection with Nemo/Moriarty/Larsen/von Hessel/Karl. We know from Farmer's biography of Doc Savage that Savage, Sr., Hubert Robertson, and Ned Land were present at Doc's birth on the schooner Orion off the coast of Andros Island. We also know that Doc's mother is Aronnaxe Larsen, who is Ned Land's granddaughter and Wolf Larsen's daughter.[60]

In all probability, events occurred as follows: Doc's father had long ago become involved with a secret society, which Farmer calls the Nine, a society which controls human society and possesses an age-slowing elixir. He attempted to distill the elixir himself, but was unsuccessful because of unanticipated sideeffects which made him prone to violence. Now at odds with the Nine, he raised his son to fight them, but never had the chance to inform Doc of his mission. Savage, Sr. enlisted the help of Ned Land in his designs against the Nine. Ned Land was at odds with the Nine for several reasons. For one, Wolf Larsen, aka. XauXaz, etc., had married his daughter and then left her destitute. Two, Ned Land also knew about the Nine from his experiences on board the *Nautilus*. He knew that Nemo was the same man as Wolf Larsen. That Nemo—who he had grown to hate with a passion while onboard the *Nautilus*□had married his daughter was the ultimate blow to Land. That his great-grandson would be raised to defeat Nemo must have given Land a great feeling of satisfaction. The three men had gathered on the *Orion* to discuss their plan of attack against the Nine. Farmer states that Doc's birth was not registered in the ship's log because he "had good reason to leave it unrecorded." We now know why: he wished to leave no clue that the Nine could trace. Something went wrong, however, when Doc was born on that stormy night off Andros Island. The *Orion* was driven onto a reef. Farmer speculates that Doc's mother was drowned. Savage, Sr. must have worried that his well-thought-out plans were going to come to a quick end. But his son survived the mysterious demise of the *Orion* and would later take on his "doubtful heritage."

We know from *Escape from Loki* that Doc's father *did* know about von Hessel. Doc once overheard his father speak of the baron "to some cronies." These cronies may have been Ned Land and Hubert Robertson. Savage, Sr. mentions his informants, who were apparently keeping tabs on von Hessel.

But who, ultimately, is von Hessel? Having demonstrated that the baron is changing identities down through the ages, what did he mean when he told Doc that he was conceived in an illegitimate liaison between a Danish lady and the Crown Prince Frederick and that he, von Hessel, was really half brother to the Kaiser Wilhelm? If we compare von Hessel's supposed lineage with Doc Caliban's lineage in *A Feast Unknown*, we see remarkable similarities. The same genealogical relationships are presented in both cases, but with different names filled in the blanks. Again, von Hessel was sending a coded message to Doc. This time it was a blueprint for his own true lineage, which differs considerably from the lineage he had been told by his father. So while von Hessel states that he is half-brother to the Kaiser, he is sending a coded message that Doc Savage is really half-brother to Tarzan. Like von Hessel, Tarzan's father isn't who he thinks he is. Farmer, in *Feast*, goes into great detail to show that Grandrith's (read Tarzan's) father-in-name did not have intercourse with Tarzan's mother. We can guess that, like Grandrith's (Tarzan's) grandfather, his father-in-name was also sterile. This would match what von Hessel says about his own father-in-name's sterility.

The God of a Thousand Names

A final note on von Hessel's name provides some more shocking conclusions. According to the *New Dictionary of American Family Names*, Hessel—in addition to meaning "hazel"—indicates "One who came from Hessle… villages in both the East and West Ridings of Yorkshire." A pivotal event in the Farmerian Monomyth occurs in this area of England. I am referring to the crash of the Wold Newton meteorite, in the East Riding of Yorkshire, which irradiated and mutated the genes of Doc Savage's and Tarzan's ancestors. In connection with this Farmer, in *Tarzan Alive*, states that the Greystokes can trace their ancestry back to "the great god Woden in Denmark of the third century A.D." He also says, "The founders of the Greystoke line were secret worshippers of Woden long before their neighbors had converted to Christianity." Then Farmer curiously adds, "Perhaps the great god of the North is not dead but is in hiding. It pleased the Wild Huntsman to direct the falling star of Wold Newton near the two coaches. Thus, in a manner of speaking, he fathered the children of the occupants. The mutated and recessive genes would be reinforced, kept from being lost, by frequent marriages among the descendents of the irradiated parents." This, he says, created at least fourteen near-superhumans.

So we find that von Hessel, by his name, is indicating to Doc not that he is *like* Wotan but that he *is* Wotan, and that he is responsible for the mutated genes in Doc's lineage. Von Hessel caused the Wold Newton meteorite to fall where it did, thus irradiating Doc's ancestors. Remember von Hessel, under the identity of Professor Moriarty, was the author of the acclaimed *Dynamics of an Asteroid.*

The Golden Elixir

In *Escape from Loki*, Doc recalls that von Hessel also once made quite a stir in scientific circles with "His monograph on the mutations of the bacteria *Treponema pallidum* after bombardment by Roentgen rays while suspended in diluted *Cannabis sativa*." Von Hessel, of course, must have been working on experiments involving the elixir. Translated into everyday language, what does von Hessel's monograph mean? *Treponema pallidum* is the bacterium which causes syphilis. Roentgen rays are X-rays. *Cannabis sativa* is marijuana. Therefore the subject of von Hessel's monograph, in layman's terms, is about the bacterium which causes syphilis after bombardment by X-rays while suspended in diluted marijuana. This provides us with a clue as to what the elixir is and how it is administered.

Von Hessel is a man who loves cigars, and his cigars are "of the zeppelin class." It would only be fitting that he is literally displaying the elixir under his and everyone else's nose. The reverse pun on Freud must have appealed to the baron as well. The chemical composition of the elixir must involve marijuana, as indicated by his early experiments. What better way to disguise the powerful aroma of *Cannabis sativa* than to hide it under the even more potent odor of cigar smoke? There are indications in *Feast* that the elixir may be administered through smoke. When Lord Grandrith and Doc Caliban are in the caves of the Nine, they are certain that they are being administered the elixir. However, they do not know how this is done or what form the elixir takes. Doc Caliban suspects that it is in the mead-tasting drink which all initiates are given, but Lord Grandrith is not so sure. Farmer mentions "nine giant torches of wood and pitch projecting from moveable stone pillars." It is possible that the elixir is dispensed within smoke from these torches. Observe the Baron von Hessel's curious behavior in the first banquet scene. As he taunts Doc about the Countess and thought of escape, he laughs and throws "his half-smoked cigar into a corner. An orderly hastened to pick it up," writes Farmer. "Instead of placing it in a waste container, he stubbed it out and placed it in his jacket pocket." The reader is left thinking that the orderly is just hoarding the leftovers of the wasteful baron. But might we not conclude that the orderly was acting under von Hessel's directions to retrieve and save any of his discarded precious elixir-bearing cigars?

In *Feast*, Caliban and Grandrith find out that exposure to the elixir is reacting to their genetic makeup with violent sideeffects. This greatly affects their sex life, only allowing them pleasure when they erupt in violence. The elixir seems to be intimately connected with the sexual act. This makes sense historically, as traditions interested in developing an immortality elixir, such as Taoist alchemy, place a great emphasis on the transformation of generative or sexual energy into vital energy, or *chi*, in the distillation of the elixir. In fact, Taoist alchemists use the term "Golden Elixir" to describe their immortality potion. In this tradition, generative energy, which is produced in relation with the sexual center, is blended with other energies in the body to produce the elixir. This makes one wonder about the baron's designs to get Doc to sleep with his mistress, the Countess Idivzhopu. Doc has strong suspicions that the baron wanted him to have sex with the Countess, but he cannot fathom the reason. Perhaps von Hessel needed Doc and the Countess to have sex in order to distill the elixir. This would explain why, the day after Doc's intimacy with Lily Bugov, the baron smiles widely at Doc as he strolls by with the Countess, even though the baron knows that Doc has slept with his mistress. Doc's mutated genes may also be a factor in the recreation of the age-slowing formula.

There are parallels between the baron's manipulation of Doc and other books by Farmer. *Fire and the Night* is seemingly a mainstream novel about the problems of black/white relations among even the well educated and liberal. However, a strong case may be made that it is actually thinly cloaked science fiction, dealing with Farmer's recurrent themes of immortality and secret societies. A character in the story, Vashti Virgil, bears an identical resemblance to the Egyptian Queen Nefertete, wife of the pharaoh Ikhnaton. This in itself could be coincidence, but other strange events occur in the novel. Danny Alliger, the protagonist of the story, has visions of a "Lady in White." Later in the story Alliger encounters Mr. Virgil, Vashti's husband, whose father had been involved in an interracial rape, referred to as "The Case of the Lady in White." This indicates that Alliger has had a genuine premonition. At the end of the novel, Alliger is lured to Vashti's house, where the two have an intimate encounter. When they kiss, sparks fly between their lips. Eventually Alliger discovers that his encounter with Vashti has been prearranged, a set up to fulfill the psychological needs of Mr. Virgil, who desires Alliger's "whiteness" to rub off on his wife so that he can sleep with the "Lady in White." When Alliger leaves Vashti's house, he runs into Mr. Virgil, who reaches out with a finger and shocks Alliger with a static charge. But the story may not be just a psychological study of interracial issues. There are references to initiation into a secret society in a boyhood story which Mr. Virgil relates to Alliger. We can speculate that the Virgils were members of a secret society which dates back to ancient Egyptian times. Alliger, in his strange intimate encounter with the Virgils, may have been undergoing some sort of ancient initiation ritual akin to that of which Lord Grandrith and Doc Caliban partake in *A Feast Unknown*. Or Mr. Virgil may have been using Alliger to distill the elixir, just as von Hessel did with Doc. Certainly the novel ends with Alliger as baffled as Doc. (The Alliger family, by the way, appears more recently in Farmer's hard-boiled, Peoria-based detective novel *Nothing Burns in Hell*.)

There are also a great many similarities between Farmer's elixir and Doyle's Holmes story "The Adventure of the Creeping Man." This story, in which a man injects himself with monkey hormones to increase his vitality and youthfulness, also bears a striking resemblance to the events of Robert Louis Stevenson's *The Strange Case of Dr. Jekyll and Mr. Hyde*. In both of these stories, as well as in Farmer's Grandrith/Caliban books, the elixir brings on violent reactions in its subjects. If the baron is exposing Doc to the elixir in *Escape from*

Loki, we may better understand Doc's recurrent emotional outbreaks in the novel.

A Most Mysterious Game of Bridge

In *Escape from Loki*, Doc Savage is baffled by more than just the baron and his mistress. He also cannot fathom the details behind the events leading to the deaths of Duntreath, Cauchon, and Murdstone. The sequence of events is certainly somewhat confusing. Doc Savage assigns Johnny Littlejohn the task of keeping tabs on Murdstone, the entomologist, who, because of his slight accent, Doc suspects is a German spy. Just before the scene in which the three men die, Doc asks Johnny where Murdstone is. "In the colonel's room," replies Johnny, "playing bridge with him, Major Wells, and Deauville." However, when Renny Renwick, assigned to follow Cauchon, announces that Cauchon, Murdstone, and Duntreath are locked in Duntreath's burning office, Major Wells and Deauville seem to have vanished. They are never mentioned again. Doc rushes in and stabs the pain-blinded Murdstone, who then croaks out a number of fragmentary sentences. These few words leave Doc thinking that Duntreath was really a German agent and that he has mistakenly given Murdstone a fatal wound.

But some of Murdstone's final utterances do not make sense. He seems to indicate that Cauchon had spied on Doc and his followers and reported their plans for escape from Camp Loki. But he also seems to indicate that Duntreath, the supposed traitor, had been fighting with Cauchon. Why would Cauchon and Duntreath, who are supposedly both German agents, be coming to blows with one another? Doc questions Murdstone if it is Cauchon or Duntreath who is the German agent. In fragments, Murdstone replies:

> The colonel… a plant. Cauchon… must've… colonel stabbed him… I… we struggled. Lamp fell, broke… fire… stabbed me… shot me… killed… colonel… couldn't see, thought he might still be alive… attacked… shot, stabbed, got me. Or somebody else?

We assume that Murdstone means to say that Colonel Duntreath was a plant, a German spy. But we still do not know who Cauchon was and what he was doing. He is definitely not innocent, as when Doc asks Murdstone about Cauchon, he replies, “Went to… reported… you… others.” How can we come to terms with these facts in the light of Murdstone’s final testimony?

First of all, we must look at what these men had in common. All of them, Duntreath, Murdstone, and Cauchon, were in the habit of playing bridge together in Colonel Duntreath’s office. Doc observes that Murdstone had been getting on an intimate footing with Duntreath by playing bridge with him and two other cronies. These latter must be Deauville, who is Duntreath’s assistant, and Major Wells, about whom we know nothing. Doc also observes that Cauchon, who is a Belgian infantry captain, was in the habit of playing bridge with them when a regular was absent. Those who know anything about the history of card games might remember that bridge evolved out of the once popular game of whist.

Here we must pause and consider where the game of whist appears in winding tunnels of the Farmerian Monomyth. In *The Other Log of Phileas Fogg*, the card game plays a pivotal role among agents of an extraterrestrial secret society. Members of this society use the individual cards and their varying combinations to communicate esoteric information among one another. In this way, Fogg knows that he should proceed as ordered on his mad rush around the globe. Whist also appears in Doyle’s “The Empty House” in a game involving the notorious Colonel Moran, Moriarty’s cohort, who also appears in *Other Log*.

Now things begin to take shape. It is reasonably safe to assume that there was more than meets the eye in Duntreath’s game of bridge. Unquestionably the men were using the game to send signals to one another. That Murdstone was involved probably means that Doc’s original suspicions that the entomologist was not innocent were correct. If there are two opposing secret societies involved, as in *Other Log*, we might guess that Murdstone belonged to one and Duntreath to the other. But we should not be so hasty. When Murdstone, in his final testimony, refers to the “colonel,” he may be referring to von Hessel, who is the Baron *Colonel* von Hessel. If so, it may be the Baron Colonel who is a plant, not Colonel Duntreath. In fact, it is possible that the baron made a brief appearance at Duntreath’s game of bridge. Recall that the train steams up and halts on Doc’s side of the enclosure right before Duntreath’s office bursts into flames. Doc thinks, “The train was standing by. For whom? Why?” Maybe it was waiting for the baron, who had one last errand to perform before he left camp. That the baron was on the train we discover later. When he boarded it, we do not know.

Benedict Murdstone is still one big question mark. Farmer has connected Murdstone to the family of the same name who appear in Charles Dickens' *David Copperfield*. We may guess that he is the offspring of either sibling, Edward or Jane Murdstone. He does bear the family proboscis. Further, we must wonder about his relation to the Countess Mary Anne Liza Murdstone-Malcon who appears in Farmer's "The Adventure of the Three Madmen." Her stage name, Liza Borden, is strikingly reminiscent of "Lily Bugov." That Murdstone-Malcon appears in the story juxtaposed with the von Hessel-like Von Bork (who is also one-eyed, like Odin) is equally curious.

Earlier in *Escape from Loki*, Murdstone tells the suspicious Doc that he was never in Germany except on one summer holiday but later contradicts this by stating, as he is dying, that he was "born Bremen… ten years old… raised Berk…" This discrepancy is difficult to fathom.

A Worm Unknown to Science

Sherlockians must have been baffled and amused by a certain aspect of what is perhaps the most important scene in *Escape from Loki*. In this scene, Doc enters the abandoned chateau of Baron de Musard. He soon locates a secret chamber bearing all the gruesome accoutrements of a satanic ritual. This scene is important for two reasons. One, it gives Doc a taste of true evil, which later inspires his journey to do good acts and punish evildoers. Secondly, what Doc encounters in this room of horrors is the biggest clue of all in unraveling the tangled skein that is his dubious legacy.

To explain this statement, I shall cite two passages. The first comes from this crucial scene in *Escape from Loki*:

> Savage leaned over the stone basin to see better what was inside it. Old dried bloodstains spotched its cavity. The bones of an infant, perhaps six months old, lay in the center. Beside them was a large sharp knife.
>
> Savage was horrified.
>
> What horrified him even more, while also mystifying him, was a long whitish worm moving slowly over the spine bones.
>
> He thought that he had a thorough grounding

> in the invertebrate phyla. But he could not classify this creature. It was, as far as he was aware, a worm unknown to science.

The second passage, which must be read in conjunction with the above quotation, comes from one of Doyle's classic Sherlock Holmes stories, in which Dr. Watson recounts three cases left unsolved by the Great Detective. This is from "The Problem of Thor Bridge":

> A third case worthy of note is that of Isadora Persano, the well-known journalist and duellist, who was found stark staring mad with a match box in front of him which contained a remarkable worm said to be unknown to science.

It is too bad that the great Holmesian scholar William S. Baring-Gould did not live to read Doc Savage's first adventure. Imagine the look on his face had he compared the above two passages! In any event, Farmerian scholars must have been equally stunned, for there is a third story which not only mentions the "worm unknown to science" but which revolves entirely around it.

This third story is Farmer's "The Problem of the Sore Bridge—Among Others," a companion to Doyle's "Thor Bridge" in that it solves the three mysterious cases which so perplexed Holmes. This is Harry "Bunny" Manders' account of how he and his fellow gentleman burglar, A. J. Raffles, race one step ahead of Holmes to solve the cases of the disappearance of James Phillimore, the disappearance of the cutter *Alicia*, and the strange, unknown worm.

In the story, placed in 1895, Manders and Raffles discover that James Phillimore is in reality a shape-shifting extraterrestrial, who manages to disappear from his house by turning into a chair. He has come to earth to lay his offspring, which begin their incubation in a crystalline state resembling star sapphires, later transforming into a hideous worm with a dozen needle-like tentacles and tiny pale-blue eyes. This is the worm which drives Isadora Persano "stark staring mad" and undoubtedly the same creature which Doc Savage encounters in de Musard's chateau. Doc does not mention the tentacles, but his descriptions are vague. Either Farmer just failed to mention the tentacles in Doc's encounter or the worm was in a pre-tentacle transitory state between crystal and worm. Later Manders and Raffles come across the parent creature in its apparently true form, which looks like an enlarged version of Isadora Persano's tentacled worm. It has the ability to split itself into smaller entities which still have the ability to shape-shift.

The conjunction of these three stories, one edited by Doyle and two by Farmer, is quite shocking and absolutely beyond coincidence. But even more ominous comes the realization that the entities which Doc, Manders, and Raffles encountered appear in several more recorded accounts. We may recall from Manders' account that the Phillimore creature arrived from the heavens in a ship which plunged into the English Channel off the Straits of Dover. The ship was most likely a submersible vessel not unlike Nemo's *Nautilus*, which Farmer, in *Other Log*, reveals was really built with extraterrestrial technology. With this in mind, recall one of the most memorable scenes in *Twenty Thousand Leagues under the Sea*, in which the *Nautilus* is attacked by a giant tentacled Kraken. Nemo himself takes axe in hand to battle this fearsome creature. Who can but doubt that Nemo's giant squid is a larger version of the shape-shifting entity witnessed by Manders?

What is more, there are two more stories in which Doc Savage encounters the mysterious worm being. By this time, however, he has begun to understand the nature of the threat which challenges him. In John W. Campbell's classic 1938 story "Who Goes There?," which was the basis for the movie *The Thing*, Doc Savage makes a disguised appearance as the giant bronzed scientist McReady. Doc, as McReady, heads a team of scientists who discover a shape-shifting extraterrestrial which has been hibernating at the South Pole until it was disturbed. The creature appears at the end of the story in its original form: as a writhing, tentacled monster, identical with the one run across by Manders and Raffles. Doc must have been following some lead to the Antarctic continent which connected the monster he encounters there with the whitish worm he saw when he was sixteen. With just a little more digging we can trace what clue this probably was.

Farmer, in his biography of Doc Savage, mentions a curious item. He states that Johnny Littlejohn, Doc's geologist aide, was the narrator of H. P. Lovecraft's tale of terror *At the Mountains of Madness*. The story, occurring in 1929, chronicles the ill-fated expedition sent by the Miskatonic University to conduct geological tests in Antarctica. The team accidentally awakens a group of "Old Ones" (note this is the same phrase used to describe the extraterrestrials in Farmer's *Other Log*), who are none other than tentacled extraterrestrial entities. Here we wonder if it was really the lost continent of Atlantis which Nemo shows Professor Aronnax or really "the frightful stone city of

R'lyeh." Whatever the case, the Old Ones were also the creators of shape-shifting beings known as shoggoths, who sometime seem to appear as giant rubbery spheroids. There is also mention of "a land race of beings shaped like octopi and probably corresponding to the pre-human spawn of Cthulhu."[61] This tale, recounted by Johnny to Doc, most certainly provided Doc with enough clues to connect his unknown whitish worm with the beings the Miskatonic expedition found in Antarctica. It is revealing that one member of the team was named Larsen. Could this have been a code left in Johnny's manuscript by Lovecraft? If so, it probably indicates that our slippery baron was tagging along with the expedition. Or perhaps it was a code that Doc's father, who had married a Larsen, accompanied Johnny in disguise. There is also a character named Lake in Johnny's account. *Other Log* reveals that agents of the secret society of immortals bear names which have certain coded meanings, such as Fogg or Head. (We may wonder about the name "Farmer," if we dare…) Lake may have been an agent of the Nine, sent to Antarctica to awaken the Old Ones or perhaps Cthulhu himself. Farmer's fragmentary Doc Caliban novel *The Monster on Hold* indicates that the Nine awakened a Cthulhu-like entity, called Shraask, in order to destroy renegade agents. The clues, whatever they are, were there for Doc to see. Thus we find Doc investigating the entities at the South Pole in the 1938 story "Who Goes There?"

Doc, however, did not solve the riddle of his doubtful heritage on the Antarctic continent. Perhaps he never did. But he does come closer than before in his last recorded adventure, *Up from Earth's Center*. It is fitting that Doc's first adventure, *Escape from Loki*, begins with the phrase "Spiders, men, and Mother Nature make trap doors," for his last adventure begins with a man making "a crude thatched trapdoor which he could close against the black things of the night." This is surely Farmer's indication that these two stories are intimately connected.

To illustrate how they are connected, we bring forth the last Karl of this article, Dr. Karl Linningen. Strangely, Dent quickly drops the name Linningen, referring to the man as simply "Dr. Karl." Karl, as has been shown, is another name for Wotan, the Norse All-Father god. It literally means "Old Man," which was one of Wolf Larsen's names. Therefore, we may immediately suspect that there is something peculiar about Dr. Karl. Like H. W. Starr's contention that Nemo/Moriarty was really only an amateur sailor, so Dent portrays Dr. Karl. He constantly seems to be toying with Doc, prodding him on. When he meets Doc, he takes out a cigar, the tobacco wrapper of which he notices is broken, and remarks to Doc without looking up, "You seem to know me by sight." Doc counters by saying "Why shouldn't I know you?" Doc at this point probably realizes that the game is afoot, that he is dealing with the same forces that he encountered in 1918 when he was sixteen. But Doc is much more experienced now, much more adept at reading the signs. Thus he knows that the doctor has signaled him with the broken tobacco wrapper. The cigar has been tampered with. It is a sign that the elixir is at hand, and the elixir, working in conjunction with Doc's mutated genes, often produces undesirable results. It is no wonder that the bronze man's usually impregnable calm poise is broken and that he screams aloud at the novel's end.

Dr. Karl dogs Doc on his most bizarre adventure, constantly asking his opinion of what is going on in the strange affair. It is almost as if he is mocking him, or testing Doc to see how much of the puzzle he has pieced together. The possible devil, Mr. Wail, apparently has the ability to appear and disappear at will. This very much resembles the shape-shifting Phillimore's ability, and we can guess that Wail is also a shape-shifter. Wail even admits that he is only temporarily in human form. Doc becomes very alarmed at the strange developments in the case and gives an impassioned speech to his aides that this may be the real thing, their toughest case ever. He prods them with more force than he ever has to keep on the lookout for anything unusual. Right after this, Doc and his aides are drugged, although Doc cannot understand how —he was looking for it, but still missed it. Doc then proceeds to follow Wail into the New England caverns which Wail claims lead to Hell. Doc and Monk test for gas as they descend the caves, but neither of these two experts in chemistry finds anything unusual. Then all Hell does break loose. Doc is attacked by shapeless boulder creatures, like Lovecraft's rubbery spheroids. Doc and his crew are chased by these beings, whose "clicking and hissing, a sound that was rage and hunger and bestiality" must truly have been what Lovecraft and Poe attempted to depict by the utterance "Tekeli-li! Tekeli-li!" Finally, Doc's defenses break, and, as he is attacked by a tentacled being, he screams, "probably the first shriek of unadulterated terror that he had given in his lifetime."

Up from Earth's Center ends with no explanation except that provided by Dr. Karl that the caves had been filled with hallucinogenic gas. No mention is made of the fact that Doc and Monk, two of the world's greatest chemists, had tested for gas and found none. Doc is in great doubt as his final adventure closes, and little wonder. As warm sunlight melts the snow on the roof of the lodge where the story ends, Doc stares into space and frowns as icicles form on the eaves. There is beyond contention something supernatural at work.

And so we finally see that the Farmerian Monomyth is a complex pattern of meaningful, though subtle, hints. While Farmer is Jungian in the use of his symbols, he is also Levi-Straussian in that many of his symbols make sense only when considered structurally within a larger framework of myths. Truly it is with a sense of the eerie that one reads a description of the city of the Old Ones as portrayed by H. P. Lovecraft in *At the Mountains of Madness*. It shows best what is at play in the work of a certain Peorian:

> Naturally, no one set of carvings which we encountered told more than a fraction of any connected story; nor did we even begin to come upon the various stages of that story in their proper order. Some of the vast rooms were independent units as far as their designs were concerned, whilst in other cases a continuous chronicle would be carried through a series of rooms and corridors. The best of the maps and diagrams were on the walls of a frightful abyss below even the ancient ground level—a cavern… which had almost undoubtedly been an educational centre of some sort. There were many provoking repetitions of the same material in different rooms and buildings; since certain chapters of experience, and certain summaries or phases of racial history, had evidently been favorites with different decorators or dwellers. Sometimes, though, variant versions of the same theme proved useful in settling debatable points and filling in gaps.

The Farmerian Monomyth certainly is a *mono*-myth: its intricate labyrinth tells many stories, but the maze as a whole—winding as it does through dark depths, occasionally opening upon awe-inspiring, glittering vistas—tells The Story, a single Grand Adventure. Anyone who doubts this should consider the fact that Kickaha, the protagonist of Farmer's *World of Tiers* series, has Phileas Fogg for a great grandfather,[62] while remembering Red Orc's insistence that Kickaha was half-Lord. There is always more to The Story than meets the eye…

Bibliography

Campbell, John W. "Who Goes There?" *Science Fiction: The Science Fiction Research Association Anthology*. New York:HarperCollins, 1988.

Carey, Christopher. "Farmer's *Escape from Loki*: A Closer Look." *The Bronze Gazette*, February 1996.

---. "Loki in the Sunlight." *The Bronze Gazette*,June 1998.

Dent, Lester (Kenneth Robeson). *Fortress of Solitude*. New York: Bantam Books, 1968.

---. *The Man of Bronze*. New York: Bantam Books, 1972.

---. *Doc Savage Omnibus #13, Up from Earth's Center*. New York: Bantam Books, 1990.

Dickens, Charles. *David Copperfield*. New York: Signet Books, 1962.

Doyle, Sir Arthur Conan. "The Adventure of the Empty House," "The Adventure of the Creeping Man," and "The Problem of Thor Bridge." *The Complete Sherlock Holmes*. New York: Doubleday, 1988.

Eckert, Win Scott. "The Malevolent Moriartys, or, Who's Going to Take Over the World When I'm Gone?" *An Expansion of Philip José Farmer's Wold Newton Universe*.. Win Scott Eckert, ed. 2001. <http://www.pjfarmer.com/woldnewton/Articles3.htm#Moriarty>. Revised as "Who's Going to Take Over the World When I'm Gone?": A Look at the Genealogies of Wold Newton Family Super-Villains and Their Nemeses. *Myths for the Modern Age: Philip José Farmer's Wold Newton Universe*. Austin, TX: MonkeyBrain Books, 2005.

Farmer, Philip José. *The Adventure of the Three Madmen.The Grand Adventure*. New York: Berkley Books, 1984.

---. *Dayworld*. J.P. Putnum's Sons, 1985.

---. *Doc Savage: His Apocalyptic Life*. New York: Bantam Books, 1975.

---. *Escape from Loki: Doc Savage's First Adventure*. New York: Bantam Books, 1991.

---. *A Feast Unknown*. New York : Playboy Paperbacks, 1980.

---. *Fire and the Night*. Evanston, Regency:1962.

---. *Lord of the Trees / The Mad Goblin*. New York: Ace Books, 1980.

---. *The Monster on Hold. Program to the 1983 World Fantasy Convention.* Oak Forest: Weird Tales, 1983.

---. "The Problem of the Sore Bridge - Among Others." *Riverworld and Other Stories*. New York: Berkley Books:, 1981.

---. *The Other Log of Phileas Fogg*. New York:Tor Books, 1982.

---. *Tarzan Alive*.New York : Playboy Paperbacks, 1981.

Levi-Strauss, Claude. *Structural Anthropology*. New York:Basic Books, 1963.

London, Jack. *The Sea-Wolf.* New York:Signet Books, 1962.

Lovecraft, H. P. *At the Mountains of Madness* in *The Annotated H. P. Lovecraft.* New York: Dell Books, 1997.

Murray, Will. "The Genesis of John Sunlight, Parts 1 & 2." *The Monarch of Armageddon*. Millennium Comics, 1991.

Orchard, Andy. *Cassell Dictionary of Norse Myth and Legend.* London: Cassell, 1997.

Poe, Edgar Allen. "The Narrative of Arthur Gordon Pym of Nantucket." *The Tell-Tale Heart and Other Stories*. New York: Bantam Books, 1982.

Reaney, P. H. *The Origin of English Surnames*. New York: Barnes & Noble, 1957.

Smith, Elsdon C. *New Dictionary of American Family Names*. New York: Harper & Row, 1973.

Stevenson, Robert Louis. *The Strange Case of Dr. Jekyll and Mr. Hyde*. New York: Washington Square Press1995.

Vellutini, John L. "The Good Ship Orion." *The Bronze Gazette*.February 1995.

Verne, Jules. *The Mysterious Island.* New York: Signet Books, 1986.

---. *Twenty Thousand Leagues under the Sea*. New York:Bantam Books , 1981.

The Two Lord Ruftons
By Philip José Farmer

Baker Street Journal, December 1971

Holmes, in "The Disappearance of Lady Frances Carfax," notes that Lady Frances is the unmarried daughter of the late Lord Rufton. The famous Napoleonic soldier, Brigadier Étienne Gerard, also writes in his memoirs of a Lord Rufton. (Gerard's literary agent and editor, A. Conan Doyle, was also Watson's.) Lord Rufton, in Gerard's "How He Triumphed in England" (title by Doyle), was the English nobleman who, in 1811, was the host of Gerard while he was waiting to be exchanged for an English prisoner. In his autobiography, the Frenchman gives an account of his adventures which are, as usual, highly self-revealing and amusing. We need concern ourselves here only with the relationship of Gerard's host to Lady Frances, though we won't ignore certain implications or suggestions.

Holmes's case occurred 1 July to 18 July 1902, according to W.S. Baring-Gould in his *The Annotated Sherlock Holmes*. However, he admits that others have a good case for 1897. For our purposes any time between 1897 and 1902 is acceptable. Holmes says that Lady Frances was "still in fresh middle age," which would mean anywhere between forty and forty-three by late Victorian (or early Edwardian) standards. If she was forty-two at the time of the case, she would have been born in 1855 or 1860.

Gerard's Lord Rufton seems to have been anywhere between twenty-five and thirty, though he could have been older. Gerard does not mention any wife or child of his, and, while Gerard was one to stick to the essentials of his story, he surely would have said something about Rufton's wife if she had existed. The brigadier was too conscious of the fair sex not to have done so.

Gerard says that Lord Rufton came to Paris five years afterwards (in 1816) to see him, and Gerard does not mention any Lady Rufton in connection with this visit. Thus, it seems likely that Lord Rufton did not get married until after the visit, though he would have gotten a wife within a year or two if he were the ancestor of Lady Frances Carfax.

It's pleasing to think that Lord Rufton met and married Gerard's sister while in Paris, but we may be sure that this event would have been commented on at length by the Brigadier.

Holmes said that Lady Frances was "the last derelict of what only twenty years ago was a goodly fleet." He also said that she was the only survivor of the direct family of the late earl. Thus, a number of the earl's children, and perhaps the earl himself, still lived in 1882 (or 1877). Any sons the earl may have had had predeceased him. Lady Frances apparently did not begin her wanderings in Europe until four years before the case began. This would indicate that the last tie to her ancestral home had died at that time and that this tie was a sister or her father. I opt for the earl himself, since the money and, presumably, the ancestral seat, went to the distant male relatives. Lady Frances would have been forced to leave home sooner than four years before if the earl had died much earlier.

If Gerard's Rufton was the ancestor of Watson's,[63] he would have been Lady Frances's grandfather. Her father would have been born circa 1817-1840, and his father would have been born circa 1785.

An objection to the theory of the Ruftons' being of the same family is Gerard's reference to the lord's sister. He called her Lady Jane Rufton, whereas he should have said Lady Jane Carfax, if she was of the same family as Lady Frances. But Gerard consistently shows in "How He Triumphed in England" and in other chapters of his memoirs, a deep ignorance of British titles. Indeed he displays a deep ignorance of other things British, especially British sports. It would not have occurred to him that the earl's sister would be called by her family name, not her brother's title. And it is likely that he had never heard Lord Rufton's family name.

Gerard's account and Watson's illuminate each other so that what one lacks in data the other supplies. Thus, combining the data, we know that Lord Rufton was an earl, that the ancestral seat was High Combe, located near the north edge of Dartmoor, and that it was near enough to Tavistock to get there on the north-south highway in an hour or two on a fast horse. High Combe is close to Baskerville Hall, and it is possible that Lady Frances's grandfather (or father or both) had married a daughter of the Baskervilles.

Of course, neither "Rufton" nor "Carfax" is genuine. Gerard doubtless gave the real title of his house in his memoirs, but his editor, Doyle, changed it to avoid embarrassing an old and highly placed family. Later, as literary agent for Watson (and, undoubtedly, a collaborator on some occasions), he recognised that Lady Frances was a descendant of Gerard's lord. Doyle had changed the name of Rufton in editing the memoirs, and now he could not resist changing

Watson's original pseudonym for Lady Frances's father to Rufton also. (No doubts he did so with Watson's permission.)

Doyle (or Watson) chose Carfax as the fictitious family name because of association with another name or object. I suggest that Doyle derived Carfax from the actual family's coat-of-arms, probably through a reverse use of canting, or punning, arms. The family's shield may have borne a *quadriga* (a Roman two-wheeled chariot with a team of four) and a fox, hence, *car* plus *fax*. Or perhaps, knowing that Carfax Square in Oxford is believed to be an Anglicization of the ancient Roman *quadrifurcus*, and knowing that the shield bore four shakeforks (or pitchforks or eel spears), or even a cross moline voided, Doyle chose the family name. At this moment I am going through Burke's *Peerage* for such arms in an effort to identify the real Carfaxes.

We know that the issue of the Carfax case was successful and even happy, since Lady Frances and the Hon. Philip Green were reunited. Apparently, they got married and had issue. Watson does not take the story far along. But he may have referred to it, with typical Victorian obliquity, when he put into Holmes's mouth the comment that Lady Frances's middle age was "fresh." This would be another example of Watson's humour.

Kiss of the Vampire
By John A. Small

"...Hee saw hir lipps were wet wi' blude,
And hee saw hir lufelesse eyne,
And loud hee cry'd, 'Get frae my syde,
Thou vampyr corps uncleane!'
Bot no, hee is in hir magic boat,
And on the wyde, wyde sea;
And the vampyr suckis his gude lyfe blude,
Sho suckis hym till hee dee.
So now beware, who'er you are,
That walkis in this lone wood:
Beware of that deceitfull spright,
The ghaist that suckis the blude."
(From "The Vampyre" by James Clerk Maxwell;
written in 1845, when he was fourteen years of age.)

She is known by many names and appears, in one form or another, in the legends and folklore of nearly all cultures of the planet: the nocturnal demoness who can change form and who is especially feared in homes where a birth has just taken place. The evil that has been attributed to her is far too great to attempt to catalog here; there are those who say she roams the world still, preying upon the bodies and souls of the innocent.

Amongst the Malays she is known as the *penangglan*, or living witch; the ancient Greeks referred to her alternately as the *strigae* or *lamiae*; the Arabs knew her as the *algul*, the "man-devouring demon of the waste" (known as the "goule" or "ghoul" in translated editions of *The Arabian Nights*). And the ancient Babylonians and Assyrians knew her as a demon who "dwelled in desolate places."

But it is the name bestowed upon her by the Hebrews—Lilith—by which she is best known, and so it is by this name that we shall refer to her here.[64]

According to the best-known (or at least most oft-quoted) legends, Lilith was the first wife of Adam—and the mother of Kane the Immortal. At some point she was banished from the tribe of Adam and sent into exile. The exact nature of her transgression, like so much else regarding Lilith, has become lost in the mists of time; what little is known about this period has been handed down in the form of conflicting legends and folk tales which describe her variously as an insubordinate wife, a child-killer and even a demon-lover. (It is generally assumed that—whatever the circumstances that resulted in Lilith's banishment—they took place some time prior to those events in which her son Kane rebelled against Yog-Sothoth and murdered his brother, which in turn resulted in the disbursement of humanity by the angry entity.)[65]

Lilith's exile led her to dwell in an area near the Red Sea which, according to legend, was the home of all manner of otherworldly creatures.[66] Whether these beings were indeed supernatural "demons" or representatives of some star-faring race which had taken an interest in the development of this world is a matter of conjecture; whatever their origin, it is generally accepted that these beings were well versed in certain black arts and included cannibalism among their many dark rituals. Angry and embittered towards those who had cast her out from her home, Lilith in time came to be fully accepted as a member of her new "tribe"; her "indoctrination" included a series of rituals which bestowed upon Lilith the gift of immortality.

But immortality came at a great price, in the form of a savage bloodlust (the reason, no doubt, behind the cannibalistic practices of those beings who bestowed this immortality upon Lilith in the first place). But whatever horror she might have felt was no doubt quickly replaced by the realization that she now wielded a great power she never could have believed existed prior to her transformation.

Lilith saw in her new existence a means to exact great revenge upon the tribe of Adam and his descendants. She would feed upon the most innocent and vulnerable of their number, and in doing so would create a race of beings like herself: creatures of the night, neither alive nor dead, but possessing great powers.

Thus did this castaway from the tribe of Adam become this world's first vampire, many millennia before the word "vampire" would even be coined.

As the ages passed and the tribes of Man spread out to establish new cultures over the four corners of the globe, Lilith's powers grew and her army of minions grew ever larger. In time her powers became so great that she acquired the ability to create "soul clones"—that is, to infect the spirits of certain victims with portions of her own psyche, making them in effect an extension of her personality.[67] One of the most chilling accounts of one of Lilith's "soul clones" was related by the writer Fornari in his *History of Sorcerers*:[68]

In the beginning of the fifteenth century there lived at Bagdad an aged merchant who had grown wealthy in his business and who had an only son to whom he was tenderly attached. He resolved to marry him to the daughter of another merchant, a girl of considerable fortune, but without any personal attractions. Abul-Hassan, the merchant's son, on being shown the portrait of the lady, requested his father to delay the marriage till he could reconcile his mind to it. Instead, however, of doing this he fell in love with another girl, the daughter of a sage, and he gave his father no peace until he consented to the marriage with the object of his affections. The old man stood out as long as he could, but finding that his son was bent on acquiring the hand of the fair Nadilla, and was equally resolute not to accept the rich and ugly lady, he did what most fathers under such circumstances would do—he acquiesced.

The wedding took place with great pomp and ceremony, and a happy honeymoon ensued, which might have been happier but for one little circumstance which led to very serious consequences.

Abul-Hassan noticed that his bride quitted the nuptial couch as soon as she thought her husband was asleep, and did not return to it till an hour before dawn.

Filled with curiosity, Hassan one night, feigning sleep, saw his wife rise and leave the room. He rose, followed cautiously, and saw her enter the cemetery. By the straggling moonbeams he saw her go into a tomb: he stepped in after her.

"The scene within was horrible. A party of ghouls were assembled with the spoils of the graves they had violated and were feasting on the flesh of the long-buried corpses. His own wife, who, by the way, never touched supper at home, played a no inconsiderable part in the hideous feats.

> As soon as he could safely escape Abul-Hassan stole back to his bed.
>
> He said nothing to his bride till next supper was laid, and she declined to eat; then he insisted on her partaking, and when she positively refused he exclaimed roughly: 'Oh yes, you keep your appetite for your feasts with the ghouls.' Nadilla was silent; she turned pale and trembled, and without a word sought her bed. At midnight she rose, fell on her husband with her nails and teeth, tore his throat, and, having opened a vein, attempted to suck his blood; but Abul-Hassan, springing to his feet, threw her down and, with a blow, killed her. She was buried next day.
>
> Three days after at midnight she reappeared, attacked her husband again, and again attempted to suck his blood. He fled from her and on the morrow opened her tomb, burnt her to ashes and cast the ashes into the Tigris…"

Similar stories can be found throughout history. One tale has it that Lilith assumed the guise of an asp—that is, she created the mesmeric (or hypnotic) illusion that she was an asp—and bit the Egyptian queen Cleopatra; this gave rise to legends claiming that Cleopatra herself continued to roam the earth after death as a vampire herself.[69]

And at Waterford, in Ireland, there is a little graveyard under a ruined church near Strongbow's Tower; legend has it that underneath the ground at this site there lies a beautiful female vampire—another of Lilith's minions—still ready to kill those whom can be lured thither by her beauty.[70]

Lord of the Vampires

With the passage of time, it became inevitable that there would arise other powerful vampires who would challenge Lilith's dominion over their race. Of these, none was more powerful than he who would one day become known as "The Lord of the Vampires"—the being known as Dracula.

He was Vlad Tepes, a 15th Century Wallachian prince whose cruelty towards his enemies has been the subject of much Romanian,

Turkish, German, Slavonic and Byzantine folklore. He is remembered by most historians as "Vlad the Impaler"—a name derived from his favorite method for imposing death—but he was also known to the simple peasants of his native Romania as "Dracula," a diminutive meaning "son of the devil." (His father, an equally bloodthirsty ruler whose birth name had also been Vlad, had been known as "Dracul," the Romanian word for "devil.")[71]

That this Dracula continued to walk the earth as a vampire following his death in battle against the Turks outside the city of Bucharest in 1476, and has periodically returned to continue his campaign to spread the vampire cult throughout the world, has long been a matter of record. Most accounts agree that Dracula's vampirism is the result of some pact he made with "the Evil One";[72] while the common perception is that this refers to Satan, there are those who have theorized that the "Evil One" in question may in fact have been none other than Lilith herself.

If this is so, then there would seem to be no better evidence of the strength of Dracula's will than the fact that he was able to break free of Lilith's control and rise to domination over the vampire cult she had founded so many millennia before.

The many tales and legends of Dracula—including his rise to the aforementioned title of "Lord of the Vampires"—are far too numerous to discuss in detail at this time. However, one exploit that does bear mention here took place in 1805, when Dracula found himself engaged in battle with one Don Diego de la Vega, the Old California nobleman who, as is now well known, was the first to don the mask of The Fox, El Zorro. It was the most dangerous exploit of the original Zorro's career, one from which he just barely escaped with his life before finally defeating Dracula.[73]

Several years later, following his return to California and after the unfortunate death of his bride, de la Vega unwittingly found himself embroiled in the affairs of a thrill-seeking young woman who assumed a masked identity apparently inspired by his own. When Anita Santiago first adopted the guise of Lady Rawhide in that year of 1808, it was at least partially out of revenge; she blamed Zorro for horrendous injuries suffered by her beloved brother, but upon encountering Zorro while in her Lady Rawhide identity she found herself torn between her need to avenge her brother and her sudden attraction to the masked caballero.[74]

Lady Rawhide eventually became something of an ally of Zorro and went on to a brief career of her own—a career that was cut short by her encounter with a woman from Zorro's past, a woman with a dangerous secret.

That woman was Carmelita Rodriguez, whom Zorro had encountered during his battle against Dracula in 1805. She had been one of Dracula's victims—no doubt he planned on taking her as his "bride," another addition to his entourage of female vampires—and although The Fox managed to help Carmelita break free of any hold Dracula may have had on her, he could not have known that she had become transformed all the same.

Two years after her own first encounter with Zorro, in 1810, Lady Rawhide became involved in an escapade that saw her locked in battle against a crew of cutthroat pirates. Following a particularly fierce battle on board the pirates' ship off the coast of California, as Lady Rawhide lay bleeding and near death, she was confronted by Carmelita Rodriguez, who had been a passenger on board the ship. After years of struggling to overcome the vampiric urges that were the legacy of her encounter with Dracula, Carmelita gave up trying to resist further and fed upon Lady Rawhide's blood. The encounter actually served to revitalize Lady Rawhide and, when last seen, she had seemed to have regained her health and was rushing off to further battle. However, she was apparently never seen again after this encounter and it was long assumed that she had fallen in battle.[75]

Saddened and sickened by what she had become—and driven to depression by the apparent disappearance of Anita Santiago—Carmelita returned to her native Spain and, in a fit of anger and remorse, committed suicide. But rather than bring peace to what had in the past few years become a very tortured life, Carmelita's action only served to hasten her transformation into a full vampire;[76] she continued to roam the European continent for many years before eventually returning to North America.

At some point during the late 1860s, the Irish author J. Sheridan LeFanu—who had built his career on works based upon "ghost stories" and similar legends from throughout Europe—became aware of events that occurred some time after Carmelita's return to Spain and used them as the basis for his most famous work, the novella *Carmilla*.[77] In fictionalizing the tale, LeFanu transferred the action from Spain to Austria—he was undoubtedly more familiar with the various vampire legends to have been reported in this part of the world—and changed both the time period in which the events occurred and the era in which "Carmilla" (the fictional counterpart to Carmelita) was reported to have died; he also altered the circumstances surrounding Carmilla's death and transformation, though whatever reason he may have had for this has been lost to the ravages of time.

Whatever his reasons for such alterations, the success of LeFanu's novella later helped to convince another Irish author named Bram Stoker to publish his own famous fictionalized account concerning Prince Dracula.[78]

The Fate of Lady Rawhide

As for Anita Santiago—her own revival as a vampire and the realization of just what her encounter with Carmelita Rodriguez had wrought produced a shock to her psyche so intense that it apparently affected her mind, to the point that she lost all memory of her former life as Anita and her short-lived career as Lady Rawhide. Over the course of the next century and a half, accounts of a female vampire roughly matching Anita's description circulated throughout the world.

At one point she took the name Nadina and took up residence on an isolated island, where she enticed a number of victims in order to satisfy her bloodlust.[79] Several years later, in Europe, she encountered an archeologist and his brother, who were searching for the legendary Ring of the Nibelungen; the brother fell into Anita's clutches and was turned into a vampire himself, forcing the archeologist to destroy his brother along with a number of Anita's vampiric slaves.[80]

By the 1920s, Anita—now traveling under the name Lemora—had returned to America where she met a thirteen-year-old girl named Lila, the daughter of fugitive gangster Alvin Lee; Anita/Lemora's attempts to initiate Lila into the "delights of vampirism" were ultimately unsuccessful, and she was forced to flee.[81]

Several years later, she adopted the name Nicole and became the ward of a lugubrious stage director named Darvas. When a series of vampiric murders occurred, Darvas—who had become known for sideshow-like spectacles—became the prime suspect; but after Darvas himself turned up as one of the victims, a family friend discovered "Nicole's" vampirism and triggered a final confrontation which—like the previous incidents listed above—seemed to end with Anita's death.[82] Like Dracula and Lilith before her, however, Anita survived and continued her bloody quest to regain her past.

Later still, in the 1960s, Anita took refuge in the cellar of a large castle-like mansion which was the residence of a pair of hippies and the mistress they both shared. All four became involved with a honeymooning couple who due to circumstances quite beyond their control, found themselves having to take shelter in the mansion for the night. Anita made victims of the couple, the hippies and their mistress.[83]

It was not very long after this incident that Anita happened to save the life of Urthona, a member of a dimension-hopping race known as the Thoans. Realizing that his savior was a vampire, a grateful Urthonia—aware that Anita had no memories of her past life and certain he might be able to help—offered to "take her home." During his many voyages across the dimensions, Urthona had once found himself upon a planet inhabited by vampire-like beings. This planet—which Urthona referred to as Drakulon—had a bizarre geology with rivers and oceans of blood. (It would appear that Drakulon may have actually existed within one of several so-called "pocket universes" reportedly created for the entertainment of the Ancients;[84] there have been reports that the time-traveling being known simply as The Doctor and one of his many companions, Romanadvoratrelundar—Romana for short—found themselves on Drakulon during their voyages in the netherverse referred to by the Doctor as "E-Space," where they helped a band of rebels overthrow a trio of tyrannical vampire leaders living in a lost spaceship.)[85]

The amnesiac Anita, thinking she might at last have found a definite link to her past, agreed to travel to Drakulon with Urthona. He deposited her on Drakulon and departed, leaving Anita to face the possibility of a new life on a "homeworld" she had never known. It would not be a lengthy sojourn, however; another spaceship landed on Drakulon, and upon encountering Anita the ship's captain explained that he and his crew were one of several which had been dispatched to follow the flight trajectory of an interstellar ship manned by one Colonel George Taylor and his crew, a ship that had disappeared shortly after it had left the planet. Although neither Anita nor the ship's crew had any way of knowing it, this crew and the ship they were searching for were actually from an Earth that existed in an alternate universe separate from the one which Anita Santiago had been born into; Taylor's ship and those sent out in search of him had each become ensnared in some sort of space/time anomaly which had plucked them from their flight paths and sent them into parallel dimensions.

Realizing that their quest for Colonel Taylor had been fruitless, the crew set about repairing their ship and began making preparations to return to Earth; unhappy with her new life on Drakulon, Anita hid aboard their ship and accompanied them back to Earth—her Earth, not the Earth from whence the space travelers had come (quite unbeknownst to them). Although she managed to remain in hiding for most of the flight, as the ship approached Earth she found herself once again unable to resist her vampiric urges and the unfortunate crew became her victims.[86]

The Coming of Vampirella

Shortly after her return to Earth, the former Anita Santiago turned up in—of all places—Hollywood, where she found herself assuming yet another new identity: that of Vampirella, the host of one of those late-night horror movie programs that seemed to dominate the UHF airwaves from the 1950s through the late 1970s. Utilizing a gift for acting that she had picked up during her time with her former mentor, the stage director Darvas, she used her new, false "memories" as a supposed native of Drakulon as a part of her new character; in time, no doubt as a result of the celebrity that accompanied her role as a television personality, she came to consider the "Vampirella" role as an extension of her actual personality and actually began using the name as her own.[87]

But Vampirella's television career came to a halt when she fell into the clutches of an evil sorcerer named Ethan Shroud and the acolytes of an otherworldly being operating under the guise of the dread god Chaos. Even as Vampirella found herself in the unexpected position of having to defend the human race against the threat of Chaos, she was also confronted by dangers of a more personal nature. Conrad Van Helsing and his son Adam—descendants of the same Dr. Abraham Van Helsing who had devoted so many years of his career to battling Dracula—had taken up their famous ancestor's cause of hunting down and destroying evil supernaturals and pursued Vampirella for murders which she did not commit.

Eventually the Van Helsings would realize Vampirella's innocence and become her allies—and, in Adam's case, her lover. It was also during this period that Vampirella first met another ally, "The Great Pendragon," a stage magician for whom sad circumstances had resulted in alcoholism and estrangement from his family. The battle against the being known as Chaos—who, it has been speculated, was a member of the same ancient race which had originally bestowed upon Lilith the gift of immortality—eventually culminated in an epic clash with none other than Dracula himself.[88]

Shortly afterward, Vampirella ran afoul of a mysterious, mystic presence known as The Conjuress, who used her magical powers to send both Vampirella and Dracula back in time to 1897; here she encountered none other than Abraham Van Helsing, who found himself working to find a way to return Vampirella to her own time period. Their efforts succeeded, and Vampirella (and Dracula) were returned to the present. Vampirella was soon reunited with the modern-day Van Helsings and Pendragon, who found himself confronted by demons from his own past; during this series of adventures it was revealed that Pendragon's wife, daughter and grandson—all long believed dead—were in fact still alive but had become part of the notorious Granville organized crime family.[89]

Vampirella and Pendragon then embarked on a series of adventures that took them around the world to face a variety of weird and dangerous menaces. It was during this period that she encountered such creatures as the Traveler, an immortal gambler whose eternal life continued only so long as he acted heartlessly; the Devastator, a zombie rock star who remained alive by feasting upon the blood of his fans; and a being who claimed to be Huizitopochili, a Central American sun god, and who had fallen in love with Vampirella.[90] Upon her return to America, Vampirella was reunited with the Van Helsings and faced new confrontations with the Granville family and Chaos. At one point, she even briefly encountered the masked crimefighter known as The Spirit.[91]

In what proved to be the single most unusual of her recorded exploits as Vampirella, she and Pendragon were nearly killed by an evil entity calling herself the Blood Red Queen. One version of the story has it that, during the course of this conflict Vampirella's eyes were torn out and Pendragon's heart was actually ripped from his chest. Given that Pendragon is known to have survived this encounter, it seems reasonable to assume that the extent of his injuries may have been exaggerated for dramatic effect. On the other hand, who knows?

In any event, both were saved in the nick of time by a band of dimension-roving physicians named Starpatch, Quark, Mother Blitz and Crouchback, who assisted in the healing and rehabilitation of Vampirella and Pendragon. Upon learning that Vampirella was supposedly a native of Drakulon, a world with which they were familiar, Starpatch's group arranged for her to return to her false homeworld to recuperate from her injuries; it was here that Vampirella met the woman named Pantha, a lycanthrope from whose race of prehistoric Drakulonian cat-people the planet's vampiric race had apparently evolved! When Starpatch and company returned Vampirella to Earth a short time later, Pantha came along and became for a time Vampirella's companion.[92]

For a brief time Vampirella returned to show business, as she and Pantha embarked on a career as actresses in a series of low-budget horror movies similar to those she had hosted on her old television program. After the first few films, Pantha gave up acting to concentrate instead on serving as Vampirella's manager. Although Vampirella's films quickly became a favorite among fans of that sort of thing, behind the scenes she found herself facing a whole new series of dangers and adventures: confrontations with crazed former child stars, villainous prop men and special effects specialists, various monsters, robots, and even at one point a species of flesh-eating aliens posing as film producers! Whether disillusioned by the movie industry or fed up with the strange experiences she had endured during this period, Vampirella again left show business—presumably for good this time.[93]

Conrad and Adam Van Helsing came back into Vampirella's life around this time, and together they battled an evil occult conspiracy known as the Council of Wizards; Adam, still very much in love with Vampirella, proposed but was turned down; stung by Vampirella's rejection, he struck up a brief relationship with Pantha and they set out on a series of adventures of their own. Around this time Vampirella struck up a friendship with Cryssie Collins, a young woman possessed by demons; during this period she found herself battling such menaces as the assassin squad known as Apocalypse Incorporated, an evil scientist named Countess Vorlok, and an enigmatic, dimension-transcending alien known as the "Walker of Worlds." She also endured new confrontations with the Granville family and the Council of Wizards, and was briefly reunited with Adam van Helsing after his break-up with Pantha.[94]

New Beginning

At some point after this Vampirella again confronted her old foe Ethan Shroud, who managed to drug her and keep her his prisoner for the better part of a decade. During this period, while under Shroud's spell, Vampirella served as a sort of tutor to a teenaged girl named Chelsea, whom Shroud had kidnapped and made a pawn in his campaign to create a "replacement Vampirella" for his own pleasure. It was also during this period that Vampirella first came to learn that her memories of Drakulon were indeed false. Vampirella was eventually freed, with the timely assistance of her old friends Pendragon, Conrad Van Helsing and his son Adam—now a U.S. Senator—but not before Chelsea's first surge of bloodlust resulted in the deaths of Conrad van Helsing and Chelsea herself. Like Vampirella before her, however, Chelsea returned from the grave to walk the earth as a full-fledged vampire—a fact not known by Vampirella and her friends for some time.[95]

Now aware that she was not truly a native of Drakulon after all, but still unaware of her true origins and her past life as Anita Santiago/ Lady Rawhide, Vampirella once again set out on a quest to learn the truth about her past; this quest occasionally led her to cross paths again with Pendragon, Adam van Helsing and Chelsea. And it was during this period that Vampirella finally encountered Lilith, the mother of all vampires, who enlisted her assistance in tracking down and defeating other forms of supernatural evil—presumably so that Lilith could regain her former stature as "Queen of the Underworld."[96]

At one point Vampirella's wanderings even brought her and Pendragon to Gotham City, where they briefly allied themselves with a costumed adventuress who had seemingly adopted the guise of Catwoman first created by Selena Kyle Wayne half a century before. (Although it cannot at this time be fully substantiated, I have reason to believe that Bruce Wayne and Princess Khefretari of Memnon—the "Cat-Woman" Wayne encountered during a 1939 adventure which also involved the Eighth Earl of Greystoke, aka. Tarzan—may have developed a more intimate relationship than had been previously suggested, and that the Catwoman encountered by Vampirella in 1997 was in fact their descendent.) Together this Catwoman and Vampirella battled a female private investigator-turned-werecat to solve a series of violent cat-themed burglaries.[97]

Whether or not Vampirella remained loyal to Lilith or ever learned the true story of her past has, at least as of this writing, not yet been told.[98]

Name of a Thousand Blue Demons
By Cheryl L. Huttner

Jules de Grandin was one of the premier occult detectives of his era, with a career that lasted until at least 1951, and yet Mr. Farmer never directly connected him with the Wold Newton lineage. I have always believed that such a connection must exist. Until recently, I was unable to prove this connection. Now, however, I believe that I have located information on the de Grandin line that successfully integrates it with Mr. Farmer's main Wold Newton information. I have also been able to clarify some aspects of my original research regarding the lineage, thanks to the help of other researchers such as Matthew Baugh, Rick Lai and Jean-Marc Lofficier. Mr. Lofficier's research into the French branches of the Wold Newton family tree has been most helpful and I heartily recommend his book *Shadowmen: Heroes and Villains of French Pulp Fiction* (Black Coat Press, 2003) for those who wish to learn more.

First, some notes. Grandin in its many forms (Legrand, Grandet, Grandin, etc.) is a fairly common French name. For example, another member of this family was Eugenie Grandet, whose life Balzac chronicled.

I began my research with information provided by Philip José Farmer in his discussion of Sir William Clayton's vast contribution to the spreading of the Wold Newton mutations. Mr. Farmer used information provided by Sir William in his memoirs, *Blood and Love Among the Redskins*, which includes a brief mention of Sir William's third marriage to Marie Grandin during his trip to the American Rockies with the expedition of Prince Peter Rubinroth of Lutha. He returned to England after his wife apparently drowned in a mountain stream. Marie is described as the daughter of — Grandin, a French trapper, and of a Crow woman. No date is given but the timeframe of the work sets it between 1827 and 1831. I wondered about the connection and, with some of the serendipitous luck that seems to accompany Wold Newton research, was able to acquire an old, handwritten journal, which seemed to be an early attempt at a de Grandin family tree. The journal refers to that incident and gives the name Anatole de Grandin to the trapper. The journal also describes his return to France at his father's behest, bringing with him a young son. I traced genealogical records in the United States and found no record of such a child born to

Anatole and Snow Cat or any other woman. The only record of a male Grandin was a record of a son born to a Marie Grandin, and I believe that this boy, actually Anatole's grandson, was the child who became Jules de Grandin's grandfather. My researches into the records of the expedition indicate that there was indeed an accident while traversing that mountain stream, in which Marie and her mother were believed to be lost. However, only Snow Cat's body was found and when the expedition members returned to the village with her body, Anatole turned on his son-in-law in a blind, grieving rage, driving him away and never notifying him when Marie was found. Marie survived long enough to bear a son, but died in childbirth. Anatole took the child, named Phillippe-Guillaume, back to France, claiming the boy was his own child.

Research in France and in M. de Grandin's own memoirs, as chronicled by Seabury Quinn, indicates that the de Grandin line that leads to Jules de Grandin can be traced back to the early 1200s. One Ramon Nazara y de Grandin of Languedoc became involved in the events surrounding Simon de Montfort. Later Ramon began the family's association with the occult in a battle with werewolves in Germany. At that time a prophecy was made that Ramon's descendents would be champions against supernatural entities. Several generations later, the family surfaced again when a de Grandin successfully escaped Paris and the St. Bartholomew's Massacre of Huguenots on 24 August 1572.

The family next appeared during the French Revolution, when Josce-Pierre de Grandin married Isabelle Hugonin. The Hugonins appear to be an old Anglo-French family with at least one known tie to Mr. Farmer's research, as a member of that family married into the Litchfield lineage described by James Branch Cabell. There is also a possible linkage with a branch of the Hugonins who served on the side of Queen Maud during the reign of King Stephan, as described in *The Virgin in the Ice* by Ellis Peters.

What I have been able to discover of the de Grandin family follows.

First Generation:

Josce-Pierre de Grandin married Isabelle Hugonin.

Isabelle gave birth to twins, Jacques-Yves and Anatole, in 1785. The family fled to England during the French Revolution. Afterwards, the family returned to help rebuild the nation and Jacques, the elder twin, inherited the family lands, while Anatole went to the American continent to make his own fortune. There he settled among the Crow nation, marrying a Crow maiden named Snow Cat.

Second Generation:

Jacques-Yves de Grandin married Seraphine Austin in 1803.

The Austins married into both the Delagardie and the Challenger/ Rutherford families, yet Mr. Farmer made no mention of any of them as having been present at the Wold Newton meteor strike. However, I have found records of an Etienne Austin and his sister Seraphine having been among the people rescued from the French Revolution by Sir Percy Blakeney, aka the Scarlet Pimpernel. Etienne seems to have been hired as a postboy to the Greystokes. I have some evidence that I believe places Etienne with the coaches on the night of the Wold Newton strike. Etienne himself later married Ange Lecoq, a daughter of one of the other coachmen. There are letters, transcribed into the journal I acquired, that describe the meteor strike by an eyewitness, which seem to have been written to his family by Etienne.

Third Generation:

Laurent de Grandin, born in 1805, married Helene Gerard in 1826.

I find Helene Gerard an interesting person. While there are few official records concerning her, her daughter Gerardine claimed that Helene was a sister of Brigadier Etienne Gerard, whose adventures A. Conan Doyle chronicled. This, however, is a fairly common, and usually unsubstantiated, claim in French genealogies. The birthdates involved also make this claim unlikely. While I believe that there is a relationship to Brigadier Gerard, I have found no textual evidence to back this up. However, recent research by Jean-Marc Lofficier has provided an interesting possibility. He discovered that a sister of the Brigadier married Armand Chauvelin, the Scarlet Pimpernel's enemy. I suspect that Helene was born of this union, but used the Gerard name rather than Chauvelin. This possibility is further increased by Mr. Lofficier's discovery that another daughter of that marriage, Arlette, was raped by the creature known as Gouroull, also known as the Frankenstein Monster (seemingly one of several) and gave birth to a disfigured son, Erik, who was to become known as the Phantom of the Opera. Evidence indicates that Erik was born c. 1830. My research has shown that in 1829 Laurent and Helene were reported as having been murdered by bandits. I suspect that Arlette was visiting her sister at the time and that the bandit story was a cover for the attack by Gouroull, with only Arlette surviving to bear his son.

Fourth Generation:

Philippe-Guillaume married Gerardine de Grandin.

With the death of his son, leaving no male heir, Jacques-Yves contacted his brother Anatole. Anatole returned to France with his supposed son, who was actually his grandson Philippe-Guillaume. In France, Philippe, a brilliant young man, became a lawyer-physician and married his cousin Gerardine. While it may have been an arranged marriage, it also seems to have been a fertile one, as I have located records of at least seven surviving offspring. They seem to have had at least three sons, Jean, Nicholas, and Jules, and four daughters named for the seasons: Ete, Printemps, Automne, and Hiver. Jean would marry Serene Delagardie and name one of his sons for his twin brother, Nicholas.. Three of his sisters married into families whose names would become familiar in the field of French detectives. Much like Anatole, Nicholas seems to have emigrated to the U.S. where he Americanized his name to Grandon. While I have as yet been unable to learn the name of his wife, his son Robert was to have some very interesting travel experiences. I believe Gerardine to be the author of the journal I found, and that Robert brought the copy I now possess with him to America.

Fifth Generation:

Jean married Serene Delagardie.

Jean and Serene were the parents of Jules de Grandin. Interestingly enough, Serene Delagardie, described as "convent bred," implying she was Catholic, opposed her son's marriage to a Catholic girl, after which Jules remained single his entire life. I have found some interesting notes, which may explain her attitude. This information surfaced while I was investigating a comment on the slight resemblance between the famous Belgian detective Hercule Poirot and Jules de Grandin. Poirot's mother was a Vernet, related to the Violet Vernet who married Mycroft Holmes and was Sherlock Holmes' grandmother. What I discovered was that while Violet Vernet was the daughter of Antoine Charles Horace "Carle" Vernet, she was illegitimate, being the daughter of Vernet's lover, one Philippa Delagardie. Philippa bore two children to her lover: Violet Vernet and a son, Carle. Carle Vernet married a cousin, Marguerite Delagardie, and had two daughters. Their first daughter, Felicite, married a Belgian named Poirot, becoming the mother of Hercule Poirot. The other was Serene. I believe that Philippa Delagardie was, in fact, that same Philippa Drummond who married Honore Delagardie and was present at the Wold Newton incident. While Mr. Farmer claims that both Philippa and Honore died in an accident while visiting relatives in Paris, I suspect that Philippa survived the so-called accident, placing her children with the Vernets and going into hiding.

Why do I believe that what happened was no accident? Honore came to England with "coachmen" who have been shown, through Mr. Lofficier's untiring research, to be members of the infamous Black Coats gang which ruled the French underworld for many years. This does seem the sort of thing that might make enemies. I suspect that these enemies eventually caught up with Philippa Drummond-Delagardie while she was residing with her son, resulting in the deaths of Carle and Marguerite. She placed her granddaughters in separate convents under the Delagardie name. The Vernets were able to locate and adopt Felicite, who was raised using the Vernet name, but never located Serene. Unfortunately the convent in which Serene grew up was one in which no child should have been placed. Serene never forgot or forgave what she saw as abandonment or her treatment in the convent and it was this attitude that caused her to reject her religious upbringing and disrupt her son's romance.

I am appending a simple chart of what my research indicates is the true de Grandin family line. As a sideline, I have given de Grandin's birth year as 1874 for thematic reasons; the spacing is suggestive when you consider the birth years of his cousins through the Vernets, Sherlock Holmes (b. 1854) and Hercule Poirot (b. 1864).

1st Generation
Josce-Pierre de Grandin - Isabelle Hugonin

2nd Generation:
Children of Josce-Pierre & Isabelle
1. Jacques-Yves de Grandin b. 1785 - Seraphine Austin
2. Anatole Grandin b. 1785 - Snow Cat (Crow)

3rd Generation:
A. Children of Jacques-Yves & Seraphine
1. Laurent de Grandin b. 1805 - Helene Gerard

B. Child of Anatole (de) Grandin & Snow Cat
1. Marie Grandin b. 1813 m William Clayton

4th Generation:
A. Child of Laurent de Grandin & Helene Gerard
1. Gerardine de Grandin b. 1828 m Phillippe-Guillaume de Grandin b. 1830

B. Child of Marie & William
1. Philippe-Guillaume de Grandin b. 1830 m Gerardine de Grandin b. 1828

5th Generation:
Children of Phillippe-Guillaume & Gerardine
1. Jean de Grandin b. 1848 m Serene Delagardie
2. Nicholas de Grandin (Nick Grandon)
3. Jules de Grandin
4. Ete m Picard
5. Printemps m Maigret
6. Automne m Leqoc
7. Hiver

6th Generation:
Children of Jean & Serene
1. Jourdain-Renaud de Grandin (untraced)
2. Jules de Grandin b. 1874 [99]

NOTE: For clarification I am appending a chart of the Vernet links.

1st Generation
Children of Antoine Charles Horace "Carle" Vernet & Philippa Drummond-Delagardie
Violet Vernet m Mycroft Holmes
Carle Vernet m Marguerite Delagardie

2nd Generation
Children of Carle Vernet & Marguerite Delagardie
Felicite Vernet m Poirot
Serene Delagardie m Jean de Grandin

The Great Korak-Time Discrepancy
By Philip José Farmer

ERB-dom No. 57, April 1972

Some Problems in Writing A Tarzan Biography
Part I "THE SON OF TARZAN"

Tarzan is a living person.

This is the basic premise of my *Tarzan Alive, A Definitive Biography of Lord Greystoke* (Doubleday, April, 1972, $5.95).

This premise that Tarzan is not a fictional character makes inadmissible any speculation about the literary origin of Tarzan. Romulus and Remus, Kipling's Mowgli, Prentice's *Captured by Apes* and the dozen or so other sources so far advanced as the sources from which Burroughs derived his idea of Tarzan have no relevance to reality.

Since this premise removes Tarzan from the realm of fantasy it requires that the stories about him be examined for their fidelity to fact. Or to what we can classify as fact, admitting that evidence may be uncovered in the future which will force us to reclassify.

With this in mind, we can reread the Tarzan epics by Burroughs. And we can place some in the category of largely fictitious, some in the half-true, and some in the nearly all true. Few, for instance, would deny that almost all of *Tarzan at the Earth's Core* and most of *Tarzan and the Ant Men* is fiction. The reasons for these conclusions will, however, be dealt with in separate essays.

This essay is devoted to the epic about which the most controversy has raged in the world of Tarzanic scholarship: *The Son of Tarzan*. This storm is not due to ambiguous or obscure statements by Burroughs or lack of pertinent data. No, certain facts are clear enough. But certain scholars have refused to admit these facts, and they have done so because of emotional factors.

These people cannot admit that Jack Clayton, or Korak, cannot be Tarzan's son.

The Great Korak Time-Discrepancy Controversy must be old ground for most of the readers of this publication. For the benefit of the new, I'll go over the familiar material. However, I'll introduce some aspects not considered before. And I'll then go on to an examination of other features of the book. (My textual source is the 1918 A. L. Burt reprint edition.)

The Son of Tarzan, written in 1915, is a sequel to *The Beasts of Tarzan*. In *Beasts*, Tarzan and Jane's son is a babe in arms, and, from all internal evidence, is less than a year old. Burroughs does not say so, but it is evident that Jane is nursing the baby she carries with her in her flight from Rokoff. This baby is the same age as little Jack.

The events in *Beasts* must take place in 1911 or, at the earliest, in late 1910. In *Son*, Sabrov, a Russian, is rescued after ten years as a captive in an African cannibal village. Burroughs says that his real name was Paulvitch, though he does not say how he could have known that. Sabrov never told anyone that his real name was not Sabrov. Thus, if Burroughs is writing a novel based on certain events which did, in fact, happen, he had no way of knowing that Sabrov was Tarzan's old enemy. But it would make for a fine dramatic point to have Sabrov be Paulvitch, and Burroughs, first and foremost a story teller, would not be likely to let such drama go by.

Burroughs does state that it is ten years since the events in *Beasts*. This means that Sabrov is rescued from the cannibals circa 1921.

In *Son*, Jack (Korak) must be ten or eleven years old. He is a remarkably powerful youth, since he can subdue his young male tutor with ease. A few months after this, he strangles to death with his bare hands an adult black savage. This man is presumably much more powerful than the tutor and is fighting for his life.

A year later, Korak, himself only eleven or twelve years old, throws the eleven-year-old Meriem across his shoulder and leaps nimbly into the lower branches of a tree. A year or two later (Burroughs is vague about the exact time), Korak fights a mighty mangani male with his bare hands and teeth and rips open the great bull's jugular vein. Immediately after follows a scene in which it is obvious that both Korak and Meriem are well into puberty. This is succeeded by a scene in which Korak uses fists to beat another giant bull into near-unconsciousness.

All of the above except one are just barely credible. It's possible that Korak could carry Meriem as easily as Burroughs says, that Korak and Meriem were coming into sexual maturity, and that Korak was skilled enough and powerful enough to hammer a bull great ape into submission. But it is difficult to believe that any human's teeth, let alone a twelve-year-old male's, could bite through the hair and thick skin and jugular vein of a massively muscled anthropoid the size of a gorilla. Especially while the anthropoid was tearing away with his hands at Korak. The great apes are described by Burroughs as being equal to a gorilla in strength, and a gorilla's strength has been estimated as equal to at least ten men's strength.

I don't doubt that Korak did win in his fights. But I think it's likely that Burroughs was gilding the lily for story purposes and that Korak used his knife and may even have had some help from Meriem and her spear. Even so, these feats would be remarkable and would need no exaggerating to get our admiration and respect.

Meriem, or Jeanne Jacot, is ten years old when Korak is forced to flee London with Akut, the great ape. When the book ends, she is sixteen. Thus Korak would have been in the jungle for almost six years. He was also sixteen. It would not be discreet to ask why Korak's parents permitted their son to marry at such an early age.

It is permissible to wonder about the Honourable Morison Baynes. He must have been at least twenty-one years old and was probably at least twenty-five, judging from his considerable hedonistic experience on the Continent and his sophistication. Yet he estimates that Korak was his own age or possibly older. This can be explained as due to Korak's unusual large size, an accelerated maturity due to the rigors of jungle living, and the possibility of a beard. Burroughs says nothing about Korak shaving, so we can at least speculate that he could have had facial hair. Some youths do get rather heavy beards at sixteen. Tarzan didn't; he does not seem to have had to shave until he was about twenty.

In *Tarzan the Terrible*, Korak is old enough to fight during the Meuse-Argonne operation (September-November 1918).

Peter Ogden, editor of *ERBANIA*, has published a theory to account for the Korak Time Discrepancy. He says that Burroughs could have given the wrong date for Tarzan's birth in *Tarzan of the Apes*. He would have done this as one more cover for the true identity of Lord Greystoke. And, working backwards from 1914, so that the chronology of *Son* will be consistent with reality, Ogden figures that Tarzan was probably born in 1872.

(It's not relevant, but is interesting, to note that 1872 was the year of Phileas Fogg's amazing dash around the world and of the mysterious case of the *Marie Celeste*. I am presently working on a book which will tie the two together[100].)

Thus, Tarzan could have met Jane by 1893 and married her in 1895. Korak would have been born in 1895 and would be ten years old in 1905. He and Meriem would've married in 1911.

Ogden's theory raises more problems than it solves, and these will be dealt with in my essay on *Tarzan of the Apes*. However, after all the evidence for the 1888 or 1872 theories is in, neither can be "proved." The reader is free to choose whichever he prefers. What he is not free to choose as the truth, if he insists on being logical, is Burroughs' version of *Son* in its entirety.

The central insurmountable fact that *Son* was written in 1915 means that all events in *Son* have to have taken place before Burroughs started writing it. Korak married Meriem before 1915, when both were sixteen. If Korak were sixteen in 1914, he would have been born in 1898. Tarzan did not meet Jane until February 1909 (See *Tarzan of the Apes*).

The Burroughsian has two choices. Believe Ogden's theory or believe Harwood-Starr's. If you choose the latter, then you must accept as a fact the adoption of a boy born about 1898 by Tarzan and Jane. Probably, he would have been a close relative who had been orphaned. In my book *Tarzan Alive*, I opt for Bulldog Drummond's younger brother, John. (That is, for the younger brother of the man on whom the fictional character of Bulldog Drummond was based. Do not, however, be misled by the statement of McNeile that this man was Gerard Fairlie.) My reasons for this are developed in *Tarzan Alive*; to present them here would expand this essay to too great a length. But the reader may examine the evidence presented in my biography and say yea or nay to it.

Harwood and Starr also suggest that Tarzan's son really was the baby who died in *Beasts* and that Burroughs suppressed this and distorted other facts to give the book the happy ending which he knew his readers would demand. I reject this. Otherwise, how do you account for the "youthful Jack" in *The Eternal Lover*?

I believe that Tarzan's real son lived but that we shall never know anything about him except what Burroughs tells us in *Beasts* and *Lover*. Because of having presented Korak as Tarzan's true son in *Son*, Burroughs was obliged to leave out any reference to the true son thereafter in the novels. At the time, Burroughs may have thought that this was a small price to pay, since Jackie was a baby and it would be many years before he, too, could have adventures and so become a worthy subject of Burroughs' fictionalized biographies. But I wonder if, around the time of World War II, he did not regret this. Surely, the real Jack Clayton III, first in line to the title of Greystoke, must have been a remarkable man in his own right. Nor do we have to suppose that Tarzan and Jane had no other children after him just because Burroughs does not mention them. If the Claytons had daughters, for instance, we may be sure that they would have been tall, lovely, and grey-eyed and very capable of taking care of themselves.

The Son of Tarzan has to end in 1914, before August of that year. From August on, Tarzan was looking for Jane until after the end of World War I. The chronology of *The Eternal Lover* indicates clearly that the Custers were visiting the Greystokes at their plantation in 1914 not too long before WWI broke out. Tarzan's baby son and Esmeralda were present then; Korak and Meriem, if present, are not mentioned by Burroughs. But they were undoubtedly still in Europe, visiting Meriem's parents. Tarzan and Jane would have accompanied them to England first, as indicated at the end of *Son*, and then would have returned to Africa, where they were visited by the Custers. For some reason, Esmeralda took young Jackie to England, since the two were not at the plantation when it was destroyed by the Germans (in *Tarzan the Untamed*). Perhaps the "business" which Tarzan was attending to in Nairobi when *Untamed* opened was sending Esmeralda and Jackie away to England or France.

Beasts seems to have ended about the middle of 1912. Since *Son* would have started not too many months later, it is obvious that Paulvitch could not have been a prisoner of the cannibals for ten years. And it is obvious that Sabrov is not Paulvitch. Harwood-Starr's surmise that Burroughs identified Sabrov as Paulvitch for dramatic reasons is the only reasonable theory so far advanced. Even if Paulvitch had disguised his appearance, he would not have been able to conceal his individual body odor, and Tarzan would have identified him immediately.

What did happen to Paulvitch?

We'll never know. If his name had been Pyotrvitch (Peterson), I'd be inclined to think that he had made his way back to Europe, had become a master at disguise, no doubt to ensure that Tarzan would never hear of him, had become as powerful as the late Professor Moriarty, and died (supposedly) in a flaming dirigible in 1927 after he'd tangled once too often with Korak's older brother.

Paulvitch, by the way, is not a standard Russian name. It should be Pavlovitch or Pavlitch. However, it is possible that Paulvitch's grandfather was a Frenchman, perhaps a captured French soldier who settled down in Russia after Napoleon's defeat, and Paulvitch was his hybrid Gaul-Russian name.

Many opponents of the "adopted relative" theory point to the numerous references in *Son* to Korak's inheritance of his father's traits. But Burroughs would have made these up and inserted them in the novel to strengthen the premise that Korak was Tarzan's issue. The novel is consistent within its own framework, though there are some curious things to consider.

Captain Jacot, Meriem's father, is a grey-haired general at the end of the book, an "old man." In nine years he has gone from a seemingly vigorous young man and captain to an aging general. And d'Arnot, a naval lieutenant in *Apes*, which ended in 1909, is, in 1914, an admiral.

John F. Roy, in *ERB-dom* #18, has explained the latter promotion. He says that Admiral d'Arnot could be the father of Tarzan's good friend. As for Jacot, it is true that Burroughs does not specify his age at the time when Meriem (Jeanne) was kidnapped. He could have been a vigorous fifty or so. And that he could see further than his men, that they called him for this reason the Hawk, may have been due to the long-sightedness brought on by middle age. And it is possible that a combination of fortunate events, good connections, and his outstanding military record, did advance him to a generalship.

Another problem. How did Korak, who was only ten when *Son* began, according to Burroughs (but fourteen according to my estimate), manage in one day to get false passports for himself and Akut? He had the money to flee England, but how did he make the necessary connections with the criminal world?

Also, Burroughs says that Tarzan would not tell Korak the location of his African plantation. Would not a boy with Korak's driving interest in such matters have found out?

The *Marjorie W.*, which picked Sabrov up, was chartered by a scientific expedition. Why would the scientists aboard have permitted Sabrov to walk off with Akut, obviously a specimen of a hitherto unknown genus of great ape? (Or, if my theory is right that the mangani were hominids akin to *Australopithecus robustus*, the uniqueness of Akut would have been even more apparent.)

It is probable, however, that the scientists were botanists and chemists, so unqualified in anthropoid identification. And Sabrov's claims to Akut as his property could easily have prevented any attempt by the scientists to obtain Akut for their uses. But Sabrov and his property did have considerable publicity after getting to London. It is difficult to understand why scientists there would not have known that Akut was something new in the zoological world. Perhaps they did, but, again, Sabrov refused to recognize anything but the jurisdiction of private property.

This matter can be cleared up by examining the London *Times* of this period (say, from 1911 through 1913 to cover a broad enough area). If no such case is mentioned in the papers, then the next step is to admit that perhaps Ogden's theory of Tarzan's birth in 1872 is right. The *Times* for the period of 1893 through 1896 should be covered for items about Akut or a reasonable facsimile thereof.

Would anyone, even in the slums of London, have taken in such a lodger as Akut? Especially when Akut does not seem to have been locked up in a manner to satisfy the public as to its safety? Would not the police have been called in by the terrified tenants of the house where Sabrov and his "pet" lived?

Perhaps not, if Sabrov had greased enough palms. And it is possible that Akut was much more restrained during transit between the East End lodgings and the theater than Burroughs implies. It was only during the theater shows and in Sabrov's room that Akut had any comparative freedom.

Another problem is Jane's concern about Korak's clothes after hearing that he has been found. She wants Tarzan to take to Korak one of his "little suits" that she has saved. This would indicate that a long time has elapsed, since Tarzan says that Korak has grown so big that he would fit only into one of Tarzan's own suits. But this little scene is, again, one of the fictions of Burroughs to make the novel consistent in its own framework. Even so, it's doubtful that Korak, big enough at the age of ten to overpower his tutor, would have been wearing a *little* suit when he disappeared.

The ability of the monkeys and the baboons (who are really monkeys and not apes) to speak should be examined. But this will be taken up in a separate essay.

There are some problems about the location of the Greystoke plantation, but this will be dealt with in the essay on *Tarzan the Untamed.*

Meriem, at ten, is the Sheikh's prisoner in a small native village "hidden away upon the banks of a small unexplored tributary of a large river that empties into the Atlantic not so far from the equator…" (*Son*, p. 63). Here the Sheikh's tribe collects goods and twice a year carries them on camels to Timbuktu. An examination of the (Michelin) maps of African fails to locate any river which will fill the above requirements. The only large river near the equator which empties into the Atlantic is the Congo. Any small tributary of the Congo which emptied into the Atlantic would be about 1800 miles on a straight line from Timbuktu. A caravan route would cover two or three times that distance, perhaps four times 1800 miles. Moreover, no camels could traverse the thousands of miles of heavy jungle, rugged hills, and many rivers between the tributary and Timbuktu (which is in the present nation of Mali). Burroughs could not have meant that the tributary was one of the Congo's inland rivers, because Korak found Meriem in a village near the coast. The text clearly indicates this.

However, about 1500 miles from the equator (northwards), in the German Kamerun (the Cameroons), ibn Khatour's tribe might have had a headquarters. They would have been fairly close to Korak, who probably disembarked at Douala. Even so, the tribe still would have had to travel through considerable jungle and it would have been about 1200 miles (in a straight line) from Timbuktu. A year later, both Meriem and Korak were on the other side of Africa, near the Greystoke plantation. To get there, they had to round the great lake of Victoria and cross steep mountains. What ibn Khatour's tribe was doing in this area is not explained. Probably it had been driven out of western African because of its criminal activities and was headed for fresh opportunities for ivory poaching and slave raiding.

But on page 325 of *Son* is a phrase which seems to indicate that the tribe and Meriem, after a few days' march, are back at the village on the tributary of the Congo, back on the west coast. Meriem is brought back "to the familiar scenes of her childhood…"

Obviously, this is impossible. Burroughs must have meant for the reader to interpret this as the people and type of buildings with which she had been familiar during her childhood. But it could not have been the same location.

Why did not Tarzan recognize Malbihn when he showed up as Hanson? Meriem might have failed to recognize him because Malbihn had changed his appearance. But Tarzan should have recognized his odor. On the other hand, his contact with the Swede had been very brief. And no doubt Malbihn as Hanson not only bathed frequently when he was to be with Greystoke, he also used a strong cologne.

The river on which Meriem escaped and on which Malbihn was wounded could be the Mara River of lower western Kenya and upper western Tanganyika. It is not, however, "a great African" river (p. 333) nor is it in jungle territory. But inasmuch as it seems the only candidate reasonably near the Greystoke plantation and since *Untamed* indicates the plantation is in southwestern Kenya, then the river should be the Mara. That it is a jungle river in *Son* can be due to Burroughs' tendency to romanticize. Also, Burroughs often deliberately confuses locations so that the true site of the Greystoke plantation cannot be found from a reading of the novels.

In conclusion, I sympathize with the fundamentalists' desire that Korak be Tarzan's real son. But I do not find that the Harwood-Starr theory of an adopted relative spoils *The Son of Tarzan* for me. It is one of my favorites, and it contains several scenes which still bring tears. Such as Meriem's joy on finding a mother's love again in My Dear's arms or in Korak's reunion with Jane. When I am not reading *Son* to analyze it, I read it as a novel. And I accept, for the time being, the internal premises of the story.

No reader should be disappointed that Korak is not Tarzan's real son. After all, as Korak himself says,

"THERE IS BUT ONE TARZAN…THERE CAN NEVER BE ANOTHER."

Asian Detectives in the Wold Newton Family
By Dennis E. Power

This article was written to redress the issue of at least two underrated members of the Wold Newton family, Mr. Moto and Charlie Chan.

Mr. Moto

Mr. Moto's membership in the Wold Newton Family was speculated upon by the great genealogist Philip José Farmer himself. In *Doc Savage: His Apocalyptic Life*, Farmer stated that it was quite likely that Mr. Moto was the son of Wolf Larsen and a Japanese woman who he had abducted, raped and abandoned in an incident depicted in *The Sea Wolf.*

Although Farmer speculated that Wolf Larson was Doc Savage's grandfather I find it odd that Farmer never made any direct connection with Wolf Larsen and the Wold Newton family, considering Larsen's genius, physique and close genetic connection to one of his primary biographical subjects. It is my opinion that Wolf Larsen, supposedly a Norwegian sailor of Danish descent, was in fact the son of James Moriarty.

Consider this. James Moriarty, as Captain Nemo, traveled the world gathering materials and men for his great ship the *Nautilus*. It is not beyond the realm of speculation to entertain the possibility that he either wed or had a child by a Danish woman who died in childbirth. It is even possible that Wolf Larsen was a member of the *Nautilus*, albeit a very young one. Both Larsen and Moriarty (at least in his early career) had a nautical predilection. Wolf was a genius—without any formal schooling he designed a starscale, thus demonstrating a talent for mathematics and astronomy, as had Moriarty. They were both very amoral and both suffered from a strange neurological condition.

If my speculation has any merit at all, then Mr. Moto deserves a place in the Wold Newton family through his descent from Wolf Larson.

Mr. I. A. Moto was probably not his real name, Moto being the suffix for a Japanese name such as Morimoto. Mr. Moto was the superlative espionage agent of the Japanese Intelligence service. In all of his adventures, save one, he brilliantly manipulated the characters and various competing interests so that in the end Japan's interests would be best served. Hints of Mr. Moto's abilities and the various roles he played during his role as an espionage agent are suggested in the books. He stated that he had worked as a valet for many young men in New York. He also stated that he could navigate and manage small boats, that he knew carpentry, surveying, and five Chinese dialects. He had also studied at two foreign universities, including one in the United States. His primary area of operation was in the Far East, primarily in China.

He is portrayed as a diminutive man with a Prussian hairstyle and gold-filled front teeth. Mr. Moto also has a taste for loud clothes and patent leather shoes. Considering his occupation, he is not only well known but seems rather easy to spot. One would think that this would be not only a foolish thing for an espionage agent but rather dangerous as well, unless of course it was deliberate. This public flashy image may have been designed to make Mr. Moto noticeable so his fellow agents could work better in the background.

Evidence of Mr. Moto's acting ability and his mastery of disguise are available in the source by which he is probably best known, the film series that bears his name. The film series, despite borrowing titles from the novels, does not follow any of their storylines. Mr. Moto is portrayed quite differently than he is in the novels. He has slicked back hair, wire frame glasses, regular teeth and dresses conservatively. One could easily believe that they were entirely different people. However there are quite a few things that both the film and novel versions of Mr. Moto share. These are their basic personalities, their mastery of jujitsu and a certain ruthlessness.

In the film series Mr. Moto is ostensibly a private detective or a police detective of unknown affiliation, yet even so in his first couple of films there are flashes of the ruthlessness that characterized the novel version of Mr. Moto. In the first film, *Think Fast, Mr. Moto,* Moto discovers that one of the stewards on an ocean liner is part of a smuggling crew. Mr. Moto fights with the man and easily subdues him, then rather than turn him over to the ship's Purser, Mr. Moto throws the man overboard.

In *Thank You, Mr. Moto*, Mr. Moto is gathering seven sections of a map that will lead to the treasure of Genghis Khan. Moto is in disguise as an Arab trader when his guise is discovered by one of the caravan guards who had entered Moto's tent. Moto kills the man and buries him in the dirt beneath his own tent.

Through the film series Mr. Moto's abilities to disguise himself are highlighted. One wonders then if the flashy image in the novels is also a disguise of sorts, one designed to draw attention to Mr. Moto.

The only real difference between the two depictions of Moto are the manner in which he dresses, combs his hair and the gold-filled teeth, which could be a set of dentures.

It is likely that the private detective Moto was also one of the roles that the espionage agent Mr. Moto played. One of his degrees was probably in criminology or police science. He was proficient enough in criminology to teach a short course at a university, as depicted in the film *Mr. Moto's Gamble*. In a sense this film bridges the first section of this article with the second section, for one of the students in Mr. Moto's criminology class was Lee Chan, Charlie Chan's Number One Son, at least in the films.

Mr. Moto was acquainted with Charlie Chan because he had honed his criminology and acting skills under his tutelage. Mr. Moto had worked as Charlie Chan's assistant under the name of Kashimoto. He had perfected his ability to create a credible persona by playing upon Chan's well-known disdain for the Japanese and acting like a bumbling buffoon. Chan had, however, penetrated the persona early on and deduced that Moto worked for Japanese intelligence. Rather than turn Mr. Moto in, he offered Moto a deal. He would allow Moto to remain free so long as Moto did not actively work against United States interests and if Moto agreed to help keep China destabilized. Chan did not hate his homeland but feared who would rule a united China. Moto agreed to the bargain so long as the interests of Japan would not be compromised.

It was to keep this promise that Moto spent most of the Thirties in the Far East in the China area, destabilizing China while aiding Japanese interests there. The events depicted in the film *Thank You, Mr. Moto* were part of Mr. Moto's direct attempt to prevent Charlie Chan's father from gaining the relics of Genghis Khan. Charlie Chan's father's quest for these relics is depicted in the film version of *The Mask of Fu Manchu* (1932).

The last Mr. Moto film to be released prior to World War II was *Mr. Moto Takes a Vacation*. With Japan making great incursions in the East, and rumors of atrocities, the public lost its taste for these films which gave a positive portrayal of the Japanese.

In 1942, the novel *Last Laugh, Mr. Moto* was released. In it Mr. Moto was directly in confrontation with an agent from the United States over a device that would aid in flight navigation. This was the first case in which Mr. Moto failed to achieve his objective and instead the agent from the United States won out. While it is certainly true that this could simply be a case of author John Marquand's patriotism symbolically defeating the Japanese, or the fact that even a superlative agent as Mr. Moto does not win out every time, it could also be that Moto was keeping his promise to Chan of not working directly against the United States.

The next appearance of Mr. Moto was in the 1957 novel, *Right You Are, Mr. Moto* or *Stopover: Tokyo*. Mr. Moto worked with the American occupation forces to keep Japan from being taken over by the Communists.

However there had been another film appearance by Mr. Moto, although he appeared under a different name. In the 1942 film *Invisible Agent* a group of German agents, accompanied by a lone Japanese agent, visited a printing shop in New Jersey. This shop was owned by Frank Raymond. Raymond was the son of the Invisible Man. The lone Japanese agent was named Baron Ikito. In the film he was portrayed by Peter Lorre in the same way he had portrayed Mr. Moto. Ikito also had a ruthless streak, threatening to cut Raymond's hand off in a paper cutter unless Raymond revealed the invisibility formula. Further clues that Baron Ikito was probably Mr. Moto are that Marquand referred to Moto as I. A. Moto. "I" possibly stood for Ikito. Another is that Mr. Moto was "a suave scion of Japanese nobility" according to *Your Turn, Mr. Moto*. In *Right You Are, Mr. Moto*, Mr. Moto and an American agent stayed at a house loaned to them by Mr. Moto's cousin, a Baron. The house was an odd mixture of Western and Japanese styles. When Jack Rhyce admired a sake pot, Moto gave it to him. This may have actually been Moto's home, although he did not want to reveal this to the Western agents.

Raymond escaped from the clutches of the Germans and Baron Ikito. When Raymond freed himself the German agents began firing at him but Baron Ikito spoiled their aim by pretending to trip. The foreign agents were forced to flee the country. Raymond eventually went to work for the U.S. government using his invisibility formula. His first mission was to infiltrate Germany and prevent a massive air strike on the United States. During the course of the mission, Raymond once again ran into the German agent who had visited him in New Jersey, and Baron Ikito who was also in Germany. While Ikito competed with the Germans to get his hands on the Invisible Agent, his primary concern was over a code-book that he had placed in the hands of the German agent who was his contact. This book contained the names of the Japanese and German agents in the United States. When Raymond learned of this book, he stole it.

Baron Ikito told the German agent that if the book were not located then Ikito would have to commit *seppuku*, ritual suicide. He promised the German agent that the agent would precede him in death.

Raymond transmitted the information in the book to the allies and prevented the air strike. Baron Ikito shot the German agent and committed suicide.

Yet Mr. Moto was alive and well in the post-war era, as evidenced by Marquand's *Right You Are, Mr. Moto*.

Moto had set in motion an elaborate ploy that revolved around the code-book that he had given the Germans. The book purportedly contained the names of the German and Japanese agents in America. It is not believable that the Japanese would know all of the German agents in the United States. If the book had been authentic, Moto would never have given it to the Germans. And if it had contained information about German agents, the S.S. or Gestapo would have had it destroyed. So the book probably only contained the names of the purported Japanese agents in the United States. However the Japanese-Americans were distressingly loyal to the United States and there really was not a full-fledged Japanese Sixth column in the United States. Moto planted the book to mislead the Nazis as to Japanese strength and motives in the United States. Also he felt that the book would be good bait for the German resistance or American espionage agents. Besides, should the book somehow fall into the hands of the Allies, it would send the various United States Intelligence agencies on a wild goose chase.

Baron Ikito's *seppuku* was depicted in the film for two reasons. Due to the propagandistic nature of the war films of that era, the Japanese villain would have had to die in some fashion. The other reason is that as far as the Germans were concerned, Ikito actually did kill himself. However, this was staged to get Moto out of the country since his mission had ended.

Mr. Moto's last appearance was in the novel *Right You Are, Mr. Moto*. There was a film called *The Return of Mr. Moto* (1965) but it merely used the character's name and had no connection to the previous film series or the novels.

Bibliography of Mr. Moto novels by John P. Marquand:

Your Turn, Mr. Moto. 1935. Boston: Little, Brown and Company, 1985.
Thank You, Mr. Moto. 1936. Boston: Little, Brown and Company, 1985.
Think Fast, Mr. Moto. 1936. Boston: Little, Brown and Company, 1985.
Mr. Moto Is So Sorry. 1936. Boston: Little, Brown and Company, 1985.
Last Laugh, Mr. Moto. 1942. Boston: Little, Brown and Company, 1986.
Right You Are, Mr. Moto. 1957. Boston: Little, Brown and Company, 1986.
Also published as *Stopover Tokyo*.

Filmography:
Think Fast, Mr. Moto (1937)
Thank You, Mr. Moto (1937)
Mr. Moto's Gamble (1938)
Mr. Moto Takes a Chance (1938)
Mysterious Mr. Moto (1938)
Mr. Moto's Last Warning (1939)
Mr. Moto in Danger Island (1939)
Mr. Moto Takes a Vacation (1939)
Invisible Agent (1942; As Baron Ikito)

Charlie Chan

There is one detective that I believe deserves to be in the Wold Newton Universe, if only for his brilliant detective reasoning, yet like many others in the Wold Newton family he was also greatly traveled. I speak, of course, of Charlie Chan, who I propose is the son of Fu Manchu.

According to Philip José Farmer, Fu Manchu was likely the son of William Clayton and Ling Ju Hai, a green-eyed Chinese beauty born in Vietnam circa 1840.

Farmer tells us that Fu Manchu as a young man was named Hanoi Shan. He was a tall, good-looking man with a kindly character who was governor of a province in Tongking, China. While supervising the roundup of wild elephants he was smashed against a tree by an elephant. He went to Paris hoping surgeons there could repair his twisted spine. When they could not, he went on a crime spree in Paris of 1906. Farmer says that between 1906 and 1918 Fu Manchu had his spinal injury repaired.

Having unearthed some additional information, I propose that Fu Manchu was the son of William Clayton and Ling Ju Hai, and that he was born in Hanoi under the name of Shan Ming Fu. Having discovered that she was pregnant, Ling Ju Hai's father sent her to Hainan Island in disgrace. Once there, Ling Ju Hai found herself a suitable husband, the scion of a Mandarin family whose family name was Shan. She gave birth to his son, Shan Ming Fu. When Shan Ming Fu was a young man the Self-Strengthening Movement was very popular in China. Its philosophy was to use Western ideas and technology to strengthen Chinese traditions and values. As part of this philosophical movement, Shan Ming Fu was educated at four western universities.

According to Sax Rohmer, Fu Manchu was the governor of the Province of Honan under the dowager Empress Tzu-Hsi and Farmer apparently concurs with this, stating that it must have been in the 1870s.

It more likely that Fu Manchu was an advisor to the Governor-General of that province from about 1864-71, during the Taiping and Nien rebellions. By 1871, Shan Ming Fu saw that the Self-Strengthening movement was doomed to failure and tried to take steps to salvage the movement and effectively reorganize the Imperial government to best suit China's needs. In doing so, he created enemies and was abruptly dismissed from his government post, nor was he allowed another. Effectively shut out of the government as an insider, Shan Ming Fu found alliances outside the government, determined to save China at all costs. To this end he formed alliances with several secret societies such as the Sublime Order of the Peacock, the White Lotus Society and the Si Fan.

On hiatus from government service, Shan Ming Fu/Fu Manchu encountered Sherlock Holmes for the first time during the adventure "The Musgrave Version" as written by George Alec Effinger. Through his connections with the secret societies he again succeeded in gaining positions in government, and served as the advisor to the Governor-General of the disputed province of Tongking. It was this posting which led to some confusion between him and another individual. Farmer speculated that Fu Manchu and the individual known as Hanoi Shan were the same man. Hanoi Shan was a hunchbacked man who terrorized Paris with a brilliant crime spree in the early 1900s. According to Farmer's source on Hanoi Shan, H. Ashton-Wolfe in *Warped in the Making* and *The Thrill of Evil*, Hanoi Shan had been the governor of the Tongking province until he had been slammed against a tree by an elephant and crippled. His mind had twisted along with his spine and he had become evil. Farmer suggested that Fu Manchu would have his spine straightened but the twisted nature remained. Farmer was correct Fu Manchu did use the name Hanoi Shan; however Ashton-Wolfe was incorrect in attributing the elephant attack as the cause of Hanoi Shan's injury. The elephant attack occurred against Dr. Sun Ah Poy. When he was writing *Warped in the Making,* H. Ashton-Wolfe filled in the scant information that the Parisian police had on Hanoi Shan with the information released about Dr. Sun Ah Poy, an Asian villain recently captured in the United States. Ashton-Wolfe believed, without solid evidence, that they were the same man. Dr. Sun Ah Poy was from the Tongking province and had been crippled in an elephant incident which had warped his character. Dr. Sun Ah Poy also used spiders and snakes as a means of eliminating his foes. The similarity of these methods with those used by Fu Manchu gave tentative evidence to some law enforcement organizations that there was a connection between Sun Ah Poy and Fu Manchu. In this they appear to be correct. However, Sun Ah Poy was a member of the Si Fan and so associated with Fu Manchu. They were not the same man, nor did Sun Ah Poy ever have a career as Hanoi Shan.

Fu Manchu left the position in Tongking in 1883 and began to seriously pursue his study of the medical uses of plants, seeking the elixir of life. The Si Fan sent him on a mission to dispatch the Mahdi. Officially the Mahdi died of typhoid. While Shan Ming Fu was away his principle wife gave birth to a son, whom Shan Ming Fu would name Shan Shilin Li. Although Shan Ming Fu never publicly or even privately stated so, he had doubts about his parentage of the child, considering the differences in their height and general body structure. However, it seems that Shilin Li's height and lack of green eyes was determined by his mother's side of the family. The child had a brilliant mind and was drawn to the Confucian philosophy at an early age.

In the ensuing years as Shan Shilin Li grew up, Fu Manchu once again gained a position in the imperial administration and became the Governor-General of the Honan province. A peasant revolt broke out in 1898 against Manchu misrule in the province of Shantung. It was linked to the anti-dynastic White Lotus Society. The dissident movement spread rapidly through the Shantung province, fueled by a rural economic depression and severe drought. Although it was, in reality, a general uprising with many various groups and no binding ideology other than hatred for the Manchus and the foreign devils, the most vocal and visible members of the uprising were The Righteous and Harmonious Fists, called the Boxers, who used marital arts.

Shan Ming Fu, as the governor of the Honan province, which bordered on Shantung, could have crushed the movement in its early stages had he been so inclined. Yet he and the Si Fan believed that they could use the combined anti-dynastic and anti-foreign credo of the uprising to remove the Dowager Empress from power, restore the Emperor, and if not drive away the Westerners, then at least make a start at removing some of Western influence by instilling a sense of national unity to the Chinese masses.

Shan Ming Fu was able to damp much of the anti-Manchu sentiment of the popular rebellion and heighten the anti-Westerner hatred. Like a cat with nine lives, however, the Dowager Empress once again managed to turn this circuitous attack on her position to her personal advantage, although to the great detriment of China as a whole. She supported the Boxers' rebellion by taking no action against them and having Chinese troops aid them in their attacks on foreign legations and missionaries. In reality, the Boxer rebellion could hardly be classified as either a rebellion or a war against the Europeans. The Provincial Governor-Generals ignored the Empress Dowager's instructions and put forth every effort to prevent disorder or any harm coming to foreigners. The Boxer Rebellion, then, was only limited to a few places, but concentrated itself in Beijing. The Western response was swift and severe. Within a couple months, an international force captured and occupied Beijing and forced the imperial government to agree to the most humiliating terms yet: the Boxer Protocol of 1901. Under the Boxer Protocol, European powers got the right to maintain military forces in the capital, thus placing the imperial government more or less under arrest. The Protocols suspended the civil service examination, demanded a huge indemnity to be paid to European powers for the losses they had suffered, and required government officials to be prosecuted for their role in the rebellion. In addition, the Protocols suspended all arms imports into the country. To maintain her personal power, the Dowager Empress had in effect made China a client state to the Western Powers.

At the close of the Boxer rebellion and after the Boxer Protocols had been enacted, Shan Ming Fu was designated as one of the Mandarins to be executed for their part in the Boxer rebellion. Leaving his post as Governor-General of Honan to avoid being arrested by Imperial troops, Shan Ming Fu barely escaped with his life but his wife and son were not so lucky. They were shot by the Chinese army. Shan Ming Fu's son survived his shooting and made his way across China from Honan to Hong Kong on horseback. The trek was long and arduous and he vowed never to be hungry again. He found passage to Hawaii where he began work as a houseboy in a mansion owned by the Phillimore family. Knowing of his father's connection to the Boxer Rebellion and his father's subsequent notorious acts, he cut all ties with his homeland and viewed his father as dead. He Anglicized his name from Shan Shilin Li to Charlie Chan. Those who state that Charlie Chan does not resemble Fu Manchu are correct. However, the difference between their height and eye color as been addressed above. Charlie's weight was the result of overeating rather than an inherited glandular condition. Once he had started to slim down a bit, the resemblance between Shan Shilin Li and Fu Manchu would become more pronounced. Cementing the resemblance, the actor who most popularized Charlie Chan first played Fu Manchu in the films.

When Charlie Chan first appeared in print in 1925, he was Sergeant Chan. We can surmise that he was about forty years old, which would have made his birth date around 1885. He had a child in college at the time of his first recorded case.

Charlie Chan never gave many details about his background in China. We only learn that he emigrated to the United States territory of Hawaii as a young man. We can speculate that his character was formed at an early age and that he was rather disgusted at his father's machinations of Chinese society. He would learn how his father had forced his half sister into a leadership role in the Si Fan because he did not have a son. Charlie knew that if his father knew that he were still alive, he would be forced to leave his home and family and serve the wishes of Fu Manchu as his only male heir.

We can surmise that he took the opportunity to escape from his father's clutches once and for all by eluding his Si Fan guardians, making his way to Hawaii and assuming a new identity. He served as a houseboy in the Phillimore Mansion. The Phillimores' sponsored him and helped him get his citizenship papers. He joined the police department and worked his way up the chain of command. Naturally he never revealed any of his real background for fear of retaliation against his family by his father. His giant girth may have been part of a natural disguise or it may be that he and his wife were voracious eaters; she had started out as "slender as the bamboo is slender" yet she was nearly as plump as Charlie in the depictions in the novels. According to the novels Charlie also brought his mother from China to Honolulu so she could spend her final years with him. This was not his mother, since his mother was had been killed in China in the aftermath of the Boxer Rebellion but rather his wife's, Lotus Blossom's, mother.

As demonstrated in the Earl Derr Biggers biographies, during the early part of Charlie Chan's career he was involved in routine police investigations centered in Honolulu, Hawaii, with some excursions to the United States mainland. His career in the novels actually covered a very short time period. They were published from 1925-1932, so the actual time period that that covered was probably 1923 or 1924 to 1931. However a slight change in his character was noted in the novels: he lost weight. In the early books he was corpulent, in the later books he was merely called plump. Something had either caused him to loose his great appetite, become more physically active, or both.

In the 1930 novel, *Charlie Chan Carries On*, Charlie befriended Inspector Duff of Scotland Yard. After Duff was wounded in Honolulu, Charlie Chan continued Duff's investigation and revealed the killer aboard an ocean liner en route to San Francisco. This brought him accolades from Scotland Yard, made him famous in San Francisco, and so brought up his stock in Hawaii. He was promoted to Lieutenant. However Charlie's encounter with Inspector Duff of Scotland Yard and his trip to San Francisco made him aware that a sleeping giant had awakened. During Chan's early career, that is, during the time period recorded in the novels, Fu Manchu was in retirement. Fu Manchu had gone into retirement after his encounter with Dennis Nayland Smith in Egypt in 1917, as recorded in Cay Van Ash's *The Fires of Fu Manchu.*

Charlie learned how quickly his father had seized control of the entire Si Fan organization and how far reaching and pervasive the Si Fan had become under Fu Manchu's leadership. He began investigating the Si Fan by establishing contacts in various police agencies throughout the world and by using his status as a celebrity detective to study police techniques in various foreign countries. His status grew as in every place he visited he solved a high profile criminal case, yet his true purpose at first was to investigate the trail of his father. In 1931, shortly after the conclusion of the case called *The Keeper of the Keys* by Biggers,[101] he traveled to London, Paris and Egypt. These journeys were recorded in the films *Charlie Chan in London*, *Charlie Chan in Paris* and *Charlie Chan in Egypt.*

Although he solved mysteries in each of these cases, his main purpose was to seek out information about Fu Manchu in the Limehouse district of London. This led him to Paris where a contact in the Sûreté informed him about the criminal career of the hunchbacked Hanoi Shan. From the pieced-together physical descriptions, Charlie was able to discern that this was his father, who had been wearing a disguise or had suffered a back injury that had been corrected by surgery. From Paris he went to Egypt. In Egypt he learned of the current plan of Fu Manchu, which was to use the relics of Genghis Khan to unite all of Asia under Chinese rule. Although he doubted that this could be done, he invoked his agreement with Moto to stop Fu Manchu. Moto did not directly confront Fu Manchu, but he was able to destroy some of the key pieces of the map to Khan's tomb, while Denis Nayland Smith and Lionel Barton more directly confronted Fu Manchu and thwarted this particular plan, as was seen in the film version of *The Mask of Fu Manchu*, (MGM 1932).

Charlie Chan next traveled to Shanghai via ocean liner. He had contacted Colonel Watkins, a man he had met when working with Scotland Yard, who was now the Commissioner of Police in Shanghai. He wished to combine a business trip and pleasure trip, if he could assist Watkins in any way. While on board the ship he had sung a short song about the Princess Ming Lo Fu who had an audience before the Emperor Fu Manchu. After the song was done, somebody slipped a note into his pocket, telling him that Shanghai was not healthy for him. At the dock, Charlie was met by his son Lee Chan, who had preceded him to China. Charlie assisted the British Secret Service and the United States Secret Service in breaking an opium smuggling ring. One of the ringleaders was American, the other was a Russian, and yet Charlie knew that this was but one of the many small operations controlled by the Si Fan. After the opium ring had been smashed, he assisted Colonel Watkins in solving a series of thefts. Radium had been stolen from a bank vault. Cobra bites lead to a number of murders. Given the object of the theft and the use of venomous snakes as weapons, Charlie was certain that his father was behind this plot. Although he and Lee thwarted it, there was no direct evidence of the hand of Fu Manchu.[102]

Clues discovered in China had Charlie and Lee Chan travel to Monte Carlo. Ostensibly Charlie Chan was on a gambling vacation in Monaco. Due to his celebrity, he was called upon to aid in the investigation of two murders. One victim was a casino messenger on his way to Paris with a million dollars in bonds. The other was a two-bit Chicago gangster who had recently been tending bar in a Monte Carlo hotel. The events of this case were depicted in the film *Charlie Chan in Monte Carlo* (Paramount, 1937), although the events themselves occurred in 1932.

In addition to the crimes in this case, Charlie Chan was also diligently searching for clues to the presence of Fu Manchu. However, the events that would be depicted in the novel *Bride of Fu Manchu* had already been completed and Fu Manchu had escaped from police custody. His resources in London informed him that Fu Manchu's quest for power seemed to be finished once and for all, with Fu Manchu on the lam and cut off from the resources of the Si Fan. Believing that the struggle against Fu Manchu was at least in recess, Charlie and Lee Chan returned to Honolulu. Lee returned to college on the mainland. During the 1933-late 1934 period, Charlie Chan's cases were primarily once again in Hawaii or on the United States mainland. They were depicted in the films, *Charlie Chan in Honolulu*, which transpires just as Charlie is returning to Honolulu, and *Charlie Chan's Secret*, which takes him to San Francisco. In San Francisco, Charlie was offered a position with the San Francisco Police Department. Although Hawaii would always be his home, he realized that resources on the mainland would be very useful in his struggle to bring his father to justice.

Without selling the house on Punchbowl Hill, he accepted the position and bought a home in San Francisco. This is one of the reasons many of the later films depict Charlie as being either on the mainland or in San Francisco. In San Francisco he solved the Opera case, *Charlie Chan at the Opera*, and a few others that were not filmed.

In late 1934 he received information about possible Fu Manchu activity in South America. He went to investigate, and was once again called upon to solve a couple of puzzling murders (*Charlie Chan in Rio*). However, he could not find any discernable evidence of Fu Manchu's presence in South America. Rick Lai, in his "Some Chronological Observations on the Fu Manchu Series" (available on *The Wold Newton Universe* website), speculates that Fu Manchu was involved in either the border dispute between Peru and Columbia or The Chaco War, so Fu Manchu must have hidden his trail quite well.

In late 1935, Charlie Chan got wind that Fu Manchu was in the mainland United States, attempting to subvert the political process. In the novel *President Fu Manchu*, Fu Manchu attempted to place his own puppet candidate into the Presidency. This candidate was based in part on Huey Long. Rick Lai speculates that Fu Manchu had Long assassinated and took over Long's organization with his own candidate, Paul Salvaletti. Charlie went to New Orleans to investigate, and was drawn into an investigation of mysterious goings-on at the La Fontanne Chemical Company. He learned that Mr. La Fontanne's partners were manufacturing poison gas, which Fu Manchu intended to use to help his candidate get elected by staging a crackdown on the poor by the current administration. Charlie thwarted that plan. His investigation into Salvaletti revealed that Salvaletti was having an extramarital affair with his Si Fan contact, Lola Dumas. When this was revealed on a radio program, Fu Manchu's political plot was thwarted.

In 1936, Charlie returned to San Francisco and had a few months of regular police duties. He spent time with his children (*Charlie Chan at the Circus*), and was involved in two cases in the desert, which were filmed as *Charlie Chan in Reno* and *Castle in the Desert*. In 1936, Fu Manchu once again began operations that would culminate in a grand design. Fearing how China would fare in the coming great war, Fu Manchu planned to assassinate the war-mongering leaders of Europe and Asia. Yet he also knew that merely killing these men would not stop the machinery of either politics or war, so other measures had to be taken. Fu Manchu set about to cripple the ability of the great nations to war with one another.

Lee Chan was a member of the United States swimming team at the Berlin Olympics in 1936. While there, Charlie Chan found himself drawn into a case concerning murder over an invention which would allow an aircraft to be flown by remote control. Fu Manchu was attempting to get this device to control the air forces of the great nations. Although Chan kept the device out of the hands of Fu Manchu's agents, it was discovered that the device did not work. (*Charlie Chan at the Olympics*.)

Returning to New York, Charlie Chan attended a police convention, and learned of sabotage slowing down production in aircraft plants. He was certain that agents of Fu Manchu were behind this and aided the local police in smashing the sabotage ring. (*Murder Over New York.*)

During the New York investigation Charlie Chan learned of aplot involving espionage to destroy part of the Panama Canal, trapping a Navy fleet on its way to the Pacific after maneuvers in the Atlantic. Working with the OCI, Charlie impersonated an employee of the U.S. government to foil this plot. (*Charlie Chan in Panama.*)

While Charlie Chan was preventing Fu Manchu from crippling the United States's military power and its ability to mobilize in case of war, Dennis Nayland Smith prevented Fu Manchu from assassinating Adolf Hitler and Benito Mussolini, as described in *The Drums of Fu Manchu*, although Hitler and Mussolini were called by different names in that novel. Charlie Chan learned that Fu Manchu had suddenly changed gears and instead of plotting against Fascists, he was now considering using them as a means of uniting Europe under one totalitarian rule which could then be more easily toppled. As part of this change in policy, the Si Fan planned to destroy Leon Blum, the Premier of France, through scandal.

In 1937, Charlie Chan had been invited to a reunion of World War I veterans in France and he decided to attend. This was the first time that Chan's wartime service had been revealed. Once in Paris, he uncovered the plot of the Si Fan, which was to link Blum to the murder of a munitions manufacturer who had been supplying arms to the enemy during the Great War. This was filmed as *Charlie Chan in the City of Darkness*. However the connection between Blum and Chan was excised for political considerations, the same considerations that caused Rohmer to change the name of Leon Blum to Marcel Delibes in *The Drums of Fu Manchu.* Unfortunately, neither Rohmer's account nor the film relates the only time that Chan and Smith worked together against Fu Manchu, to prevent the assassination of Marcel Delibes. The Si Fan had decided to assassinate Blum when the scandal ploy failed.

Eventually Blum was ousted from power by the political process of his own country, through Si Fan backers of the radical fascists. Smith and Chan learned that Fu Manchu had also been replaced as President of the Si Fan, which accounted for the abrupt change in policy from working against Fascists to working with them.

This near-encounter with Fu Manchu was the closest Charlie Chan would get to bringing his father to justice. During the war years he worked on regular, although often times bizarre, police cases and assisted the United States Secret Service a few times. The Chan family was living in San Francisco during this time and so escaped the horrific events of Pearl Harbor. The last of the Charlie Chan film series was released in 1949, but the film series ended prior to the end of his career. Charlie retired from detective work in 1950 at the age of sixty-five, although he remained available as a consultant. Charlie was getting old and suffered from heart disease as a result of his years of obesity. Although he knew that his father had achieved some form of longevity due to his discovery of the Elixir of Life, had it been offered to him, Charlie would have rejected the offer. He would have been philosophically opposed to accepting anything from his father. He also believed that immortality prevented one from taking their place among the honorable ancestors.

In the 1950s Fu Manchu once again began plotting to dominate the world and Charlie was too ill to aid in the fight against him. He felt extremely guilty about this when the machinations of Fu Manchu struck close to home. Charlie's nephew, Tony McKay, who had been inspired by Charlie to not only become a law enforcement official, but to fight against Fu Manchu, was killed in the attempt to bring Fu Manchu down. Tony McKay was the son of Lotus Blossom's sister.

Charlie Chan's second son, Jimmy Chan, would also carry out the fight against Fu Manchu, first as an FBI agent and then as a member of a government antiterrorist and intelligence agency. He would discover however, that the man called the Yellow Claw, who he fought most strenuously against, was not Fu Manchu, but one of his lieutenants in the Si Fan. Jimmy Chan was called Jimmy Woo in the published accounts of his battle against the Yellow Claw.

Charlie lost quite a bit of weight due to his illness and was positively svelte in early 1963 when he was consulted by a United States Intelligence agency on two cases. The name of the agency, the real names of the agents, and even Charlie's name was changed in the television series based on the adventures of agents 86 and 99. In the first episode, Charlie was introduced thusly: "Mr. Smart, this is the famous Hawaiian detective, now serving with the San Francisco police force. Inspector Harry Hoo." The actor portraying Charlie was much younger than Charlie and since the show was a parody the characterization of Charlie was broadly humorous.

In 1970 Charlie Chan underwent bypass surgery and he felt reinvigorated at the age of eighty-five. It should be remembered that many Wold Newton Family members often display great vitality and long lives despite not receiving any form of longevity treatment.

Upon a visit to New York in 1974, Charlie became involved in a case involving his son Tommy Chan, who had become a New York City police officer as depicted in the novel *Charlie Chan Returns* by Dennis Lynds. Although Charlie's son in the book is called Jimmy, he was also referred to as the third son, who was Tommy Chan in most accounts. By the character's age and mannerisms as depicted in the novel, and the fact that Jimmy was working for the government at the time, this was probably Tommy Chan.

Charlie was not able to enjoy retirement for very long because he was hired to solve a murder that had taken place aboard a Greek shipping magnate's yacht in 1975, as seen in the film *The Return of Charlie Chan*. Assisting him in this case were his grandson and granddaughter, Peter and Doreen Chan. Although the film depicts these two characters as his offspring, they were too young to have been his son and daughter.

In his last recorded case, Charlie teamed up with his grandson, Lee Chan, Jr. Lee Chan had become a criminologist but his true vocation was art. He became an illustrator of some renown, and married into the Lupowitz family. Charlie and his grandson pursued one of Charlie's old adversaries and a former agent of Fu Manchu, Lola Dumas, known now the Dragon Queen. It is perhaps fortunate that Charlie Chan did not live to see the travesty that depicted his last great adventure, filmed as the rather unfunny comedy, *Charlie Chan and the Curse of the Dragon Queen*. Shortly after defeating Lola Dumas in 1977, Charlie Chan joined his honorable ancestors.

Bibliography of Charlie Chan novels by Earl Derr Biggers:

The House Without a Key. New York: Avenel, 1925.
The Chinese Parrot. New York: Avenel, 1926.
Behind the Curtain. New York: Avenel, 1928.
The Black Camel. New York: Avenel, 1929.
Charlie Chan Carries On. New York: Avenel, 1930.
Keeper of the Keys. New York: Avenel, 1932.

By Dennis Lynds:
Charlie Chan Returns. New York: Bantam Books, 1974.

Filmography:
House Without a Key (1926)
The Chinese Parrot (1926)
Behind That Curtain (1929)
Charlie Chan Carries On (1931)
The Black Camel (1931)
Charlie Chan's Chance (1932)
Charlie Chan's Greatest Case (1933)
Charlie Chan's Courage (1934)
Charlie Chan in London (1934)
Charlie Chan in Paris (1935)
Charlie Chan in Egypt (1935)
Charlie Chan in Shanghai (1935)
Charlie Chan at the Opera (1936)
Charlie Chan's Secret (1936)
Charlie Chan at the Circus (1936)
Charlie Chan at the Race Track (1936)
Charlie Chan at the Olympics (1937)
Charlie Chan on Broadway (1937)
Charlie Chan at Monte Carlo (1938)
Charlie Chan in Honolulu (1938)
Charlie Chan in Reno (1939)
Charlie Chan at Treasure Island (1939)
Charlie Chan in City in Darkness (1939)
Charlie Chan at the Wax Museum (1940)
Charlie Chan in Panama (1940)
Murder over New York (1940)
Charlie Chan's Murder Cruise (1940)
Dead Men Tell (1941)
Charlie Chan in Rio (1941)
Castle in The Desert (1942)
Charlie Chan in the Secret Service (1944)
The Chinese Cat (1944)
Black Magic (1944)
The Jade Mask (1945)
The Scarlet Clue (1945)
The Shanghai Cobra (1945)
The Red Dragon (1945)
Dark Alibi (1946)
Shadows over Chinatown (1946)
Dangerous Money (1946)
The Trap (1947)

Chinese Ring (1947)
Docks of New Orleans (1948)
The Shanghai Chest (1948)
The Golden Eye (1948)
The Feathered Serpent (1948)
The Sky Dragon (1949)
The Return of Charlie Chan (1979)
Charlie Chan and the Curse of the Dragon Queen (1981)

"This shadow hanging over me is no trick of the light"

By Jess Nevins

In 1637 King Charles I of England was faced with several crises. He had dissolved Parliament in 1629, and the outcry from the common people and the English noblemen had grown louder every year until 1637 when it had reached deafening levels. After the dissolution King Charles lost support for his political goals from those noblemen, not least because of his belief in the divine right of kings and his marked unwillingness to compromise on any of the political or religious reforms that the former members of Parliament had demanded. The Chancellor of the Exchequer faced continual shortfalls in funding, so that many of Charles' dearest projects were all but impossible to achieve or even begin. Earlier in the year he had imposed a revision of the Prayer Book on the Scottish Kirk (Church); this new, "Laudian" form was seen by the Scots as a subversion of God's words and the foisting upon them of "Popery and superstition." This revision acted as the catalyst for the Scottish rebellion in 1639 and led to the victory of Oliver Cromwell and the death of Charles. But in 1637 all that could be seen and heard were the angry words and midnight assaults of affronted Scotsmen.

Charles was intent on a pet project, the construction of a new royal palace at Whitehall to rival the Louvre or the Escorial. He could ill-afford many distractions, and when he was approached by an upset nobleman demanding to be appointed "Ambassador Extraordinary" to Constantinople, Charles agreed. The Ottoman Empire was in a state of great upset, with Emperor Murad IV fighting a war against the Persians to retake Baghdad. Charles no doubt saw an opportunity to gain trade advantages and create goodwill by sending an ambassador to Constantinople to forge an alliance between the Empire and England. The Battle of Lepanto was over sixty years in the past and the war with Venice seven years in the future; relations between the Empire and England had thawed enough for a desultory trade to develop between the two countries. Charles seemed to have thought that a new treaty, one advantageous to England and the Crown, would boost his popularity at home. Charles further anticipated that Murad, busy campaigning in Persia, would have neither the time nor the energy to devote to the treaty to make it more than adequate for his own purposes.

The English "Ambassador Extraordinary" is one of the minor mysteries of recorded history. We know of him because of his biographer, but even she was unable to cast light on the darkened areas of his life. His name was Orlando, and he was extraordinarily long-lived. He first comes to notice as the particular favorite of Queen Elizabeth I, and more than a favorite if contemporary rumors are to be believed.[103]

Accounts of Orlando's childhood and early years are spotty at best, and all that can be ascertained with any certainty is that he approached Charles with his request for the ambassadorship following an unsuccessful love affair with Arch-Duchess Harriet Griselda of Finster-Aarhorn and Scand-op-Boom in the Roumanian territory.

What occurred in Constantinople following Orlando's arrival there, however, remains obscure. To quote from Orlando's biographer,

> It is, indeed, highly unfortunate, and much to be regretted that at this stage of Orlando's career, when he played a most important part in the public life of his country, we have least information to go upon. We know that he discharged his duties to admiration—witness his Bath and his Dukedom. We know that he had a finger in some of the most delicate negotiations between King Charles and the Turks—to that, treaties in the vault of the Record Office bear testimony. But the revolution which broke out during his period of office, and the fire which followed, have so damaged or destroyed all those papers from which any trustworthy record could be drawn, that what we can give is lamentably incomplete. Often the paper was scorched a deep brown in the middle of the most important sentence. Just when we thought to elucidate a secret that has puzzled historians for a hundred years, there was a hole in the manuscript big enough to put your finger through. We have done our best to piece out a meagre summary from the charred fragments that remain; but often it has been necessary to speculate, to surmise, and even to make use of the imagination.

This account, and especially its final sentence, will resonate with anyone who has tried to research the tangled history of the Wold Newton Family.

Orlando seems to have completed the treaty, for in 1638 Murad abolished the Ottoman tribute in Christian children, a significant victory for England. At some point following the signing of the treaty, after the end of Ramadan, the Order of the Bath and the title of Duke (though which Dukedom is not clear) were conferred on Orlando, and a frigate, commanded by Sir Adrian Scrope, arrived in Constantinople to deliver the Order and the Dukedom to Orlando. The English Embassy was host to an enormous party, a masque of proportions unknown to Constantinople, full of the nobility and politicians stationed in Constantinople at that time. At midnight a salute by the Ottoman Imperial Body Guard was staged, and Orlando acknowledged the salute and received the Star and Collar of the Most Noble Order of the Bath. The masque ended at two in the morning, and Orlando retired, to be joined an hour later by a woman.

This woman, Penelope Hartopp, daughter of the General of the same name, achieved what so many other English and Ottoman women of Constantinople had desired and schemed for in vain: an evening of love with Orlando. Hartopp vanished from his room that morning, *enceinte*. Orlando lapsed into a coma, and a week later awoke as a woman, his sex somehow changed.

Orlando's personal history following this event is irrelevant to this article; those interested in him may read his biography for further information.[104] It is Ms. Hartopp who we will now follow. She was visiting Constantinople with friends and family on a "mind-broadening" trip, the young ladies' version of the Grand Tour. Ms. Hartopp was originally scheduled to spend only a few weeks in the Mediterranean before returning home to Leicestershire. Instead she stayed in Constantinople for an additional year. It is clear that once her pregnancy became known to her guardians they kept her in Constantinople rather than having her shame become known in London.

Hartopp's child was left at a local orphanage and she and her guardians fled, never to return. Her child was given the name "Hasan" at the orphanage and grew quickly, exhibiting the attractiveness of Orlando and the physical hardiness of the Hartopps (who, it must be remembered, were cousins of the enormous Ridds of Exmoor). By age eighteen Hasan was a physical marvel. He enlisted in the forces of Mohammed Kiuprili, the Grand Vizir from 1656-1661, and was at the forefront of the effort to rein in the Janissairies and execute those army commanders whom Kiuprili found "incompetent." Hasan distinguished himself afterwards under Mohammed Kiuprili's son, Ahmed Kiuprili, the Grand Vizir from 1661-1678. It was Hasan who was responsible for capturing Bajazet, the son of Sultan Amurat, and for guarding him during his imprisonment. Hasan won numerous commendations for his actions in the wars against Austria, Poland, and Russia. He was a standout in the Battle of St. Gotthard, the sieges of Candia and Vienna, and the battle of Slankamen, in which he died protecting Grand Vizir Mustafa Kiuprili.

Hasan was also a sadist, glorying in the torture and execution of Christian prisoners, the maltreatment of Christian women, and the kidnapping of Christian children. It might be said that this was customary among Ottomans and for the time period, and that Hasan was no worse (or better) than many Christian warriors. But Hasan seems to have been notable even by the standards of the day, and unfortunately this cruelty left its mark. It was not present in his children: Hasan's son Mahmut, who became infamous in Europe when the notes from his espionage mission to Europe on behalf of the Sultan were published in 1684, was a gentle man. But Hasan's cruelty returned in full force centuries later, to the sadness of many.

Unfortunately, a gap of evidence exists between Hasan and the other figures in this article, and although there is substantial circumstantial evidence to link them, there is no direct evidence, and attempts to exhume Ms. Hartopp for DNA testing have been denied.[105]

We now skip ahead two centuries, to the reign of Sultan Abdülhamit II (1876-1909). This was a time of great unrest in the Ottoman Empire, with the establishment and later dissolution of a Constitutional government—a time of insurrections, terrorist acts, rampant crime and corruption, and the development of the Young Turk Movement. Although it is little known in the West, the Sultan did employ certain extraordinary individuals to help him in the fight against crime and various violent terrorists and insurrectionists. One of these men was Gavur Memet (1841-?), an enormously capable man who was extremely successful in his role as special agent to the Sultan and whose feats spawned numerous folk legends and even, it is said, attracted the attention of certain agents of the British government.

Most of Memet's feats remain classified by the Turkish government. The secrets of Memet's personal life have not been kept nearly so discrete, however, and I have discovered the names of five of his children (all fathered on different women, none of whom Memet married).

The first, Adil (1873-?), entered government service as a young man and is rumored to have been active in the 1890s in the suppression of the rebellion in Sassun and later, in 1897, in the war against Greece. His actions on Crete gained him the attention of the Sultan, who in 1900 awarded Adil the hand of the Sultan's niece, Vecihi (1877-?). Vecihi had gained a small amount of fame in England, where she was known as "Princess Dullah-Veih" during her association with the lady detective Loveday Brooke, who attended Vecihi's wedding to Adil in 1900. Adil was wily enough to survive Abdülhamit's deposition in 1909 and remain in government service, entering the espionage department of Sultan Mehmed V in 1910 and working overseas in the guise of "Demetrius Rackapolo, agent of the Turkish secret service." Adil used this identity to befriend the famous American detective Nick Carter and assisted Carter on several of his cases early in the decade while also spying on America and Europe.

The union of Adil and Vecihi was a fruitful one and produced a number of notable figures, more than equaling that of Memet himself. Undoubtedly they would have followed their father and grandfather in serving the Sultan, but after Abdülhamit's deposition in 1909 Adil's children followed different paths, for good or evil. Adil's sons Kara Hüseyin (1901-?), Recai (1902-?), Kartal Hsan (1903-?), Elegeçmez Kadri (1904-?), Civa Necati (1904-?), Kandökmez Remzi (1904-?) and daughter Çekirge Zehra (1906-?) all became detectives, working in the major cities of Turkey as policemen or private detectives. Adil's son Nahit Sami'ni Sergüzeştleri (1902-?) turned to crime, modeling his methods and activities on the infamous French gentleman thief Arsène Lupin and plaguing the Middle East with their crimes. When Lupin visited Istanbul in 1940, apparently to see how his imitator was getting along, Nahit's brother Recai jousted (in a friendly fashion) with Lupin.

Memet's second son, Avni (1877-?), did not enter the police force as his father did, but instead used the money that his father (anonymously) left him on attaining his majority to become a "consulting investigator." By 1912 Avni was well established in Constantinople as "Merciless Avni," the best private investigator in the city. There is some evidence that Avni rendered service even to the Grand Vizir, and that during World War I Avni worked for, or ran, the Vizir's intelligence service, dueling with British and Russian spies in Constantinople. The Turkish government refuses to make available any documents describing Avni's single recorded defeat, at the hands of British adventurer Richard Hannay and the American spy John Blenkiron in 1916. Avni's heyday as investigator was from 1912-1920, after which he faded from the public eye and newspapers of Constantinople.

Memet's third child, Zihni (1890-?), followed his brother's path (although there is no indication that they knew of their shared parentage) and became a private investigator, using a gift (again anonymous) from his father to establish an investigation agency in Constantinople in the mid-teens. By 1922 Zihni's reputation as a devious and masterful detective was secure and he had supplanted Avni in the mind of the Turkish public and government as the foremost consulting detective of Constantinople. "Quickwitted Zihni" was extremely active from 1922-1928, with nearly forty recorded cases, all completed successfully. His use of disguises and advanced (for the day) science, and his superior intelligence, led him to victory in every case. But, like his half-brother, Zihni also disappears from the public record, and I have been unable to find any evidence of his existence after 1929.

Memet's fourth child, Orhan Çakiroglu (1890-?), entered the police force, following his father's model, although it must be said that there is no solid evidence that he knew his father's identity. Çakiroglu worked his way up through the ranks of the Constantinople police, and by the late 1930s and early 1940s he was solving a number of surprisingly violent cases.

Memet's fifth child, Meshedi (1891-?), was legally adopted by Gavur and raised as his own child. Gavur trained Meshedi in all the skills that he had learned fighting crime and instilled a love of justice in his son. On graduating from college Meshedi decided to become a policeman, to best serve the public. Like Memet's other children Meshedi received a sizeable monetary gift from his father once he became an adult. Meshedi used his father's money to support himself while he worked in Constantinople as a policeman. He was thus able to resist the many attempts at bribery and corruption proffered to him and to rise through the ranks quickly, using his intelligence and the training his father gave him to solve the crimes he encountered. Meshedi was active as a police sergeant and later detective from the mid-1920s through the beginning of World War II, after which time he disappeared. He was known, in Istanbul, as "Honest Meshedi," a term of praise rarely given by the average Turk to the police of Istanbul during that time; the common men and women in Istanbul saw him as a man of unimpeachable integrity, and loved him for it.

Meshedi, however, had one momentary moral blemish, a spot on his escutcheon, although he successfully kept it a secret from everyone at the time. He cheated on his wife. It only happened the once, in 1931, but that one slip led to no small amount of misery, both in Turkey and around the world.

Meshedi was called in to investigate a poisoning case. A wealthy British businessman, Evelyn Windsor, visiting Istanbul with his daughter Vivian, fell sick and died while visiting the local baths. Meshedi was called in to investigate and discovered a curious entry wound along Windsor's left shoulder blade. The wound was quite small, but it was visible, and had left a surprising amount of blood. This led Meshedi to order an autopsy, which revealed that the businessman had been poisoned with the venom of a hamadryad.

While investigating the crime Meshedi became romantically involved with Vivian. The closer he came to tracking down the poisoner the more insistent Vivian became that he leave Istanbul with her. After substantial legwork Meshedi discovered that Vivian had met with a local representative of the dreaded criminal organization the Si Fan. From there it was a simple thing to determine that the goal of the Si Fan and their mysterious leader was the death of Vivian's father, a heavy contributor to the British Labour Party, and that they had paid Vivian to murder her own father.

One of the policemen who assisted Meshedi on this case confirmed that when Meshedi confronted Vivian with evidence of her crime she tried to kill him and then, when that failed, told him that she was pregnant with his daughter. Neither attempt to dissuade him from seeing justice done worked, and she was convicted of murder and imprisoned in 1932. She gave birth to Aynur late in 1931. Vivian escaped from prison in 1938 and, having learned her lesson, never again left any evidence behind that might link her to her crimes. The only thing she left behind her, from that point forward, were bodies, as she became the infamous "Vivian LeGrand," the "Lady from Hell," a criminal mastermind and adventuress, poisoner, blackmailer, and thief.

Meshedi seems to have been ashamed, as much for being seduced by a woman involved in a case he was working on as for cheating on his wife. Aynur was placed in one of the city orphanages and raised as a ward of the state, although Meshedi was diligent about sending the orphanage money. She left the orphanage at age eighteen, intending to become an actress, but had little luck gaining stage or screen roles, and by 1954 was reduced to bellydancing for Western tourists. It was then that she met her future husband, and following a whirlwind romance married him, with a child following some months afterwards.

Aynur's husband is of extremely distinguished lineage, and to adequately describe it we must lay aside Aynur's story for the moment.

In the early 1890s an amateur investigator calling himself "Victor" set up practice in Cologne. The exact dates of his practice are unknown, as is the extent of his stay in Cologne, but it is known that by New Year's Eve 1892 Victor was an accepted part of the city. He was well respected by both the police of the city as well as its upper classes. He had a remarkable success rate at solving crimes. He was tall, thin, possessed of a pronounced nose and close only to one man, who was continually dumbfounded (as, it should be said, were the rest of the men and women of Cologne) by Victor's erudition, his skills of detection, and his ability to accurately deduce vast amounts of information about a person simply by looking at them. Victor often traveled and treated his rooms in Cologne more as a waystation than as living quarters, and by early 1894 he was gone for good from Cologne, his rooms once again being let and his best and only friend left feeling deserted.

If "Victor" sounds familiar, it is for a reason. He may have been one of two men: Sherlock Holmes or Sexton Blake. Both men shared the physical characteristics and personality of "Victor," and the personal histories of both Blake and Holmes have large holes in them from 1890 to 1893. Holmes was presumed dead by English society during this time, his "Great Hiatus," and he was traveling abroad, enjoying the relative freedom from responsibility. But, as with his joust in 1892 with Adolphus Zecchino and his trip to "Wonderland" in 1893, Holmes never felt himself totally liberated from stopping criminals and evil, and it is entirely in character that he should temporarily work in Cologne. For Blake's part, he did not begin work in London as a consulting detective until late in 1893, and his early adventures, as recorded by "Hal Meredith," contain several chronological gaps.

It would be in character for either of them to have become involved with a local woman. Neither Holmes nor Blake was a committed bachelor, regardless of what their companions and literary agents wished the Victorian public to believe. It is a demonstrable fact that Holmes was involved with Irene Adler and fathered two children on her, and it has been shown elsewhere that Holmes became romantically involved with other women. Blake's marital status has long been a subject of dispute among historians; his literary agent let slip the existence of a "Mrs. Blake," but so far no one has been able to discover who this woman might be. Blake's relations with some of his female clients and enemies, including Olga Nasmyth, the "Girl of Destiny," and the spy "Mademoiselle Yvonne," seemed much closer than simply businesslike. And it makes sense, from a psychological standpoint, that both gentlemen would use their time in Cologne to explore freedoms not so easily available in Victorian society, freedoms that involved women.

While in Cologne "Victor" was briefly involved with Anna Lugoff, a respected concert violinist. Her diary reveals that she consulted with "Victor" on a case and immediately recognised him as Sherlock Holmes. (If "Victor" was actually Sexton Blake, he was undoubtedly either enraged or flattered by her mistake.) She made a conscious decision to seduce him. For his part he was initially amused but acceded to it; Anna was young, beautiful, learned, witty, and excellent company. The relationship was developing well, but after a month Anna suddenly broke it off. According to her diary she had determined that she was pregnant and realized that if she informed "Victor" of this he would feel duty-bound to remain in Cologne. Anna felt that she could not have that on her conscience, as the world needed him more than she did. The thoughts of "Victor" regarding her departure remain unknown.

Lugoff returned to her native Berlin and gave birth to twins, supported by her earnings as a performer and her parents' largesse. The first child, Jurgen, entered the Berlinischer Polytechnicum and graduated with advanced degrees in physics and archaeology. After commanding his own unit in France during World War I Jurgen briefly returned to Germany before emigrating to the United States, where he carried out a series of experiments designed to prove the Simesian "Hollow Earth" theory. In 1935 his efforts were rewarded when he discovered a fantastic kingdom beneath the surface of the Earth. With the help of his two young assistants, Matt Haynes and Don Dixon, Jurgen ventured to this land, which he called "Pharia."

Interestingly, "Pharia" is a transliteration of "ffar-yia," the word in the language of the Xexot people for "Pellucidar," the subterranean land explored by Professor Lidenbrock, David Innes, Abner Perry, Lord Greystoke, and Jason Gridley. The only conclusion that can be reached is that Jurgen, Haynes and Dixon explored a so far unchronicled section of Pellucidar, perhaps in the company of one of the Xexots.

Jurgen's life after 1941 is a mystery. It may be that, like the Japanese and Italians in America at the time of America's entry into World War II, he was interned, and died in the camps. Or, perhaps, he was offered a job with the American government.

Anna Lugoff's second child, Arno, joined a military academy in Dusseldorf, acquired a scar in a dueling match at age sixteen, and entered the German army at age eighteen. He quickly drew notice from the officers for his superior hand-eye coordination, his intelligence, and his dignified bearing. Arno was transferred into the Air Force, and at the beginning of hostilities volunteered for combat duty. Arno became one of the most feared aces of World War I, shooting down sixty-six Allied pilots before finally being shot down and captured at Ypres in 1918. (The man who bested him—the only pilot to do so—was the famous British airman Biggles.)

After the war Arno initially took to crime and had several memorable mid-air battles with, among others, Tommy Tomkins, Jack Martin, and, most often, the American adventurer and pilot Rick "Scorchy" Smith. Eventually, however, Arno was convinced to leave crime and wrongdoing behind him, and he became Smith's best friend and wingman.[106]

It was while flying with Smith that Arno first met the blonde adventuress Mickey Lafarge. Mickey first clashed with Smith and Arno, then began romancing Smith, but she was finally won over by Arno's courage and greatness of heart, and they married in 1936. Arno and Mickey fought for the Allies during World War II and afterwards, with their son John, returned to Germany.

John turned eighteen in 1954 and, using the money he was given as a graduation present, traveled around the Mediterranean. While in Istanbul he encountered a beautiful Turkish girl. The two were smitten with each other, and after a week-long romance were married. The girl was Aynur, and she gave birth to a child a few months after marrying John Lugoff.

Unfortunately, I have had little luck tracking their movements following the birth of their child. In large part this is because the child, as an adult, obscured his origins, erasing all records and making himself extremely hard to find. It is even conceivable that he killed his parents. Even his name is unknown, although his pseudonym is somewhat recognizable, to those who have done their research.

This child, who I will call "X" for the moment, was involved with crime from the very beginning, although only two events can be confirmed with any degree of certainty. By his early twenties he was involved in an opium-smuggling operation in Istanbul. In 1977 a Hungarian gang, attempting to wrest control of the drug ring from X, attacked his home, raped his wife, and threatened to kill his children unless X turned control of the operation over to them. X reportedly killed his own wife and children rather than have them used against him in that matter. He then killed all but one of the Hungarian gang and went on a campaign of terror. In the words of one possible witness,

> He lets the last Hungarian go, and he goes running. He waits until his wife and kids are in the ground and he goes after the rest of the mob. He kills their kids, he kills their wives, he kills their parents and their parents' friends. He burns down the houses they live in and the stores they work in, he kills people that owe them money. And like that he was gone. Underground. No one has ever seen him again. He becomes a myth, a spook story that criminals tell their kids at night.

It was following the murder of his family that X began his meteoric rise to power. Within a decade he had become one of the most powerful crime lords in the world.

The second confirmed event occurred in 1995, when X settled affairs with a man set to betray him and with five American thieves who had stolen from him in the past. The exact details of X's revenge remain unclear—the files have been sealed by the New York City police and by the FBI—but the end result was twenty-seven corpses and an exploding ship on a New York City pier.

X's name, the one he was known to criminals and certain crimefighters alike as, was "Keyser Soze." However, a moment's reflection reveals this to be an obvious pseudonym, and my investigations have revealed a disturbing fact.

Consider his name. Although the common spelling of his first name is "Keyser," it is obvious that the name X actually chose for himself is "Kaiser," a title befitting his role as a preeminent crime lord. His last name, "Soze," is slightly more challenging. *Soze* is meaningless in Turkish, X's putative background. Likewise, in German *soze* has no meaning. However, *sozi* does have a meaning in German. It is pronounced the same as *soze*, and so we may reasonably assume that it is "Sozi," and not "Soze," which X took as his last name. "Sozi," in German, means "Red" or "Communist." X's chosen name, roughly translated, is "Kaiser of Communists."

The implication is clear. X was motivated by more than mere greed and pride in his drive to become a crimelord, and SPECTRE had good reason not to eliminate him as an unwelcome rival. X was not just a Capo of a world-wide crime network, responsible for hundreds, perhaps thousands, of deaths every year by murder, drugs and prostitution. X was a top agent for the Soviet government and for SMERSH (and perhaps SPECTRE via SMERSH), responsible for helping to destabilize the West through crime. We might speculate that X went into business on his own following the fall of the Soviet Union, or that he remains an agent for a SMERSH/SPECTRE now independent of the Soviet Union, but we have no way of knowing for sure, and there are few investigators who are foolhardy enough to press the issue.

Bibliography

Ali, Ebüssüreyya, and S. Sadi. The "Nahit Sami'ni Sergüzeştleri" stories (1920s). (Nahit Sami'ni Sergüzeştleri).

Author not known. The "Civa Necati" stories (1940s). (Civa Necati).

Author not known. The "Elegeçmez Kadri" stories (1930s). (Elegeçmez Kadri).

Author not known. The "Kandökmez Remzi" stories (1940s). (Kandökmez Remzi).

Author not known. The "Kara Hüseyin" stories (1920s). (Kara Hüseyin).

Blackmore, R.D. *Lorna Doone* (1869). (The Ridds of Exmoor).

Böttcher, Maximilian. "The Detektiv" (*Willkommen!*, v10, 1899). (Victor).

Bourne, Mark. "The Case of the Detective's Smile" (*Sherlock Holmes in Orbit*, 1995). (Holmes' trip to Wonderland).

Buchan, John. *Greenmantle* (1916). (Richard Hannay, John Blenkiron).

Burroughs, Edgar R. *At the Earth's Core* (1913). (Pellucidar, David Innes, Abner Perry, Jason Gridley).

Tarzan at the Earth's Core (1927). (Lord Greystoke's trip to Pellucidar).

Chaffin, Glen, and Hal Forrest. *Tailspin Tommy* (1928-1942). (Tommy Tomkins).

Dey, Frederic van Rensselaer Dey. "The Inspector's Iniquity, or Nick Carter's Policeman Foe" (*New Nick Carter Weekly* #761, 29 July 1911). (Nick Carter, "Demetrius Rackapolo").

Fleming, Ian. *Thunderball* (1959). (SPECTRE).

Johns, William E. *The Camels are Coming* (1932). (Biggles).

Kaye, Marvin. "Too Many Stains" (*Resurrected Holmes*, 1996). (Holmes's clash with

Adolphus Zecchino).
McQuarrie, Christopher. *The Usual Suspects* (1995). (Keyser Soze).
Marana, Giovanni Paolo. *Letters Writ by a Turkish Spy* (1684). (Mahmut).
Moseley, Zack. *Smilin' Jack* (1933-1973). (Jack Martin).
Nadir, Hüseyin. *Fakabasmaz Zihni* (1922). (Zihni).
Pfeufer, Carl, and Bob Moore. *Don Dixon and the Hidden Empire* (1935-1941). (Dr.
Jurgen Lugoff, Matt Haynes, Don Dixon, and Pharia).
Pirkis, C.L. "A Princess's Vengeance," *Ludgate Monthly* (May, 1893). (Vecihi, aka.
"Dullah-Veih," and Loveday Brooke).
Racine, Jean. *Bajazet* (1672). (Bajazet).
Rohmer, Sax. *The Mystery of Dr. Fu Manchu* (1913). (Si Fan).
Safa, Peyami. *Alnimin kara yazisi : roman* (1926). (Recai).
Arsen Lupen Istanbul'da (1940). (Recai's duel with Arsène Lupin).
Göztepe Soygunu (1935). (Çekirge Zehra).
Kartal Pençesinde (1921). (Kartal İhsan).
Sakir, Ziya. *Mahmut Sevket Pasa* (1939). (Gavur Memet).
Sami, Ebu-Süreyya. The "Avni" stories (1912-1920). (Avni).
Shelly, Bruce, and David Ketchum. "Tuttle" (*M.A.S.H.*, episode 1.15, 14 January 1973).
(Berlinischer Polytechnicum).
Blyth, Harry, *e. al.* The "Sexton Blake" stories (1893-1968). (Sexton Blake)
Sickles, Noel. *Scorchy Smith* (1930-1961). (Scorchy Smith).
Talu, Ercüment Ekrem. *Meshedî'nin hikâyeleri* (1926). (Meshedi).
Thomas, Eugene. "The Lady From Hell" (*Detective Fiction Weekly*, 9 Feb. 1935).
(Vivian LeGrand).
Verne, Jules. *Voyage au Centre de la Terre* (*Journey to the Center of the Earth*, 1864).
(Professor Lidenbrock).
Woolf, Virginia. *Orlando* (1928) (Orlando, Penelope Hartopp)

The Lord Mountford Mystery
By Philip José Farmer

ERB-dom No. 65, December 1972

As almost everybody knows, Tarzan does live, and most of the stories told about him by Edgar Rice Burroughs (ERB) are true. However, ERB did mix some fiction in his biographies of the immortal apeman. H. Rider Haggard (HRH) was also not above falsifying some accounts of Allan Quatermain. Unlike ERB, though, he never concocted a story. His deviations from reality were confined to giving some of his real-life people fictional names or falsely locating the fabled cities which the great hunter and explorer of Africa found. Just as ERB used pseudonyms to protect some persons from unwanted publicity and gave hopelessly confused directions for finding Opar, so HRH used fake names and made it impossible to track down Kor, Zuvendis, and Waloo by following clues in *She*, *She And Allan*, *Allan Quatermain* and *Heu-Heu*.

The American, ERB, and the Englishman, HRH, never met. HRH probably heard of ERB as they both had stories in *New Story Magazine* in late 1913. It's highly likely that ERB had read some of Haggard's very popular works, and he probably did research on one of HRH's minor protagonists before writing one of his Tarzan tales.

It's the purpose of this essay to show just where a work by each intersected in a certain English noble family.

"The Lord of the Jungle is abroad" in *Tarzan the Magnificent*. He's far north of Lake Rudolf (which is near the northern border of Kenya) on a mission for Haile Selassie I, King of Kings, Lion of Judah, and emperor of Ethiopia (Abyssinia). (As an aside, Tarzan, like Selassie, is descended from King Solomon, as may be seen by referring to addendum 3 of my *Tarzan Alive*. Greystoke, however, is lord of far more than Selassie can claim, since all Africa is his domain.)

Tarzan finds a skeleton of a black message-bearer and in the runner's cleft stick, a nineteen-year-old letter. Since *Tarzan the Magnificent* occurred in 1934, the letter was written in 1915. Its writer, Lord Mountford, and his wife had disappeared twenty years before while exploring this vast, arid, and mountainous area. Mountford says that he and his wife were captured by a tribe of white women who live on the plateau of Kaji. Kaji, ERB says, is not far from where the Mafa River empties into the Neubari River. A study of detailed maps of Ethiopia and several encyclopedias and atlases fails to locate these. We can assume that ERB is using fictional names for real rivers. The only large river in the area northwest of Lake Rudolf (they are specified by ERB) is the Omo (sometimes spelled Umu). The Omo forms the eastern border of the northwest area. The only town of any consequence in this area is Maji, which has an airport now. The similarity of Kaji to Maji is no doubt a coincidence.

Possibly, the confluence of two rivers which ERB described may be, in reality, the point where the Akobo River branches into two streams. Certainly, this territory is rugged and unpopulated enough to still conceal the cliff-dwellings of the Kaji and the small village and two-story building of the Zuli, the enemies of the Kaji.

Lord Mountford says in his letter that his wife bore a daughter a year after they were captured. His wife was killed by the Kaji because she had not delivered a son. The Kaji amazons needed white males to keep the "white blood" in the tribal veins. This murder seems to be illogically motivated. Why not allow Lady Mountford to have more babies, some of which might be male? However, as we know, all societies, literate or preliterate, often proceed on illogical and nonsurvival grounds, and this seems to have been the case with the Kaji.

A little later, Tarzan finds a refugee from the Kaji. He is Stanley Wood, a travel writer who has capitalized on his "natural worthlessness, which often finds its expression and its excuse in wanderlust."

It may be that ERB put these words into Wood's mouth. Every now and then, in his books, ERB pokes fun at his own profession.

Wood and a friend had led a small safari to search for the long-lost Mountfords. On the way, Wood finds Mountford, who has just escaped from the amazons and their chief, a male witch doctor. After some delirious statements, Mountford dies. He is a man well under fifty, and so, if he's in his early forties, would have been born circa 1892. This point is made here because it's relevant to the chronology of my theory.

Tarzan later encounters Mountford's daughter, a beautiful nineteen-year-old blonde. She is known only as Gonfala. After many adventures, aided by Tarzan, Gonfala and Wood escape to civilization and are, presumably, married there. They'll be wealthy, since Tarzan is going to give them the enormous emerald of the Zulis or some share of it.

Tarzan the Magnificent does not give many details about the

Mountfords. It says nothing, for instance, of their family background or history before their disappearance. Nor are the Mountfords mentioned in the other Tarzan Epics.

But Allan Quatermain, in *Finished*, Haggard's 1917 novel, meets a member of the Mountford family in 1877. And from this story, we can fill in the background which ERB left blank.

Quatermain, while in Pretoria, then a frontier town, runs into a Maurice Anscombe. He is a younger son of Lord Mountford, one of the richest peers in England. He is tall and loosely built and between thirty and thirty-five years old. He has steady blue eyes with a humorous twinkle. His face is attractive, though the features are too irregular and his nose is too long for good looks. He served in a crack cavalry regiment, resigned, and went to South Africa to hunt big game. He is brave, but a bad shot.

Anscombe has inherited much money from his recently dead mother. His father is also dead. An older brother is the present Lord Mountford. None of his brothers have any children.

Anscombe goes to the Kashmir in India to hunt wild sheep but returns on October 1, 1878 to hunt with Quatermain. While they're tracking a wounded gnu, they run into the alcoholic and terrible-tempered Marnham and his sinister partner, Doctor Rodd. These recruit native labor for the Kimberley mines but get most of their money from smuggling diamonds and running guns for rebellious natives. Marnham once served with Anscombe's father in the Coldstream Guards but was cashiered for striking a superior officer during a card game. He had married a beautiful Hungarian, but she died a year after giving birth to a daughter, Hedda.

The daughter is almost twenty-one, is tall and slender, and has auburn hair and large dark-grey eyes. Rodd is in love with her but is killed while trying to do away with Anscombe and Quatermain.

A weird black dwarf, the wizard Zikali, the Opener-of-Roads, the Thing-that-should-never-have-been-born, predicts that Hedda will have five children. Two will die, and one will give her so much trouble she'll wish it had died, too. Inasmuch as all of Zikali's prophecies come true in other Quatermain tales, it can be assumed that this one is valid.

Zikali then makes a strange statement. "But who their father will be I will not say."

Whatever this means, Anscombe and Hedda do get married. After many years, Quatermain hears they're still alive and spend most of their time in Hungary, where Hedda has inherited property.

"Lord Mountford" is as fictional a title as "Lord Greystoke." Mountford, to the best of my knowledge, is not to be found in any book on extant or extinct peerages. The real title is a matter for future research.

But ERB, when writing of the peers who figure in *Tarzan the Magnificent*, decided to use HRH's title, since they were both writing of the same family.

Since Maurice Anscombe's brothers would have died childless, he would have inherited the title, perhaps late in life. One of Hedda's sons, born when she was about thirty-four, would have become Lord Mountford when Maurice Anscombe died. It was this son who was the Lord Mountford of *Tarzan the Magnificent*.

It is possible that, since he was raised in Hungary a good part of this time, he married a girl of that country. Their daughter, Gonfala, could be one of the beautiful Hungarian blondes typified by the Gabors. Probably, Gonfala's mother was of that ancient aristocracy which, like Baroness Orczy, biographer of The Scarlet Pimpernel, traces its ancestry back to Arpad, the Magyar conqueror of that area to be called Hungary. (Lord Greystoke himself, as shown in *Tarzan Alive*, could do the same through the founder of the Scots family of Drummond, a Maurice by the way.)

Whether or not Gonfala could lay claim to the title is not known. When her father disappeared into Africa, the title may have gone to a male relative, a brother, a nephew, or cousin. If there were no male relatives, the title may have become extinct. If, however, the patent permitted a female in the direct line of descent to inherit the title, as some English patents do, Gonfala could have become a peeress.

If this were not the case, she probably went to the USA as just Mrs. Stanley Wood. The latter seems more likely, since there is nothing in the various chronicles of the years circa 1934 indicating that the daughter of a long-lost peer suddenly appeared out of Africa.

In any event, there is evidence that Henry Rider Haggard did write the story of the parents of Edgar Rice Burroughs' Lord Mountford.

The Magnificent Gordons

By Mark K. Brown

In the annals of the Wold Newton families, there is one family which has not yet received the attention it deserves. This would be that ancient and noble lineage: the Gordons. The family originates in Berwickshire, but Sir Adam of Gordon was granted the castle of Strathbogie, in Aberdeenshire, by Robert the Bruce. The Gordons were powerful and very involved in British politics over the centuries. Among the famous members of the clan are George Gordon; Lord Byron, the notorious poet; and General Charles Gordon of Khartoum, the hero of Africa. One branch of the Gordons who lent their blood to the Wold Newton families is the line stemming from the above Lord Byron, a line described by noted genealogist Philip José Farmer, which includes Lord John Roxton, Richard Wentworth, and as others than Farmer have speculated, Mack Bolan

Here I am concerned with a different line, descended from Orion Gordon, who has been described as "a printer and intelligence operative for the crown," and Dorothy Blake, of Boston. We pick up the trail a few generations after Orion and Dorothy.

Charles Gordon (born 1786) married his distant cousin, Antonia Drummond. Antonia was the daughter of Sir Hugh Drummond, baronet, and Georgia Dewhurst. Charles' father was a descendant of Orion Gordon. His mother was a Glenmore, descended from Robert Glenmore, Earl of Dalbright. Robert had two sons, Robert II (who followed his father as Earl), and Edward. Edward went to Germany and then Sweden, ca. 1631. Among his many children, his first son remained in Sweden and became the ancestor of the mother of Matt Helm, the American assassin whose memoirs have been edited by Donald Hamilton. Robert II was the ancestor of Charles Gordon, and of Sir Hugh Drummond's mother.

Sir Hugh and his bride had been among those present when a meteorite fell to earth in the village of Wold Newton in 1795. Georgia had been pregnant at the time, and gave birth, several months later, to a son, John. John Drummond married Oread Butler. Farmer describes Oread as "of that distinguished family of Charleston, South Carolina." This is not entirely accurate. Although her grandfather had been a hero of the Revolutionary War, Oread's father had been a loyalist and had moved back to Britain when the Colonies won their freedom. Oread's brother, Nathaniel was the ancestor of the noted British composer, Christopher "Kit" Butler, who figures in Colin Wilson's novels, *The Glass Cage* and *The Black Room*. John and Oread's descendants have been described at some length by Farmer in both *Tarzan Alive* and *Doc Savage: His Apocalyptic Life*, and include Sir Richard Hannay, Bulldog Drummond, and John Drummond Clayton, known as Korak.

In 1797, Sir Hugh and Georgia had a daughter, Antonia, named after Georgia's brother, Anthony Dewhurst, a member of the League of the Scarlet Pimpernel. Antonia married Charles Gordon, a man ten years her senior, and gave birth to, firstly, James Gordon. James was a successful military man. He married a niece of the Earl of Burlesdon. His son, Richard, followed in his footsteps and entered military service. He married a Victoria Smiley in 1873. Their oldest son, Stanley, emigrated to the United States, where he made a small fortune delivering merchandise to the then rather new department stores. Stanley married Caroline Jones of Connecticut, and their son David became an inventor of some note, earning a good deal of money from several patents. His son, Raymond, born in 1911, became well known as a fencer and polo player at Yale, earning the nickname "Flash," for his speed. Shortly after his graduation, Flash disappeared during the so-called "Rogue Planet" crisis of 1933.

David's third child, Alan, had a son in 1937. Bruce Gordon became a noteworthy physicist.

Stanley Gordon's younger brother, John, became an agent of the British Secret Service, serving his country from Egypt to China. John learned his trade working under Sir Denis Nayland Smith, and later worked alongside the American agent James Schuyler Grim. In the mid 1920s, John Gordon became aware of that evil mastermind known as Kathulos, or Skull-Face. His war on Kathulos is related in several stories by Robert E. Howard.

The second son of Charles Gordon and his wife, Antonia, was named Hugh. Hugh moved to the United States and married Francesca Cooke, a descendant of Henry Burlingame, and a distant relative of the Gordons. They had four children, the oldest of whom was Evelyn Gordon. Evelyn married Erica Dale. Evelyn was killed at the Battle of Gettysburg, leaving behind two children, Richard and Eliza.

Try as I might, I have been so far unable to ascertain the maiden name of Richard's wife, Delores, but I do know that the couple had at least two children, John and Cyril. It is evident that the two brothers were close, as Cyril's son was named John, and John's grandson was named after Cyril. Cyril's son, John, was born in 1920. He grew up to be an accountant clerk for an insurance office in New York City. During World War II, John served as a bomber pilot in the Pacific, flying a large number of successful missions deep into Japanese territory. After the war was over, John returned to his career in insurance, but had a tremendous difficulty adjusting to peacetime after spending so many hours living on the edge and was constantly restless. This period of his life came to an end in 1946, when, according to his account, he was contacted mentally by Zarth Arn, a scientist from 200,000 years in the future. John Gordon claimed that he had switched bodies with Zarth Arn, and become embroiled in the political intrigues and warfare of that far-off time. Upon being returned to his own time, he related his adventures to Edmond Hamilton, who edited them for publication. The story appeared as *The Star Kings* in 1949.

Cyril's brother, John, married one Joan Roark and moved to Ohio, where he bought land. His son, George, married Heather Goodwin. George and Heather's son, the above-mentioned Evelyn Cyril, was born in 1940. George joined the army and served in both World War II and the Korean War, where he was wounded during the Inchon March. In the years following his return from Korea, George's health deteriorated, and eventually he died. Although his family believed that his death was the result of his wounds, the government disagreed and refused to pay full benefits. Despite this, Evelyn joined the military himself, in the hopes of earning the money for medical school, and became one of the first "military advisors" in the conflict in Southeast Asia. After being slashed in the face by an enemy guerrilla during hand-to-hand combat, Evelyn gained the nickname "Scar," and was discharged for the injury. While bumming around Europe, he was selected by Star Balsamo (who claimed to be the niece of Cagliostro) to be her champion. His tale was related by Robert Heinlein in *Glory Road* and *The Number of the Beast.*

Richard Gordon's sister, Eliza, married one Calvin Rogers of Pittsburgh, Pennsylvania. Their oldest son, Joseph, married a woman named Sarah, and moved to Brooklyn. Calvin and Eliza's second son, Anthony, was born in 1898, and enlisted in the Army Air Service at the outbreak of World War I. He fought in the skies over France for eighteen months. After the war ended, Anthony returned to the U.S. Taking up work as a surveyor for the American Radioactive Gas Corporation, he periodically visited his older brother in New York, where he enthralled Joseph's son with war stories and tales of patriotic valor. These stories were very influential in shaping the sickly young Steven's world outlook. On December 15, 1927, while exploring an abandoned coalmine near Wyoming Valley, PA, Anthony was apparently buried in a cave-in. His body was never found, although Philip Francis Nowlan wrote a book purporting to be the memoirs of Anthony Rogers' life in the world of 2419 AD, 492 years after his death.

The loss of his beloved uncle, coming shortly after the death of his father, Joseph, cemented the patriotic fervor in young Steve Rogers (his mother would die a few years later). When it seemed inevitable that America would join the European War in 1941, he attempted to enlist in the army. His sickly youth had left him weak and underdeveloped and he was rejected as unfit for military service. However, he was eventually able to serve his country in a greater capacity, as a volunteer for Project: Rebirth, the experiment that turned him into the living symbol of his country, Captain America.

The Evelyn Gordon who died at Gettysburg had a brother, Artemus. I have been able to learn little about his life, excepting the fact that he was part of the Secret Service, and apparently served with the exceptional agent, Jim West. Shortly after his time with West, he retired and settled down in Chicago to have a family. His oldest son, Walter, married one of the Blythes of Prince Edward Island, and had a son, James W. Gordon. James was born on January 5, 1900 in Chicago. When he was a small child, his father and uncle Clifford made an unsuccessful attempt to start a business together. They failed miserably and lost everything they had. Walter found good work in New York and moved his family there.

Young James Gordon made it into law school, but while there something happened which caused him to decide to pass up a law career and, upon his graduation in 1924, he became a police officer instead. He married maverick socialite, Barbara Lane (granddaughter of rancher and miner Hondo Lane) in 1927, but the marriage was short-lived. His rise in the force was meteoric. In 1934, James W. Gordon became the youngest police commissioner in New York history, earning the nickname "Wildcat." However, he often found his attempts at crimebusting stymied by bureaucratic red tape and, in 1935, inspired by the legendary heroes of times past—such as Zorro and the Lone Ranger, stories of whom he had heard as child—as well as by rumors of newer nemeses of the underworld such as The Shadow, Commissioner Gordon created a masked crime-fighting identity of his own, the Whisperer.

In 1936, Gordon married his sweetheart of some years, Tiny Traeger. In 1937, the legendary Batman appeared on the scene. For some years, Gordon seemed to regard the Batman as a menace, but in 1941 or '42, he apparently decided that the Batman was doing a better job as a masked avenger than the Whisperer. Gordon retired his alter ego, and began to accept and even work closely with the Batman.

Walter Gordon's brother, Clifford, was hit much harder by the failure of their business. He had two small sons, Matt and Robert, to support, his wife's early death being one of the things which prompted Walter's suggestion that the two brothers combine their fortunes. Clifford and his sons were forced to take lodgings in a poorer section of town, a locale Matt was never completely able to escape. Robert enlisted in the army when the United States joined the hostilities in Europe in 1917, and was soon flying over France. He was wounded and taken to England to recuperate. While there, he met a nurse named Margaret Dundee, an Australian working in the hospital, and after the Armistice they were married. The young couple honeymooned in Australia, visiting her parents. Robert rented an airplane and the two were flying over a range of mountains in the north central portion of the continent when the craft went down, and for over twenty years nothing was heard of them. In 1940, Alan Hunter, an American, was exploring the region known as Lost Land and discovered the answer to the mystery of the Gordons' fate. Both husband and wife had survived the crash. Margaret Gordon had been pregnant at the time, and a few months later had given birth to a healthy boy, named John. As a toddler, young John Gordon had had trouble pronouncing his own name, and he became known as "Jongor" as a result of his stumbling efforts. Even though life was difficult in Lost Land, which was one of those locations where there have been survivors from earlier ages (as described in the books Robert Moore Williams wrote about Hunter's expedition to Australia), Robert and Margaret Gordon managed to keep their family safe for nearly ten years. In 1931, both parents were killed by pterodactyls, leaving poor Jongor on his own until the arrival of Alan Hunter and his sister, Anne.

Matt Gordon married a woman named Rose and had two children, Charles and Norma. Young Charlie was born in 1926, and was mentally retarded. As an adult, he had an IQ of 68. On March 3, 1958, Charlie joined the research program of Professor Harold Nemur, who was working to increase intelligence. The project had spectacular, but unfortunately short-lived success, turning Charlie into a genius of previously unheard-of ability. However, by November of that year, Charlie had not only returned to his previous low IQ, but had died as a result of the experiment.

The third son of Charles Gordon and Antonia Drummond was born in 1817 and named Arthur. In 1836, at the age of nineteen, Arthur went to Texas, where he led a gang of brigands who committed crimes in the name of Texas' rebellion against Mexico. While there, he had two sons, William L. and James, by a woman who is currently unidentified. In 1837, Arthur Gordon became a sailor in the slave trade, reportedly under the slaver John Charity Spring. Gordon eventually rose to the position of captain of his own slave ship.

Arriving in Paris in 1843, Arthur became the lover of Hermine de Chalusse. After wounding her brother, Raymond, in a duel, Arthur and Hermine fled to the United States, where they married. The following year, a son, Wilkie, was born to them in Richmond, Virginia. In 1850, the Gordons returned to Paris. Once there, Hermine fled from Arthur, taking her son with her. The lives of Hermine and Wilkie are recorded in *La Vie Infernale*, by Emile Gaboriau.

Arthur's older sons, William and James, remained in the American West. James died under unusual circumstances in Dodge City, Kansas on the night of November 3, 1877. Earlier that year, William had a son, Francis X. Gordon, in El Paso, Texas. For a few years, William Gordon and family moved back and forth between that city and Antioch, before settling in El Paso. Francis became a famous gunman and eventually traveled much of the orient, becoming well known in Iran and Afghanistan as El Borak. Several stories about him were written by Robert E. Howard.

Although I am still trying to discover the antecedents of the American journalist Sydney Gordon, whose adventures were chronicled by Richard Bessiere in 1957, my Wold Newton colleague Jean-Marc Lofficier is undoubtedly correct in asserting that Sydney is a member of this family.

Bibliography

Bessiere, Richard. *Sydney Gordon*, 1957.

Eckert, Win Scott. "The Amazing Lanes." *The Wold Newton Chronicles*. Mark K. Brown, ed., 2000. < http://www.pjfarmer.com/chronicles/Lane.htm>.

Eclipso series. DC Comics.

Farmer, Philip José. *Tarzan Alive*. New York: Doubleday & Co., 1972.

---. *Doc Savage: His Apocalyptic Life*. New York: Doubleday & Co., 1973.

Fraser, George MacDonald. *Flash for Freedom*. New York: Alfred A. Knopf, 1971.

Gaboriau, Emile. *La Vie Infernale*. 1870.

Hamilton, Donald. The Matt Helm series. Greenwich, CN: Fawcett Gold

Medal Books.
Hamilton, Edmond. *The Star Kings*. New York: Warner Books, 1967.
Heinlein, Robert A. *Glory Road*, New York: Avon Books. 1964.
---. *The Number of the Beast*.New York: Fawcett Books, 1980.
Howard, Robert E. *Lost Valley of Iskander*. New York: Zebra Books, 1974.
---. *Skull-Face*. New York: Berkley Books, 1978.
---. *Sons of the White Wolf*. New York: Berkley Books, 1978.
---. "The Dead Remember." *Argosy*, 1936.
Kane, Bob. *Batman* series. DC Comics.
Keyes, Daniel. *Flowers for Algernon*. New York: Bantam Books, 1967.
Lai, Rick. "The Monsieur Lecoq Chronology." *An Expansion of Philip José Farmer's Wold Newton Universe*.. Win Scott Eckert, ed. 2001. <http://www.pjfarmer.com/woldnewton/Lecoq.htm>.
L'Amour, Louis. *Hondo*. Greenwich, CN: Fawcett Gold Medal Books, 1953.
Le Carré, John. *Tinker, Tailor, Soldier, Spy*. New York: Alfred A. Knopf, 1974.
Lee, Stan and Jack Kirby. *Captain America* series. Marvel Comics.
McConnell, Arn. "The Case of Commissioner Gordon." *The Wold Atlas* v1, n3, Fall 1977. *The Wold Newton Chronicles*. Mark K. Brown, ed., 2000. <http://www.pjfarmer.com/chronicles/gordon.htm>.
Merritt, A. *The Moon Pool*. New York: Collier Books, 1961.
---. *The Metal Monster*. New York: Avon Books, 1966.
Montgomery, L.M. *Anne of Green Gables*.
Moorehead, Alan. *The White Nile*. New York: Dell Books, 1960.
Nowlan, Philip Francis. *Armageddon 2419 A.D.*. New York: Ace Books, 1978.
Power, Dennis E.. "The Wold, Wold West." *The Secret History of the Wold Newton Universe*. Dennis E. Power, ed., 1999. <http://www.pjfarmer.com/secret/woldwest/wold-wold-west-revised2.htm>.
Rand, Ayn. *The Fountainhead*. New York: Signet Books, 1996.
Raymond, Alexander. *Flash Gordon* comic strip. King Features Syndicate.
Williams, Robert Moore. *Jongor of Lost Land*. New York: Popular Library, 1970.
---. *Return of Jongor*. New York: Popular Library, 1970.
---. *Jongor Fights Back*. New York: Popular Library, 1970.
Wilson, Colin. *The Black Room*. New York: Pyramid Books, 1975.
---. *The Glass Cage*, New York: Bantam Books, 1955.

The Legacy of the Fox
Zorro in the Wold Newton Universe
By Matthew Baugh

> "Oppression—by its very nature—creates the power that crushes it. A champion arises—a champion of the oppressed. He will be there. He is born—" *The Mark of Zorro*, 1920

Zorro is one of the most charismatic and enduring of all costumed heroes, and also one of the most mysterious. Everyone knows that El Zorro; the masked avenger of Spanish California was actually Don Diego Vega[107], a young *caballero* who posed as a meek poet to avoid suspicion. Beyond that though, it is very difficult to say much about his true personality. Don Diego was as much a disguise as the black costume of Zorro.

In Don Diego's case, the problem with writing an accurate biography comes from too much information rather then too little. Many authors and filmmakers have tried to write the story of Zorro's adventures over the years and the result is a confusing morass. Most of the presenters try to encapsulate the whole career of the first Zorro into one story. The problem is that details like the name of the villainous *comandante*, the name of Diego's true love and many other details change from telling to telling. The fact that so many different love interests are mentioned seems to have led to the erroneous assumption that Diego was a compulsive womanizer (an idea taken to the extreme in the 1972 film *The Erotic Adventures of Zorro*). While it is true that Diego loved and married several women over the course of his life there seems to be little basis for the idea that he was a seducer.

Don Diego's foppish act was not entirely a pretext. He was a highly intelligent man who loved to read and admired men of genius from Cervantes to da Vinci. Neither was his disdain for the traditional recreation of a *caballero* completely feigned. He secretly loved fencing, courting beautiful women and racing horses, but found a life devoted to those things hopelessly shallow. Diego lived in a time and place where there was considerable injustice, especially for the Indians and the peons of the community. He was frustrated by the fact that the other *caballeros* were too immersed in their own selfish pursuits to try to change their world for the better.

As Zorro, Diego found a way to combine the pleasures of the *caballero* life with his own quest for justice. He fought for the oppressed, gaining the love of the poor and of the Franciscan friars, but he did it in a way that caught the admiration of the *caballeros*. As Zorro, Diego could out-ride, out-fence, out-charm and outwit any of his peers.

Though he was a progressive thinker, Diego was also a product of his time and his culture. He was a devout Roman Catholic who saw the Christianization of the California Indians as a good thing. He was also a *caballero* who believed in the superiority of "good blood" and who often boasted that his was as blue as that of anyone in California. More modern retellings of the story have attempted to soften this edge by introducing the ideas of religious tolerance, sexual equality and the removal of class distinctions. In fairness to them, Diego was as receptive to these ideas as any man of California in the early 1800s could be. If some of his sensibilities offend us we should remember that he stood up to the worst social problems of his time with unflinching courage.

The question of Diego's time is a difficult one. The California of Zorro's time seems to combine elements of several periods of California history ranging from the 1780s to the 1840s. The Disney series and most subsequent versions have taken the sensible approach of using the 1820s as their setting. More of the elements of the Zorro stories can be seen in this period than in any other. For this article I have taken a different approach and started with the dates actually given in the works of Zorro's first chronicler, Johnston McCulley.

What follows is not just a biographical timeline of Don Diego Vega. It is a chronology of Diego's family and of all who have worn the mask of El Zorro. In writing this I have tried to give equal consideration to all sources except those which I had no access to or which seemed obvious parody.

A Chronology of Zorro

1513
On September 15 or 17 Nunez Balboa and his expedition cross the Isthmus of Panama to become the first Europeans to gaze on the Pacific Ocean. At Balboa's side is a member of the Vega family. (Mentioned in *Don Q, Son of Zorro*, 1925.)

1520
The Aztecs rise up against Hernan Cortez in Tenochtitlan. A young Vega in armor is one of the hundreds of conquistadors killed on this "Night of Tears." (Mentioned in *Don Q, Son of Zorro*, 1925.)

1532
Francisco Pizarro leads his men in the capture of the Inca Emperor Atahualpa. As Peru falls to the conquistadors, a Vega is at Pizarro's side. (Mentioned in *Don Q, Son of Zorro*, 1925.)

c. 1600
Zorro Contro Maciste: Long before the time of Don Diego Vega, another man becomes the first Zorro. He is the poet Ramon, who becomes the Fox to help the noble Isabella reclaim her rightful lands. Unfortunately, the lady's evil sister Malva has persuaded the heroic strongman Maciste to help her. The two champions clash before finally joining forces to restore Isabella. Ramon weds Isabella and becomes the Count of Seville.[108] (The story is told in the in the 1963 film *Zorro Contro Maciste*, which was released in English as *Samson and the Slave Queen*. Maciste is one of the longest-lived of all cinematic heroes. He first appeared in the 1914 Italian film *Cabiria*, and was the hero of more than fifty movies. *Zorro Contro Maciste* establishes Maciste as a part of the Wold Newton Universe. The date comes from the fact the story is set shortly following the death of King Philip II of Spain.)

c. 1620
Zorro E I Tre Moschietteri: Spain is at war with France and agents of Cardinal Richelieu gain an advantage in the conflict by capturing Isabella, the cousin of the King of Spain. Ramon's son, the young Count of Seville, travels to Spain to trade Spanish military secrets for Isabella's release. Actually this is a ruse, enabling the Count to don the mask of Zorro and to rescue Isabella. Richelieu's enemies, Athos, Porthos, and Aramis, join with Zorro in this adventure. (This 1963 film was released in English as *Mark of the Musketeers*. The fact that D'Artagnan is not present suggests that this adventure takes place before the events of *The Three Musketeers*, the novel by Alexandre Dumas. The connection between Ramon of *Zorro Contro Maciste* and the Count in this film is speculative but makes sense given their proximity in time.)

1610-1770
There is a long period during which there are no recorded adventures of the man called El Zorro[109], and his story becomes the stuff of legend.[110]

1771
The mission of San Gabriel Arcangel is established in the area that will become Los Angeles. The Franciscan priest, Fray Filipe, who heads the mission, will become one of Zorro's closest allies.

Don Alejandro Vega and his wife Isabella[111] arrive in Alta California to settle. Isabella is pregnant during the long voyage and gives birth to a son, Diego, not long after arriving in their new home. Fray Filipe baptizes Diego. (The year of Diego's birth is established by the fact that he is twenty-four in *The Curse of Capistrano*. That Fray Filipe was the priest who baptized Diego is told in the McCulley stories. The connection with Fray Filipe establishes that Diego is almost certainly born in California.)

As Diego grows up his friends include *caballero* boys his own age like Ricardo del Amo, Audre Ruiz, and Rafael Reyes. He also befriends peons and Indians, including the elderly medicine woman Gray Owl (*El Búho Gris* in Spanish). (Don Audre Ruiz first appears in the novel *The Further Adventures of Zorro* by Johnston McCulley. Rafael Reyes is from the story "Zorro Fights a Friend," also by McCulley. Ricardo del Amo is from several episodes of the Zorro television series by Walt Disney Productions. His first appearance was in the episode "The Practical Joker." Gray Owl appeared in the animated Zorro series by Warner Brothers.)

1777
Lolita Pulido is born to Don Carlos and Doña Catalina Pulido; she will grow up to become Don Diego's first and greatest love. (The year of Lolita's birth is established by the fact that she is eighteen in *The Curse of Capistrano*.)

1781
The Pueblo of La Reina de Los Angeles is established in Alta California. Los Angeles will be the center of El Zorro's activities for most of his career. (The Los Angeles of Zorro's world boasts a military *presidio* run by a cruel *comandante*. This is different from the Spanish Los Angeles of our world, which was run by a civil government and which never featured a *presidio*.)

c. 1783
The Vegas move into a *hacienda* originally built by another *caballero*. They will expand it greatly over the years, but Don Alejandro will never discover the secret escape passage created in case of Indian attacks. (The date is speculative; the story of the passage[112] is told in *Zorro: The Dailies* by Don MacGregor.)

c. 1785
Doña Isabella Vega dies[113] and Don Alejandro never remarries. (The report of Isabella's death comes from the novel *Zorro and the Jaguar Warriors* by Jerome Priesler. The date is speculative, though Priesler says Diego was an adolescent when his mother died.)

Also this year, a hurricane forces the evacuation of the coastal island of San Nicholas. Several of the leaders of the Los Angeles community including Don Alejandro Vega, Fray Filipe and the young Lieutenant Monastario supervise the evacuation. One local woman goes back to find her daughter and the ship is forced to leave her behind. She screams curses at the men and promises that her spirit will not rest until she has had her revenge. (The date is thirty years prior to the events of *Zorro and the Witch's Curse*.)

1786
Don Diego witnesses a number of incidents of violence and oppression against the Franciscan friars, the Indians, and the peons. He decides that the poor and helpless need a champion, and resolves to become that champion. (In *The Curse of Capistrano* Diego mentions that he was fifteen when he first became aware of the injustices around him.)

Around this time Diego discovers the secret passage in the hacienda. He tells no one about it. (The date is speculative, though the Disney television episode "Zorro's Secret Passage" mentions that Diego was a boy when he discovered the passage.)

1788
Don Diego is sent to the University in Madrid to complete his education. While there, he perfects his skills at fencing, riding, marksmanship and the other talents he will need as Zorro. He also creates a persona for himself as a foppish and ineffectual poet. (The studies in Madrid are not mentioned by McCulley but are featured in every other version of the story. The fact that Diego was seventeen when he left for Spain is mentioned in the novel *Zorro and the Jaguar Warriors* by Jerome Priesler.)

1791-1795
The unrecorded adventures of Diego in Spain take place during this period. In one of these adventures he becomes the enemy of the young Don Ramon Castillo. They will meet again years later. (Don Ramon appeared in the Disney television episode "Auld Acquaintance.")

1795
Diego returns to Los Angeles with a mute servant named Bernardo.[114] He finds the oppression in California even worse than he had remembered it, with a corrupt governor named Luis Quintero[115] in power and a wicked military ruler, Capitán Juan Ramon, and his assistant, Sgt. Pedro Gonzales in control. Don Diego poses as harmless poet but by night he becomes the masked El Zorro, avenger of injustice and protector of the weak. Only Bernardo and Fray Filipe are privy to his double identity.

Early in his adventures Zorro gains the magnificent black stallion Tornado[116] as his steed.

The Curse of Capistrano: After a series of adventures Zorro gathers together many of the local *caballeros* and forms a masked band of 'Avengers' (*Los Vengadores* in Spanish.) Together they force Governor Quintero to back down and Zorro humiliates Capitán Ramon in a duel. Zorro then reveals his identity to Lolita Pulido and her parents. He also reveals his secret to Don Alejandro, and to Don Audre Ruiz, the leader of the Avengers. Diego believes that there is no longer a need for Zorro. He plans give up his adventuring and marry Lolita. (A distorted version[117] of these events appears in the novel *The Curse of Capistrano* (also published as *The Mark of Zorro*) by Johnston McCulley.)

The Further Adventures of Zorro: Several weeks later the vengeful Quintero and Ramon act to disrupt Diego's wedding plans. Though he has been humiliated and now wears the mark of Zorro on his cheek, Capitán Ramon is still in charge of the *presidio*. The villains hire a pirate named Bardoso to loot Los Angeles and to abduct Lolita. Diego becomes Zorro again and rallies the *caballeros* to defeat the pirates. Bardoso is defeated, but not before he kills Capitán Ramon. (These events are told in *The Further Adventures of Zorro* by Johnston McCulley. This novel was rewritten by D.J. Arneson and distributed as *Zorro and the Pirate Raiders*. Arneson's version is mostly true to the original but keeps Zorro's identity a secret. For the purposes of this article it must be counted as more accurate than the original story.)

Following this adventure, Governor Quintero is forced to resign and return to Spain. Sadly, Don Diego's wedding must be postponed when Lolita falls ill and must return to Spain. Diego is led to believe that she will never recover.[118]

1796-1798

This marks a period of relative inactivity for Zorro. At the beginning of *Zorro Rides Again*, Sgt. Pedro Gonzales comments that Zorro has not ridden in three years. This is an exaggeration and Gonzales would have done better to say that Zorro had hardly ridden in three years. The honest Capitán Torello assumes command of the *presidio* and Gonzales remains as his aide.

1796

Bardoso escapes from captivity and resumes his pirate career. He retires shortly after losing an eye in a fight with another pirate. While Bardoso is recovering from his wound he meets the kindly Fray Fransisco who reforms him.

Around this time Zorro becomes blood brother to the warrior José of the Cocopahs. Both Bardoso and José will prove valuable allies of Zorro in the future.

The adventures recorded in the McCulley stories "Zorro Saves a Friend" and "Zorro Hunts a Jackal" take place this year.

1797

There is a change of command and Capitán Marcos Lopez replaces Capitán Torello as comandante. Lopez suspects Don Diego of being Zorro. He persuades Don Miguel Sebastiano to pose as the Fox and incite the natives to rebellion, hoping this will trap the real Zorro. The plan fails but it will be only the first of many such "false-Zorro" plots over the years. (This story is recounted as "Zorro Deals with Treason" by Johnston McCulley.)

Also this year Deigo travels to San Diego de Alcala where he assumes the identity of the mysterious "Don Miguel" to expose a planned rebellion. It fits with Zorro's sense of humor that he uses a variation of Lopez and Sebastiano's plan for himself. He seems even to have lifted Don Manuel Sebastiano's name for his own alias. In the course of this adventure Diego meets and courts Señorita Carmelita Ramon. By the end of the story she has learned that he is El Zorro and the two seem to be heading for an engagement. (The story was published as "Mysterious Don Miguel" by Johnston McCulley.)

1798

Zorro Rides Again: A miraculously healed Lolita Pulido returns to Los Angeles. Diego breaks off his romance with Carmelita and renews his engagement to Lolita. A ruthless new military commander named Capitán Valentino Rocha has replaced Lopez as comandante. He and his ally Don Estaban Rodriguez try a variation of the "false-Zorro" ploy. (This adventure is found in the novel *Zorro Rides Again* by Johnston McCulley. In the original version Diego had already revealed his identity and everyone knew he was Zorro. D.J. Arneson rewrote the story, changing this detail so that Zorro's identity remained secret. It was also published as *Zorro Rides Again*. For the purposes of this article, Arneson's version is treated as more accurate than the original. McCulley lists the year of the story as 17—; Arneson fills this out as 1798.)

Following this adventure Diego hangs up his Zorro costume and marries Lolita.

1799

Twin sons are born to the Vegas but Lolita dies from the stress of childbirth. The midwife, Inez Resendo, secretly steals one of the boys. Diego names his son Cesar and mourns for Lolita. (In the opening chapter of *The Sign of Zorro* Diego is mourning his wife, who "...died of a fever before they had been wed a season." Though the wife is not named, I interpret this as a reference to Lolita. That Lolita dies in childbirth is a logical assumption if we accept that she is Cesar's mother.)

Inez names the stolen child Gilberto and returns to Spain to raise him. (The twin brother is established in the New World television series, though the series mistakenly says he is Diego's brother rather than Cesar's.)

Also this year Diego's younger cousin, Antonio de la Cruz, is born. Antonio is the son of Diego's maternal uncle, Don Estivan de la Cruz. (Antonio's existence is revealed in an unsold pilot for a television series called *The New Adventures of Zorro*.)

1800

The Sign of Zorro: Diego is still mourning the death of Lolita when he is called into action once again. In the course of this adventure Don Diego pays court to Señorita Panchita Cancholes. Diego and Panchita have become engaged by the end of the story, but there is no evidence that they ever marry. We can only speculate at why their engagement may have been called off. Perhaps Diego realized that any woman he loved would be in danger so long as he still rode as Zorro. (The date is given in the story as "…evening in mid September, about 1800.")

Following the events of *The Sign of Zorro*, Don Diego resumes adventuring as El Zorro. During this year Sgt. Pedro Gonzales retires to become a tavern keeper and Sgt. Pedro Garcia[119] takes his place. A new *comandante*, Capitán Ortega, comes to the *presidio*. With the exception of Capitán Monastario, Ortega is the most determined of the *comandantes* when it comes to capturing Zorro. (Capitán Ortega and Sgt. Garcia become fixtures in the Zorro stories beginning with "Zorro Strikes Again.")

El Zorro's adventures this year are all written by Johnston McCulley and are as follows:
"Zorro Draws his Blade"
"Zorro Upsets a Plot"
"Zorro Strikes Again"
"Zorro Saves a Herd"
"Zorro Runs the Gauntlet"
"Zorro Fights a Duel"
"Zorro Opens a Cage"
"Zorro Prevents a War"
"Zorro's Hour of Peril"
"Zorro Lays a Ghost"

1801
This is probably the year that the following adventures occur. As of the date of this writing only the first two of these adventures have been reprinted, so it is impossible to be precise. The stories are all by Johnston McCulley and are as follows:
"Zorro Frees Some Slaves"
"Zorro's Double Danger"
"Zorro's Masquerade"
"Zorro Stops a Panic"
"Zorro's Twin Perils"
"Zorro Plucks a Pigeon"
"Zorro Rides at Dawn,"
"Zorro Takes the Bait"
"Zorro Raids a Caravan"

1802
This year is the probable setting for the following Johnston McCulley stories:
"Zorro's Moment of Fear"
"Zorro Saves his Honor"
"Zorro and the Pirate"
"Zorro Beats a Drum"
"Zorro's Strange Duel"
"A Task for Zorro"
"Zorro's Masked Menace"
"Zorro Aids an Invalid"
"Zorro Saves an American"
"Zorro Meets a Rogue"
"Zorro Races with Death"
"Zorro Fights for Peace"

1803
This year is the probable setting for the following Johnston McCulley stories:
"Zorro Serenades a Siren"
"Zorro Meets a Wizard"
"Zorro Fights with Fire"
"Gold for a Tyrant"
"The Hide Hunter"
"Zorro Shears Some Wolves"
"The Face Behind the Mask"

1803
This year is the probable setting for the following Johnston McCulley stories:
"Zorro Starts the New Year"
"Hangnoose Reward"
"Zorro's Hostile Friends"
"Zorro's Hot Tortillas"
"An Ambush for Zorro"
"Zorro Gives Evidence"
"Rancho Marauders"
"Zorro's Stolen Steed"

"Zorro Curbs a Riot"
"The Three Strange Peons"

1804
This year is the probable setting for the remainder of the Johnston McCulley stories:
"Zorro Nabs a Cutthroat"
"Zorro Gathers Taxes"
"Zorro's Fight for Life"
"Zorro Rides the Trail"
"The Mask of Zorro"

Also this year, Don Diego travels to Santa Cruz where a Prussian mercenary named Sebastian Golle has been named *comandante.* Golle has the new civilian administrator killed by an assassin posing as Zorro. He then tries to force the man's daughter, Señorita Isabella Palma, to marry him. Diego poses as a wandering gentleman to win the confidence of Golle then rescues Isabella and breaks his oppressive rule. (This story is found in the 1936 film *The Bold Caballero*. The placement in the chronology is speculative and several details must be considered fictional for this article's purposes. Diego does not marry Isabella at the end of the movie, and Diego is not using his own name in this adventure. The Vegas were far too well known in California for Don Diego to get away with posing as a penniless wanderer. Possibly he was using his old "Mysterious Don Miguel" alias.)

1805
Dracula Vs. Zorro: Don Diego travels to Spain where he commissions a special sword from the brilliant Moorish metalsmith Rambak. His new sword contains iron, silver and other blended metals and is far superior to an ordinary weapon. On this trip Zorro runs afoul of Count Dracula, who has been forced from his homeland by Napoleon's armies. (The details of their conflict are found in the two-part *Dracula vs. Zorro* comic from Topps Comics. The Topps comics do not give a more specific date than the early 1800s for any of Zorro's adventures. The reference to the Napoleonic Wars places the story some time in the years 1803-1815.)

1806
Don Diego returns to California, stopping on his way to deal with the

villainy of a man called Lucien Machete at Pico de Orizaba, Sierra Madre. (Recounted in issue n1 of the Topps Comics series.)

***Zorro* (The Walt Disney Series)**: Diego reaches Los Angeles to find a new *comandante*, Capitán Enrique Sanchez Monastario. Capitán Monastario will prove to be the Fox's most tenacious foe[120]. Monastario's second-in-command is Sgt. Demetrio Lopez Garcia[121], an overweight buffoon with a heart of gold. Eventually Zorro humiliates Monastario in front of the visiting Viceroy. The disgraced officer is stripped of his command. (The conflict with Monastario can be seen in the Disney television series, episodes 1-13.)

No sooner has Monastario been removed, than Zorro discovers a new threat. A secretive mastermind known as the Eagle (*El Aguila* in Spanish) has started a conspiracy to seize the government of California. The Eagle communicates with his minions through coded messages sent in the form of eagle feathers. Eventually Zorro unmasks the Eagle, who is actually the aristocratic Don Sebastian Varga. (The conflict with the Eagle ran from episodes 14-39.)

1807

Zorro travels to Monterey where he defends Don Gregorio Verdugo and his lovely daughter Anna Maria from bandits. Don Diego has romantic ideas about the Señorita but ultimately decides there is no place in his life for romance while Zorro is needed. Zorro also picks up a second steed in Monterey; a white stallion called Phantom (*Fantasma* in Spanish.) (The trip to Monterey took place over episodes 40-44 of the Disney series.)

Back in Los Angeles Zorro spends time struggling with rebels and the military 'Especiales' sent to defeat them. (Episodes 45-48 of *Zorro*.)

Diego's boyhood friend, Don Ricardo del Amo, comes to Los Angeles to catch Zorro for the sport of it. He also becomes a rival for the attentions of Señorita Anna Maria Verdugo. (*Zorro*, episodes 49-52.)

In unconnected adventures, Zorro helps two indentured servants in love, and protects Sgt. Garcia from bandits. (*Zorro*, episodes 53-54.)

Zorro's uncle, Don Estivan de la Cruz, comes to Los Angeles. Don Estivan is now a widower looking for looking for a wealthy woman to wed. He sets his sights on the Señorita Margarita. After Zorro spoils his romance and his other get-rich-quick plans Don Estivan leaves Los Angeles for Santa Fe.[122] There he is actually able to catch and wed a wealthy Spanish heiress. (*Zorro*, episodes 55-58.)

Zorro helps a vengeful peon then aids a young *señorita* whose *hidalgo* father seems to have disappeared without a trace. (*Zorro*, episodes 59-62.)

An American mountain man named Joe Crane comes to Los Angeles and promptly gets into trouble with a local *caballero*. It takes El Zorro some time to straighten things out. (*Zorro*, episodes 63-65. Joe was also a regular on another Walt Disney series, *The Saga of Andy Burnett*, which ran in 1957. Actor Jeff York played the burly mountan man in both series. This crossover brings Andy Burnett into the Wold Newton Universe.)

An official representing the King of Spain arrives to raise money for the war effort. The official abuses his power until Zorro stops him. (*Zorro*, episodes 66-69.)

In unconnected adventures Don Diego is challenged to a duel, and Sgt. Garcia has to guard a golden chalice during a measles outbreak. (*Zorro*, episodes 70-71.)

The governor of California is injured and is forced to stay at the Vega *hacienda* to recuperate. Zorro must foil the repeated assassination attempts of an insurrectionist group called the *Rebatos* before the governor is safe to leave. (*Zorro*, episodes 72-75.)

In unrelated adventures Zorro stops a fortuneteller in league with bandits, aids a young boy who turns out to be a kidnapped member of the Chinese imperial family, and saves Bernardo from a false accusation of robbery. (*Zorro*, episodes 76-78.)

As the year closes, El Zorro foils the bandit leader known as *El Chuchillo* (the Knife), rescues a young *señorita* from a manipulative suitor, and deals with his old enemy Don Ramon Castillo. (These adventures were all shown as special one-hour programs by Walt Disney productions after the cancellation of the *Zorro* series.)

1808

Zorro In Old California: Capitán Monastario is reassigned to the Presidio of Los Angeles[123]. The years have made him even harsher than before and he sets about gathering exorbitant taxes and skimming profits for himself. Zorro faces Monastario several times trying to stop him. (These adventures are recounted in the collection *Zorro in Old California* by Nedaud and Marcello.)

***Zorro* (Topps Comics Series)**: Monastario has an Indian blacksmith named Felix Quintero whipped for asserting that his people's religion has as much validity as Christianity. The man retaliates by forging special weapons to strike back against all Europeans. He discards his Christian name and becomes Moonstalker (*El Cazador de la Luna* in Spanish.)

While chasing Zorro, Monastario accidentally shoots Don Ramon Santiago, blinding him and terribly scarring his face. Ramon's sister, Anita Santiago, creates the scantily costumed identity of Lady Rawhide *(La Dama de la Cuera* in Spanish) to wreak vengeance on both Monastario and Zorro.

While Zorro, Moonstalker and Lady Rawhide are trying to sort out their complex relationships, Lucien Machete comes to Los Angeles as the new "Regency Administrator." (All of this is seen in issues 2-12 of the Topps Comics series. It was suggested that Lady Rawhide and Moonstalker would eventually become the Fox's allies, but the series was canceled before this possibility could be explored. The date is established as two years after Zorro's first encounter with Machete. By leaving the two-year gap in his story, author Don MacGregor is probably signaling that his stories are meant as a continuation of the two-season Disney television series.)

1809

Zorro, The Dailies: After Lucien Machete is out of the picture, Monastario hires a mercenary called Quickblade (*La Navaja Rápida*[124] in Spanish) to deal with the Fox. Their conflict ranges over several stories involving the tar pits at Rancho La Brea. (These stories, "Tusk Envy" and "Dead Body Rising," are collected in *Zorro, the Dailies* by Don MacGregor.)

1810-1813

Zorro has a series of unrecorded adventures during these years. At some point during this time Lady Rawhide and Moonstalker drop out of the picture and do not return. Their final fates are unknown.

1810

***Zorro* (Animated Series)**: Zorro has a series of adventures involving Monastario (spelled "Montacero" in this version), Sgt. Garcia and an assortment of colorful villains (including Bigfoot.) He receives aid from his old friend Gray Owl and a new friend, Señorita Isabella Torres, both of who learn his double identity. (These events are recounted in episodes 1-25 of the Warner Brothers animated series. Isabella is the daughter of a *hildalgo* who is a neighbor of the Vegas. This probably means that she is the daughter of Don Nacho Torres and the younger sister of Elena. Nacho and Elena were recurring characters in the first season of the Disney series.)

1811
A daughter is born to Don Estevan de la Cruz and his new wife. She is Don Antonio's half-sister and will become the mother of Jeff Stewart. (There is no hint of Don Estevan's daughter in any of the stories, but she is necessary to explain Jeff Stewart's connection to Zorro. Dennis Power has researched the genealogy of the De la Cruz branch of the family in great depth. For more on them, see his article "All That Glitters" on *The Secret History of the Wold Newton Universe* website.)

1814
Don Diego is now forty-three years old and realizes that he cannot keep going forever as El Zorro. He decides to train his son Cesar in the skills of the Fox.

***The New Adventures of Zorro* (Animated Series)**: Don Cesar shares a number of adventures with his father using a costumed identity of his own. When Cesar is in costume Zorro refers to him as "Amigo." Their main enemies are Capitán Monastario and Sgt. Garcia. (These adventures can be seen in episodes 1-13 of the animated series *The New Adventures of Zorro* by Filmation. In the series the main villain is actually called Capitán Ramon; his assistant is Sgt. Gonzales, and Amigo's true identity is Miguel. For the purposes of this article I am assuming these names are not accurate.)

Alejandro Mesones is born to a peon family. Alejandro and his brother Joaquin (who is two years older) will play a crucial role in Don Diego's life years later. (Alejandro is said to be eight and Joaquin ten years old in the opening scenes of *The Mask of Zorro*. Joaquin and Alejandro are surnamed Murietta in the film and are supposed to be the legendary California bandits Joaquin and Alejandro Murietta.[125] The semi-legendary Joaquin Murietta is thought to have lived approximately 1831-1853, so the brothers in the film cannot be these Muriettas. I have given them name Mesones for its similarity to the American name Mason.)

1815

Zorro And The Jaguar Warriors: Zorro has several very strange adventures centering on a new enemy, a descendant of Hernan Cortez with great mental powers who calls himself Hidalgo El Cazador. Don Cazador begins by starting up a cult devoted to the Aztec gods outside Los Angeles.[126] (The story is told in *Zorro and the Jaguar Warriors* by Jerome Priesler. The year 1815 is mentioned in the story, as is the fact that the action begins during the closing days of *Carnival*, the annual celebration that precedes the Church season of Lent.)

Zorro And The Dragon Riders: Angered by his defeat, Don Cazador hires four deadly warriors from Japan[127] to put an end to El Zorro. Fortunately Diego has purchased a manual on the Japanese martial arts.[128] With this and the advice of a ninja-trained Cossack named Yuri he gains enough insight to defeat them.[129] (This adventure, recounted in *Zorro and the Dragon Riders* by David Bergantino, transpires only weeks after Zorro's first encounter with Cazador.)

Zorro And The Witch's Curse: A mysterious woman claiming to be the legendary Witch of San Nicholas (*La Bruja de San Nicholas* in Spanish) and her crew of pirates terrorize Los Angeles. Zorro defeats the witch and she flees. Her ship vanishes mysteriously in a storm, giving rise to a new legend that she has magically escaped and will one day return.

Some time following this adventure Sgt. Garcia retires, Don Alejandro dies and Capitán Monastario is transferred to another position. (These characters are not seen in later versions of the story so it is reasonable to assume that they have all moved on in one way or another.)

1816

Zorro And Son: Diego concludes Cesar's training, then retires and marries Isabella Torres.[130] With nothing to worry about in Los Angeles, Don Cesar travels to Madrid to attend the University. (The adventures of Diego and Cesar were told in a highly distorted form[131] in the television series *Zorro and Son*, which lasted only five episodes.)

c. 1816

***Zorro* (1974)**: The villainous Col. Huerta sends assassins to Spain to kill the newly-appointed governor of Nuova Aragon[132] so that he can seize control of the nation for himself. A soldier-of-fortune named

Diego takes the governor's place. He poses as the foppish Miguel Vega de la Serna while fighting Huerta's tyranny as Zorro. He is the first of a number of heroes who have no connection to the Vega[133] family but who assume the identity of El Zorro to fight oppression. (This story is told in the 1974 film *Zorro*. The date is conjecture based on Huerta's comments about insurrection in the interior. This probably sets the story in the period of 1810-1822 when the Spanish possessions in the New World were swept with rebellions.)

1817

Don Q, Son of Zorro: In Madrid, a jealous rival frames Don Cesar for the murder of an Archduke. Cesar becomes a fugitive and adopts the alias of "Don Q"[134] while attempting to clear his name. Don Diego hears of his son's plight and sails to Spain to help him. While Cesar is fighting for his life in the ruins of the ancestral Vega Castle, he is joined by Zorro. Fighting side –by side, father and son triumph. (This adventure is told in the 1925 film *Don Q, Son of Zorro*, starring Douglas Fairbanks as both Don Cesar and Don Diego.)

Don Cesar remains in Spain and becomes engaged to Dolores del Muro. Don Diego returns to Isabella in California.

1818

***Zorro* (New World Series)**: A new *alcalde* is appointed to Los Angeles. Luis Ramon is a harsh man who has resumed Monastario's corrupt taxation policies. Diego sends for Don Cesar, who breaks off his engagement to Dolores and returns to Los Angeles. Once there he assumes the identity of El Zorro. He also meets Victoria Escalante, the owner of the local tavern. Victoria is not of *hidalgo* blood but she has an independent spirit that causes Cesar to fall in love with her. (The New World series is meant to be an updated version of the original story but many details have been changed. Zorro's romance with a woman not of noble blood, the substitution of the young servant Filipe for the familiar Bernardo, the different villains, and even the fact that there are quite a few Americans in Los Angeles make it difficult to reconcile with other versions. For our purposes it is easier to assume that "Don Alejandro" is really the older Don Diego[135] and "Don Diego" is really Don Cesar. A slightly distorted version of the new Zorro's origin is seen in episodes 8-11 of the New World Television *Zorro* series.)

As Zorro, Don Cesar has a series of independent adventures. (These are seen in episodes 1-7 and 13-25 of the first season of the New World series.)

An American inventor arrives in Los Angeles and tries to capture Zorro using technological devices. This is noteworthy because of the possibility that Dr. Henry Wayne is an ancestor of Bruce Wayne, the Batman. (New World, season two, episode 1, "The Wizard." Adam West, who also played Bruce Wayne on the 1966-1969 *Batman* series, plays Dr. Wayne.)

Another string of adventures ends in a final confrontation with Luis Ramon in the stronghold known as the "Devil's Fortress." Ramon unmasks Zorro but is so startled by what he sees that he slips and falls to his death. (New World, season one, episodes 2-23.)

1819
The villainous Ignacio De Soto becomes the new *alcalde* of Los Angeles. Zorro fights De Soto and fends off various other menaces. In one of these adventures a sharp-shooting American woman named Annie takes an interest in the bounty on El Zorro's head. (These events are told in the second season of the New World series, episodes 1-25. Episode 18, "They Call Her Annie," implies that Annie is actually the famous Wild West markswoman Annie Oakley. The historical Annie Oakley (1860-1926) had not yet been born in the time of Zorro.)

Elena Vega is born to Don Diego and Isabella. (Elena is two years old in the opening scenes of *The Mask of Zorro*.)

Zorro has another string of adventures. (New World, season four, episodes 1-9.) Part way through the year, Cesar's twin, Gilberto Resendo comes to Los Angeles as an emissary from the Spanish throne. He seizes control of the *pueblo* and mounts a campaign against the Vegas. For years Inez has told Gilberto that his parents rejected him and now he burns for revenge. Eventually Gilberto is killed, but not before Diego and Cesar learn who he really is. (This storyline came about in episodes 10-13 of the New World series.)

Saddened by recent events, Don Cesar Vega travels to France for a vacation. While there he meets the descendants of Athos, Porthos and D'Artagnian and shares an adventure with them. (This story was titled "One for All" parts 1 & 2 and was broadcast as episodes 24-25 in season two of the New World series. I have moved them to the end of the series where they make better chronological sense.[136])

1820
While Don Cesar is traveling and incommunicado Don Diego's worst nightmare comes true. Enrique Sanches Monastario[137] is made the new governor of California. Diego must resume the role of Zorro to fight Monastario once again.

1821
Zorro faces Monastario in a series of unrecorded adventures.Also this year, the War of Mexican Independence begins.

1822
Mexico gains its independence from Spain and California becomes a part of Mexico.In California Governor Monastario realizes he will have to flee to Spain. He makes a final desperate effort and manages to unmask Don Diego. Isabella is accidentally killed as Diego is arrested. Monastario burns the Vega *hacienda* and has Diego locked in the terrible prison at Talamantes. He reports that the entire Vega family was killed in the fire and departs for Spain, taking Elena to raise as his own daughter. (These events are seen in the opening scenes of *The Mask of Zorro*.)

Zorro, The Gay Blade: In Santa Fe, Don Antonio de la Cruz hears of Don Diego's supposed death. He travels to Los Angeles and takes up the identity of Zorro. Monastario is gone but the evil Alcalde de Soto is still in the *pueblo*. Before long Don Cesar returns from his European travels. The two men realize that they look enough like one another to pass as twins and use this to their advantage. After a short series of adventures they oust de Soto and set things right in Los Angeles. (The story of Antonio's return to avenge Don Diego comes from the unsold television pilot, *The New Adventures of Zorro*. The idea of the twin Zorros fighting to avenge their "father" is seen in distorted form in the movie *Zorro, the Gay Blade*.[138])

After the fall of de Soto, Antonio returns to Santa Fe. He takes his Zorro costume with him in case it is ever needed again. Cesar and Victoria marry and Cesar retires as Zorro.

1824
Zorro's Fighting Legion: Members of the San Mendeleto regional council in Mexico conspire to seize control of the region. Don Pablo, the Minister of Justice[139] assumes the guise of a Yaqui god named Don del Oro[140] to stir up revolt among the native peoples. Presidente Guadalupe Victoria sends for Don Cesar in the hope that Zorro can help. Don Cesar poses as a timid member of the council by day. By night he organizes the *caballeros* into a masked legion. Eventually Zorro and the Legion are triumphant and the conspiracy is smashed. (The adventure is told in the Republic serial *Zorro's Fighting Legion*. In the serial several names are changed. Don Cesar is referred to as "Don Diego" and Guadalupe Victoria is referred to as "Benito Juarez".[141])

1825
Despite the best efforts of El Zorro, the Yaquis begin a savage war against the Mexicans, which will last for many years. Discouraged by the state of affairs in Mexico and California, Cesar and Victoria move to Spain to live on the ancestral Vega lands. Cesar never had the heart to rebuild the Vega hacienda and it remains in ruins.

1830
Don Manuel Parides seizes control of Baja California, exercising dictatorial powers. One of the patriots who oppose him is Juan Ortiz who assumes the name (though not the costume) of Zorro. Ortiz may have been one of the members of Zorro's Legion a few years earlier. Parides retaliates by murdering Ortiz's wife and burning down his home with his infant son inside. The baby is rescued and is raised by a widow named Clara. He is baptized with the name Diego Guadalupe. (This is seen in the film, *Three Swords of Zorro*. The date is given in the film.)

1835
Jeff Stewart is born in Santa Fe, New Mexico territory. Jeff is the son of Don Estevan's daughter and her husband, an American named Stewart. Jeff is the second cousin of Don Diego on his mother's side.[142] (The date is speculative based on the probable age of Jeff in *Son of Zorro*. He had received a law degree before becoming an officer in the Union Army during the Civil War. This suggests that he must be about thirty at the beginning of the serial.)

Cesar and Victoria become parents fairly late in life. Victoria gives birth to twin boys named Diego and Bernardo. (These sons do not appear in any version of the Zorro stories. They are my own invention to establish the family line that leads to Jim Vega.)

1836
With Diego in prison and Cesar back in Spain there is a period in which oppression flourishes in Mexican California. That is, until a mysterious new rider dressed as Zorro appears to oppose the nefarious Comandante Santiago. This new Zorro seems literally able to disappear into thin air, but the comandante finally manages to trap him in an ambush. This Zorro's final fate is unknown. (This Zorro is actually the time-traveling scientist Allan Lucas whose adventures were seen in the story "Uncle Zorro" by Bill DuBay and Jose Ortiz. The story appeared in issue n11 of *The Rook* magazine. For more information on this Zorro see the entries for 1961 and 1981.)

1839
Don Manuel Parides captures Juan Ortiz and locks him in prison. He believes this will end the threat of Zorro forever. (This is seen in *Three Swords of Zorro*. The date is given in the movie.)

1842
The Mask of Zorro: Monastario returns from Spain with a byzantine plot to make California into his own independent country and to exploit its hidden gold. His ally is an American named Harry who helps him by tracking down the bandit Mesones brothers and killing Joaquin. Alejandro Mesones swears vengeance on Harry.[143]

Don Diego escapes from prison and allies himself with Alejandro Mesones. He trains the young man to pose as a fop named Don Alejandro del Castillo y Garcia. He also teaches Alejandro to fight with all the skills of Zorro. Working together the two Zorros thwart the villains' plot. Monastario, Harry, and Don Diego all die in the final conflict but not before Diego is reunited with his long-lost daughter Elena.

(These events are all seen in the 1998 movie *The Mask of Zorro*. The dates are given in the movie.)

The Treasure of Don Diego: As the new Zorro, Alejandro begins the fight against oppression again. He opposes the corrupt representatives of the Mexican government, especially the new military commander in Los Angeles, Capitán Augustín Landovar. In his first solo adventure as Zorro, Alejandro gains a new ally in young Mateo Cantua. He also finds a will written by Don Diego, which voids all earlier wills and leaves the vast Vega holdings to him. As Diego's heir, Alejandro changes his name to Vega.

The Secret Swordsman: A dangerous new enemy named Sir Nicholas Thorne arrives form England and Elena must become a second Zorro to help defeat him. This novel also establishes that Zorro's old ally, Fray Filipe, is still alive and active.[144]

Skull And Crossbones: Zorro foils a plot by some local Dons and the pirate Elijah Bone, called *El Fuego,* to kidnap General Santa Anna and make California a rogue nation. (The involvement of Santa Anna and references to U.S. President Zachary Tyler help to confirm the date of this adventure.)

1843
Alejandro and Elena marry early in the year. Before the year is out a son named Joaquin is born to them. Joaquin is the grandson of the first Don Diego. (The infant Joaquin is seen in the closing scenes of *The Mask of Zorro*.)

1846
A daughter named Luisa is born to Alejandro and Elena. (Luisa is not hinted at in any of the stories, she is my invention and is necessary to connect the Vega family tree to the Merediths of *Zorro's Black Whip*.)

1848
Traces of Monastario's lost gold mines are found at Sutter's Mill. This begins the famous "Gold Rush" which floods California with American settlers.

1852
Jeff Stewart journeys east to attend college and law school.

1854
Three Swords of Zorro: Diego Guadeloupe is grown. Posing as a simple-minded young man he assumes the identity and the costume of Zorro to fight Paredes. Eventually he frees his father, Juan Garza, from prison. The two men and Diego's adopted sister, Maria, all don the costume of Zorro and put an end to Paredes' tyranny. (This is seen in *Three Swords of Zorro*. The date is given in the film.)

1859
After gaining his law degree, Jeff Stewart buys a small ranch in Utah and opens up a practice. His family's retainer Pancho joins him to serve as the foreman of the ranch. Unknown to Jeff, Pancho brings Don Antonio's Zorro costume with him.

Around this time Don Cesar's and Elena's branches of the family learn of each other's existence. The reactions range from delight to disbelief to shock. Unfortunately, Alejandro and Cesar have a serious falling-out. Cesar claims that, as the firstborn son, it is his children who should inherit the California lands and that Alejandro and Elena are "squatters." Alejandro tells Cesar that Diego's will clearly voided all of his son's rights and that the Spanish Vegas are not welcome in California.

Joaquin is sympathetic to Cesar's family, and that leads to a dispute with his father. When Alejandro insists that Joaquin is only true heir, Joaquin reacts by disowning this claim. He even drops the name Vega and goes back to his "true name" of Mesones.

1860
Joaquin travels to the East Coast to enter school. He finds that there is a strong undercurrent of prejudice in the eastern schools and he must hide his heritage to be accepted. He Americanizes "Joaquin Mesones" to "Ken Mason" and is accepted into a prestigious college of engineering. (All of Ken's earlier life, including the conflict between Alejandro and Cesar, is speculative. It is needed to explain how Don Diego Vega has a grandson named Ken Mason.)

Around this time a son named Manuel is born to Diego and his wife in Spain. He is the great-grandson of the first Don Diego. (Don Manuel Vega is seen in the Republic serial *Zorro Rides Again*—he is the uncle of Jim Vega.)

1861
The Civil War begins. Jeff Stewart and Ken Mason both enter the Union Army. Ken has not completed his college education but his time in the army gives him first-rate training as an engineer.

1864
Luisa Vega marries an American named Meredith and travels with him to the Idaho territory.

1865
The Civil War ends and both Jeff Stewart and Ken Mason return to their chosen careers. Jeff leaves the army as a Captain. Ken's rank is never mentioned.

Son of Zorro: Jeff returns to his small ranch in Utah[145] where he plans to open a law practice. His plans are interrupted by the actions of corrupt officials who seized control of the county in the 1862 elections. Jeff assumes the identity of Zorro and, after many adventures, smashes the gang. Jeff is different from most of the people who have assumed the mantle of Zorro in that he does not pretend to be a harmless fop in his regular identity. (Jeff's adventures are seen in the Republic serial *Son of Zorro*. The date comes from the fact that he is seen returning home from the war in the opening scenes.)

Ghost of Zorro: Ken Mason leaves the army and begins work as an engineer. His first assignment is to help with the installation of telegraph lines in the wild New Mexico Territory. There is a local gang run by the blacksmith in Twin Buttes who is giving shelter to outlaw gangs[146] and does not want better communication in the region. When they act to sabotage the project Ken sends for Moccasin, the grandson of Bernardo. Moccasin sets up a secluded cave hideout for Jeff and equips him with the costume and tools of Zorro.[147] Working together, the pair brings down the gang. (Ken's adventures are seen in the Republic serial *Ghost of Zorro*. The year is seen on a telegram dated July 1865. The telegraph line is completed in November of the same year.)

Randall "Randy" Meredith is born to Luisa Meredith and her husband. Randy is the great-grandson of the first Don Diego.

1866

Jeff Stewart marries Kate Wells and begins a prosperous law practice. Nothing is known about his adventures or his branch of the family after this. The fact that he was a successful lawyer may have been an influence on some of his younger relatives.

Ken Mason marries Rita White and the two eventually return to Los Angeles. Wold Newton researcher Dennis Power lists attorney Randolph Mason as their son and Buck Mason and Perry Mason among their grandchildren.[148]

1867

Barbara Meredith is born to Luisa Mason and her husband. Barbara is the great-granddaughter of the first Don Diego.

c. 1870

A son named Ramon is born to Don Bernardo Vega and his wife in Spain. He is the great-grandson of the first Don Diego. (Don Ramon is alluded to but never seen in the Republic serial *Zorro Rides Again*. He is the father of James Vega. The serial never gives his name; "Ramon" is my own invention.)

c. 1874

The Ysabel Kid[149] encounters a mysterious character called El Zorro in an adventure on the Mexican border. The Kid deduces that this Zorro is actually a local man named Diego.[150] He shows up the Fox in their encounter and defeats the villains himself. (This adventure is recounted in the short story "Comanche Blood" by J.T. Edson and is collected in the volume *The Hard Riders*. Fellow Wold Newton scholar Brad Mengel provides the date of this story.)

c. 1885
Alejandro and Elena die within a short interval of each other. Ken Mason tries to persuade Diego and Bernardo to return to California and take over the Vega holdings. The twins refuse, but their sons Manuel and Ramon do come back to the *hacienda*.

1888
A group of outlaws who want to keep Idaho from achieving statehood begins a campaign of terror. Randy Meredith adopts the Zorro-like guise of "the Black Whip"[151] to fight them. Randy also uses his position as editor of the local newspaper to push for statehood. Randy's younger sister Barbara ably assists him from behind the scenes. (Randy's adventures as the Black Whip are alluded to but never seen in the Republic serial *Zorro's Black Whip*. The date is conjecture.)

1889
Zorro's Black Whip: Randy Meredith is fatally wounded while riding as the Black Whip. Barbara takes over both the newspaper and the identity of the masked vigilante. The criminals are unaware that she is not the original Black Whip. With the help of government agent Vic Gordon[152] Barbara defeats the gang and Idaho's plans for statehood are realized. (The story is told in the Republic serial *Zorro's Black Whip*. The date is given in the movie.)

c. 1890
Barbara Meredith marries Vic Gordon and the two probably settle down in Idaho. Nothing more is known of the adventures of their branch of the family. It is possible that Vic is connected to the heroic Gordon family, whose members include Artemis Gordon, Flash Gordon, and Police Commissioner James Gordon, but this has not yet been established. (For more on the Gordon family, please see Wold Newton researcher Mark Brown's article, "The Magnificent Gordons," on *The Wold Newton Chronicles* website.)

c. 1895
Don Ramon Vega meets and marries a California woman.

c. 1900
A son named James Vega is born to Don Ramon and his wife. James is the great-great-grandson of the first Don Diego. (James is said to be the grandson of Don Diego in *Zorro Rides Again*, but given the time that has elapsed between Diego's era and the 1930s this is not possible. Don Manuel tells James that he is the last of the line of Zorro. This is an odd statement in light of the Mason, Stewart and Meredith branches of the family. Probably Manuel simply meant that James is the last to carry the name of Vega.)

c. 1917
James Vega goes off to school. After completing college and law school James becomes a lawyer in a major East Coast city. (James' career is not specified but he is seen sitting in an office with what appear to be law books on the shelves.)

1918
Johnston McCulley is given access to the Vega family records. McCulley uses the information to write a fictionalized biography of Don Diego and El Zorro which he titles *The Sword of Capistrano*. (In our universe the story was *The Curse of Capistrano*, but the title *The Sword of Capistrano* appears in the story "Uncle Zorro," establishing the fact that, in the Wold Newton Universe, McCulley's story had a different title.)

c. 1930
Zorro Rides Again: Don Manuel Vega is involved in the construction of the California-Yucatan[153] railroad, which will be a boon to both Mexicans and Spanish-descended Californians. Unfortunately a greedy businessman named Marsden hopes to buy up the railroad and develop it himself. He hires a gang of thugs led by Brad "*El Lobo*" Dace to sabotage the building of the line. Don Manuel is killed but not before Jim Vega has returned to take up the mantle of El Zorro. After facing many perils, Jim defeats the gang and the railroad is completed. (This story is told in the Republic serial *Zorro Rides Again*. While the technology and costumes suggest some time in the early 1930s, there are no clear clues to help date this movie. Marsden may be a descendent of Sgt. Pedro Gonzales, who first appeared in *The Curse of Capistrano*.[154])

Jim Vega retires as Zorro and marries Joyce Andrews. At the time of this writing, he is the last known member of the Vega family to have assumed the identity of Zorro.

1961
Physicist Allan Lucas invents a time machine and uses it to travel back to the California of 1836. Lucas is a romantic who knows of Zorro's adventures from the novel *The Sword of Capistrano*. He decides to become Zorro himself and uses his time machine to stage Zorro's miraculous escapes. The only other person who knows Allan's secret is his young nephew, Chik Lucas. When Allan fails to return after one of his adventures, Chik spends the next twenty years wondering what could have happened. (This is related in "Uncle Zorro.")

c. 1975
An unknown person adopts the identity of El Zorro to fight for justice in the tiny republic of Tijada. CIA agent Vincent J. Ricardo and hapless dentist Sheldon S. Kornpett travel to the nation in a complex attempt to depose the tyrannical General Garcia. When they meet Garcia, Sheldon notices that he has a "Z" shaped scar[155] on his cheek. Was this the work of a Vega, or the action of some other fighter for justice who was inspired to take up the Fox's identity? The answer is unknown, but the incident illustrates that wherever there is injustice, Zorro will rise up to oppose it!

1981
Now an adult, Chik Lucas sets out to learn what happened to his time-traveling Uncle Allan. The story ends before we learn what happens, but it is implied that Chik learns how to use his uncle's time machine to travel back to 1836 and try to rescue him. While we do not know whether Chik was successful, we do know that there are no further adventures of this Zorro. (The story is told in "Uncle Zorro" by Bill DuBay and Jose Ortiz in issue n11 of *The Rook* magazine. The story was intended to be the first of two parts and the second part was never written.)

From ERB To Ygg
By Philip José Farmer

Erbivore, August 1973

All persons of North European ancestry, and the majority of those of South European extraction, are descended from Charlemagne. Charlemagne, or Karl the Great (742-814 A.D.), was the king of the Franks and emperor of the West (Holy Roman Empire). Most American blacks can also claim the distinction of descent from this famous monarch, since very few lack white ancestors. Furthermore, those belonging to Indian tribes whose original habitat was east of the Mississippi can make a similar claim. Further, anybody whose forebears were of old British stock also has as ancestor Alfred the Great (849-899 A.D.), king of the West Saxons. This includes many Dutchmen, Belgians, French, and Germans, since the British, in their many, many wars and travels, have left a trail of babies behind them in western Europe and elsewhere.

Unfortunately, few of us in the United States know who our great-grandfathers were. We can only show that Alfred and Charlemagne are in our lineage by arithmetic. Suppose you were born in 1950 A.D. Assuming twenty-five years per generation, you had sixteen ancestors living in 1850. Doubling each generation as you go backwards, you had 256 ancestors living in 1750. By the time you get to 1040 A.D., you have 23,873,978,368 ancestors.

The world population today is about 3.4 billion, the highest by far that it has been since the human species began. The world population in 1 A.D. was somewhere between 200 and 300 million. Obviously, you could not have had over 23 billion ancestors living in 1040 A.D. Marriage between cousins, near and far, is the only explanation of this discrepancy. The world is, and has been, a hotbed of incest.

It's no exaggeration to say that we're all related and that all of us have noble and royal ancestors. The difference between the majority of us and a small minority is that the latter can offer documentary proof of their descent from kings and nobility. They can give the names, step-by-step, ancestor by ancestor, of those in their lineage.

Edgar Rice Burroughs (ERB) belongs to this minority. His lineage is distinguished indeed. In fact, it can be traced back to the great Germanic God Woden, known in various languages as Odin, Wuodan,

Wodan, Wuotan, etc. One of his epithets in Old Norse was Ygg, hence the name in the title of this essay. Ygg means "The Terrible One," and Yggdrasil, the great ashtree or worldtree of the Old Norse, means "Odin's Steed."

But let's go to a son of Odin, the man whose lineage is the subject of this article. He was born in Chicago on the first of September 1875. Neither his environment nor his immediate ancestry smacked remotely of the divine. Yet this man, Edgar Rice Burroughs, had an imagination which would carry his readers further than Woden ruled, to the center of the Earth and beyond Earth itself, faster than Odin's eight-legged steed, Sleipnir, could travel.

His parents were George Tyler Burroughs (1833-1913) and Mary Evaline Zieger, married 23 February 1863. George was a major in the U.S. Army during the Civil War and a successful businessman afterwards. He was the son of Abner Tyler Burroughs (1805-1897) and Mary Rice, married 16 December 1827.

Abner Tyler Burroughs was the son of Tyler Burroughs (1771-1845) and Anna Pratt. The ancestors of Tyler Burroughs are not known to me, though Mr. Porges, in his biography of ERB (still unpublished[156]) may extend the genealogy in the Burroughs line.

However, it is the purpose of this article to trace ERB's lineage through the Rices. The genealogy of ERB's other American ancestors, the Ziegers, Colemans, McCullochs and Innskeeps, is not covered here.

Mary Rice (see above), ERB's paternal grandmother, was born in 1802 in Warren, Massachusetts, and died in 1889 in Chicago, Illinois.

Her parents were Thomas Rice (1767-1847) and Sally Makepeace, both of Brookfield, Massachusetts.

Thomas's parents were Tilly Rice and Mary (Baxter) Buckminster of Brookfield.

Tilly Rice was the son of Obadiah Rice (born in Marlboro, Massachusetts) and Esther Merrick.

Obadiah was the son of Jacob Rice (born in Marlboro) and Mary ___[157]

Jacob Rice (died 1746) was the son of Edward Rice, born in Sudbury, Massachusetts. Mary Evaline Zieger, ERB's mother, says in her booklet on the family, *Memoirs of a War Bride* (1914), that Jacob Rice married Mary □. *Burke's Landed Gentry*, 1939, states that his wife was Mary, daughter of Christopher Bannister of Marlboro.

Edward Rice (died 1712) married Anna □, according to *Memoirs of a War Bride*. Burke says that Edward's wife was Agnes, daughter of

John Bent of Marlboro.

Edmund, called Deacon Rice, father of Edward, was born about 1594 in Berkhampstead, Hertfordshire, England. He emigrated to the colonies and settled in Sudbury, Massachusetts, in 1639. Edmund was one of the founders of Sudbury, a proprietor and selectman, a freeman and a deputy to the General Court. He had a twin brother, Robert, who followed him to America.

Edmund's father was Thomas Rice of Boemer, county of Buckinghamshire. There seems to be no record available of Edmund's mother.

Thomas' father was William Rice, born 1522 in the same town as Thomas. William was important enough to be granted a coat of arms in 1522. These arms are illustrated in color in *Burke's Landed Gentry* of 1939. Their blazoning: Argent on a chevron engrailed sable between three reindeers' heads erased gules as many cinquefoils ermine. As descendants of William Rice, ERB and his posterity are entitled to bear these arms.

William Rice was a younger son of Rice ap-Griffith FitzUryan and Katherine, daughter of Thomas Howard, 2nd Duke of Norfolk. It is through these two that noble and royal blood enters the Rice family. Let's consider the Welsh line before we go to the English line.

First, though, it must be admitted that William Rice is a weak link in the genealogical chain. *Burke's Peerage* in the section on *Dynevor* gives only a son, Griffith apRice FitzUryan, and a daughter, Agnes, as the children of Katherine Howard and Rice apGriffith FitzUryan. *Burke's Landed Gentry* states that it is said that William Rice was a younger son of Katherine and Rice. Dr. Charles Rice of Alliance, Ohio, a genealogical writer, indicates that there is no doubt about William Rice being their son. Since Burke often does not mention children who founded "unimportant" lines, the omission in the *Peerage* may be due to this. This may also account for the omission of Obadiah Rice in *Landed Gentry*. Obadiah (ERB's great-great-great-grandfather) was "unimportant" to *Landed Gentry*. This is ironic, since *Gentry* lists in detail the accomplishments and novels of two of the descendants of Edmund Rice; but who today has ever heard of Cale Young Rice and Alexander Hamilton Rice? Yet, in 1939, Edgar Rice Burroughs was a world-famous writer and the creator of a character, Tarzan, whose only close rival in literary stature is Sherlock Holmes. I have no hesitation in saying that these are immortal characters, literarily speaking—the best known in the 20th century, and undiminished by time. As the years go by, they grow bigger.

Again, the family of Doyle is not even listed in *Landed Gentry*, though A. Conan Doyle came of ancient and distinguished stock from both sides. But then, neither Doyle nor Burroughs were considered to be "respectable" writers. And they are still vastly underrated by the literati.

The Welsh line of ERB's ancestry is studded with knights, princes and gentlemen. Those who are interested can refer to the section on the barons of Dynevor in *Burke's Peerage*. This begins the Rice lineage with Uryan Rheged, Lord of Kidwelly, Carunllou, and Iskennen in South Wales. He married Margaret La Faye, daughter of Gerlois, Duke of Cornwall, and he built the castle of Carrey Cermin in Carmathenshire, Wales. He had originally been a prince of the North Britons, but was expelled by the Saxons in the 6th century and fled to Wales.

His great-grandfather's sister was supposed to be Helena, mother of Constantine the Great. However, Helena's origin as a Briton is based on legends which are not backed by records contemporary to Constantine.

Uryan Rheged's great-great-grandfather was Coel Codevog, King of the Britons. Coel, who lived in the 3rd century A.D., seems to be the original of the nursery song, "Old King Cole." (See *The Annotated Mother Goose* by William S. and Ceil Baring-Gould, Clarkson N. Potter, 1962.)

Let's return now to the English line of ERB's family tree. Katherine Howard, William Rice's mother, came of a line which had many kings in its pedigree. The present head of the family, the Duke of Norfolk, is the Earl Marshal of England and the premier noble. Katherine was the daughter of Thomas Howard, 2nd Duke of Norfolk, and of Agnes, daughter of Hugh Tilney. Thomas led the English to their great victory over the Scots at Flodden Field, 9 September 1513.

Thomas' father, Sir John Howard, first Duke of Norfolk, married Katherine, daughter of William, Lord Moleyns, and died fighting for Richard III on Bosworth Field.

The first duke was the son of Margaret, eldest daughter of Thomas, Lord Mowbray, and of Sir Robert Howard.

Sir Robert's lineage started with a John Howard of Wiggenhall St. Peter, 1267, who married a Lucy —. Sir Robert was also descended from King John of England, Duke of Normandy, through Joan, daughter of Sir Richard de Cornwall, a bastard of Richard Cornwall, second son of King John.

Margaret, Sir Robert's wife, was the eldest daughter of Thomas,

Lord Mowbray, and of Elizabeth FitzAllen, daughter of the Earl of Arundel. Her brother, be it noted, was the ancestor of Isabel Arundell, the wife of the great explorer, writer and anthropologist, Sir Richard Francis Burton. Another item of interest is that some of the present branches of the Howard family are descendants of the barons of Greystoke. (See Burke, *Extinct Peerage*.) The de Greystock blood, alas, entered the Howard veins too late for ERB to claim them as forefathers. Captain Stafford Vaughan Stepney Howard-Stepney is the present Lord of Greystoke Manor in Cumberland and a distant relative of ERB.

Thomas, Lord Mowbray, was the son of John, Lord Mowbray, and of Elizabeth Segrave.

Elizabeth Segrave was the daughter of John, Lord Segrave, and of Margaret Plantagenet.

Margaret was the daughter and heiress of Thomas de Brotherton, Earl of Norfolk and Earl Marshal of England.

Thomas was the eldest son of King Edward I by Margaret, daughter of Philip the Hardy, King of France. Philip's dynasty will be described in Part II, along with other ancestors of ERB, the rulers of Scotland, Normandy, Norway, Hungary, and the Swedish Norsemen rulers of medieval Russia.

Edward I was the son of Henry III and of Eleanor, daughter of Raymond Berengaris, Count of Provence. Edward, be it noted, was the brother of Richard, also called Norman of Torn or the Outlaw of Torn. ERB says that Richard was a legitimate son, but there is plenty of evidence that *The Outlaw of Torn* is a semifictionalized account. Richard was probably one of Henry III's "natural"[158] children. The identity of the mother is a subject for a separate article. I may also mention that Alice Pleasaunce Liddell, the real-life model for Lewis Carroll's Alice, was a descendant of Edward I. Her line came through John of Gaunt, Edward I's grandson. But she, along with Old King Cole, is a relative of ERB's.

Henry III's father was King John, who's had such a bad press that no king of England has ever been named John since. Actually, John was no worse than any of the medieval monarchs and a lot better than many. His brother, Richard the Lion-Hearted, was a thorough rotter who probably couldn't even speak English, but writers (until recently) made a hero out of him.

John married Isabel, daughter and heiress of Aymer, count of the French province of Angouleme. John's parents were Henry II and Eleanor, daughter of William, Duke of Aquitaine.

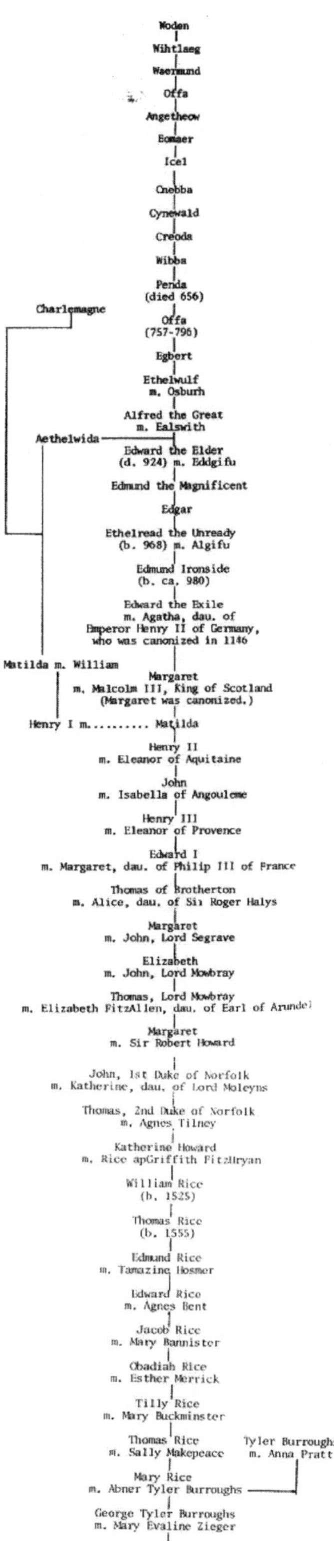

Henry II's father was Geoffrey, Count of Anjou and son of John, King of Jerusalem. Henry's mother was the empress dowager of England and daughter of Henry I.

Henry I married Maud, daughter of the king of the Scots, Malcolm III, surnamed Caennmor. Maud, also called Matilda, was directly descended from Alfred the Great.

The father of Henry I was William (1027-1087), called the Bastard or the Conqueror. He and his Normans defeated King Harold of England at Hastings in 1066 and so won the rulership of England. William was the illegitimate son of Robert I, Duke of Normandy, also known as Robert the Devil. His mother was Arletta, daughter of a tanner of Falaise, and the story is that she caught the Devil's eye while he was riding past a brook where she was washing clothes. Robert dismounted and mounted. And thus was created another link in the blood-chain which resulted in ERB. Little William was raised in Robert's house and, since Robert had no surviving legitimate sons, became Robert's heir. In those days, the upper crust often took in their natural children to rear as their own. There was no stigma attached to bastardry.

What if Robert the Devil had not happened to be riding by that particular spot on that particular day? Quite probably the Norman conquest of England would not have occurred. The world, especially the English-speaking world, would be different in many respects. The English speech would not quite be what it is today, nor would our political and social institutions. Most of us (North American and European readers) would not exist. Our places would be taken by entirely different individuals. The works of Edgar Rice Burroughs would not exist, and this article would not have been written.

William the Conqueror was the descendant of Rollo, or Hrolf, the Norseman who conquered that part of France which became Normandy. Rollo was called the Ganger, or Walker, because he was so huge that no horse could bear his weight. His ancestry will be described in Part II.

William married Maud, or Matilda, daughter of Baldwin, Count of Flanders. She was descended from Alfred the Great and Charlemagne.

Skipping a few Old English kings, we come to Alfred the Great. He was the son of King Ethelwulf (died 857) and of a lady named Osburh. Ethelwulf was the son of Egbert, King of Wessex, also titled Bretwalda, "ruler of Britain", deceased in 839.

The line of descent from Offa (reigned 757-796), King of the Mercians and of all England, is uncertain. But since there was much giving in marriage of sons and daughters among all the early Old English kings, it's highly probable that Egbert was descended from Offa.

Offa, according to a traditional genealogy, was a descendant of Penda, a king of Mercia. Penda's ancestral line consisted of Wibba, Creoda, Cynewulf, Cnebba, Icel, Eomaer, Angetheow, Offa, Waremund, Wihtlaeg, and the great god Woden.

(The latter Offa is quite likely the Offa mentioned in *Beowulf.*)

No one today is claiming that a god actually begat Wihtlaeg. This founding of a royal line by a deity was traditional and common to all the kings of Kent, Eastanglia, Essex, Mercia, Deira, Bernicia, Wessex and Lindesfaran. But, according to some modern authorities (Jacob Grim, among others), Woden was probably a hero of the early Germanic peoples who became deified after his death.

He would have lived, however, somewhere between 1000 B.C. and 800 B.C., not the 4th century A.D.

This early date means that the majority of those who read this article are also the many times great-grandchildren of that ancient proto-Germanic speaking hero.

The descendants of ERB are living today, but the scope of this article ends with ERB. As it is, it's been a long journey from Woden to Tarzan.

Who's Going to Take Over the World When I'm Gone?

A Look at the Genealogies of Wold Newton Family Super-Villains and Their Nemeses

By Win Scott Eckert

Part I: The Malevolent Moriartys

The Notorious Noels

The saga of the malevolent Moriartys and their various criminal offspring begins with the Wold Newton meteor event in 1795. Among others present was Sebastian Noel, a young medical student accompanying Siger Holmes and the third Duke of Greystoke.

The prolific Sir William Clayton was the son of the third Duke. Dr. James Noel was the son of Sebastian Noel, which brings us to the 1830s and the beginning of our story. (The background on Sir William Clayton is given in Philip José Farmer's *Tarzan Alive* and *Doc Savage: His Apocalyptic Life*. James Noel's membership in the Wold Newton Family is described in Rick Lai's "The Secret History of Captain Nemo.")

Dr. James Noel, the father of Professor James Moriarty, travelled to Germany under the alias of Von Herder. While there, he fathered a son, Julius Von Herder. This son was brilliant but also blind. He became a mechanic and designed weapons, such as airguns, for the Moriarty gang.[159] After the break-up of the first Professor Moriarty's gang in 1891, Julius Von Herder joined German Intelligence. In the late 1890s, Von Herder was eventually posted to China, under the guise of a missionary, where he came into contact with Dr. Fu Manchu. Fu Manchu cured Von Herder's blindness.

Julius Von Herder eventually became a member of a trio of spies known as the Black Stone. During 1907-1909, several members of the Kaiser's court, including one Graf Otto Von Schwabing, were accused of being homosexuals. Forced to flee, Von Schwabing was recruited into German Intelligence by Von Herder. The third member of the Black Stone was an unknown German. In 1914, the Black Stone discovered that the Serbian Black Hand planned to start the Great War by killing Archduke Franz Ferdinand. Rather than warn their German superiors, the Black Stone kept this knowledge to themselves as part of a scheme to steal British naval plans. The tale of the Black Stone's defeat by Richard Hannay was told in John Buchan's *The Thirty-Nine Steps*. However, Buchan altered the facts slightly to make it appear that the Black Stone caused the war by assassinating a Greek politician, Constantine Karolides. In any event, Von Herder was executed by a British firing squad. Von Schwabing escaped, but met his end in 1918, as told in John Buchan's *Mr. Standfast*.

Throughout the years, Julius Von Herder had maintained contact with Fu Manchu. In gratitude for his cured blindness, Von Herder fed Fu Manchu intelligence, including information regarding the impending Great War.[160] There is also another explanation for the continued relationship between Von Herder and Fu Manchu. During his time in China, Von Herder had fathered a son by one of Fu Manchu's female operatives, Madame de Medici. Madame de Medici (b. 1883) was the daughter of Fo-Hi, from Sax Rohmer's *The Golden Scorpion*, and Princess Sonia Omanoff.[161]

This son of Von Herder and Madame de Medici was born in 1899 and became involved in the Tongs in Shanghai at a very young age. He was eventually smuggled to the United States, where he took up residence in New York. By 1929, he was the treasurer of the Hip Sing Tong. He was involved in the great Tong Wars of New York City, and ultimately went to ground with one million dollars in Tong gold. When the Tong killers caught up with him, they tortured and maimed him, cutting off his hands, and then shot him through the heart, leaving him for dead. The Tong killers didn't know that his heart was on the right side of his body, rather than the left, and so he survived what would otherwise have been a fatal attack.

Von Herder's son disappeared, changing his name to Julius No: "Julius" after his father and "No" for rejection of the father and all authority. It is also possible that he knew of his paternal grandfather: "No" is part of the name "Noel." In 1943, after years of cosmetic surgery and the study of medicine, Doctor Julius No resurfaced long enough to purchase the Caribbean island called Crab Key.[162]

Doctor No certainly lived up to the Noel penchant for criminality. In 1956, he made a move to extend his power base beyond Crab Key. The story of the titanic struggle between Doctor No and British agent James Bond was told by Ian Fleming in *Doctor No*, at the conclusion of which it appeared that No had died, buried in a pile of bird guano. However, he somehow survived and resurfaced in 1971 to again plague Bond, as told in "Hot Shot."[163]

There is another likely candidate for the Noel family. Dorus Noel was also descended from Sebastian Noel.[164] Dorus Noel's yellowed skin was supposedly acquired from years of living in China. In fact, he was part Chinese. As will be seen below, twins ran strong in the Noel lineage.

Dorus Noel, the twin brother of Doctor Julius No, was also the son of Julius von Herder and Madame de Medici. Dorus Noel chose to establish a career as a police detective. In order to distance himself from the name Von Herder, he reverted to the Noel name. He must have been unfamiliar with his grandfather's role as a master criminal, or else he probably would have avoided using the Noel name. He also spread the cover story that he was born in New York City, but had spent considerable time in the Far East. He did this in order to conceal his Chinese heritage. If his mixed heritage were known, it would have been impossible for him to get a high post as the secret officer charged with maintaining the peace in New York's Chinatown in the 1930s. Noel's arch-enemy was the Chinese called Chu Chul, also known as the Cricket, but one cannot help but wonder if Noel also encountered his twin brother while policing New York's Chinatown.

The Three Moriartys

The world knows by now that there were three brothers named James Moriarty. The first son, Colonel James Moriarty, was the son of Sir William Clayton and Morcar Moriarty (for convenience let us refer to him as James Clayton Moriarty). He was born in 1835.

Morcar Moriarty's second and third sons were also named James Moriarty, and were fathered by Dr. James Noel.

The full name of the second son was James Robert Moriarty. This is the man who for a period of time adopted the name "Captain Nemo," and was also known as the first Professor Moriarty. He was born in 1836.

The third son's full name was James Noel Moriarty. (Rick Lai, in "The Secret History of Captain Nemo," calls him simply Noel Moriarty.) He was born in 1840. He was the "station-master" referred to by Dr. Watson in *The Valley of Fear*, and went on to become the second Professor Moriarty, as seen in John Gardner's semi-accurate accounts, *The Return of Moriarty* and *The Revenge of Moriarty*.

Jerrold Moriarty, Morcar's brother, has sometimes been mistakenly identified as their father.[165] In fact he was a beloved uncle and father figure to the three boys.

One Brother Moriarty

Little is known of Colonel James Clayton Moriarty, except that in 1872 he was assisting in the schemes of his younger half-brother (the first Professor Moriarty, aka the second "Captain Nemo") in the ongoing Eridanean-Capellean conflict.[166] He was also seen in Robert Louis Stevenson's "The Suicide Club" in 1878.

After the purported death of his brother, Professor James Robert Moriarty, James Clayton Moriarty started to write letters to various newspapers attempting to clear his brother's name. It was these letters that prompted Dr. John H. Watson to formally write and publish "The Final Problem" in the December 1893 issue of *The Strand Magazine*.[167]

Shortly after this, Colonel James Clayton Moriarty immigrated to America, where he had at least two sons. Like his father, the first son joined the military. During World War II, he joined a tank battalion and became known as a genius at fixing mechanical items. Unfortunately, the only record of his adventures, the motion picture *Kelly's Heroes*, never gives us his first name, although one wonders if it was also James.

The second child of James Clayton Moriarty was named Dean Moriarty. Dean Moriarty was a tinsmith and a drunk. Dean's son, also named Dean, was born on the road in 1926. Dean Jr. inherited something of the Moriarty intellect but was never formally schooled. His full story was told by Sal Paradise in *On the Road*, edited by Jack Kerouac.[168]

Two Brothers Moriarty

Of the three James Moriartys, James Robert Moriarty (the first Professor) has been the subject of the greatest amount of genealogical research.

His first sons, twins, were born in 1858 to Emily Caber. Throughout his extended life, one son was known by various identities, such as "Wolf Larsen," "Baron Karl von Hessel," and simply "Baron Karl."[169] The other was known as "Death Larsen." We shall return to the Larsens later.

James Moriarty and Emily Caber had three additional children. The third and fourth children were also twins, James and Emile Caber. (As we now know, twins are common in the family.) The fifth child was named Urania Caber Moriarty and was born in 1862.

In 1863, Emily Caber and the twin children, James and Emile, were killed, setting in motion James Robert Moriarty's scheme of revenge. This eventually led to his theft of one submarine *Nautilus* and his masquerade as "Captain Nemo."[170] His sons, "Wolf Larsen" and "Death Larsen," served as cabin boys on this *Nautilus*, before it was finally sunk in 1868 by Phileas Fogg.[171] It could have been during his travels and masquerade as "Captain Nemo" that Moriarty fathered the child known later as Rasputin, as revealed in John T. Lescroart's *Rasputin's Revenge*.

Urania Caber Moriarty became known as Patricia Donleavy in 1872, after her father took up with a woman named Donleavy. Surely, however, this was but one of a host of aliases. Urania's first son was born in 1883, of a liaison with John Clay.[172] This son would later be known as Dr. Caber, and would become the nemesis of Wold Newton family member Joseph Jorkens. Lord Dunsany related their tales in three stories: "The Invention of Dr. Caber" (found in *Jorkens Has a Large Whiskey*), and "The Strange Drug of Dr. Caber" and "The Cleverness of Dr. Caber" (both in *The Fourth Book of Jorkens*).[173]

In 1889, the second grandson of Professor Moriarty was born. Again, he was a child of Urania Moriarty and John Clay. He later went by the name Carl Peterson and was the arch-nemesis of Bulldog Drummond. Peterson was an archfiend and criminal who could present himself as of any nationality or none. His constant companion was the sinisterly beautiful Irma, who was originally presented as Peterson's "daughter." Irma Peterson lived on to seek revenge on Drummond after Carl Peterson died in his fourth meeting with Drummond in 1926, as told by H.C. "Sapper" McNeile in *The Final Count*.

Peterson came back to life in *The Return of the Black Gang*, in 1954. Mr. Farmer writes in *Doc Savage: His Apocalyptic Life*:

> Carl Peterson was the greatest villain Drummond ever encountered. Peterson was about five times as intelligent as Drummond, but he kept tripping himself up because he expected Drummond to do the sneaky and the devious. Drummond was not bright enough for this; he always did the obvious. Besides, they had a mutual, if unconscious, liking for each other, which may explain why they didn't kill each other when each had so many opportunities:
>
> "We readers were saddened when Carl Peterson seemed to have perished in a flaming dirigible, caught in his own trap. But Gerard Fairlie, who continued the Drummond series,

> revealed in the last one, *The Return of the Black Gang*, that Peterson was alive and well, though not good. Peterson failed once again to kill Drummond but escaped once again. What happened thereafter has not been recorded. But both Bulldog Drummond and Carl Peterson were getting old and tired. It may be that both just decided to retire."

However, Hugh "Bulldog" Drummond's biological brother was John "Korak" Drummond-Clayton, the adopted son of Tarzan. The whole Tarzan family had access to an immortality treatment.[174] It is doubtful that Korak would have withheld this treatment from his brother.

Mr. Farmer continues:

> Irma, Carl's wife or mistress, was every bit as villainous and innovative as Carl. It was she who kept the feud going while Carl was convalescing from the dirigible disaster or just engaged in his rotten, but colossal, projects elsewhere. Irma seems a fit candidate for inclusion in the Wold Newton family. Carl posed as Irma's father during some of their nefarious activities, so I wouldn't be surprised if she really was his daughter. Incest certainly would not have been below them; they tackled with enthusiasm anything wicked.

However, Rick Lai, in his "*A Brief Biography of Dr. Caber (1883-1945?)*," persuasively theorizes that Irma was actually the daughter of Dr. Caber, making Carl Peterson Irma's uncle, and for our purposes we accept this theory as true.

It has been postulated elsewhere that the Drummond-Peterson battle continued to a new generation, with Hugh Drummond, Jr., battling Carl Peterson, Jr., as seen in the films *Deadlier Than the Male* and *Some Girls Do*.[175] Although I agree that the Hugh Drummond seen in *Deadlier Than the Male* and *Some Girls Do* is of a different character, and thus must be Hugh, Jr., I still maintain Hugh, Sr., and wife Phyllis did have access to the immortality treatment. They most probably went underground, changing their identities in order to conceal their rather unnatural longevity.

The Carl Peterson seen in *Deadlier Than the Male* and *Some Girls Do* was also a junior. And he was the son of Irma Peterson, giving him the rather dubious distinction of having the same father and great-uncle.

Turning our attention back to Carl Peterson's and Dr. Caber's mother, Urania Moriarty, we find that during the latter part of 1918 and well into the year 1919, she, as Patricia Donleavy, gave Sherlock Holmes and his student, Mary Russell, quite a run for their money before her death.[176]

And now we shall deal with the first Professor Moriarty's other surviving children, "Wolf Larsen" and "Death Larsen." Wolf Larsen was born in 1858, as established in Farmer's *Escape from Loki*, and Larsen's other identity as Baron Karl von Hessel has been well documented elsewhere.[177] The twin relationship between Wolf and Death is my own conjecture, although they are described as brothers in Jack London's *The Sea Wolf*. Thus, I theorize that Death Larsen was also born in 1858.

Death Larsen had a daughter, Lorelei Larsen. Lorelei's mother was Zarmi of the Hashishin. Lorelei was the mistress of Emmanuel Dumas. They had a daughter, Lola Dumas. Both Emmanuel and Lola Dumas were seen in Sax Rohmer's *President Fu Manchu*. Lorelei then became the priestess of a sinister octopus cult and married a Si-Fan leader, Fo-Hi.[178] Lorelei Larsen and Fo-Hi had a daughter, Zarmi. Zarmi was also known by the nickname Lo Lar. Zarmi apparently was killed, as related by Dr. Petrie in *The Hand of Fu Manchu*. However, it has been demonstrated that she actually survived. As Lo Lar, she later came in to conflict with her cousin, Doc Savage, as related in Lester Dent's *The Feathered Octopus*.[179]

Meanwhile, as Mr. Farmer has demonstrated in *Doc Savage: His Apocalyptic Life*, in 1884 Wolf Larsen married and then deserted Arronaxe Land, the daughter of Ned Land from Jules Verne's *Twenty Thousand Leagues under the Sea*. A daughter, Arronaxe Larsen, was born in 1885. At a very young age Arronaxe Larsen married James Clarke Wildman, Sr. (aka Clark Savage, Sr.), the illegitimate son of the sixth Duke of Greystoke. Their son, Clark Savage, Jr., was born on November 12, 1901. Thus, Doc Savage is the grandson of the notorious Wolf Larsen and the great-grandson of the infamously evil Professor Moriarty.

Wold Larsen, during the despicable events that occurred in 1893 and recounted by Jack London in *The Sea Wolf*, begat another child, Mister Moto. Moto was born in 1894 and his adventures were told by

John P. Marquand.

Doc Savage and Mister Moto are certainly aberrations in the annals of the incredible Moriarty lineage. As Farmer said, "Every family barrel has its rotten apples."

The Moriarty influence reasserted itself with the April 1919 birth of the man known as "John Sunlight." As demonstrated by the following entry from the *Crossover Chronology*, Sunlight could have been the son of Clark Savage, Jr., and Lily Bugov, the Countess Idivzhopu:[180]

> April 1919—Nine months after Doc Savage's escape from the prison camp Loki, a child is born to Lily Bugov, the Countess Idivzhopu. The child is raised as the son of Baron Karl von Hessel (Doc's grandfather, who will go by the moniker Baron Karl by the time of the Doc Savage novel *Fortress of Solitude*). However, given young Clark Savage's intimate encounter with the Countess Idivzhopu in July 1918, there can be little doubt as to the *true* parentage of this child, who will grow up to menace the world, not to mention his own hated father, as "John Sunlight."
>
> Wold Newton researcher Christopher Carey, in his article "The Green Eyes Have It - Or Are They Blue? or Another Case of Identity Recased," gathers and documents an incredible amount of evidence about the Countess, von Hessel, and Doc's arch-enemy "John Sunlight." Mr. Carey concludes that John Sunlight is either Lily Bugov posing as a man, or that she underwent a sex-change operation to become Sunlight. Mr. Carey evocatively points out both Bugov's and Sunlight's unusually long fingers. Keeping in mind all the physical similarities between Bugov and Sunlight that Mr. Carey documents, as well as the behavioral differences, I am lead to a different conclusion. I believe Sunlight is Lily Bugov's son.
>
> However, if Sunlight were born in April of 1919, he would be only eighteen years old in August

of 1937 (*Fortress of Solitude*). This could pose a problem, in terms of his believability as a villain. On the other hand, Baron von Hessel / Baron Karl has been mentoring him in the ways of evil for those eighteen years. And Doc made a believable hero at age sixteen, just as many other Wold Newtonites started their careers early in life. There is a statement that, "He was not a young man...," but I believe this to be blatant misdirection on Lester Dent's part, in order to help Doc conceal the terrible secret of Sunlight's parentage. In short, Sunlight's age is not an insurmountable issue. (It is interesting to note that, based on textual evidence in *Fortress of Solitude*, Sunlight escaped from the Siberian gulag at approximately age sixteen or seventeen – the same age at which his father escaped from a similar inescapable prison camp.)

Further, I do not believe that Farmer would have noted the sexual encounter between Clark and Lily without reason. Sunlight, like Doc, emits a strange sound in times of excitement or stress, although Sunlight's takes the form of a low, evil growl, rather than Doc's cool, exotic trilling. Sunlight's inhuman strength, derived from unspecified sources, and his incredible stamina and will power, a result of his magnificent brain, are extensively described in *Fortress of Solitude*. The derivation of Sunlight's formidable intelligence is easily understood once it is revealed that he is of the Moriarty lineage, as well as that of the Savages-Claytons. In my estimation, the physical similarities between Countess Idivzhopu and Sunlight, coupled with Sunlight's Savage-like strength, vocal habits, and brain power, undoubtedly point to a familial relationship, one made possible by Doc's indiscretion with the Countess.

As has been demonstrated elsewhere,[181] Sunlight could have been the son of Clark Savage, Jr., and Lily Bugov, the Countess Idivzhopu. Further research indicates that Lily Bugov was the granddaughter of Sir William Clayton and Sir William's wife, a Russian woman named Natalie, daughter of the Prince of Kiev, who disappeared shortly after their wedding in 1855. Given the double influx of the foul Wold Newton genes, it was inevitable that John Sunlight, the great-great-grandson of the first Professor Moriarty, and the great-grandson of Sir William Clayton (who, after all, had also spawned the insidious Doctor Fu Manchu), would embark upon a career as a super-criminal. Of course, it also helped that John Sunlight was raised by his rather wicked grandfather, Baron Karl von Hessel (Wolf Larsen).

What was Von Hessel doing between the mid-1890s, when he abandoned the Larsen identity, and 1918, when he encountered his grandson Clark Savage at Camp Loki? We can only speculate. However, he does seem to have some connection with Russia, as shown by his close relationship with the Russian woman, Lily Bugov. After the events of *Escape from Loki*, when he became persona–non grata with the German High Command, it seems likely that he escaped to Russia. This is evidenced by the fact that when we first meet Von Hessel's grandson, John Sunlight, he is being sentenced in Russia to a Siberian prison camp, for unspecified crimes.[182]

Based on Von Hessel's Russian connections, and based on extensive research in the files of MI6, it has been determined that Larsen/Von Hessel spent the first decade of the 20th century living under a Polish identity. Poland, at the time, was under Russian control, and remained so up to the end of World War I. During his time in Poland, Von Hessel met a Greek woman and, following pattern, married her. This Greek woman also brought the notoriously contaminated genes of Sir William Clayton to the table: she was the granddaughter of Aspasia Clayton, who was the daughter of Sir William and Ermione Khatamagos.

Their child was born in Gdynia on May 28, 1908. By World War II, he was selling information to the Germans, Swedes, and Americans. After the war, with half a million in Swiss banks, he disappeared to South America. He reappeared in 1959, and the world's intelligence communities first heard of SPECTRE, The Special Executive for Counterintelligence, Terrorism, Revenge, and Extortion. It was not until a while later that intelligence services learned the identity of SPECTRE's leader, Ernst Stavro Blofeld.

British Double-0 agent James Bond foiled Blofeld's plans on several occasions. The first was related by Ian Fleming under the title

Thunderball. When Blofeld and Bond crossed swords again, in late 1961, Blofeld ruthlessly murdered Bond's wife, Tracy, as told in Ian Fleming's *On Her Majesty's Secret Service*. In 1963, Bond finally tracked Blofeld down in Japan, where Blofeld was hiding under the name Doctor Shatterhand. The story of this final encounter was revealed in Fleming's *You Only Live Twice*.

However, the legacy of Blofeld and SPECTRE lived on. From the late 1960s until the mid-1970s, a woman known as Madam Spectra was controlling SPECTRE.[183] It seemed that James Bond had smashed the organization once and for all, but in 1981 it reared its head again. And Blofeld was once again in charge of SPECTRE.

It turns out that Ernst Stavro Blofeld had a daughter, who was born with a particular deformity: she had only one breast, as told in John Gardner's *For Special Services*. Though she went by the name Nena Bismaquer, she was really Nena Blofeld. She was truly her father's daughter, as well as the great-granddaughter of the first Professor James Moriarty.

Professor James Robert Moriarty did have one other child, who was born in 1881. James Ian Moriarty was a genius mathematician like his father. In 1907 he was using the name Ian Murdoch and serving as a Mathematics coach at The Gables, when he had a run-in with Sherlock Holmes.[184] Thereafter, he moved to America, adopted the name of James Murdock, and had twin sons. In 1921 he became an agent of the Nine, operating under the alias of James Murtagh, as told in *Lord of the Trees* by James Cloamby, Lord Grandrith, edited by Philip José Farmer.[185]

The first twin son of James Murdock/Murtagh had one son named Hamish M. Murdock (b. 1947). "H.M.," as he preferred to be called, served in Vietnam, where his fearlessness in a helicopter earned him the nickname of "Howling Mad" Murdock. Later, Murdock was the helicopter pilot for a bank raid by a commando unit known as the A-Team. Intriguingly, the leader of the A-Team, John "Hannibal" Smith, is the great-nephew of Sherlock Holmes[186] making this perhaps the first time that a member of the Holmes family and a member of the Moriarty family worked together.

The second twin had two children, a boy born in 1948 and a girl, Ashton, born nearly ten years later. In 1960, this man, his wife, and their daughter Ashton were in a car crash. The parents were killed and Ashton was adopted by a couple named Cooke. The boy was taken into the care of Nicolas Hellman, a director of Homicide International Trust (HIT), and became known only by his surname, "Murdoc." (HIT was possibly related to the earlier Moriarty criminal organization or one of its offshoots, such as Krafthaus or THRUSH. Perhaps the auto accident was not so accidental after all.) In any event, Murdoc became one of HIT's best assassins and was a master of disguise. But in 1980 he failed on a mission for the first time. Appropriately enough, the man who stopped him, Angus MacGyver, was related to Sherlock Holmes, thus bringing the feud to a new generation. MacGyver and Murdoc faced off against each other several times, but neither ever succeeded in stopping the other.[187]

Three Brothers Moriarty

We now turn to the third James Moriarty, who adopted the identity of his older brother and became the second Professor Moriarty in the 1890s. In 1876, James Noel Moriarty started working as an assistant to his brother, the first Professor. He became involved with Katherine Koluchy in the mid 1880s. Koluchy had already begun her evil activities in 1884, as told in *The Brotherhood of Seven Kings* by L.T. Meade and Robert Eustace. In 1886, Dominick "Medina," the son of James Noel Moriarty and Kathryn Koluchy was born.[188]

James Noel Moriarty took over as the second Professor Moriarty in 1894. He was responsible for directing the infrastructure of his "late" brother's vast criminal empire toward the creation of the Circle of Life cult, contacting Martian Sarmaks residing in a parallel dimension, and attempting to bring Martian destruction to the parallel Earth called Annwn, as recounted in George Smith's *The Second War of the Worlds*.

The second Professor Moriarty's humiliating defeat in that incident lead to the metamorphosis of the Circle of Life into the Krafthaus organization, a "secret nation" bent on world domination. In 1903, Moriarty created a new, respectable identity for himself, Andrew Lumley. When Edward Leithen inadvertently stumbled upon Krafthaus in 1910, and Moriarty's exposure was inevitable, Moriarty/Lumley killed himself.[189] The Krafthaus organization lived on as the super-criminal empire THRUSH; however, with the death of Moriarty/Lumley, there was a leadership vacuum in THRUSH.[190]

In 1897, Koluchy had been blinded in a fire and became known as "the Blind Spinner." In the years following Moriarty/Lumley's death, the Blind Spinner and her son, Dominick Medina/Moriarty, had a very tenuous grip on the reins of THRUSH. This was compounded by the fact that during 1914-18, Medina was in Central Asia studying mesmerism.[191] In an effort to strengthen their power base and reaffirm their leadership role, the Blind Spinner communicated with her son, instructing him to travel to China in order to court the leaders of the Si-Fan for the purpose of forging an alliance. This occurred in mid-1914, shortly after the final events of *The Hand of Fu Manchu.* While it represented the first time that the powers-that-be of THRUSH attempted to win the favor of Doctor Fu Manchu, it was not to be the last.[192]

Fu Manchu had no intention of forging an alliance with this upstart Western criminal organization, and in any event was too busy attempting to maintain his own power base.[193] He gave Dominick over to his daughter, Fah Lo Suee, the Lady of the Si-Fan, for disposal. However, Fah Lo Suee, in what was perhaps the first of many betrayals of her honoured father, took an immediate interest in Dominick and proceeded to seduce him rather than dispose of him. Fortunately for Fah Lo Suee, her father did not learn of this particular indiscretion and the resulting child was placed with an "aunt" in Pekin. Later on, Fah Lo Suee did have further offspring, as will be seen presently in this article.

The child of Dominick Medina/Moriarty and Fah Lo Suee was born in 1915. She was the granddaughter of the second Professor Moriarty and the granddaughter of Fu Manchu. She was later known by the name "Myra Reldon." The name "Myra" is from a Latin derivation and means "scented oil," which is interesting considering that Fah Lo Suee's name is supposed to mean "sweet perfume."

Myra Reldon, also known as "Ming Dwan," was first encountered Walter Gibson's novel *Teeth of the Dragon*. The Shadow encountered her in San Francisco and did not know for whom she was working, although it later was revealed that she was working for the FBI under the guidance of Vic Marquette. How Myra Reldon came to be recruited as a Special Agent for the FBI, and the details of her assignments in different parts of the country (mostly in the Chinatown areas of San Francisco and New York), is a story that has yet to be told.

Meanwhile, Dominick Medina/Moriarty had escaped from China with Fah Lo Suee's help, and eventually went back to England—and THRUSH—empty-handed. He and his mother were overthrown in a coup, but managed to escape with their lives. In 1921, Medina/Moriarty and his mother resurfaced with a plan to make Medina the Prime Minister of Great Britain. Sir Richard Hannay defeated the plans of Dominick Medina and his mother, and Medina was killed at the end of this adventure.[194] However, before his death, Dominick Medina/Moriarty had at least two more sons. The identity of their mother is currently unknown.

The first son also had a son, named Edgar Moriarty. The second son of Dominick Medina/Moriarty had a son named Thomas. Edgar Moriarty inherited his family's evil tendencies, whereas his cousin Thomas seemed relatively undistinguished. Edgar was killed in late 1986, while attempting to recreate one of the schemes of his illustrious great-granduncle, the first Professor Moriarty. (However, Edgar seemed to be somewhat confused and thought that the first Professor, James Robert Moriarty, was his great-grandfather rather than his great-granduncle.) Thomas Moriarty married Mary Watson, a great-granddaughter of Doctor John Watson[195] and Nylepthah, who in turn was the daughter of Sir Henry Curtis.[196]

Part II: The Dynasty of Fu Manchu

Among the various Wold Newton articles which focus on Sax Rohmer's Oriental mastermind Fu Manchu, due attention has been paid to the Devil Doctor's ancestry and descendants.[197] Less attention has been focused upon the other rich characters that populate the universe of Fu Manchu novels, stories, and comics. While the research presented here hopefully rectifies this oversight, it nevertheless also reveals a bit more about the family of the Devil Doctor himself.

The Smiths

Fu Manchu's primary nemesis for over seventy years (from 1911 to 1982) was Sir Denis Nayland Smith. In *Tarzan Alive*, Philip José Farmer proposed that Nayland Smith (b. 1883) was the nephew of the famed detective, Sherlock Holmes of Baker Street. Smith's mother was Sigrina Holmes, an older sister of Sherlock. However, Mr. Farmer never identified Nayland Smith's father. A likely candidate is John Vansittart Smith, F.R.S., seen in Arthur Conan Doyle's "The Ring of Thoth."[198]

Vansittart Smith was a man who excelled in many areas, such as zoology, botany, and chemistry, before finally settling on Egyptology. In October of 1889, while conducting research at the Louvre in Paris, Smith had a very strange experience. He encountered an Egyptian called Sosra, who claimed to be 3,600 years old. This man, whose father had been the chief priest of Osiris in the temple of Abaris, had discovered a chemical mixture which conferred immortality. Unfortunately, the great love of Sosra's life died of a plague before Sosra could administer the elixir to her. The elixir acted in such a way that Sosra could not die, even if he attempted suicide. Thus, he was condemned to near-immortality until the elixir wore off, or until he could find the antidote to the elixir concealed in the Ring of Thoth.

"The Ring of Thoth" also mentions that, at the time of the events, Vansittart Smith was a married man, and that his wife was "an Egyptological young lady who had written upon the sixth dynasty." I can find nothing in Mr. Farmer's work to indicate that Sigrina Holmes was not an Egyptologist in her own right. As the editor of numerous case files regarding Sigrina's brother, Sherlock Holmes, Arthur Conan Doyle must have been pleased at the synchronicity which brought the events of "The Ring of Thoth" to his attention and allowed him a further view into the detective's family background. However, Doyle respected the Great Detective's wish for privacy and did not identify the "Egyptological young lady" as Sigrina Smith, née Holmes, in the story.

Nayland Smith was also quite well versed in Egyptological matters, and we may surmise that he learned a great deal from his parents, and his uncle, as will be seen below. Nayland Smith also met a man obsessed with immortality, although Fu Manchu's elixir of life never worked quite as well as the one described in "The Ring of Thoth" and required repeated doses. It is probable that growing up on his father's accounts of Sosra gave Nayland Smith the open mind and worldview required to recognize and counter Fu Manchu's fantastic schemes.

Sir Arthur Conan Doyle also chronicled stories involving other members of the Smith family. As Rick Lai has pointed out in "The Savage Reversion" section of his *The Complete Chronology of Bronze*,[199] Doyle's and Watson's "The Adventure of the Dying Detective," collected in *His Last Bow*, concerned Sherlock Holmes' investigation of the murder of Victor Savage by Victor's uncle, Culverton Smith. William S. Baring-Gould's *Sherlock Holmes of Baker Street* places this case in November 1887. Rick Lai proposes that Smith murdered Victor Savage in order to gain access to the Frankenstein notebooks, as part of the reversion described by Watson.[200]

Culverton Smith had three sons: the aforementioned John Vansittart Smith, Francis Smith, and Abercrombie Everett Smith. It is possible that they spent at least a portion of their childhoods in Sumatra, where Culverton Smith had a plantation and became an amateur expert in Far Eastern diseases. Fortunately the three sons did not take after their father. It should also be noted that John Vansittart Smith's mother (Culverton Smith's wife) was the sister of the John Vansittart who drowned at sea in 1872, as told in Sir Arthur Conan Doyle's "De

Profundis."[201] According to the tale, "John Vansittart was the younger partner of the firm of Hudson and Vansittart, coffee exporters of the Island of Ceylon, three-quarters Dutchman by descent, but wholly English in his sympathies."

Arthur Conan Doyle told the tale of Abercrombie Smith in "Lot No. 249."[202] Denis Nayland Smith clearly spent a good deal of time with his uncle, Abercrombie Smith, with whom he shared more than a few character traits, such as smoking a briar-root pipe and their clipped manner of speaking. While it would be possible to identify Abercrombie Smith as the father of Nayland Smith (b. 1883), there is nothing in the text of "Lot No. 249," which takes place in May of 1884, to indicate that Abercrombie Smith is married or has a child at the time. Indeed, he is described as a bachelor, although that could refer to his residential status at University. Abercrombie Smith is in his freshman year at Oxford as a medical student, although he has studied four years previously at Glasgow and at Berlin. It is probable that a man such as Abercrombie Smith, who was so focused upon his medical studies, would defer marriage and fatherhood until those studies were completed and his practice established.

Thus, between Vansittart Smith and Abercrombie Smith, Vansittart is the more likely candidate for identification as Nayland Smith's father. In any event, children often take after their uncles or aunts, thus explaining some characteristics which Nayland Smith shares with his uncle. And Uncle Abercrombie surely would have regaled young Nayland Smith with the brave tale of his defeat of the evil Edward Bellingham and the 4,000 year-old mummy which was at Bellingham's command.

In 1889, Abercrombie Everett Smith immigrated to America and set up his practice in Athens, Ohio. He married Elsie Wheeler and their son Henry was born on April 13, 1892. Henry Smith was a small, dapper, but rather colorless man who started as an office boy with the Phalanx Insurance Company in Cincinnati in 1910. He eventually worked his way up to investigator for the company, and displayed remarkable powers of observation and deduction similar to those of his great-uncle, Sherlock Holmes. Six of his cases were documented by Fredric Brown in the 1940s.[203]

Nayland Smith's other uncle, Francis Smith, is described in "Lot No. 249" as an elder brother of Abercrombie Smith. Further research indicates that Francis Smith had three sons: Aurelius Smith, James Ebenezer Smith, and T.B. Smith.

Although Aurelius Smith, aka "Secret Service Smith," is described as an American Secret Service agent, he could have easily been a British national. He was extremely well travelled, working in India, in Britain for the Criminal Intelligence Department (CID), and in Paris. In pulp tales told by R.T.M. Scott through the 1910s and 1920s, it was revealed that he finally settled as an amateur criminologist in New York City.

James Ebenezer Smith fell under a dark cloud in his younger years and became estranged from his family. Despite the adversity he experienced as a young man, he eventually made his fortune and, following in his forebears' footsteps, became an ardent Egyptologist. His strange experience in the Cairo Museum was told by H. Rider Haggard in "Smith and the Pharaohs."[204]

T.B. Smith went on to become a high official with Scotland Yard. His exploits were publicized by Edgar Wallace in *The Nine Bears* (1910), *The Secret House* (1917), and *Kate Plus Ten* (1919), as well as one of the short stories in *The Admirable Carfew* (1914).

Although Mr. Farmer does not explicitly identify any of Sir Denis Nayland Smith's siblings, he must have been one of three children. As revealed in Dr. Petrie's *Ten Years Beyond Baker Street* (edited by Cay Van Ash), Nayland Smith had a brother, probably born in 1884 or 1885. Whereas Nayland was lanky and lean, like his uncle Sherlock, Nayland's brother took after the stockier, more heavyset Holmes line, such as Mycroft Holmes and Nero Wolfe. *Ten Years Beyond Baker Street* also reveals that Nayland Smith's brother was thought killed in the *Titanic* tragedy. Research indicates that in fact he survived and had his own reasons for failing to inform his family. He started a new life in America, but Smith was a sufficiently generic name that he may not have felt compelled to change it.

The call of crime detection was in this man's blood. Although one of his cases was first recorded by Dashiell Hammett in 1923, "The Whosis Kid" describes him as starting with the Continental Detective Agency in 1917. However, the story "This King Business" mentions that he was an American intelligence officer in the Army during the Great War. Arriving in America in 1912, he would have become eligible for citizenship in 1917. He must have joined the Continental Detective Agency in 1917, and then left briefly to serve in the American army during 1917-18.

The Continental Detective Agency imposed a condition upon Dashiell Hammett in return for allowing publication of Smith's cases: Smith's identity must not be revealed in the tales. Of course Hammett agreed, but found the whole notion of being forced to conceal the true identity of a man with the rather nondescript name of "Smith" highly amusing. He responded by declining to identify his hero by any given name. Hammett called his man "the Continental Op." It is possible that the Continental Op, after retiring from the Continental Detective Agency, took the name of "Brad Runyon" and set up his own private detective agency.

The Op's son, Algernon Heathcote Smith, was born in 1914. Like his father, in size and girth he took after the large, stocky members of the Holmes lineage, such as his great-uncle Mycroft and his cousin Nero Wolfe. At age twenty-two he graduated from Massachusetts Tech with a degree in electrical engineering. However, he was framed shortly thereafter for the disappearance of $8,000 worth of platinum from the lab in which he was employed. He spent a year in prison. Upon his release, the gigantic "Smitty" could only get employment as a chauffer. In 1938, he met up with Richard Henry Benson (aka The Avenger), and joined him in a life of adventure as a member of Justice, Inc.[205] Smitty probably eventually married fellow Justice, Inc. member Nellie Gray, aka Penelope Alice Clayton, the daughter of Lord Greystoke.[206]

Denis Nayland Smith also had a sister. In the pages of the comic book series, *The Hands of Shang Chi, Master of Kung Fu*, it is revealed that Smith had a nephew called Lancaster Sneed. Sneed would also be the great-nephew of Sherlock Holmes. We must presume that Nayland Smith had a much younger sister—let us call her Violet Smith—who married a man named Sneed. Sigrina Smith would still be of childbearing age in the late 1890s, although just barely. If Violet Smith was born in the late 1890s, her son could have been born in 1945, putting him in his thirties during the mid-1970s events depicted in *Master of Kung Fu*. Lancaster Sneed originally followed his uncle's footsteps in working for the British Secret Service. However, after an accident unhinged his mind, he went freelance and adopted a new identity, calling himself "Shockwave."

Lancaster Sneed had a few cousins, the children of Denis Nayland Smith. Sometime before his first chronicled adventure, *The Insidious Dr. Fu Manchu*, Nayland Smith had two children. He probably met his wife, Joan Blakeney, in England before his first posting to Egypt in approximately 1903. Joan Blakeney was the great-great-granddaughter of Sir Percy Blakeney, the Scarlet Pimpernel. Her mother, Joan Fielding, was a descendant of the Hornblower line.

The two sons of Nayland and Joan Smith were likely born in Egypt sometime between 1903 and 1907, but their mother must have died well before the 1911 events of *The Insidious Dr. Fu Manchu*. The children were probably sent to live with family members, either their grandparents Vansittart and Sigrina Smith, or perhaps their great-uncle Francis. They also could have been raised by their grandmother, Joan Fielding.

One son, Horatio Smith, was an archaeology professor at Cambridge who emulated the exploits of his illustrious ancestor, the Scarlet Pimpernel. He used his digs, under cover of seeking evidence of an ancient Aryan civilization, to enter Nazi Germany and help dissident scientists, journalists, artists, and others escape.

Professor Horatio Smith's story was told in the 1941 film *Pimpernel Smith*,[207] covering a period from spring to September 1, 1939. Despite the fact that neither Sir Percy Blakeney nor the Scarlet Pimpernel was ever mentioned in the movie, there is the obvious allusion of the film's title. Horatio Smith was also in line to inherit a title. Horatio's older brother, Sir George Smith, was the British ambassador in Berlin. It is likely that Sir George was knighted for the performance of some service, in addition to being an heir. If he was actually titled at the time of the film's events, that means that his uncle, John Blakeney (b. 1893), great-uncle, Peter Blakeney (b. 1863), and his distant cousin, Peter Blakeney (b. 1891), would all have pre-deceased him.[208] This is possible, but unknown.

Horatio Smith displayed many characteristics which demonstrate his worthiness of inclusion among the Smiths and Blakeneys. He managed to outwit the Gestapo at every turn, and showed great courage, even remaining completely silent and motionless after being wounded by a rifle. He had great physical endurance, had a natural capacity for melting into the landscape, and pulled off his dual-identity scheme faultlessly. He ultimately rescued twenty-eight people. Upon his escape from Germany, on the night before the Nazi invasion of Poland, he left his nemesis, General von Graum, with these words: "Don't worry, I shall be back. We shall *all* be back."

According to fellow Wold Newton researcher Brad Mengel, in "Watching the Detectives, Or, The Sherlock Holmes Family Tree," Sir Denis Nayland Smith had another son, John "Hannibal" Smith, who was born almost thirty years after his half-brothers Horatio and George. In the early 1980s, Hannibal Smith was the leader of the A-Team and displayed a flair for disguise, as did his father and other members of the Holmes line. As might be expected, Hannibal Smith bore some resemblance to his distant cousin, Archie Goodwin.[209]

What Mr. Mengel does not mention is the identity of Hannibal's mother. In Sax Rohmer's *The Trail of Fu Manchu*, which takes place in January 1933, it is strongly implied that the daughter of Fu Manchu, Fah Lo Suee, had an intimate encounter with Nayland Smith, for whom she professed her love. A child would have been born in October 1933. The child's existence almost certainly would have been kept secret from Fu Manchu. Fah Lo Suee was presumed killed in this adventure, but we know she was not from her later appearances in the Fu Manchu series. Fah Lo Suee survived, went into hiding, and after her child's birth, she turned the child over to Nayland Smith to be raised. Hannibal Smith was raised by Nayland Smith's relatives for two reasons: Smith himself was too busy tracking Fu Manchu to raise a child, and the child had to be kept secret from Fu Manchu.

At this point it is worth a brief digression to discuss the parentage of Fah Lo Suee, as established by researcher Rick Lai. Fah Lo Suee was the daughter of Fu Manchu and an unnamed Russian woman, as told in Rohmer's *The Daughter of Fu Manchu*. Rick Lai postulates that the unnamed Russian woman was also the mother of Madame de Medici, making Fah Lo Suee (b. 1897) and Madame de Medici (b. 1883) half-sisters. Madame de Medici, whose father was Fo-Hi from Sax Rohmer's *The Golden Scorpion,* was featured in Rohmer's "The Key to the Temple of Heaven" in *Tales of Chinatown* and "The Black Mandarin" in *Tales of East and West*.[210] Mr. Lai further posits that the "unnamed Russian woman" was Princess Sonia Omanoff. Princess Sonia was also the mother of Talbot Mundy's Yasmini of India, and the grandmother of Doctor Julius No.

Returning to the Smiths, John "Hannibal" Smith had a daughter, named Leiko, who was born in the mid-1950s. Leiko's mother was probably Chinese. Apparently John and Leiko's mother divorced, or else Leiko's mother fled to her native country. In any event, Leiko grew up in poverty and suffered at the hands of an abusive step-father. The tales of Leiko Smith, also known as the "Black Lotus," were told in the *Mike Shayne Mystery Magazine* in the early 1980s.[211] The first story was "The Black Lotus."

In second story, "Death From the Sky," Leiko makes several references to her grandfather, speaking of him as a great man who cast his shadow over the entire East and who might have ruled the world. It is also revealed that she may have been born "Leiko Gordon." If so, this could tie in with Matthew Baugh's identification of Nayland Smith with Robert E. Howard's "John Gordon,"[212] under the theory that many pulp writers refer to their subjects by various "code names."

In her third and final appearance, in "Doomsday Island," the Black

Lotus reveals that she survived a lethal radiation exposure because her blood is special. She also tells Mike Shayne that she thought her grandfather was dead, but that they have found each other again. The three Black Lotus stories, which take place during 1980 and 1981, strongly imply that Leiko Smith is the granddaughter of Fu Manchu. The Smith name is also telling. A further connection is the reference by British detective Solar Pons to Fu Manchu as "the insidious mastermind of the Si-Fan and the Brotherhood of the Lotus."[213] Of course, in this genealogical reconstruction, it is evident that Fu Manchu is really her great-grandfather, but it is not unlikely that in the course of normal speech, this would be shortened to "grandfather."

The first Mike Shayne novel by Brett Halliday (a pseudonym for Davis Dresser), *Dividend on Death*, appeared in 1939.[214] The last Shayne story was published in 1985. The 1939-1985 stories may really cover the cases of Mike Shayne and Mike Shayne, Jr. Red-haired Miami private investigator Mike Shayne was married in the very early novels; his wife Phyllis died giving birth to their son, Mike Jr. After his wife's death, Mike Sr. acquired a secretary sidekick, Lucy Hamilton, who continued to appear into the 1980s stories. However, Mike Shayne, Jr. probably had his own secretary, and the use of the Lucy Hamilton character was just a fictionalization to continue the premise that there was only one Mike Shayne.

It is hard to say that Mike Shayne, Jr. and the Black Lotus were in love, although she did love him in her own way. She made sure that he never came to permanent harm. They even made love once. However, this was in the first story, "The Black Lotus," which took place in 1980. If a pregnancy resulted from this encounter, it is not discernible in their subsequent meetings. Nevertheless, any child of this union would be coming of age at the time of this writing.

Finally, returning to Leiko Smith's grandfather, Nayland Smith, it is interesting to note that he shares a characteristic with British detective Solar Pons, namely, the habit of tugging on the left earlobe in times of stress or deep thought. Brad Mengel proposes that Nayland Smith and Solar Pons are distant cousins, related through Pons' mother, Roberta McIvor, a descendant of the Holmes line.[215] It is significant that Solar Pons would also cross swords with Dr. Fu Manchu, although not to the same degree that Smith did.

The Grevilles

This was not the first instance that Fah Lo Suee found herself pregnant and in the position of concealing the child's existence from her father.

Her first child was born in 1915. Her daughter did not follow in her mother's footsteps; instead, she took a much different path and was eventually known as Ming Dwan, aka Myra Reldon.

The other instance was in 1930, when the child of Shan Greville and Fah Lo Suee was conceived, as implied in *The Mask of Fu Manchu*. In 1931 a child was born of that union. Fu Manchu, given Fah Lo Suee's constant betrayals, felt that her blood was tainted, and wanted nothing to do with his grandchild.

What happened to the child is unknown, except that he was a former bishop turned high-tech entrepreneur.[216] However, this may be an exaggeration. In any event, we do know that he was the Asian-Anglo father of the man identified as "John Rossi." (We know that this man is Asian-Anglo because Fu Manchu himself is only half Chinese, therefore his daughter, born of a Russian woman, is only one-quarter Chinese.) We may speculate that he was placed in an orphanage in Hong Kong and grew up there, perhaps the very same orphanage in which his son, the second man to call himself The Saint (b. 1964), would later grow up.

Robert Greville was the son of Shan Greville and Rima Barton.[217] He appeared in *The Hands of Shang Chi, Master of Kung Fu* comic series from Marvel Comics, but was quickly dispatched by Fah Lo Suee in an adventure which took place in the mid-1970s. (Obviously, despite the earlier intimate encounter between Shan and Fah, or perhaps because of it, there was no love lost between Fah Lo Suee and the Grevilles.) Rima Barton was the niece of Sir Lionel Barton, a central figure in the Fu Manchu novels.

According to the *Master of Kung Fu* series, Melissa Greville was the niece of Shan Greville. Melissa's mother was married to Shan's younger brother, Bertram Greville. Melissa's mother also knew Clive Reston's father, James Bond. What is more, it is implied that the knowledge was carnal.[218] This begs the question: who was Shan's sister-in-law (Melissa's mother)? Or, to put it another way, which "Bond girl" married Bertram Greville after a liaison with Bond?

Melissa Greville was in her mid-twenties in 1977, making her year of birth somewhere in the early to mid-1950s. There are several likely candidates for Melissa's mother from this time period. Tiffany Case, from *Diamonds Are Forever*, is a possibility. Ian Fleming's *From Russia, With Love*, reveals only that Tiffany sailed for America after the end of her relationship with Bond. John Pearson's *James Bond: The Authorized Biography of 007* expands on this, imparting that she married an American military man named Nick.

From Russia, With Love's Tatiana Romanova is another possibility. However, in *Master of Kung Fu* n108, it is divulged that Romanova is the mother of "Dark Angel," a Russian spy who has just defected to the West. It is unlikely that Tatiana Romanova is also the mother of Melissa Greville. *Moonraker*'s Gala Brand can be eliminated due to the fact that she was set to marry a Detective-Inspector Vivian. We may exclude *Doctor No*'s Honeychile Rider on the basis that Pearson's biography tells us that she married a rich man named Schultz.

Of course, perhaps Melissa's mother was one of the many women Bond courted, but who was not revealed in one of Fleming's semi-biographical novels. However, one possibility does remain, *Live and Let Die*'s Solitaire. *Live and Let Die* takes place in January and February 1952. Afterward, Solitaire is not heard from again. It is certainly conceivable that after she met Bond, she met Bertram Greville and married him. Solitaire could have had a daughter, Melissa, by 1954, which would make Melissa twenty-three in 1977, certainly well within Melissa's age as portrayed in *Master of Kung Fu*. It should be noted that Melissa Greville also had a younger sister, Mandy.

The Petries

One of the sons of William Petrie and Margaret Mitten, William Petrie, Jr., married Anne Flinders, daughter of Ann Chappell and Captain Matthew Flinders, the explorer and cartographer of Australia. Their child, William Matthew Flinders Petrie, was born on June 3, 1853.

Sir William Matthew Flinders Petrie (1853-1942), the celebrated Egyptologist who has been called "the father of modern archaeology," was the father of Dr. Petrie, Nayland Smith's closest compatriot and the narrator of the first several Fu Manchu novels.[219] However, Dr. Petrie's mother was not Hilda Mary Urwin, later Lady Hilda Petrie. Dr. Petrie was born in Egypt in 1884, when his father was excavating at Tanis. Hilda Petrie, the wife of Sir Flinders, was born in 1871. She would be too young for Dr. Petrie's birth date of 1884. Sir Flinders must have been previously married to a woman who died in childbirth.

Although never revealed in the Fu Manchu books, research indicates that Dr. Petrie's full name was Dexter Flinders Petrie, based on the possibility that "Dr." was an abbreviation for both "Doctor" and "Dexter," with the name "Flinders" coming from the theory that Dr. Petrie's father was the noted archaeologist.[220] Although Dexter Petrie flirted with Egyptology in his youth, he eventually went on to take his medical degree at Edinburgh.

An interesting mystery remains concerning Dexter's father, Sir

Flinders. After his death, he was buried in Jerusalem, or at least most of him was. His head was supposedly kept in a preserving jar at the London headquarters of the Royal College of Surgeons. However, the head in question looks remarkably like that of a younger man. The head has black hair, while Sir Flinders' hair at the time of his death was white. If this head is not Sir Flinders', then whose is it, and where is the head of Sir Flinders Petrie? Given Fu Manchu's penchant for faking the deaths of prominent scientists and then conscripting them into his service, as well as his ongoing interest in the Petrie family, one cannot help but wonder if the Devil Doctor was also involved in this mystery.

A Dr. Petrie (not Nayland Smith's cohort), an archaeologist at the Cairo Museum, was killed in the feature film *The Mummy's Hand*,[221] which researcher Chuck Loridans has dated to 1910. Could this be a relative of Sir Flinders Petrie? Although many biographers have stated that Sir Flinders was an only child, more recent research has uncovered the existence of Sir Flinders' younger brother, Major Thomas Flinders Petrie (b. 1864).[222] Although Major Petrie was a skilled engineer, it is possible that, later in life, he followed in his brother's footsteps as a professor of archaeology, meeting his untimely end in 1910.

Kâramanèh, the love of Dr. Petrie's life, was a young Arabic girl introduced in the first Fu Manchu novel, *The Insidious Dr. Fu Manchu*. She and her brother were the slaves of Fu Manchu. Fu Manchu held her brother in suspended animation, and she had to perform his nefarious deeds, because he held the antidote. She also, upon first sight, fell in love with Dr. Petrie. For the first several books, she would be rescued by Petrie and Smith, then be recaptured by Fu Manchu, and so on. Finally Petrie and Kara were married, and Fu Manchu seemed to leave them alone for a while. However, he did make it appear that their baby daughter had died. In fact, Fu Manchu had taken the baby and raised her as his own daughter. Fleurette Petrie (b. 1915) was finally reunited with her true parents many years later.

Dr. Petrie and Kâramanèh did have other children, although any mention of them was naturally suppressed in Sax Rohmer's Fu Manchu novels. Following in the family's footsteps, Louis Petrie also became a London-based archaeologist specializing in the occult, as seen in George Franju's Fantômas movie serial entitled *Shadowman*.[223] In the 1970s, Dr. Louis Petrie was enlisted to help trap Fantômas, but the plan failed and an irate Fantômas had Petrie murdered by one of his zombie-like killers.

Dr. Louis Petrie had one son, Henry Petrie, who must have

emigrated to America at a young age. In 1975, the Petries moved to a small town in Maine. Stephen King told the story of Henry's son Mark, a brave resourceful teenager, in the novel *'Salem's Lot*.

The other son of Dr. Dexter Petrie and Kâramanèh, Val Petrie, was born in 1929. Growing up on the stories of his father's exploits with Nayland Smith, Val was naturally drawn to law enforcement. By 1979 he was with Scotland Yard, in which year he had an adventure which involved Prince Zarkon and several other notables, including his "uncle" Nayland Smith.[224]

Returning to Fleurette Petrie, she and her husband, Alan Sterling, had one daughter, Fiona Sterling, who after her marriage was known as Fiona Jefferson.[225] However, they had at least one other child. Their second daughter eventually went into the archaeology and anthropology fields, like her great-grandfather, Sir Flinders Petrie. She was born on October 5, 1932 and was named Catherine. Catherine Sterling was a bit wild in her formative years, and formed a penchant for black leather suits and boots, powerful motorbikes, and judo.

Catherine did attempt to settle down and was briefly married; but it did not take. Her husband, a farmer in Kenya, was killed in the Mau Mau troubles, in which she learned to handle a gun with adroitness. She went on to earn a Ph.D. in anthropology, and fought in the hills of Cuba with Fidel Castro. However, after Castro achieved power, he deported her to Britain due to her opposition to some aspects of his government. Mrs. Catherine Gale took a position with the British Museum, and by 1961 she was "selected" by British agent John Steed to be his next regular partner.[226] After about two years, she apparently tired of Steed's brand of adventure. Following a short American holiday, she permanently returned to Africa. In 1968, Cathy Gale briefly rejoined Steed once more, along with his other talented amateur partners, and then was not heard from again.[227]

Jungle Brothers
or
Secrets of the Jungle Lords
By Dennis E. Power

In February of 1916 Sherlock Holmes and Dr. John H. Watson were summoned to a meeting with Mycroft Holmes and his aide Henry Merrivale. Merrivale would go on to have an important post in British Intelligence. He was also rather famous for solving mysteries in which he rivaled Sherlock Holmes in deductive abilities, as chronicled in the works of John Dickson Carr.

Mycroft briefed them about a new secret weapon that the Germans were trying to gain possession of, a formula for creating a bacillus that could be mutated to eat certain foodstuffs. If released on the British Isles it would cause demoralization and finally starvation. Holmes and Watson were requested by British Intelligence to travel to Egypt to track down and capture the German espionage agent Von Bork, who had the formula for the bacillus in his possession. Holmes and Watson had previously met and bested Von Bork in the adventure that Dr. Watson named "His Last Bow." Holmes and Watson were to travel to Marseilles and then on to Egypt. Holmes and Watson were informed that they were acquainted with the pilot who had been designated to fly them to France—John Drummond, the younger son of Hugh Drummond.[228] John Drummond was also the adopted son of the Duke of Greystoke, about whom many strange tales had been circulating. This led to a tangential discussion about Lord Greystoke, whose unconventional life was the basis for a trashy novel written by an American named Burroughs.[229] This discussion foreshadowed Holmes and Watson's encounter with Tarzan.

Drummond was injured and could not pilot them to France. Their substitute was a man named Wentworth, an American with a drinking problem. Their pilot suffered from either delirium tremens or some other psychological condition that caused him to hallucinate. Despite his hallucinatory state, his flying ability and his fighting skills were unimpaired. Although he believed German planes to be giant bats or flying cockroaches, he still managed to down those that attacked the plane carrying Holmes and Watson. Upon arriving in Marseilles, Wentworth was placed in a straight jacket until he dried out.[230]

The pilot assigned to fly Holmes and Watson from Marseilles to

Cairo was named Kentov. He was an American in service to the Tsar of the Russians, the French and Germans, all of whom referred to him as the Black Eagle.

Once they were underway, Kentov informed Holmes and Watson that a great storm was brewing and was threatening to blow them off course slightly. Also, intelligence had reported that a German Zeppelin was approaching Egypt, probably with the intention of picking up Von Bork.

Both the airplane carrying Holmes and Watson and the Zeppelin were blown far south. Kentov attacked the German Zeppelin, despite the raging storm that both were caught in. Kentov landed atop the Zeppelin, and he and his two passengers entered the gridwork of the Zeppelin's body, intending to sabotage it. The three men managed to do some damage to the dirigible. Rather than be captured, Kentov jumped off the dirigible. Watson claimed never to have heard what had happened to Kentov, but believed he had successfully parachuted to safety.[231] Holmes and Watson were captured by the Germans. Von Bork was indeed among German crew. Captain Victor Reich refused to follow Von Bork's suggestion that he shoot Holmes and Watson as spies and instead treated them as honored guests. Captain Victor Reich told Holmes and Watson that his orders were to travel to German East Africa, rendezvous with the forces of General Lettow-Vorbeck, and burn the dirigible. The badly-damaged dirigible limped into Africa but was so compromised that it never reached German East Africa, instead crash-landing in British East Africa. Holmes and Watson slipped away from the Germans and became lost in the African wilderness.

In the jungle, they were about to be struck by a cobra when an arrow transfixed its head. Holmes deduced that the archer was Lord Greystoke, about whom many odd tales had been told. Holmes and Watson believed that this man was the same boy whom they had rescued from kidnapping several years before, as recounted in "The Adventure of the Priory School." He had appeared to have "gone native" and told Holmes and Watson that he would hunt down and kill the crew of the Zeppelin.

When Lord Greystoke left to find something suitable for Holmes and Watson to eat, Holmes discussed with Watson his conclusion that Lord Greystoke was an imposter. Watson recounted to Holmes the tale of *Tarzan of the Apes*, as written by Edgar Rice Burroughs.

Holmes and Watson heard an odd cry in the far distance and left the spot where Greystoke had told them to stay. They were captured by men who seemed, oddly enough, dressed like ancient Persians. These strange men had also captured the Germans. Holmes and Watson were taken to what remained of Zu Vendis. Greystoke trailed them to Zu Vendis and appeared on the verge of rescuing them when Holmes made an angry remark about Lord Greystoke not being entitled to his title. Greystoke made him explain. Holmes explained how the account in *Tarzan of the Apes* was truthful and that Tarzan's father, John Clayton, had been the heir to the title; but when he had perished in Africa, his brother had become the sixth duke and his son William Cecil Clayton had become the seventh duke. Holmes surmised that Tarzan had assumed the identity of William Cecil Clayton, whose death in Africa Burroughs had fictionalized, rather than suffer through the endless public scrutiny that would ensue if his true origins were made public knowledge.

Lord Greystoke purchased Holmes' silence on this account by placing him on retainer. Greystoke also told them how he had heard of a white Englishwoman being held captive by tribe of African natives. He had discovered the woman, fought his way into the tent of the Sultan who held her—killing a dozen men—rescued her and then discovered she did not want to be rescued, but was quite content to be the wife of the Sultan.

Watson caught sight of the Priestess of the Zu Vendis, Nylepthah, whom Greystoke revealed was the granddaughter of Good and Curtis, the explorers who had discovered Zu Vendis, as seen in *Allan Quatermain* by H. Rider Haggard. Watson immediately believed that she should be rescued from the savages.

Greystoke rescued Holmes, Watson, the remaining Germans, and a somewhat reluctant Nylepthah from Zu Vendis, although they had to fight their way clear. During the battle, Greystoke was hit on the head, suffering a form of amnesia in which he reverted to a primal state. He recovered within a day and guided the party to Nairobi. Just outside of Nairobi, Greystoke suffered another blow to the head and again reverted to his primal state. This time he did not return to normal. Holmes and Watson discovered that Von Bork had hidden the secret formula for the bacillus inside his glass eye.

The Adventure of the Peerless Peer was written by Philip José Farmer in 1973, and published by Aspen Press. It was reissued by Dell in 1974. In 1984 Farmer had an offer from Byron Preiss Visual Publications to do an illustrated book of some of his best short fiction. He chose *Adventure of the Peerless Peer* as one of his selections. However, the Burroughs estate refused to allow Farmer and Preiss to reprint *The Adventure of the Peerless Peer* until 1999 when the copyright on Tarzan ran out.

Rather than write an entirely new novella, Farmer rewrote *Adventure of the Peerless Peer*, substituting Mowgli for Tarzan and changing the name to *The Adventure of the Three Madmen.*

The action of the novella *Three Madmen* is almost identical to the *Peerless Peer* up to the point when they arrive in Africa. The one early significant difference in *Three Madme*n is that in their initial discussion with Mycroft, Holmes and Watson were told Sir Mowgli, a baronet, was in Africa shooting a film. *Three Madmen* diverges from the story of *Peerless Peer* when Holmes and Watson are confronted by the cobra. Instead of killing it, Mowgli talked to Nag, the cobra, and it slithered away.

Holmes greeted the wolf-man by name and Mowgli was startled that Holmes had deduced his identity. However this was not so great a deduction as the detective seemed to make it out to be, as Holmes and Watson had been told Mowgli was in the area making a motion picture.

Hiding in the bush near Mowgli was a young woman named Liza Borden, an actress. She accused Mowgli of having ravished her, which Mowgli denied. Mowgli left them to go hunting. Liza Borden recounted how she had been making the film with Mowgli, but after the film wrapped a tribe of African savages attacked the film crew and tried to capture her. She had escaped and followed after Mowgli.

Mowgli returned to the three with a forest pig, which they ate raw. Later they heard some commotion, sounding like a group of men. Mowgli investigated; Liza Borden answered a call of nature; and Holmes and Watson left the area to get away from Liza Borden. Holmes and Watson were then captured by the Zu Vendians.

Mowgli trailed them to Zu Vendis, startling Holmes and Watson as they hid in a tree watching the isolated Queen of Zu Vendis.

Angry, Holmes stated that he doubted that Mowgli was entitled to his title. Mowgli had shown up in Bombay in 1899, claiming to be the son of a woodchopper. The woodchopper and his wife had been killed by a tiger and their child had been carried off. This woodchopper was a poor relative of Sir Jametsee Jejeebhoy, the Parsee baronet of Bombay. Mowgli had the same birthmark as the woodchopper's lost son. Sir Jametsee adopted Mowgli and when Sir Jametsee passed away Mowgli inherited the title. Holmes was convinced that Mowgli was a fraud and that his birthmark was a mere coincidence. He threatened to thoroughly investigate Mowgli once they had reached civilization.

Mowgli bought Holmes' silence by hiring him to investigate his claim. Mowgli rescued Holmes, Watson, and Nylepthah from the Zu Vendians. He suffered a blow to his head, which caused him to revert to a primitive state, as Tarzan was described as doing in *The Peerless Peer*.

This is at least the official account. It is true that Farmer had trouble with the Burroughs estate while trying to have *Peerless Peer* reprinted, but he also thought that this would be a great way to publish the Mowgli version of events, which had just recently surfaced along with several other Watson manuscripts.[232] Actually both of these accounts were versions of a singular, momentous encounter that occurred more or less as written. Tarzan and Mowgli were both present and both interacted with Holmes, Watson, Von Bork, and with each other. Incredible as this may sound, it is nevertheless true. Watson had written two versions of the incident for reasons that will be divulged in the article to follow.

The action of Holmes and Watson's adventures from February to June 1916 was generally as Mr. Farmer described it in both versions of the incident.

The meeting between Mycroft Holmes, Sherlock Holmes, Dr. Watson, and Merrivale was more accurately described in *The Adventure of the Three Madmen*, with both Tarzan and Mowgli being discussed. Farmer, however, left out the detail that even though Von Bork was in Cairo, there was a good possibility that he would be going to Africa to aid the Germans beleaguered efforts on that continent.

In such a happenstance, Mycroft Holmes informed Sherlock Holmes and Dr. Watson that they could rely on either Greystoke's or Mowgli's assistance. They did indeed end up traveling across Africa. Holmes and Watson were captured while onboard the L9 Zeppelin, but due to extensive damage and sabotage by Kentov, the zeppelin sank. Once earthbound, Holmes and Watson eventually eluded their German captors.

While in the African jungle, Watson and Holmes were attacked by a cobra.

In *Three Madmen*, Watson stated that Mowgli rescued them by convincing the cobra not to attack them. In *Peerless Peer*, Tarzan shot the cobra with an arrow. Which was true? Both. Mowgli did indeed talk the cobra out of attacking Holmes and Watson, but as it slithered away from Watson and Holmes and towards Mowgli, an arrow transfixed its head. As can be guessed, the first meeting of Mowgli and Tarzan did not go well. Mowgli was upset that Tarzan had killed the snake after Mowgli had talked to it and asked it to leave them alone. Tarzan at first disbelieved Mowgli's ability to talk to animals. However, when Tarzan began to eat the snake, Mowgli was a bit mollified. After all, the Law of the Jungle blessed eating one's kills.

Mowgli was not the first person Tarzan had encountered who had also been raised as a feral child. Tarzan had previously met Ka-Zar and Kaspa. Tarzan, however, found Mowgli's ability to communicate with animals to be astounding, even though he too possessed a lesser form of it. Mowgli, as later scientific investigation would reveal, did not really vocally talk to the animals but rather possessed a low-level form of telepathy that allowed him to communicate directly with them. As revealed in *Peerless Peer* and *Three Madmen*, both Tarzan and Mowgli had similar childhoods in that their parents died while they were infants and they were raised by wild animals. Unknown to them at the time, Mowgli and Tarzan were also similar in that they had mysteries surrounding their present stations in society.

When Holmes and Watson mentioned that there were Germans in the area, Tarzan explained that he had vowed to kill every German he could find, for they had murdered his wife.[233] He hurried off to hunt the crew of the Zeppelin. Holmes and Watson accompanied Mowgli. They soon encountered a beautiful Englishwoman in a torn gown.

This was Liza Borden, Mowgli's co-star in the film epic *Mowgli's Revenge.* She was a loud-mouthed, spoiled woman who claimed that Mowgli had ravished her many times. Watson was immediately suspicious of her story since she used dialogue from her films. Mowgli had been ordered by the British Army to report for duty in East Africa after shooting on the film had stopped. Shortly after Mowgli had departed, a native tribe had attacked the movie crew, intent on capturing Liza Borden. Despite her claims of ravishment, she had followed Mowgli after eluding the native tribe. Mowgli explained that she protested too much; he remained faithful to his mate but she persisted in trying to seduce him.

Mowgli scouted ahead to find them food, telling them to come with him. Holmes balked at being ordered about. Holmes and Watson were left with the company of Liza Borden. Despite her previous claim that she was running away from him, Miss Borden urged them, in strong language, to follow after Mowgli. They did so with some reluctance.

Mowgli had killed a boar and was eating its meat raw. Holmes and the rest, while at first recoiling at the thought of eating raw meat, soon followed suit. They heard men approaching. Mowgli told them to stay put while he checked them out. Liza Borden refused to remain, stating that she had to relieve herself.

They heard a cry that in *Three Madmen* was stated to be a wolf's cry, though in *Peerless Peer* it was the victory cry of a bull-ape.

It was both, intermingled in one strange ululating cry.

Let us examine some of the clues Farmer provided for us:

In both *Peerless Peer* and *Three Madmen* natives who resembled Persians capture Holmes and Watson and take them to their village. A day later, two of the Germans are shoved into the hut with them. The Germans tell identical stories in both *Peerless Peer* and *Three Madmen* with one minor change. The Germans had heard the strange cry and hurried to see what the cause of it was. There were five dead men lying in a clearing. Six men were running in one direction away from the clearing and four others were running in another direction. Inside the clearing was a large dark man clutching a bloody knife, his foot placed upon the chest of a dead man, screaming a strange cry. That is in the *Three Madmen* version. In the *Peerless Peer* version it is a large tanned man wearing a leopard skin with his foot planted on a dead man. He also screamed a strange cry.

Three of the dead men had been shot with arrows, two had their necks broken, and there may have been stab wounds, since there was the bloody knife to consider.

Our clues to consider here are the presence of the arrows and the two directions in which the natives were running.

Mowgli was not depicted as having a bow and arrow prior to this incident, although the German offered the suggestion that he had taken the bow from one of the natives. While it may be that Mowgli had acquired proficiency with the bow and arrow after his career was chronicled in the *Jungle Books*, in *The Jungle Books* themselves he used his teeth, nails, and knife. As he apparently did in this case, which accounts for the broken necks and the bloody knife.

However, we know that in *Peerless Peer*, Tarzan was depicted as having a bow and arrow, and he was, as any reader of Burroughs' works can attest, a superlative archer.

Captain Reich, one of the Germans, said that they were going to shoot the savage, but that he took to the trees before they could.

What evidently happened was that Captain Reich remembered the incident incorrectly; that is, he remembered the events but not the exact sequence of events. He should not be blamed for this; he had seen his beloved Zeppelin destroyed, his marriage was in a shambles, and he had been stuck in the African jungle for nearly a week. Although Farmer does not record it, Reich's men had been winnowed down as they trekked through the jungle. Someone, evidently Tarzan, was throwing nooses at and strangling the German soldiers in their nightly camps and on the trail. The noose was an old joke of Tarzan's.

Mowgli and Tarzan arrived at the clearing at approximately the same time. They had obviously heard the commotion and investigated. The natives fired arrows at them. Tarzan retaliated by shooting back, killing three with arrows. Mowgli dropped out of the tree cover and broke two of the men's necks. Both Tarzan and Mowgli then took the opportunity to sound their victory cries. Hearing the cries, the main body of the natives ran into the clearing. Mowgli and Tarzan then took to the trees, moving off in separate directions. The natives split into groups to chase them down. Tarzan and Mowgli picked them off individually, but forsook further victory cries, not knowing how many more natives were in the area.

Reich said that he and his men then headed east. An arrow pierced the neck of one of Reich's men. The angle showed that it had come from above the man. A voice in excellent German, with a perfect Brandenberger accent, ordered them to turn back and head southwest. If they did not, they would be picked off one by one.

Reich followed the voice's orders. Once again we come to a slight difference in the two texts.

In *Peerless Peer* Reich states that all of their food was stolen that night and it was evident that their stalker intended for them to starve to death. After two days Reich begged for food. Eventually a freshly killed boar was thrown into their campsite with the admonishment, "Pigs should eat pig."

However in *Three Madmen* Reich does not mention the food being stolen.

The stolen food sounds like another Tarzan joke. Considering Tarzan's deep antipathy for the Germans it is unlikely that he would have given the starving Germans a freshly killed pig. This was more likely Mowgli's action.

Reich's men were attacked by a group of the savages who captured Holmes and Watson, with only Reich and Von Bork surviving the encounter.

The bits of dialogue in *Peerless Peer* and *Three Madmen* in which Holmes, Watson, Reich, and Von Bork discuss Mowgli or Tarzan may have taken place, but it is also likely that Farmer inserted these bits of expository dialogue to move the story along. If these conversations did in fact take place, then in all probability they were not as extensive as Farmer portrays them. Holmes and Watson probably would not have discussed the private lives of British aristocrats with German soldiers.

In both versions, Holmes and Watson climbed a tree to look into the natives' great stone temple and to observe the queen. While they were in the tree a hand clamped down on Watson's shoulder. Although the narratives of *Peerless Peer* and *Three Madmen* remain almost identical from this point, with Mowgli or Tarzan being substituted for the feral jungle lord character, there are slight differences that give us a clue as to what actually happened.

It was Tarzan who greeted them in the tree. The incident that followed was as Farmer related in *Peerless Peer*. Holmes ferreted out the truth about Tarzan's assumption of his cousin's identity after William Clayton had died in the jungle. Tarzan did put Holmes and Watson on a retainer to insure their silence about this matter. Tarzan also explained to them that the territory in which they were currently incarcerated was the remnant of Zu Vendis, the great land that H. Rider Haggard had written about in *Allan Quatermain.* The High Priestess was the granddaughter of Good and Curtis.

In *Peerless Peer*, Tarzan relates how he went to check out a rumor that a white woman, an Englishwoman, had been captured by a tribe of blacks. He states he fought his way to her, killing a dozen men, and fought his way out carrying her with him, killing a dozen more men. When Tarzan removed the gag he had put on her so she would stop screaming, she told him that she was perfectly happy living with the Sultan and asked if Tarzan could please return her, immediately. This incident is not related in *Three Madmen*.

However, *Three Madmen* does leave us with one mystery: whatever happened to Liza Borden? We are told that she eventually found her way back to England, but nothing is told of her ensuing adventures. Liza Borden is the woman "rescued" by Tarzan and Mowgli. Yes, Mowgli was with Tarzan, as he had been when they were trailing the Germans. After their battle in the clearing together they had become blood brothers. It was Mowgli who convinced Tarzan not to kill the Germans outright, knowing something of Holmes and Watson's mission but not willing to disclose it to a civilian. When Tarzan told Mowgli about his wife's death and then about the captive white woman, Mowgli had agreed to accompany Tarzan and help free the woman. While we can believe that Tarzan could have held off and killed twenty-four men in a matter of minutes, in reality it was he and Mowgli who had done so. To Mowgli's dismay, the woman turned out to be Liza Borden. True to form, she demanded to be taken back to the Sultan. Tarzan refused. Mowgli agreed to take her back, mainly because he despised the idea of her accompanying them and he liked the idea of her being sequestered in a harem.

Meanwhile, Tarzan agreed to rescue Holmes and Watson, take the High Priestess, and even take the Germans once Holmes had explained why Von Bork must be taken alive.

They were forced to run from the Zu Vendians when a woman's scream alerted the village. A complement of warriors blocked their path and Tarzan and Mowgli fought their way clear. They were pursued until they came to the hives of the Zu Vendians' sacred bees. A vast cloud of bees attacked them from the front and the Zu Vendians attacked from the rear. Tarzan was knocked unconscious. Holmes used his apiarist knowledge and diverted the bees to attack the Zu Vendians.

When Tarzan regained consciousness, he had reverted to a primitive state that took hold of him every so often; however, he did not regain his memory immediately as related in *Peerless Peer*. Tarzan left, and was not seen again by either Holmes or Watson for nearly three years. But Mowgli arrived the next morning, having finished returning Liza Borden to her sultan.

Mowgli led Holmes and the rest of the party to Nairobi, although he seemed anxious to report for duty. Holmes doubted this, and when Mowgli asked him to explain his remark Holmes launched into a discussion of his deductions about Mowgli's origins. He claimed that Mowgli was not the Mowgli of Kipling's stories. He also doubted if Mowgli was in actuality the true heir of Sir Jametsee Jejeebhoy, the Parsee Baronet of Bombay, which had depended upon a birthmark on the big toe, a mark that Mowgli possessed and that Holmes believed was a remarkable coincidence.

Although Watson's account in *Three Madmen* leaves one with the impression that Mowgli did indeed have something to hide, he is shown hiring Holmes to investigate the validity of his claim for an extremely high fee. Mowgli asked them to hold their investigation until he notified them to start, but he paid the money up front. Holmes and Watson seemed to believe that this was Mowgli's manner of purchasing their silence, believing that the word to proceed would never come.

Mowgli left Holmes, Watson, Nylepthah, and Von Bork outside Nairobi and went to finally report for duty. Despite what was related in the *Three Madmen*, Mowgli never lost his memory nor was he subject to fits of amnesia. Von Bork made a dash for freedom but ran into a tree escaping from a rhinoceros. His eye popped out and it was revealed that the plans for the secret weapon were etched onto his glass eye.

Watson and Holmes became very wealthy as a result of these two big fees. Greystoke recovered his senses and personally brought Holmes two checks, one for Watson and one for Holmes, three years later. Each of the clients stipulated, out of courtesy to his jungle brother, that if Watson should ever write up a narrative based on the case, he should leave the other feral man out of the story. Watson did so, writing two separate but nearly identical volumes, which he hoped would further muddy the waters. Another example of this obfuscation technique was his raising Mowgli's true age while at the same time pretending to reveal the truth about Mowgli's origins. Mowgli was actually thirty-three in 1916, rather than forty-three. Even Rudyard Kipling hid Mowgli's true age, telescoping events over several years. He had him as seventeen in 1894, when he was actually only eleven.

The story might have ended there, if not for Mowgli's visit to Holmes' Sussex estate to ask him to start earning his fee by investigating Mowgli's claim to the Jejeebhoy estate.

Holmes was frankly astounded by what he discovered.

Not only was Mowgli entitled to the estate he was also entitled to a larger, more prominent title.

The story went that Mowgli was the son of a woodchopper and his wife. A tiger had killed them, but Mowgli had walked away from the carnage while the tiger was occupied with his parents and found refuge with a wolf pack. The woodchopper had been the only living relative of Sir Jametsee Jejeebhoy and had at one time visited his relative to show off his son. This Jametsee Jejeebhoy was either the same Jametsee Jejeebhoy mentioned by Mr. Farmer in *Tarzan Alive, Doc Savage: His Apocalyptic Life* and *The Other Log of Phileas Fogg* as being related to Aouda Jejeebhoy, or else it was his son. Records on the Jejeebhoys are either inaccurate or incomplete.[234] *Three Madmen* does state that the childless Jametsee adopted Mowgli, believing him to be his relation.

Holmes' investigation revealed that Mowgli, while a relative of the Jejeebhoys, was not the son of the woodchopper, except in the adoptive sense.

Mowgli had survived not one but *two* tiger attacks in his first two years of life. The woodchopper had seen a wounded tiger carrying a baby by its swaddling cloth. He had thrown his axe at the tiger, chasing it off, and it dropped the baby. His wife had just suffered a miscarriage. They raised the child as their own, never realizing that this child was his cousin's child. His cousin was the sister of Jametsee Jejeebhoy. Hearing that Sir Jametsee's sister and her baby had perished in a tiger attack, the woodchopper visited Sir Jametsee, partially as a condolence and partially to make Sir Jametsee aware of this child.

Shortly thereafter the formerly wounded, now lame, tiger returned to the area and killed the woodchopper and his wife. The baby walked a short distance before finding sanctuary in a wolf's den. The tiger who had been injured and then lamed was Shere Khan, who became Mowgli's mortal enemy.

Holmes dug up what he could on Mowgli's mother and her husband and berated himself when he discovered the answer. It had been staring him in the face and he had missed it. Jaya Jejeebhoy had met and married, almost upon sight, a Captain of the Pioneers of the Corps of Madras Sappers and Miners. His name was Lord John Staveley, also known as John Clayton. It was 1883 and he was nineteen years old.[235] Holmes realized with a shock that Mowgli and Tarzan had looked exceedingly similar with the same general build and similar facial features. Mowgli possessed the Indian's dark skin coloring and supraorbital ridges, but lacked the gray eyes that often cropped up in the family tree. John had kept the marriage secret from his family, partially out of apprehension of what they would think of an Indian wife, but also because Jaya had yet to tell her brother, fearing much the same reaction.

Accompanied by a companion of John's, a Colonel Moran, the young couple went on a safari to see Jametsee Jejeebhoy, believing that their newborn son would mollify Jejeebhoy's reaction to the marriage. Their small party was attacked by two tigers and an apparently crazed hyena. Jaya was killed immediately by one of the tigers. Moran killed one and shot another as it was mauling John. The wounded tiger grabbed the baby and disappeared.

When a fairly cursory search for the baby turned up nothing, it was assumed the tiger had eaten it, but the woodchopper later encountered this same tiger. Although a woman, Messua, and her husband would later claim that Mowgli was theirs, Messua's child was more than likely yet another unfortunate babe who had met his death as a victim of Shere Khan.

Colonel Moran wrote of the tiger attack in his book, *Three Months in the Jungle* (1884). As a side note, as it would later be revealed in *The Other Log of Phileas Fogg*, Moran was a Capellean agent, which begs the question: was the tiger attack an accident? If not, who was the target, John Clayton or Jaya Clayton (whose family, the Jejeebhoys, were known Eridaneans)? Since Moran shot the tiger to save John Clayton, we can only speculate at this time.

While Clayton was recovering from his tiger mauling, he was told that his wife and child had perished in the tiger attack. When he was sent to England for recuperation, he was persuaded by the East India Company for the good of the company and England not to press any of his supposed claims to wealth or property from his wife's relatives. Her family refused to acknowledge the marriage. To press the matter could lead to unnecessary unrest. While he was in England recovering from his mauling, Clayton met and fell in love with Alice Rutherford. Their union produced Tarzan, Mowgli's half brother.

Some might say that this explains Mowgli's ability to survive in the jungle, his hardiness, stamina, etc. These and his other mutant abilities can be attributed to the Wold Newton meteor event. This is certainly not the case!

The Wold Newton genes merely reinforced Mowgli's inherited abilities and gave new strength to some of the traits that were becoming latent. The Jejeebhoys were members of the Indian Jahangir meteorite family, whose extended family produced several superior persons such as Ram Singh, Chullunder Ghose, Chandra Lal, Inspector Ghote, and Hadji Singh Quest.[236]

Among the abilities derived from this meteorite were increased strength and stamina, heightened sensory abilities, and on occasion, the ability to talk to animals, something Mowgli shared with his distant kinsman John Dolittle and to some degree Tarzan. (How Dr. Dolittle came to be part Indian is a story for another article.) Tarzan, however, received his diluted ability from his ancestor Siegfried.[237]

Holmes discovered that, as the elder brother, Mowgli had a claim on the Greystoke estates and titles. When he passed this information on to his client, he was sorry for his earlier words about his character and morality. Mowgli did not want to press any claim. He did not want the publicity, nor did he have any wish for the titles and property that accompanied it. Further, he had no wish to expose his or Greystoke's feral nature and past. Mowgli was instead satisfied to know that his jungle brother was in fact his true brother.

A Language For Opar
By Philip José Farmer

ERB-dom No. 75, 1974

In *The Return of Tarzan*, Tarzan is captured the first time he enters the city of Opar. He is placed on an altar to be sacrificed, and the high priestess, La, recites a "long and tiresome prayer." At least, Tarzan presumes it's a prayer, since the language is unknown to him. Later, La addresses him. Tarzan replies in five languages, none of which she understands. The last is "the mongrel tongue of the West Coast," a *beche-de-mer* or pidgin spoken in the ports and along the shoreline of West Africa.

So far, I've been unable to identify this pidgin, though no doubt it exists and my research has not been extensive enough. The surprising thing is that Tarzan knows it. He's had the time to learn French, English, Arabic, and Waziri (to some extent, anyway). But when and where did he have opportunity and leisure to learn the West Coast pidgin? During the events of *Tarzan of the Apes* and *The Return of Tarzan*, he has been very busy and had very little contact with the natives of the West Coast.

But seek and ye shall find. Tarzan must have learned at least its rudiments while he and d'Arnot were in the port-town they found at the end of their wanderings in *Tarzan of the Apes*. Tarzan, always a magnificent linguist, could have picked up the *beche-de-mer* very quickly.

During the ceremony at the altar of this lost outpost of Atlantis, Tha, an Oparian priest, makes a complaint. Tarzan is surprised to hear him speak "his own mother tongue." This is the speech of the mangani—"the low guttural barking of the tribe of great anthropoids." La answers Tha in the same tongue.

Burroughs could not have meant that the two Oparians were emitting doglike barks. Possibly, a language could consist of clusters of long and short barks, a barking Morse code, in other words. But humans would never adopt such a speech.

Besides, Burroughs makes it evident throughout the Tarzan books that the mangani speech has definite words with consonants and vowels and that these are arranged in syntactical order. Intonation also plays an important part in the meaning. It determines whether *kagoda* means, "Do you surrender?" or "I do surrender." And intonation in a barking language is impossible.

The only way to reconcile Burroughs' two contradictory descriptions of the mangani speech is to assume that he meant something that did not accord with the conventional definition of "barking." Perhaps the force with which the words were uttered suggested to him the "barking" metaphor. Thus, in English, a drill sergeant can "bark" orders.

Burroughs' use of the adjective "guttural" must mean that the mangani used sounds not found in English and seldom found in other languages. I believe that he meant by this one of the definitions of "guttural" given by Webster: "being or marked by utterance that is strange, unpleasant, or disagreeable." Burroughs was no linguist and hence did not use "guttural" in a truly linguistic sense.

Note that the original language is "a grunting monosyllabic" tongue. What Burroughs means by "grunting" is open to speculation. He does not define the term. "Opar" and "Oah" (Cadj's fellow conspirator) are not monosyllables. But Opar must be a heritage of the period in which the language was not monosyllabic. Oah, instead of being O-ah, could be a diphthong, pronounced as our English "aw" or "oy." Burroughs doesn't tell us its pronunciation.

Whatever the sounds of the mangani language, they are not out of the range of human speech. Apparently, the mangani have teeth, oral cavities, larynxes and pharynxes much like those of human beings. And this tells us that the mangani are not as ape-like as Burroughs depicts them. But that's the subject of another article to be in *ERB-dom* soon: "The Reconstruction of the Mangani."

After Tarzan kills the madman Tha, he and La have a long conversation in mangani. La tells him of the origin of Opar and summarizes its history. And we're confronted by a problem at once.

Both La and Tarzan use many words which the mangani tongue just would not have. In the paragraph beginning "You are a wonderful man..." La uses *city* and *civilization*. Tarzan, in his reply, uses *religion* and *creed*. Some of the other non-mangani words in the following dialog are *priestess*, *temple*, *ten thousand*, *gold*, *ships*, *mines*, *slaves*, *soldiers*, *sailed*, *fortress*, *galley*, *rituals*, *sacrilegious*, and *God*.

It is probable that La used these words. But they would have been loanwords from the Oparian tongue and hence unintelligible to Tarzan. He knew only the mangani of the west coast of Africa. This, as chapter IV, "The God of Tarzan," of *Jungle Tales of Tarzan* indicates, had no concepts of, or words for, anything to do with religion. And what would the mangani among whom Tarzan had been raised know of *gold*, *galley*, *mines*, *slaves*, *civilization*, etc? Doubtless, the Oparian language had a word for *ten thousand*. But the preliterate mangani would not. For most preliterates, a word signifying "many" has to represent numbers above twenty. Some can count above that, but not very far.

How was Tarzan able to understand La???

One explanation is that he interpreted the unfamiliar words from the context. Another, the most likely, is that he interrupted La many times to ask her for the definition of a word. This would not have been easy for La, since she would have had to use the limited mangani vocabulary to make the definition. Apparently, she was successful. Tarzan's acquaintance with the vocabulary of several civilized peoples enabled him to grasp her meaning quickly.

In any event, the dialogue did not proceed as reported by Burroughs.

This linguistic difficulty may have been described to Burroughs. In this case, Burroughs just ignored the facts and described the dialogue as if it had gone smoothly. He did this for the benefit of the reader, whom he thought (rightly or not) wouldn't be interested in the mechanics of the conversation. Burroughs discarded realism for the sake of speed of narration. The essential thing was to communicate the basics of La's history of Opar.

Since the humans and the mangani of Opar were in such close linguistic contact, it is likely that some of the personal names of the humans were borrowed from the mangani. La doesn't seem to be one of these. Since she is the inheritor of a priestesshood and queenship many thousands of years old, it is probable that "La" came from the other tongue. It might have originally been a title. Perhaps every chief priestess was named La. On the other hand, Oah, during her brief tenure as the chief priestess, did not adopt the name of La. Or perhaps Burroughs did not tell us that she did because he did not want to confuse the reader with two La's.

Some ERB scholars have speculated that La might mean, simply, She. That is, The She, Ayesha, the immortal queen and high priestess of the city of Kor (see H. Rider Haggard's *She*, *She and Allan*, and *Ayesha*) is addressed as 'She' or 'She-who-must-be-obeyed.'

It's my theory that the city of Kor was founded by refugees from the same great civilization which gave birth to Opar. After the cataclysm which destroyed the mother-culture, survivors fled to various parts of Africa and founded their own tributary cultures. The cities of Athne and Cathne, Xuja, and Tuen-Baka may have been built by the refugees, and the wild Kavuru may also have been descendants of the refugees.

John Harwood and Frank Brueckel have originated this latter thesis, and it will be expounded in their forthcoming article, "Heritage of the Flaming God, an essay on the History of Opar and Its Relationship to Other Ancient Cultures." This will be published by Vernell Coriell in a *Burroughs Bibliophiles*. Harwood and Brueckel originated the idea that the lost cities of the Tarzan books may have been built by survivors of the destroyed mother-state. It is my own idea that Kor (and the civilization of the Zu-vendis, see Haggard's novel *Allan Quatermain*) was also founded by refugees.

One final speculation. The religion of Opar seems to have been monotheistic. This means that it was the end product of thousands of years of civilization. It has gone through the polytheism which is an inevitable stage of early cultures and now has one deity, the sun, the Flaming God.

The Flaming God is a male, and yet the head of the theocracy is, and apparently always has been, a woman, La.

This situation is unlike any other of which I have read. Where the dominant deity (or deities) is male, the chief theocrats are males, and almost always the temporal ruler is male. In the pre-Indo-European and pre-Semitic civilizations around the Mediterranean, the chief deity was a chthonic mother-goddess, and her chief vicars were women. Then the Indo-Europeans and Semites of the patriarchal male gods won out. Men became the chief vicars; priestesses assumed a subordinate role.

Yet, in Opar, a woman is the head of the state and the chief of a religion which worships a male god. Does this singular situation reflect a long struggle between the priestesses of a mother-god and the priests of a father-god in ancient Opar? Was the sun-god originally a son of the Great Goddess, and did he finally rise from the rank of a secondary deity to that of the primary and, finally, that of the only deity? Such seems to have been the case with the male gods in Greece and other Mediterranean countries.

And was the struggle in Opar solved by a compromise? Did the son-sun become the only deity but the priestesses retained their position as the head of the religion?

This seems the only explanation to account for the unique Oparian religion. And this indicates that the mother-state, the mighty empire stretching from sea to sea, was a matriarchy, and its chief deity at that time was an earth-goddess.

However, it is possible that she was the sun in the beginning, and that in the end the sun had to become masculinized.

In Kor (according to *She and Allan*), the struggle was still going on. She, priestess of the moon, had long been challenged by Resu, priest of the sun. Only because of the intervention of Allan Quatermain and his mighty Zulu ally, Umslopogaas, were the worshippers of the moon (a female deity) able to triumph.

The question of the ancientness of religious sacrifice of human beings in Opar is not answered in the Oparian novels of Burroughs. Apparently, it had been going on for a long time. But this does not mean that human sacrifices were a part of the religion of the mother-state at the time of the cataclysm. In ten thousand years much will change, and the Oparians had degenerated in many respects.

Watching the Detectives
or
The Sherlock Holmes Family Tree
By Brad Mengel

The purpose of this article is to collect all of the available information about the family of Sherlock Holmes. Wherever possible I have given correct names but it has been necessary to fill in gaps. Also, a number of names occur many times, so most have been given numbers to designate them in further discussion. I should also mention that not every work about Sherlock Holmes is true and a number of Holmes' relatives have had their identities used to mock the Great Detective. It is also possible that some of the people who claim to be descended from Sherlock Holmes may be lying.

We start with Dr. Siger Holmes and his wife Violet Clarke, a descendant of Micah Clarke.[238] They were present at the Wold Newton meteor strike. Siger had one elder brother, who died as an adolescent in a horse-riding accident. He had two younger siblings: a brother, Mycroft William Holmes, who married Grace Winsby, and a sister, who married a man from Canterbury and moved there. Dr. Siger had two sons, Brian Mycroft Holmes and John Scott Holmes. John Scott married Anne Routh and Brian Mycroft, the elder of the two, married Camille Francoise Josephine Lecomte-Vernet, sister of the famed French artist.[239] Brian Mycroft Holmes had six children: Mycroft Holmes (I), Siger Holmes, Henry Holmes, Dorothy Holmes, Robert Holmes (I), and Roberta Holmes (I).

Mycroft Holmes (I) married Violet Sherrinford, daughter of Sir Eric Sherrinford. It appears that William S. Baring-Gould, with all of the Violet Holmeses in the family, mistakenly stated that she was married to Mycroft's brother Siger. Mycroft (I) apparently died childless and the family estate passed in the hands of Siger.[240] Siger married Violet Rutherford, fifth child of the twelfth Baron Tennington. They had nine children, possibly more: Shirley Holmes (I), Sherrinford Holmes, Mycroft Holmes (II), William Sherlock Scott Holmes, Rutherford Holmes, Charlotte Holmes, Sigerson Holmes, Sigrina Holmes and Sibyl Holmes.

Shirley (I) married Charles Jones after her much fictionalised adventure titled "The Adventure of Sherlock Holmes' Dumber Sister in the Case of the Mislaid Pussy"[241]. Charles was the younger brother of the father of Henry Jones, Sr.[242] They had one son named Fetlock Jones and a daughter Laura Jones. A fictionalised account of a meeting between Fetlock and his uncle Sherlock was written by Mark Twain, entitled *A Double Barrelled Detective Story*.

Fetlock had two sons and a daughter. The first son named his son Jupiter after Sherlock's statement that "Jupiter is descending" when Mycroft visited him as recorded in "The Adventure of the Bruce Partington Plans." Unfortunately, Jupiter's parents died when he was very young. His Uncle Titus Jones and his wife Mathilda raised him. Jupiter started his own detective agency with two of his friends called the Three Investigators, which has to date solved fifty-four cases. He has displayed several of the family traits. Alfred Hitchcock introduces about half of the group's cases and he says that "Jupiter is known for his remarkable powers of observation and deduction," and that he is "stocky, muscular and a bit roly poly." Jupiter was also a gifted child actor. Farmer, in *Tarzan Alive*, pointed out that one of the male types of the Wold Newton Family is the "tall and obese but very strong." Certainly Jupiter ably fills these qualities and when reading the cases it feels like reading about a young Nero Wolfe or Mycroft Holmes. Jupiter lives in Rocky Beach just near Hollywood and like his relative Doc Savage has been granted special privileges by the Rocky Beach Police to investigate crimes.

Thanks to the researches of Dennis Power and Denny Hager the following information is available. Fetlock Jones' daughter Charlotte married a man named Peerless Jones. Peerless Jones first came to the world's attention when he helped Professor George Edward Challenger.[243] Peerless Jones traced his ancestry back to the foundling known as Tom Jones, who kept his name even after discovering his true parentage. Charlotte and Peerless had three sons: Barnaby, Darwin and David.[244] David went on to have a career as an operative for U.N.D.E.R.S.E.A. (The United Nations Department of Experiment and Research Systems Established at Atlantis), which was established by Professor Weston.[245] Davy later married Judith Walton, a member of U.N.D.E.R.S.E.A.'s covert ops team, the Sea Devils, and they had three children: Martin (Merlin), Frederick and Ellie. Merlin Jones' inventive genius was able to save his college from financial ruin. Freddy joined a group of occult investigators, Mystery Inc., and Ellie became an investigator for Frank Cisco's Total Security private investigation firm.[246]

Darwin Jones went on to become a noted scientific investigator. Darwin Jones' son Jebediah Romano (J.R.) went to work for his uncle Barnaby. Barnaby Jones had a long and successful career as an investigator and when he retired his son Harold took over his father's business. But on his first case Harold was murdered and Barnaby came out of retirement to assist his cousin Frank Cannon to solve the crime.

Fetlock's sister, Laura Jones, married Lord Hamish Croft and the couple had two sons, William and Jason.

William married and had two sons, Richard and Henshingly Croft. Richard and his wife had one daughter, Lara. But with the early death of Richard's wife and Richard's disappearance in 1981, the new Lord Henshingly Croft adopted his niece Lara. Henshingly tried to raise Lara to be a lady and forget about the adventures she went on with her father. This plan appeared to work and Lara eventually became engaged. It was on a plane trip with her adopted parents and fiancé that she discovered her true destiny. The plane crashed and Lara had to use her nearly forgotten skills to survive. On her return to civilisation she became a "Tomb Raider."[247]

Jason Croft astral-projected to the planet Palos, where he possessed the body of a native. Much like John Carter before him, he had many adventures and married a princess. His son, Jason Jr., was born of that union.[248]

Sherrinford Holmes was named after his aunt's father, Sir Edward Sherrinford, which partially contributed to Baring-Gould assuming that Sherlock Holmes's mother was Violet Sherrinford. The other factor was the fact that there were several women named Violet Holmes in the family. After the death of his father, Sherrinford became the squire and had three children.[249]

Richard Holmes was fathered by Sherrinford while Sherrinford was travelling in Germany. Richard's mother was from a wealthy German Jewish family. Richard went to university in Nuremberg, later moving to New York, and became a police inspector. However, he changed his last name and the name of his two sons to "Queen." His first son, Ellery, assisted his father on the first ten cases attributed to "Ellery Queen." Ellery then retired, got married, and had two sons: Ellery Jr. and Gullivar Queen. Ellery's younger brother Dan stepped in and took over the remainder of the cases attributed to his brother. Gulliver, while visiting Dan, has had three adventures. The Queen family has many things to recommend them, including grey eyes, the deductive ability, and the tall lanky build of the Holmes family. Dan, in "The Adventure of the House of Darkness," made reference to his father telling him the Queen (Holmes) clan is made of the stuff of heroes.[250]

The second son of Sherrinford Holmes became the new squire and his descendants are still the squires.

According to my research, the squire's second son, Stuart, eventually became the owner of the *Global* newspaper and in 1960 financed George Edward Challenger III on his expedition to Maple White Land. However, Stuart did so on the condition that his two children Jenny and David were able to come along.[251]

The third son, Sebastian, married a woman named Peggy. They had one son, Robert (II). Robert got involved in politics, eventually married Joanna, a Canadian woman, and moved to Canada with her. Robert (II) bore Shirley Holmes (II), and she has shown the family flair for mystery work, acting, and disguise, solving thirty-nine cases. (It should be noted here that Sebastian inherited a puzzle chest from his Uncle Sherlock. Inside the chest is a note to the solver of the puzzle in which Sherlock states that he has left no heir. Sherlock left the chest with Sherrinford before he left for the events of "The Final Problem." At that time Sherlock had only Raffles Holmes as a son and he did not hold great hope for the boy.)[252]

Mycroft Holmes (II) appears to have married twice. His first marriage resulted in two children, Andrew and Isabella Holmes.[253] Andrew was slain on the battlefield of Somme, but not before having a daughter. This daughter, like her father, was involved in espionage and politics, and married an American spymaster named Muir. The resulting son, Nathan Muir, was a great spy with many Holmesian traits, both mental (such as observation and deduction) and physical (hawk-like features, blue-grey eyes).[254] Isabella married a Christian Washington diplomat named Weston, and had a son named Geoffrey Weston. Geoffrey calls himself the world's greatest Christian detective and in *The Case of the Hijacked Moon* he is described as lanky and sporting a goatee (he must resemble Holmes in his disguise as Altamont in "His Last Bow"). In *The Case of the Invisible Thief*, the first of the series, Weston's assistant and chronicler, Dr. John Taylor, writes: "He took delight in recreating the rustic air that so characterized his grandfather Mycroft's celebrated brother. Our selection of a Baker Street office completed the picture." He apparently never married and, being Christian, never had an affair; hence, no offspring. However, his father appears to be related to Professor Weston, who was in charge of the U.N.D.E.R.S.E.A. operation.[255]

Mycroft's second marriage gave him another daughter, "Shrinking" Violet Holmes. She married Charles Beauregard but had a son to James

Bond; the son was named Clive Reston Beauregard.[256]

Sherlock Holmes has, apparently, ten children, if accounts are to be believed. These are Raffles Holmes, Mycroft Adler Norton, Nero Wolfe and Marco Vukcic, Philo and Philomina Vance, Shirley Holmes (III), Minerva Holmes, Sherlock Holmes II and Abraham Moth.

In *R. Holmes & Co*, the first chapter, set in 1883, deals with Sherlock Holmes chasing A.J. Raffles. Sherlock then falls in love with Raffles' daughter, Marjorie. Further research by Chris Davies has shown that in 1883 it would be impossible for Raffles to have a daughter old enough to marry. So it appears that Raffles, impersonating an elderly gentleman, involved his youngest sister Marjorie in this caper. This was Marjorie's one exploit in crime and shortly after marrying Holmes she died in childbirth. Sherlock was unaware of the true relationship between Marjorie and A.J., and told the one son from that union, Raffles Holmes, that A.J. Raffles was his grandfather.

Raffles had one son, Creighton Holmes, by an unknown woman.

Raffles Holmes, after World War I, succumbed to drug abuse, but before he left for the war he married a woman by the last name of Mannering. She was the sister of Terry Mannering, better known as "X Esquire."[257] This woman divorced Raffles Holmes and returned to using her maiden name. She called her son John Mannering. Mannering later adopted the guise of "The Baron" and became a daring jewel thief. (When his reputation spread to the U.S., for some reason his assumed name was changed to "The Blue Mask"). After his marriage to Laura Fauntley, he reformed.[258] The one child of this union, a daughter, became a noted actress and married an Anglo-Asian former bishop turned high tech entrepreneur. The couple had one son. His parents died in a theatre fire when he was three. He was placed in an orphanage and given the name John Rossi. Later in life, he was to adopt the name Simon Templar and the alias of "The Saint." It appears the boy half remembered tales of a gentleman adventurer in his family and fixated on the original Saint as this forebear.[259] According to my research, in 1992 John Rossi Templar (so named to avoid confusion) adopted the alias of J.T. Barker to assist and learn from expert cat burglar Karen McCoy.[260]

Like his father, Raffles Holmes eventually overcame his addiction, and lived many more years. Just before World War II, he had an affair with Jane Sherlock, a buyer for a department store and an amateur detective. It appears that when Jane Sherlock met Raffles Holmes she found him to be a better companion that her fiancé (and boss's son) Peter Blossom. However, he was forced to depart for the war, and she bore his child by herself. He was named Arthur Sherlock Holmes. Arthur Sherlock possessed many of their father's qualities: His exploits were rather comedic, he also had a drug problem, and had several near-death experiences.[261] Recently Arthur Sherlock Holmes joined the Q Branch of the British Secret Service where he was given the code name "R."[262]

Sherlock Holmes had five children with Irene Adler.[263] The first, Mycroft Adler Norton, was conceived during "A Scandal in Bohemia" and was assumed to be the son of Geoffrey Norton. Mycroft Adler Norton had one son, Mycroft Adler Norton, Jr.[264] Mycroft, Jr.'s son, James Norton, turned to a life of crime. James' daughter, Lillian "Silicon Lil" Norton, also turned to crime but assisted her great-great-grandfather in capturing a number of criminals in "The Curious Computer" by Peter Lovesy.

Twins John Hamish Adler and Scott Regis Adler were conceived in Montenegro in 1892.[265] John Hamish developed a strong resemblance to his uncle Mycroft, and became a spy code-named Auguste Lupa.[266] He later became a private detective known as Nero Wolfe.[267] He has a son, Spenser Holmes.[268]

Scott Regis, on the other hand, resembled his uncle Sherrinford, and was a traveller. (He hated his father after Professor Moriarty kidnapped him as a child.)[269] He had seven children. Using the name Redlock Regis (aka the "Scarlet Poppy", a reference to his descent from the Scarlet Pimpernel), he fathered Avalokiteshvara Melas by Devi Melas (daughter of Mr. Melas from "The Adventure of the Greek Interpreter[270]). Like his father, Avalokiteshvara was an exotic traveller and ladies' man, and he fathered Robert Goren. Robert Goren became a police detective.[271]

Later on, Scott Regis Adler adopted the name Marko Vukcic and put his cooking ability to good use as a restaurant owner. However, he never gave up his romancing escapades, and fathered Archie Goodwin by an affair with Leslie Goodwin, née McGee, of Ohio, sister of Scott McGee, who fathered Travis McGee. Archie was his Uncle Nero's assistant and biographer. Marko also had affairs with sisters Erica and Emily Russell, the granddaughters of Marshall Matt Dillon and Kitty Russell. He fathered private detective Frank Cannon[272] by Erica, and non-identical twins by Emily. One twin was District Attorney J.L. McCabe,[273] and the other was sent to Scotland for adoption. This twin was given the name David Callan and was an agent for the S.I.S.[274] until he learned of his heritage and moved back to America. McCabe was his sponsor, and as a tribute, he changed his surname

name from CALLan to McCALL, and his first name to Edward. He joined the "Company" (the CIA) until retiring and becoming a private investigator, naming his son Scott after his own father.[275]

One of Marko's last conquests before his death was Michele Wiseman. Michele bore a son, Michael Wiseman. Michael grew to be tall and obese like many members of his family; he had the grey eyes of his grandfather and a disinterest in adventure from his father. But after Michael was pushed under a train in 1999, his brain was transplanted into a synthetic body and he was given the new identity of Michael Newman. He married Lisa Schleigelmilch. They have a daughter, Heather Wiseman.[276] Holmes met Irene again in 1898, when she was posing as Mrs. Martha Hudson[277] and they again had twins (a Wold Newtonian trait). After the *Sherlock Holmes in New York* incident, Irene hid the twins, and they were raised as Philo and Philomina Vance.[278]

According to *The End of Sherlock Holmes* by A. E. P., Sherlock Holmes married a Miss Falkland, and had two children, Shirley (II) and Sherlock Holmes II.[279]

Shirley (II) married a man named Robinson. Their grandson, Dan Robinson, established his own Baker Street Irregulars, who have solved ten cases to date. Dan is constantly described as looking like Sherlock Holmes without the hat and pipe—on one occasion Dan's father looks at his son and thinks that people may be right in thinking that Sherlock is not dead, a subtle reference to the Holmes blood in the family. Nor is the resemblance purely physical, but also mental. (It appears that Dan was raised on tales of his famous family members as he often refers to Sherlock Holmes, Nero Wolfe, Richard Hannay, Fagin, and Fu Manchu.)[280]

Sherlock Holmes II had two children, Sherlock Holmes III and Richard Holmes.[281]

Richard's daughter married an East End man with the surname of Townsend and they had a son, Nigel. At age nineteen, Nigel left home and joined the Navy. Later, he gained his doctorate and worked as a trace investigator for the Massachusetts State Coroner's Office.[282]

From his affair with Vivian S. La Graine, Sherlock Holmes had two daughters, Minerva Holmes and Alice "Boomer" La Graine.[283] Alice married a Frenchman by the name of Loquot and had a son, Solomon Holmes Loquot.[284] In 1921, Holmes married Mary Russell, They produced one son: Abraham Moth (notice that he has a Biblical first name, like his mother). Moth set up his own agency at 221b Baker Street. (He also collaborated with Scotland Yard frequently, most notably with the great-grandson of Inspector Gregson.) Isaiah Cohen had an adventure with him, recorded in the graphic novel *The Woman in Red* by Byron Preiss and Ralph Reese.

There are rumours of three other daughters of Sherlock, but these may be references to Shirley and Minerva.[285] In *The Holmes-Dracula File* by Fred Saberhagen, it is revealed that Sherlock Holmes had a twin brother, Rutherford Holmes, and that Rutherford was a vampire. The reason for this is that a member of the Dracula family—Dracula's twin brother, Radu the Handsome[286]—bit Violet Rutherford. Rutherford, on occasion, stepped in for his twin brother, when Sherlock had to be away [287]unknown to the criminal community. Later in life, Rutherford started a detective agency of his own under the name Cardula.[288]

Charlotte Holmes had one son, Alexander, from a morganatic marriage to Prince Rupert of Kravonia. It appears that Rupert is descended from Sophie of Kravonia.[289] (A morganatic marriage means that Charlotte will never be Queen of Kravonia, nor will any of her heirs).[290] Sigerson Holmes' one meeting with Moriarty was turned into a farce by Gene Wilder, but most of the facts in the case are accurate. Sigerson Holmes did marry Jenny Hill, who is a descendant of Fanny Hill, a member of an early League of Extraordinary Gentlemen. They had a son, Anthony Hill Holmes, and a daughter. Anthony hated his father and as soon as he was old enough dropped his last name. He had a son, Dr. Tony Hill, Jr.[291]

Sigrina married John Vansittart Smith and had three children: Sir Denis Nayland Smith, John Smith, and a daughter Violet Smith.

Sir Denis was first married to Joan Blakeney, the great-great-granddaughter of Sir Percy Blakeney, and together they had two sons, George (later Sir George) and Horatio Smith. Horatio's adventures were chronicled in the film *Pimpernel Smith*. Sir Denis had another son, John "Hannibal" Smith. Hannibal is the leader of the A-Team and shows a flair for disguise. It has also been noted that he bears a resemblance to his cousin, Archie Goodwin. I am grateful to Win Eckert for the revelation that Hannibal Smith's mother was Fah Lo Suee, daughter of Fu Manchu. This Chinese heritage explains why one of Hannibal's favourite disguises was of Mr. Lee, an elderly Chinese man.[292] Win also reveals that that Hannibal had a daughter, Leiko Smith. It appears that Leiko's mother left Hannibal while he was serving in Vietnam. Leiko had three encounters with Mike Shayne, Jr.[293]

Sigrina and John Vansittart Smith's second son, John, appeared to have died on the *Titanic*, but thanks to Win Eckert it has been discovered that John Smith was the man known as the Continental

Op. Later in life, he was known as Brad Runyon, The Fat Man.[294]

Sigrina and John Vansittart Smith's daughter, Violet, married a man named Sneed and had son Lancaster, who became the villain Shockwave.[295]

The third son of Brian Mycroft Holmes was Henry Holmes. He married Pauline Cataflaque, daughter of Jonathan Cataflaque and great-aunt of Professor Paul Cataflaque.[296] They had one son, Jonathon Holmes. Jonathon was a scholar of the occult and had a case referred by his cousin Sherlock in *The Return of the Werewolf* by Les Martin.

The fourth child of Brian Mycroft Holmes was Robert Holmes. He married a woman named Paris. The Paris family was descended from wealthy landowner Aaron Stemple, and was consequently very rich. Robert's bride had an elder brother, Dexter Norman Paris, who had a son, Clifford Paris. Clifford named his twin sons after his father: Dexter and Norman Paris.[297] Robert had a son named Paris Holmes, who married a descendant of Artemus Gordon. They had two children: Paris Holmes, Jr., and Anthony Blake Holmes. Paris joined the Impossible Missions Force after his relative Rollin Hand (who bears a resemblance to Dexter and Norman Paris) left. Anthony Blake (named after Sexton Blake, another detective who lived on Baker Street) became a magician and detective as seen on the television series *The Magician.*

The fifth child of Brian Mycroft Holmes was Dorothy Holmes. In *Sherlock Holmes of Baker Street*, W.S. Baring-Gould suggested that Professor George Edward Challenger was the child of Siger's sister Dorothy Holmes and a cousin to Sherlock Holmes. Philip José Farmer, in *Tarzan Alive*, established that Professor Challenger was in fact Sherlock Holmes' cousin, but through Violet Rutherford's brother John and his wife Dorothy, née Swinton. Farmer admits that this contradicts Baring-Gould. My research has shown that Baring-Gould appears to have confused Sherlock's two aunt Dorothys and attributed the maternity of Professor Challenger to the wrong one.

This research has also shown that Dorothy Holmes did in fact have a son. This son so resembled his cousin Mycroft Holmes that J. Randolph Cox, in his article "Mycroft Holmes: Private Detective,"[298] mistook him for Mycroft. I am referring to Martin Hewitt. Hewitt operated prior to Holmes but his cases were edited by Arthur Morrison and published in the *Strand* at the same time as those of his more famous cousin. Dorothy also had two daughters. The first, Honoria, married firstly James Gayle, the son of Rev. and Mrs Gayle. Unfortunately, he died shortly after the wedding. It was while staying with her in-laws that Honoria met the eighth Baronet, Henry St. John Merrivale, and had two children, Henry (II) and Kitty. (All rumours of an affair between Honoria and her cousin Mycroft are slanderous).[299] Sir Henry Merrivale (II) followed his second cousin into the field of espionage where he was nicknamed "Mycroft" due to the physical and mental resemblance, but Sir Henry, who was determined to make it on his own, hated and rejected the nickname.[300] Sir Henry had one daughter, Lydia.

The second child, Kitty, married an American named Bennett, who was high up in Washington, and their son James Boyton Bennett helped his uncle solve *The White Priory Murders*.[301]

Dorothy's second daughter, Elizabeth, married a Fell and had one son, Gideon Fell. Fell certainly resembles his Uncle Martin Hewitt and his cousins Sir Henry, Nero Wolfe, and Mycroft Holmes, in bulk and intellect.

Brian Mycroft's last daughter and last child was Roberta Holmes (I). She married a McIvor and had one daughter, Roberta (II), and a son, Richard. Roberta (II) married Asenath Pons and they had two sons, Bancroft and Solar Pons. Bancroft and Solar bear such an incredible resemblance to Mycroft and Sherlock Holmes, respectively, that there can be little doubt that there is a family connection.[302]

Richard McIvor immigrated to America where, through either a clerical error or deliberate effort, his last name was changed to MacGyver. Richard then married Edwina Pratt, daughter of Ernest Pratt. Pratt was the author of the Nicodemus Legend dime novels and was frequently confused with his fictional creation. In these cases, Pratt used the inventions of Professor Eugene Bartok to uphold Legend's reputation as a scientific investigator.[303] Richard and Edwina had two children, James and Helen.

James married Ellen Jackson and the couple had one son, Angus MacGyver. Angus, or Mac, as he preferred to be called, was a former demolitions expert and Navy SEAL in Vietnam, but an incident in 1985, which recalled a childhood trauma, left him with an aversion to guns. During his time in 'Nam, his grandfather would send him Nicodemus Legend dime novels which inspired him to create his own gadgets. While Mac resembles Ernest Pratt, he has the Holmes intellect and can rapidly create gadgets out of almost anything.[304]

Helen MacGyver married Leo Schwarz and had one son, Herman Schwarz. Herman was interested in electronics from an early age and during his time in Vietnam was given the nickname "Gadgets." After returning to America he joined Mack Bolan in his infamous Death

Squad. Later, he and fellow Death Squad member Rosario “Pol” Blancanales formed Able Investigations and were joined by ex-cop Carl Lyons to fight terrorist attacks against America as “The Able Team.”

Fu Manchu Vs. Cthulhu
By Rick Lai

In a series of stories published in *Weird Tales*, August Derleth (1909-1971) refashioned the artificial mythology of H. P. Lovecraft (1890-1937) into a framework that has come to be known as the Cthulhu Mythos. Lovecraft had created a background for his tales that was based on the premise that various alien races from other planets had colonized Earth before the evolution of human beings. Eventually, these alien masters of Earth went into a state of hibernation, but legends of them persisted among various human cults that worshipped these primordial beings as gods. Most prominent of these deified extraterrestrials was Cthulhu, a giant sea creature that was lying in a sort of suspended animation in the depths of the Pacific. The ultimate horror suggested in Lovecraft's writings is that these ancient beings would emerge to devour mankind. While Lovecraft described various conflicting rivalries and alliances between his different alien life forms, Derleth imposed a system of classification that placed Cthulhu and most of Lovecraft's creations into a huge alliance of evil. To act as a counterweight to these evil entities, Derleth created the Elder Gods, a group of apparently benevolent beings from the Orion constellation. These Elder Gods were credited with exiling Cthulhu and his allies to Earth and other planets. Various human beings became pawns in the struggle between the Elder Gods and Cthulhu. If you read very carefully two of Derleth's stories, "Something in Wood" and "The Lair of the Star-Spawn," you will find hints that Dr. Fu Manchu, the malevolent master criminal created by Sax Rohmer (1883-1959), played a role in this cosmic struggle.

Derleth was clearly fond of Fu Manchu. In a series of short stories about Solar Pons, a fictional detective whose adventures were set in the 1920s and 1930s, Derleth had Fu Manchu make three appearances. The stories featuring Rohmer's creation were "The Adventure of the Camberwell Beauty" from *The Return of Solar Pons* (Mycroft and Moran, 1958), "The Adventure of the Praed Street Irregulars" from *The Reminiscences of Solar Pons* (Mycroft and Moran, 1961), and "The Adventure of the Seven Sisters" from *The Chronicles of Solar Pons* (Mycroft and Moran, 1973).

One of Derleth's Cthulhu Mythos stories was "Something in Wood" (*Weird Tales,* March 1948), a tale that was later reprinted in

The Mask of Cthulhu (Arkham House, 1958). The plot of this story need not concern us, but one of the characters did make reference to these unusual happenings:

> I could tell you things — about what happened in Innsmouth when the government took over that time in 1928 and all those explosions took place out at Devil Reef; about what happened in Limehouse, London, back in 1911; about the disappearance of Professor Shrewsbury over in Arkham not so many years ago —
>
> There are still pockets of secret worship right here in Massachusetts, I know, and they are all over the world."

The Innsmouth reference tied into one of Lovecraft's most famous supernatural tales, "The Shadow Over Innsmouth," which was first published as a slim book in 1936 by Visionary Press, and Professor Shrewsbury's disappearance was explained in Derleth's "The House on Curwen Street" (first published as "The Trail of Cthulhu" in *Weird Tales,* March 1944), but the Limehouse reference is rather curious because that district of London was frequently the headquarters of Rohmer's Dr. Fu Manchu. Neither Lovecraft nor Derleth set any of their other stories in Limehouse. Of course, there were other *Weird Tales* writers who contributed to the Mythos, or had their own myth-patterns subsumed into the Mythos by Lovecraft or Derleth. Of those writers, only Robert E. Howard (1906-1936) utilized Limehouse as a setting. Howard's *Skull-Face* (serialized in *Weird Tales* during October, November and December, 1929) featured an evil genius, Kathulos, who was clearly inspired by Fu Manchu. Like Rohmer's creation, Kathulos made his criminal base in Limehouse. The similarity between the names Kathulos and Cthulhu was noted by Lovecraft and Howard in their correspondence. As a result, the name Kathulos was briefly mentioned into two Mythos stories, Lovecraft's "The Whisperer in the Darkness" (*Weird Tales*, August 1931) and Howard's own "Dig Me No Grave" (*Weird Tales*, February 1937).

Despite a peripheral connection between the Cthulhu Mythos and Howard's Limehouse denizen, the 1911 reference in Derleth's "Something in Wood" cannot apply to *Skull-Face.* The activities of Kathulos clearly transpired in the 1920s. The hero of *Skull-Face*, Stephen Costigan, was an American veteran of World War I who had been residing in England for some years after the war concluded.

Derleth did have another Limehouse reference in the previously cited "The House on Curwen Street." The story briefly mentioned "the London scholar Follexon, who shortly after he announced himself as on the trail of important disclosures relative to certain ancient survivals in the East Indies, was inexplicably drowned in the Thames off Limehouse." As pointed out by Joseph Wrzos in his notes for the Derleth collection, *In Lovecraft's Shadow: The Cthulhu Mythos Stories of August Derleth* (Mycroft and Moran, 1998), the 1911 reference from "Something in Wood" could be tied into Follexon's death. However, Derleth gave no indication of the year when Follexon's demise occurred.

The 1911 reference is rather curious since this would seem to be the year in which the first Fu Manchu book, *The Insidious Dr. Fu Manchu* (1913), probably transpired. For the chronological issues raised in Rohmer's series, the reader is advised to consult Cay Van Ash's "A Question of Time" in *The Rohmer Review* n17 (August 1977). Although multiple misdeeds were committed in Limehouse in the course of *The Insidious Dr. Fu Manchu*, none of them would seem to have any bearing on the Mythos. If the reference in Derleth's "Something in Wood" was intended to connect Fu Manchu to the Mythos, then there must have been some unrecorded activities involving the criminal mastermind in Limehouse during 1911.

This whole question of a possible connection between Fu Manchu and Cthulhu becomes even more complicated when an examination is made of "The Lair of the Star-Spawn" (*Weird Tales*, August 1932), a story which Derleth wrote with Mark Schorer (1908-1977). The story has been reprinted in a collection of all the Derleth-Schorer collaborations, *Colonel Markesan and Less Pleasant People* (Arkham House, 1966), and in *Tales of the Lovecraft Mythos* (Fedogan and Bremer, 1992), an anthology edited by Robert M. Price. The story also can be found inside *In Lovecraft's Shadow: The Cthulhu Mythos Stories of August Derleth.* "The Lair of the Star-Spawn" featured a character, Dr. Fo-Lan, who was heavily influenced by Rohmer's Dr. Fu Manchu.

"The Lair of the Star-Spawn" supposedly transpired "almost three decades ago." Since Derleth and Schroer wrote this story in the summer of 1931, it would seem to be set around 1902. The story's narrator was Eric Marsh, the sole survivor of an American expedition to Burma. All the other members of the expedition were massacred by the Tcho-Tcho people, a dwarfish race that lived in the interior of Burma. Marsh found himself a prisoner in Alaozar, the lost city of the Tcho-Tcho people. There Marsh discovered a mysterious Oriental who claimed to be a captive in Alaozar. The man was apparently Chinese. He was slightly over six feet tall and "already well past middle-age." He wore a black gown and skullcap. This man gave Marsh the impression of being a doctor. The following exchange occurred between Marsh and the other man:

> "Doctor," I said, "you remind me of a certain dead man."
>
> His eyes gazed kindly at me; then he looked away, closing his eyes dreamily. "I had not hoped that anyone might remember," he murmured. "Yet...of whom do I remind you, Eric Marsh?"
>
> "Of Doctor Fo-Lan, who was murdered at his home in Peiping a few years ago."
>
> He nodded almost imperceptibly. "Doctor Fo-Lan was not murdered, Eric Marsh. His brother was left there in his stead, but he was kidnapped and taken from the world. I am Doctor Fo-Lan."

Doctor Fo-Lan was apparently a world-renowned scholar. He claimed to have been kidnapped by the Tcho-Tcho people three years earlier. He had allegedly been forced to help the denizens of Alaozar search in the caverns of the city for Lloigor and Zhar, extraterrestrial beings worshipped by the Tcho-Tcho people as gods. Lloigor and Zhar, tentacled monstrosities also known as the Twin Obscenities, were allies of Cthulhu. Together with various subservient alien beings, Lloigor and Zhar had been imprisoned by the Elder Gods beneath Alaozar eons ago. The Tcho-Tcho people had been seeking for centuries to unleash Lloigor and Zhar on mankind.

Through telepathy, Doctor Fo-Lan was able to contact the Elder Gods. When the Tcho-Tcho people succeeded in releasing Lloigor, Zhar and their alien hordes, the Elder Gods arrived to smite them. Fo-Lan escaped with Marsh as an incredible cosmic battle ensued.

Ten days later, an "aviator" flew from India over the site of the battle in Burma. One would assume that the aviator was using a balloon since the story took place slightly before the invention of the airplane. He observed the ruins of a city and the rotting corpses of gigantic green-black creatures unknown to science. These remains apparently belonged to the alien minions of Lloigor and Zhar. The

Twin Obscenities were apparently not destroyed because they are mentioned as dwelling on the star Arcturus in two later stories by Derleth, "The Sandwin Compact" (November 1940) and "The Dweller in Darkness" (November 1944). It could be assumed that the Elder Gods had removed Lloigor and Zhar from Earth and imprisoned them again on Arcturus.

Fo-Lan and Marsh arrived in the village of Bangka in the Chinese province of Shan-si. Although a Tokyo newspaper announced the return of Doctor Fo-Lan to the world with much fanfare, the Asian scholar became a recluse in Bangka. Eric March returned to the United States where he died in unrecorded circumstances shortly after preparing an account of his awesome experiences in Burma.

Fo-Lan's description could fit Fu Manchu. Sax Rohmer's mastermind was the same height, dressed in similar garments, and would have been about the same general age in 1902. Although numerous illustrators adorn Fu Manchu's face with a mustache, he was as clean-shaven as Fo-Lan in Rohmer's novels.

We could speculate that Fo-Lan and Fu Manchu were different names utilized by the same character. In Rohmer's *The Mask of Fu Manchu* (1932), a novel whose events were chronologically placed in 1930 by Cay Van Ash, Fu Manchu claimed to have visited Burma nearly thirty years ago. This reference would mean that Fu was in Burma around 1902, the time of the events of "The Lair of the Star-Spawn." In Burma, Fu Manchu discovered rare orchids that would eventually yield an immortality elixir. The Tcho-Tcho people seemed to possess some secret of immortality because their leader, E-poh, was reputed to be seven thousand years old.[305] Perhaps the Tcho-Tcho people had utilized the species of orchid that Fu Manchu found in Burma. Fu Manchu also demonstrated some ability to utilize telepathy for hypnotic purposes in Rohmer's novels. This ability would not be too different from Fo-Lan's usage of telepathy to contact the Elder Gods.

There are obstacles to the theory that Fu Manchu and Fo-Lan are the same man. Fo-Lan had claimed that he was the prisoner of the Tcho-Tcho people for three years. He would have been residing in Alaozar during 1899-1902. Fu's persecution of a British missionary in *The Return of Dr. Fu Manchu* (1916) strongly suggested that the infamous mastermind had participated in the Boxer Rebellion (1900), a violent insurrection by Chinese nationalists against foreigners residing in their country. Fu Manchu is clearly an alias, as it is not a proper Chinese name, and the master criminal's chief antagonist,

Sir Denis Nayland Smith, noted that the British government had been unable to trace Fu Manchu's origins in 1911 during the events of *The Insidious Dr. Fu Manchu*. Smith would have had little difficulty tracing Fu Manchu's antecedents if a Tokyo newspaper had identified him as Dr. Fo-Lan, who had mysteriously reappeared after supposedly being dead for three years. There were no suggestions in Rohmer's novels that Fu lived for any lengthy period of time in Peiping (Beijing). It was strongly suggested that he had spent most of his time in the distant Chinese province of Honan.

Fo-Lan's story of being held captive for three years also has a large credibility problem. It seemed highly unlikely that the Tcho-Tcho people could have kidnapped a noted scientist from Peiping and carried him all the way to Burma. The Tcho-Tcho people displayed an astonishing ignorance of the outside world. For example, they were ignorant of firearms. Fo-Lan could have originally gone willingly to Alaozar as an ally of the Tcho-Tcho people, and then turned against them when he learned the true nature of the beings they threatened to summon forth.

Here is a theory. In the 1890s, Fu Manchu was based in Honan. He had a half-brother, Fo-Lan, who lived in Peiping. The two half-brothers greatly resembled each other. In fact, their family connection was a closely guarded secret.[306] In Lovecraft's "The Call of Cthulhu" (*Weird Tales*, February 1928), it was mentioned that the leaders of the Cthulhu cult were a group of immortal high priests in the mountains of China.[307] In 1899, these priests of Cthulhu asked Fu Manchu to join their order. At this time, the super-criminal was using a different alias than the one by which Nayland Smith would later know him. Because he was preparing the groundwork for the Boxer Rebellion, Fu refused. The priests of Cthulhu sent an assassin to murder Fu Manchu, but mistook Fo-Lan for his half-brother and slew him instead. In 1900, Fu participated in the Boxer Rebellion. In 1902, Fu made contact with the Tcho-Tcho people. At this time, Fu sought to establish dominion over various ancient cults such as the Dacoits of Burma. The Tcho-Tcho people were vaguely allied with the priests of Cthulhu. He pretended to be Fo-Lan, and claimed that the assassin had actually slain an unimportant half-brother. As Dr. Fo-Lan, Fu Manchu claimed that he was now willing to serve the cause of Cthulhu. He entered Alaozar as a prospective ally of the Tcho-Tcho people. His real purpose was to gain control over the Tcho-Tcho people and their cult that worshipped entities from beyond the stars. He hoped to break the Tcho-Tcho people away from their alliance with the Cthulhu cult and entice them to join the Si-Fan, a confederation of various cults that he had been organizing since the failure of the Boxer Rebellion. He also hoped to use the Tcho-Tcho people to avenge himself on the leaders of the Cthulhu cult responsible for his half-brother's death. He soon discovered that Lloigor and Zhar were forces that could not be manipulated by any mortal man for personal gain. Therefore, he concluded that Alaozar and the Tcho-Tcho people needed to be destroyed. The tools chosen by Fu Manchu for his plan of destruction were the Elder Gods.

Fu Manchu did not fully take Eric Marsh into his confidence. The American could not be trusted with the true reasons that had brought the sinister savant to Alaozar. Fu erected a wall of half-truths to disguise his real motives and history. Besides using his alias of Fo-Lan, Fu lied to Marsh about the length of his stay in Alaozar, the origins of his dealing with the Tcho-Tcho people, and the true identity of the man slain in his place during 1899. Under the cover of his Fo-Lan identity, Fu pretended to retire as a recluse. He soon returned to his nefarious activities around the world.

While escaping from Alaozar, Fu Manchu took with him certain orchids. He believed that these plants were somehow used in an elixir that permitted E-poh to live for seven thousand years. Around 1929, Fu Manchu would extract from these orchids an elixir for his own usage.

Eric Marsh died under vague circumstances shortly after returning to the United States. It is possible that the Cthulhu cult had him murdered as revenge for his role in the defeat of Lloigor and Zhar. Perhaps the Cthulhu cult also discovered Fu Manchu's presence in Limehouse during 1911. Recognizing him as the former Fo-Lan, the cult sought his demise. This conflict may also have involved the scholar Follexon. An unrecorded battle transpired which was the basis for the reference in Derleth's "Something in Wood." Considering that Fu Manchu was still alive in the 1950s, there can be little doubt who emerged the victor.

There is another possible participant in the conflict between Fu Manchu and the Tcho-Tcho people. His name is Dr. Anton Zarnak, an occult detective whose exploits were first chronicled by Lin Carter, and subsequently continued by Robert M. Price, C. J. Henderson, Joseph S. Pulver and other writers. The adventures of this remarkable investigator can be found in the anthology *Lin Carter's Anton Zarnak Supernatural Sleuth* (Marietta Publishing, 2002). In Lin Carter's "Perchance to Dream," Zarnak made this utterance: "To quote an old adversary rather imprecisely, I have a doctorate in medicine from

Edinburgh, a doctorate in theology from Heidelberg, a doctorate in psychology from Vienna, and a doctorate in metaphysics from Miskatonic; my guests usually address me as Dr. Zarnak." The "old adversary" was Fu Manchu. According to *The Bride of Fu Manchu* (1933), Fu had doctorates from four universities. He was also identified as a Doctor of Philosophy as well as a Doctor of Medicine. In *Emperor Fu Manchu* (1959), three of the universities are identified: Heidelberg, the Sorbonne and Edinburgh. Since Fu cited these universities when he felt his skill as a surgeon was challenged by a subordinate, it is likely that he studied medicine and science at all three. The unnamed fourth university must be where he studied philosophy. Although Fu never made a speech like Zarnak's in Rohmer's novel, his cinematic counterpart (played by Boris Karloff in the 1932 movie version of *The Mask of Fu Manchu*) did: "I am a Doctor of Philosophy from Edinburgh, I am a Doctor of Law from Christ College, I am a Doctor of Medicine from Harvard; my friends have the courtesy to call me Doctor." Although the degrees cited in the speech are contradictory to those mentioned in Rohmer's novels, the real Fu could have uttered a more accurate variation of these remarks that Zarnak overheard. Zarnak sometimes lived in California, and he could have repeated his knowledge of Fu Manchu to a Hollywood screenwriter.

In Robert M. Price's "Dope War of the Black Tong," Dr. Zarnak professed that he had once reigned over the Tcho-Tcho people. In fact, his adoption of the Zarnak name came from an earlier alias of "Zhar-Nak, mouthpiece of Zhar." Zarnak was a benevolent scholar allied with the Elder Gods. There can be no doubt that he tried to wean the Tcho-Tcho people away from evil practices by pretending to revere Lloigor and Zhar. Zarnak was overthrown by E-poh, and consequently forced to flee Burma.

Since E-poh was seven thousand years old, and Zarnak's past is a vast mystery, it is possible that their power struggle happened centuries ago. On the other hand, Zarnak could have been ruling the Tcho-Tcho people when Fu Manchu stumbled upon them. Perhaps Fu Manchu helped E-poh overthrow Zarnak only to learn that the Tcho-Tcho chieftain had his own ambitions to release the Great Old Ones. Did Fu Manchu and Zarnak attend Heidelberg or Edinburgh together? Did they meet in Limehouse during 1911? These questions remain unanswered.

Jonathan Swift Somers III, Cosmic Traveller in a Wheelchair

A Short Biography by Philip José Farmer (Honorary Chief Kennel Keeper)

By Philip José Farmer

Scintillation No. 13, June 1977

Petersburg is a small town in the mid-Illinois county of Menard. It lies in hilly country near the Sangamon River on state route 97. Not far away is New Salem, the reconstructed pioneer village where Abraham Lincoln worked for a while as a postmaster, surveyor and storekeeper. The state capital of Springfield is southeast, a half-hour's drive or less if traffic is light.

A hilltop cemetery holds two famous people, Anne Rutledge and Edgar Lee Masters. The former (1816-1835) is known only because of the legend, now proven false, that she was Lincoln's first love, tragically dying before she could marry him. "Bloom forever, O Republic, From the dust of my bosom!"

These are from the epitaph which Masters wrote for her and are inscribed on her gravestone. Unfortunately, the man who chiseled the epitaph made a typo, driving Masters into a rage. We authors, who have suffered from so many typos, can sympathize with him. However, we have the advantage that we can make sure that reissues contain corrections. There will be no later editions in stone of Anne Rutledge's epitaph.

Masters (1869-1950) was a poet, novelist and literary critic, known chiefly for his *Spoon River Anthology.* There is a Spoon River area but no town of that name. Masters chose that name to represent an amalgamation of the actual towns of Lewistown and Petersburg, where he spent most of his childhood and early adulthood. Lewistown, also on route 97, is about forty miles from Petersburg but separated by the Illinois River.

The free verse epitaphs of Masters' best-known work were modeled after *The Greek Anthology* but based on people he'd known. These told the truth behind the flattering or laconic statements on the tombs and gravestones. The departed spoke of their lives as they had really been. Some were happy, productive, even creative and heroic. But most recite chronicles of hypocrisy, misery, misunderstanding, failed dreams, greed, narrow-mindedness, egotism, persecution, madness, connivance, cowardice, stupidity, injustice, sorrow, folly and murder.

In other words, the Spoon River citizens were just like big-city residents.

Among the graves in the cemetery of Petersburg are those of Judge Somers and his son, Jonathan Swift Somers II. Neither has any marker, though the grandson has made arrangements to erect stones above both. Masters has the judge complain that he was a famous Illinois jurist, yet he lies unhonored in his grave while the town drunkard, who is buried by his side, has a large monument. Masters does not explain how this came about.

According to Somers III, his grandson, the judge and his wife were not on the best of terms during the ten years preceding the old man's death. Somers' grandmother would give no details, but others provided the information that it was because of an indiscretion committed by the judge in a cathouse in Peoria. (This city is mentioned now and then in the *Spoon River Anthology*.)

The judge's son, Somers II, sided with his father. This caused the mother to forbid her son to enter her house. In 1910 the judge died, and the following year the son and his wife were drowned in the Sangamon during a picnic outing. The widow refused to pay for monuments for either, insisting that she did not have the funds. Her son's wife was buried in a family plot near New Goshen, Indiana. That Samantha Tincrowder Somers preferred not to lie with her husband indicates that she also had strong differences with him.

Jonathan Swift Somers III was born in this unhappy atmosphere on January 6, 1910. This is also Sherlock Holmes' birthdate, which Somers celebrates annually by sending a telegram of congratulations to a certain residence on Baker Street, London.

The forty-three-year-old grandmother took the year-old infant into her house. Though the gravestone incident seems to characterize her as vindictive, she was a very kind and probably too indulgent grandmother to the young Jonathan. Until the age of ten, he had a happy childhood. Even though the Somers' house was a large gloomy mid-Victorian structure, it was brightened for him by his grandmother and the books he found in the library. A precocious reader, he went through all the lighter volumes before he was eleven. The judge's philosophical books, Fichte, Schopenhauer, Nietzsche, et al, would be mastered by the time he was eighteen.

Despite his intense interest in books, Jonathan played as hard as any youngster. With his schoolmates he roamed the woody hills and swam and fished in the Sangamon. He gave promises of being a notable athlete, beating all his peers in the dashes and the broad jump. Among his many pets were a raven, a raccoon, a fox and a bullsnake.

Then infantile paralysis felled him. Treatment was primitive in those days, but a young physician, son of the Doctor Hill whose epitaph is in the *Anthology*, got him through. Jonathan came back out of the valley of the shadow, only to find that he would be paralyzed from the waist down for the rest of his life. This knowledge resulted in another paralysis, a mental freezing. His grandmother despaired of his mind for a while, fearing that he had retreated so far into himself he would never come back out. Jonathan himself now recalls little of this period. Apparently, it was so traumatic that even today his conscious mind refuses to touch it.

"It was as if I were embedded in a crystal ball. I could see others around me, but I could not hear or touch them. And the crystal magnified and distorted their faces and figures. I was a human fly in amber, stuck in time, preserved from decay but isolated forever from the main flow of life."

Amanda Knapp Somers, his grandmother, would not admit that he would never walk again. She told him that he only needed faith in God to overcome his "disability." That was the one word she used when referring to his paralysis. Disability. She avoided mentioning his legs; they, too, were disabilities.

Amanda Somers had been raised in the Episcopalian sect. She came from an old Virginia family whose fortune had been ruined by the Civil War. Her father had brought his family out to this area shortly after Appomattox. He had intended to stay only a short while with his younger brother, who had settled near Petersburg before the war. Then he meant to push on west, to homestead in northern California. However, he had sickened and died in his brother's house, leaving a wife, two daughters and a son. The wife died a year later of cholera. The surviving children were adopted by their uncle.

Amanda came into frequent contact with the fundamentalist Baptists and Methodists of this rural community. Though she never formally renounced her membership in the Episcopalian church, she began attending revival meetings. After marrying Jonathan Swift Somers I, she stopped this, since the "respectable" people in Petersburg did not go to such functions. Now, however, with her husband dead and her grandson crippled, she went to every revival and faith healer that came along. She insisted on taking young Jonathan with her, undoubtedly hoping that he would suddenly be "saved," that a miracle would occur, that he would stand up and walk.

This went on for two years. The child objected strongly to these procedures. The tense emotional atmosphere and the sense of guilt at not being "saved" wore him out. Moreover, he hated being the center of attention at these meetings, and he always felt that he let everybody down when he failed to be "cured." Somehow, it was his fault, not the faith healer's, that he could not rid himself of his paralysis.

During this troubling time, several things saved young Jonathan's reason. One was his ability to get away from the world into his books. The library was large, since it included both his grandfather's and father's books. Much of this was too advanced even for his precocity, but there were plenty of adventure and mystery volumes, and even fantasy was not lacking. Moreover, though his grandmother had some narrow-minded ideas about religion, she made no effort to supervise his reading. She gave him freedom in ordering books, and as a result Jonathan had a larger and more varied collection than the Petersburg library.

At this time he came across John Carter of Mars, Tarzan of the Apes, Professor Challenger and Sherlock Holmes. In a short time he had ordered and read all of the works of Burroughs and Doyle. A copy of *Before Adam* led him to Jack London. This writer, in turn, introduced him to something besides fascinating tales of adventure in the frozen north or the hot south seas. He gave young Jonathan his first look into the depths of social and political injustice, into the miseries of "the people of the abyss."

It was not enough for him to read about far-off exciting places. Unable immediately to get the sequel to *The Gods of Mars*, he wrote his own. This was titled *Dejah Thoris of Barsoom* and was one hundred pages, or about 20,000 words, quite an accomplishment for an eleven-year-old. On reading Burroughs' sequel, *The Warlord of Mars*, Jonathan decided that he had been outclassed. Years later, however, he used an idea in his story as the basis for *The Ivory Gates of Barsoom*, his first published novel. This was his first John Clayter story. Clayter is, of course, a name composed of the first syllable of Tarzan's English surname (Clayton) and the last syllable of John Carter's surname. At the time of this novel, the spaceman John Clayter has not lost his limbs.

More than books saved young Jonathan, however. His grandmother brought him a German Shepherd (police) pup. The child loved it, talked to it, fed it, brushed it, and threw the ball for it in the big backyard. Jonathan insisted on naming the male pup Fenris, after the monstrous wolf in Norse mythology. Fenris was the first of a long line of German Shepherds, Somers' favorite breed. Today, Fenris IX, a two-year-old, is Somers' devoted companion.

There is no doubt that Somers modeled his fictional dog, Ralph von Wau Wau, upon his own pet. Or is there no doubt? The Bellener Street Irregulars insist that there is a real von Wau Wau. In fact, Somers is not the real author of the series of tales about this Hamburg police dog who became a private eye. The Irregulars maintain that Somers is only the literary agent for Johann H. Weisstein, Dr. Med., and for Cordwainer Bird, the two main narrators in the Wau Wau series. Weisstein and Bird are the real authors.

When asked about this, Somers only replied, "I am not at liberty to discuss the matter."

"Are the Irregulars wrong then?"

"I would hesitate to say that they are in error."

So, perhaps, Somers is really only the agent for Ralph's colleagues.

There is one objection to this belief. How could Weisstein and Bird have written true stories about their life with Ralph since these stories took place in the future? The dog's first adventure took place in 1978, yet this appeared in the March 1931 issue of the magazine, *Outré Tales.* ("A Scarletin Study" was reprinted in the March 1975 issue of *The Magazine of Fantasy & Science Fiction.*)

Somers' answer: "There are such people as seers and science fiction writers. Both are able to look into the future. Besides, to paraphrase Pontius Pilate, 'What is Time?'"

Another of the bright lights that kept him from becoming overwhelmed by gloom was Edward Hill. This man was the brother of the same Doctor Hill who had pulled Jonathan through his sickness. Edward, however, had chosen the career of artist. Though he managed to sell some of his landscape paintings now and then, he needed extra money. At Doctor Hill's suggestion, Mrs. Somers hired him to tutor Jonathan in mathematics and chemistry. Later, Edward gave lessons in painting. During the warm months, he would put Jonathan and Fenris in his buggy, and the three would travel to a hillside or the riverbank and spend the day there. Jonathan would paint with Edward's eye on his progress or lack thereof. But they did much more than work at their pallets. Edward would bring insects and snakes to Jonathan and expound on their place in the ecosystem of Petersburg and environs.

These were some of the happiest days of young Somers' life. It was a terrible blow when Edward died the following year of typhoid fever.

Jonathan might have slid into the sorrow from which Edward Hill had rescued him if he had not met Henry Hone. Henry was the son of Neville Hone, a chiropractor who had just moved to Petersburg. A year older than Jonathan, he was a big happy-go-lucky boy, though he too suffered from a handicap. He stammered. Perhaps it was this that drew him to Jonathan, since misery is supposed to love company. But Henry, ignoring his verbal disadvantage, was very gregarious. He played long and hard after school with his schoolmates, and he did well in his classes. It was not shyness that made him spend so much time with Jonathan. It must have been a sort of elective affinity, a natural magnetism of the two.

The fact that he was Jonathan's next-door neighbor helped. He would often drop in after school or come over to spend part of Saturday. And it was he who got young Somers started with physical therapy. He talked Mrs. Somers into building a set of bars and trapezes in the backyard and constructing a little house on the branch of the giant sycamore in the corner of the yard. Every day Jonathan would haul himself out of his wheelchair by going hand over hand up a rope. At its top he would transfer to a horizontal bar and thence up and down and across a maze of iron pipes. In addition, he would pull himself up a rope which was let through a hole in the floor of the treehouse. A seat was built for him inside the treehouse, and in it he would look through a telescope at the neighborhood.

Moreover, the bars and the treehouse attracted other children. Jonathan no longer was forced to be alone; he had more companions than he could handle.

If Henry Hone aided Jonathan Somers much, Jonathan reciprocated. One of the many things that interested Jonathan was the artificial language, Esperanto. By the age of twelve he had taught himself to read fluently in it. But, wishing to be verbally facile, he enlisted Henry. At first, Henry refused because of his stammer. But Jonathan insisted, and, much to Henry's joy, he found that he could speak Esperanto without stammering. Both boys became adept in the language and for a while a number of their playmates tried to learn Esperanto, too. These dropped out after the initial enthusiasm wore out. But Henry and Jonathan continued.

On entering high school, Henry took German and found that in this language, too, his stammer disappeared. It was this that determined Henry to go into linguistics. Eventually, he got a Ph.D. in Arabic at the University of Chicago. He continued to correspond with his friend, in

Esperanto, though he never returned to Petersburg after 1930. His last letter (in English) was from North Africa, sent shortly before he was killed with Patton's forces.

It was Henry who talked Jonathan into attending high school instead of staying home to be tutored. Arrangements were made to accommodate Jonathan, and in 1928 he graduated. This decision to go to high school kept Jonathan from becoming a deep introvert. He made many friends; he even dated a few times in his senior year.

A photograph of him taken just before his illness hangs on the wall of his study. It shows a smiling ten-year old with curly blond hair, thick dark and straight eyebrows, large dark blue eyes, and a snub nose. Another picture, shot about six months after his attack of infantile paralysis, shows a thin hollow-cheeked face with dark shadows under the eyes and brooding shadows in the eyes. But his high school graduation photograph reveals a young man who has made an agreement with life. He will not sorrow about his lot; he'll make the best of it, doing better than most men with two good legs.

After getting his diploma, Jonathan thought about attending college. The University of Chicago attracted him, especially since his good friend Henry Hone was there. But that summer his grandmother broke her hip by falling out of a tree while picking cherries. Not wishing to leave her until she was well, Jonathan embarked on a series of studies designed to give him the equivalent of a university degree in the liberal arts and one in science. A room was fitted with laboratory equipment so he could perform the requisite experiments in chemistry and physics. He also took correspondence courses in electrical and mechanical engineering and in radio. He became a radio ham, and when he had a powerful set installed, he talked to people all over the world.

Jonathan had decided at the age of ten that he would be a writer of fiction. This determination firmed while he was reading *Twenty Thousand Leagues Under the Sea.* He too would pen tales about strong men who voyaged to distant and exotic places. If he could not go himself in electrical submarines or swing through jungle trees or fly dirigibles or journey in space ships, he would travel by proxy, via his fictional characters.

When he was seventeen he wrote a novel in which the aging Captain Nemo and Robur the Conqueror fought a great battle. This was rejected by twenty publishers. Jonathan put the manuscript in the proverbial trunk. But he has recently rewritten it and found a purchaser with the first submission. *The Nautilus Versus the Albatross* will appear under the nom de plume of Gideon Spilett. For those who may have forgotten, Spilett was the intrepid reporter for *The New York Herald* whose adventures are recounted in Verne's *The Mysterious Island.*

Jonathan wrote twelve works (two novels and ten short stories) when he launched into the career of freelance writer. All of these were rejected. His thirteenth, however, was accepted by the short-lived *Cosmic Adventures* magazine in December 1930. Payment was to be on publication, which was February 1931. The magazine actually appeared on a few stands here and there, but it collapsed during the distribution. Jonathan never received his money nor were his letters to the publisher ever answered. However, he did sell the story, "Jinx," to the slightly longer-lived *Outré Tales* magazine. This had had five issues, all chiefly distinguished by stories by Robert Blake, the mad young genius whose career was so lamentably and so mysteriously cut short in an old abandoned church in Providence, Rhode Island, on August 8, 1936. Somers' "Jinx" was to be featured with Blake's sixth story, "The Last Hajj of Abdul al-Hazred." But this publication also folded, and neither Blake nor Somers were paid. Jonathan corresponded with Blake about this matter, and Blake sent a copy of his story to Jonathan. As of today, it has not been published, but Jonathan hopes to include it in an anthology he is editing. "Jinx" did not go out again until 1949, when Somers dug it up out of the trunk. It was returned by the editor of the *Doc Savage* magazine with a note that the magazine was folding. Though Somers claims not to be superstitious, he decided that "Jinx" might indeed be just that. He retired the story to his files. However, it too will be included in the anthology.

Somers' second published story, and the first to be paid for, was a Ralph von Wau Wau piece, "A Scarletin Study." As noted, this was published in the March 1931 issue of *Outré Tales.* (The editor of *Fantasy & Science Fiction* failed to note the copyright in his introduction.) It is evident to the Sherlockian scholar that the title is a rearrangement of the title of the first story about Holmes, "A Study in Scarlet." The initial paragraphs are also paraphrases of the beginning paragraphs of Watson's first story, modified to fit the time and the locale of Somers' tale. All Wau Wau stories begin with takeoffs from the first pages of stories about the Great Detective and then the story travels towards its own ends. "The Doge Whose Barque Was Worse Than His Bight," for instance, starts with a paraphrase of Watson's "The Abbey Grange." "Who Stole Stonehenge?," the third Wau Wau in order of writing, begins with a modification of the initial paragraphs of Watson's "Silver Blaze."

This is Somers' way of paying tribute to the Master.

Of all his characters, the most popular are the canine private eye, Ralph von Wau Wau, and the quadriplegic spaceman, John Clayter. Those who have been unfortunate enough not to have read their adventures firsthand can find an outline of many of these in Kilgore Trout's *Venus on the Half-Shell.* This might serve as an introduction, a sort of appetite whetter. It was Trout who first pointed out that all of Somers' heroes and heroines are physically handicapped in some respect. Ralph, it is true, is a perfect specimen. But he is disadvantaged in that he has no hands. And, being a dog, he needs a human colleague to get him into certain places or do certain things. Sam Minostentor, the great science fiction historian, has also remarked on this in his monumental *Searchers for the Future.* Minostentor attributes this propensity for disabled protagonists to Somers' own crippled condition. Somers is consequently very empathetic with the physically limited.

However, Somers seldom shows his characters as being bitter. They overcome their failings with heroic efforts. They treat their condition with much laughter. In fact, they often make as much fun of themselves as their creator does of them. Some of this humor is black, it is true, but it is nevertheless humor.

"I had a choice between raving and ranting with bitter frustration or laughing at myself," Somers said. "It was bile or bubble. I drank the latter medicine. I can't claim any credit for this. I acted according to the dictates of my nature. Or did I? After all, there is such a thing as free will."

"My stuff has often been compared to my cousin's stories. That is, to Kilgore Trout's. There is some similarity in that we both often take a satirical view of humanity. But Trout believes in a mechanistic, a deterministic, universe, much like that of Vonnegut's, for instance. Me, I believe in free will. A person can pick himself up by his bootstraps—in a manner of speaking."

Jonathan was plunged into gloom when his grandmother died in 1950 at the age of ninety. There was not much time for despondency, however. She was no sooner cremated than he was informed that he would have to sell the huge old house in which he had lived all his life to pay for the inheritance taxes. To prevent this, he wrote eight short stories and three novels within six months. He saved the house but exhausted himself, and while resting his black mood returned. Then a new light brightened his life.

One of his numerous correspondents was a fan, another Samantha Tincrowder. She was his mother's cousin once removed and sister to the well-known SF author, Leo Queequeg Tincrowder.

Samantha had been born in New Goshen, Indiana, but, at the time she became a Somers aficionado, she was living in Indianapolis. Somers' letters convinced her that he needed cheering up. She quit her job as a registered nurse and came to Petersburg for an extended visit. Within two months, they were married. They have been very happy ever since, the only missing element being a child. Their interests are similar, both loving books and dogs and the quietness of village life.

Though his home is a backwater, a sort of tidal pond off the main streams of the highways, Jonathan Somers quite often gets visitors. At least once a month, fans or writers drop in for a few hours or a day or so. Bob Tucker, who lives in nearby Jacksonville, often comes by to help Somers empty a bottle of whiskey. On one occasion, he even brought his own. I live in Peoria, which is within about a two and a half-hour drive of Petersburg. I go down there at least twice a year for weekend visits. Another guest is Jonathan's relative, Leo Tincrowder. Neither Leo nor I, however, would be caught dead drinking Tucker's brand, Jim Beam, which we claim is fit only for peasants. The subtleties and the superbities of Wild Turkey and Weller's Special Reserve are beyond the grasp of Tucker's taste.

Jonathan Herowit stayed with Somers for six months after his release from Bellevue. (Somers has empathy for the mentally disadvantaged, too.) Eric Lindsay, an Aussie fan, stopped off during his motorcycle tour of the States after the Torcon. And there have been many others.

Somers' fans will be interested in his current project.

"I plan to write a novel outside the Clayter and Wau Wau canons. It'll take place almost a trillion years from now. It'll be titled either *Hour of Supreme Vision* or *Earth's Dread Hour*. Both titles are quotes from the *Spoon River Anthology*. The latter is from that fictitious epitaph Edgar Lee Masters wrote for my father, poor guy!"

"You don't have many years of writing left," I said.

He looked puzzled, then he smiled. "Ah, you mean Trout's prediction that I'll die in 1980." He laughed. "That rascal put me in his novel just long enough to kill me off. Had a boy riding a bicycle ram into me. Well, that could happen. This town in hilly, and the kids do come down the steep streets with their brakes off. I did it myself before I got sick. But the way I feel right now, I'll live to be eighty, anyway."

I drive away that night feeling he was right. His yellow hair has turned white, and his beard is grizzled. But he looks muscular and hairy-chested, like Hemingway when he was healthy. His gusto and delight in life and literature seem to ensure his durability. His readers can look forward to many more adventures of John Clayter and Ralph von Wau Wau and perhaps a host of other characters.

Somers' old mansion is only a few blocks from the corner of 8th and Jackson Street, where Masters' boyhood house still stands. A sign in front says: *Masters Home, Open 1-5 P.M. Daily Except Monday*. I wonder if someday a similar sign will stand before Jonathan Swift Somers' home. I wouldn't be surprised if this does happen. But I hope it'll be a long time from now.

John Carter: Torn from Phoenician Dreams

An Examination Into the Theories that John Carter was Phra the Phoenician and Norman of Torn

By Dennis E. Power and Dr. Peter M. Coogan

Section 1: An overview of Phra's account

Richard Lupoff initiated our exploration of Phra, albeit inadvertently, through his well-researched work on the literary influences of the creator of Tarzan, *Edgar Rice Burroughs: Master of Adventure*. While researching possible topics for his doctoral dissertation, Dr. Coogan began an in-depth look into Edgar Rice Burroughs' literary influences, intending to delve further into the subject than Lupoff had. In the course of his research Dr. Coogan read Edwin Arnold's *The Adventures of Phra the Phoenician* because of Lupoff's assertion that *Phra* directly inspired Edgar Rice Burroughs' John Carter. One passage in *Phra* sent a cold chill down his spine as Coogan remembered something he had read just a few years prior. While working on a master's degree in Arthurian literature at the University of Wales in Bangor, he came across a medieval manuscript whose title translated as *The Sleeping Saint of St. Olaf's Monastery*. The manuscript described how Archbishop of Canterbury Baldwin had blessed the bones of an unknown saint in this monastery, and in a few short years the saint's body had transformed into uncorrupted flesh and blood. The unknown saint slept from 1190 until he was physically transported to heaven in 1346. Dr. Coogan suddenly realized that the manuscript of the sleeping saint he had read years before had been about Phra!

Re-reading Lupoff's *Master of Adventure* he was struck by Lupoff's offhand concluding claim, "And Phra the Phoenician is John Carter." This simple statement inspired Dr. Peter Coogan.

He went on a short sabbatical, seeking access to the Burroughs archive. This access was granted, and the trail led to other archives of papers to which the ordinary researcher would not be granted access. Due to Dr. Coogan's great-grandfather's connection to the wealthy and generous Lamont Cranston, he was given access to various correspondences and allowed to make notes but not to borrow or photocopy.[308] He uncovered the truth of the relationship between Edgar Rice Burroughs and John Carter. He had found his doctoral topic. Yet for unknown reasons this topic was rejected by his doctoral committee, and Dr. Coogan was forced to choose another less incendiary yet still controversial topic, which he subsequently pursued at Michigan State University.

The fruits of this research did not go unused however and a small part of it was used in the article "John Carter *IS* Phra the Phoenician.[309]"

When Dennis Power contacted him with some of the information he had gathered from an exploration of diaries, court records, account books, and military records of the Carters of Virginia, they agreed to share information. The result was a series of articles on Phra the Phoenician/John Carter and his sometimes-astounding influence on history, legend and myth.

In "The Arms of Tarzan," Philip José Farmer claims that John Carter was Norman of Torn. However, in "John Carter *IS* Phra the Phoenician!" Dr. Coogan makes a strong case that John Carter was Phra the Phoenician. Coogan states, "This speculation does not contradict Philip José Farmer's assertion that Carter is Norman of Torn. Phra could have been Norman."

Unfortunately there does seem to be a contradiction between these two claims. The crux of the issue is that in Edgar Rice Burroughs' novel The *Outlaw of Torn*, the Outlaw is actually Richard Plantagenet, son of Henry III, King of England, and Eleanor of Provence. In the novel, Richard is stolen away by one of the king's servitors, Sir Jules de Vac, a master swordsman, for an imagined insult. De Vac raises the child to be an outlaw and to hate the Plantagenet kings. So the child grows up to be the infamous outlaw Norman of Torn.

In Philip José Farmer's *Tarzan Alive,* it is postulated that Norman was a natural son of Henry III of England. This is to say he was an illegitimate child of Henry by an unknown woman. Farmer may have proposed this because historically Richard Plantagenet died at the age of nine, and was interred in Westminster Abbey.

Therefore according to Farmer, Norman of Torn's name could have been Richard and he could have been a Plantagenet, but he was probably not the Richard Plantagenet who was a child of Henry III and Eleanor of Provence.

The important thing to remember is that Henry III and Eleanor identified Norman of Torn as Richard Plantagenet. How did they recognize their toddler child in the large and fearsome warrior standing before them? Richard and Norman both bore a lily-shaped birthmark. Had there also not been some family resemblance, this probably would have been considered an odd coincidence or some sort of enchantment.

In "The Arms of Tarzan," Philip José Farmer also speculated that the Outlaw of Torn was also the man who became known as John Carter of Virginia and Barsoom:

> We know that Henry III finally became aware that the famous, or infamous, outlaw was his long-lost son, Richard. But Henry died in 1272, and his son, Edward I, called Longshanks, was, though a very good king for those days, proud, jealous, and suspicious. His younger brother Richard, too popular with the common people, would have been forced to flee on a trumped-up charge of treason (nothing rare in those days). By then Bertrade de Montfort, his wife, had died, probably in childbirth or of disease, very common causes of fatality then. Richard would have taken a pseudonym again, that of John Caldwell, landless warrior. In the North of England he met old Baron Grebson. The baron had no male issue, and so, when his daughter fell in love with the stranger knight, he adopted him. This was nothing unusual; you will find similar examples throughout Burke's *Peerage*. The family name became Caldwell-Grebson, though the Caldwell was later dropped. Similar examples of this also abound in Burke.
>
> John Caldwell could not use the same arms as the Outlaw of Torn, of course. So, instead of *argent* a falcon's wing *sable*, he used *sable* a torn *or*. That he chose the torn showed he could not resist an example of "canting arms," a heraldic pun. One, indeed, that proved as dangerous as might be expected. Edward I heard of the appearance from nowhere of a knight who bore a torn on his shield, and he investigated. The king's men ambushed John Caldwell, and though he slew five of them, he, too, died.
>
> How can we be sure of this?
>
> An obscure book on medieval witchcraft, published in the middle 1600s, describes the case of a knight who was, for reasons unknown

> to the writer, slain by Edward I's men in a northern county. When his body was laid out to be washed, his left breast was found to bear a violet lily-shaped birthmark. This was thought to be the mark of the devil. But we readers of *The Outlaw of Torn* will recognize the true identity of the man suspected of witchcraft.

Farmer notes that the description of the Outlaw here applies to John Carter and proposes that Norman slew Edward's assassins, stained a lily birthmark on one, and disappeared from history. At some point, he met an adherent of the old religion who, like Tarzan's African witch doctor, administered an immortality elixir to him. He later went on to suffer amnesia and, in Farmer's words:

> Thus, on March 4, 1866, the Outlaw, a long-time resident of Virginia, an admitted victim of amnesia, left a cave in Arizona for the planet Mars. ERB called this man John Carter. Notice the J.C. I suggest that he may have been Richard Plantagenet, Norman of Torn, John Caldwell, and, finally, John Carter.

On the other hand we have Dr. Coogan's theory that Phra the Phoenician was John Carter and may also have been Norman of Torn. Although they seem mutually exclusive, both theories may actually be correct, although not in all of their particulars.

Every story must have a beginning and so we will tentatively place Phra's birth in Tyre, circa 88 BCE. It may have been earlier than this, but Phra himself is uncertain of his exact origins:

> Regarding the particulars of my earliest wanderings I do confess I am somewhat uncertain. This may tempt you to reply that one whose memory is so far reaching and capacious as mine will presently prove might well have store up everything that befell him from his very beginning. All I can say is, things are as I set them down; and those facts which you can not believe you must continue to doubt. The first thirty years of my life it will be guessed in extenuation were

> full of the frailties and shortcomings of an ordinary mortal; while those years which have followed have impressed themselves indelibly upon my mind by right of being curious past experience and credibility (p.1).[310]

Although it could be argued that Phra may have been born long before this, we have some textual evidence in *Phra the Phoenician* confirming that he was born around this time. He mentions that on his first voyage as a Phoenician merchant trader his ship was stuffed with bales of purple cloth from his father's vats. So even if he did not recall the particulars of his childhood, chances are that if his father was still alive when Phra began voyaging he could not have been very old.

On one voyage Phra purchased a red-haired British slave named Blodwen, the daughter of a chief of a coastal village in Britain. When Phra's ship was caught in a fierce storm off the British coast Blodwen offered to guide to them a safe cove.

The safe cove was Blodwen's home village, of which Blodwen was now the queen. For Phra and his men the roles reversed, and they found that they were Blodwen's captives. She bought Phra's goods and arranged for trade goods to be brought to Phra's ship. This took several months and on the day Phra was prepared to leave, his men deserted, stealing his ship and stranding him in Britain. He remained as Blodwen's consort.

For a few years Phra lived among the Britons. He married Blodwen and together they had one child. Phra was present at one of the landings of Caesar in either 55 or 56 BCE. Because of a misunderstanding, possibly a willful misunderstanding by Blodwen's jealous kinsmen Dhuwallon, Phra was accused of working with the Romans. Offered up as a sacrifice, he was wounded unto death by a bronze adz to the back of the neck. Phra slept until 408 AD. He awoke in a cavern.[311]

He shortly discovered that he had slept some four hundred years, but he quickly adapted to the new era. He became a guardsman for a lady of the Romano-British nobility and was present during the withdrawal of Roman legions from Britain in 410.

During a battling retreat against the barbarian Northmen, Phra was betrayed by a Roman noblewoman, the Lady Electra, for spurning her love. While Phra and his current lady-love Numidea were crossing a rapid stream, the guide rope was cut, sending the lovers tumbling into the rapid waters. Although Phra strove mightily to save them both, Numidea drowned before he was able to reach a safe landing.

Some friendly fisher folk gathered about him. He expired shortly after Numidea had.

Phra next awakened in 1066, finding himself in the hut of a hermit. According to the hermit cleric, Alfred the Great (847-899) had found him insensate in a fisherman's hut. Supposedly Phra had been asleep in this fisherman's hut for generations after having been dragged from the sea by the fishermen's nets. Alfred the Great ordered Phra to be taken to Canterbury. According the hermit, Phra had been kept in Canterbury until being moved to his hut just a few months prior to his awakening.

Phra was told that the Saxon invaders had in fact become the goodly rulers of England. Just two days after this awakening in 1066, Phra saw and heard Harold, the current King of England, and Phra had no trouble understanding the King's vernacular speech. A few days later Phra spoke directly with William the Conqueror and also had no trouble conversing with him. Phra later demonstrated an odd familiarity with Egyptian mythology and Norse mythology, as well as tales from the Eddas—demonstrated by his citing Mista, Skogula, and Zernebock, dark deities of the Saxons.

At the Battle of Hastings, Phra witnessed the death of King Harold, the last Anglo-Saxon King of Britain. Phra married a Saxon noble woman, Editha, a daughter of Hardicanute, and spent twelve years as a Saxon lord in Voewode. They had two children, a boy and a girl. The Normans began a poll of their subjects, and their brutal method of counting angered Phra. Although he had a fleeting vision of driving out the Norman conquerors and placing Editha on the throne, he realized this smacked of fancy.[312] However, his minor rebelliousness led to a Norman host descending upon his holdings. He and his family were forced to flee. They sought refuge inside St. Olaf's Monastery, whose abbot was Editha's uncle. The clerics at first refused to admit them. So Phra prepared to meet the oncoming Norman attackers with his sword. In the nick of time, though, the monks opened the door and admitted Phra and his family. Although not wounded, Phra inexplicably fell into one of his centuries-long naps.

Phra awoke in a chapel in 1346. He had been found as a wrapped mummy placed on a shelf by St. Baldwin and worshipped as a saint. He once again had no trouble understanding the monks as they spoke among themselves. He walked in on a feast while the monks were inebriated and was pleased at the shock he caused. Near the monastery he found a small chapel where a marble statue representing his wife and the two children stood.

Devastated by this discovery, he wandered the countryside, dependent on the charity of others to provide him food and clothing. After wandering aimlessly, or so it would appear, Phra happened upon a spot where he found a fortune in jewels scattered in a brook.

Once again Phra made a rapid acculturation to his new surroundings and, using his newfound wealth to purchase armor and become a landless knight, was able to fit into to the highly structured medieval society as a member of the lesser nobility. As a guest at the castle of Oswaldton he found himself infatuated with the eldest daughter, Alianora, yet it was Isobel, the youngest, who fell in love with him. Alianora rejected his troth, and he decided to journey to France to lend his sword arm to King Edward III. A friend of Isobel's named Flamaucoer accompanied him. Phra fought at Crecy. He met King Edward and the Black Prince Edward and ate dinner with them. Among the discussions at the table was the miraculous translation of the holy relic at St. Olaf's, which meant that the body had been missed.

In France, Phra realized that he was in love with Isobel and decided to court her by letter. Flamaucoer scoffed at this idea.

In the battle of Crecy, Phra defeated the High Constable of France in single combat. Flamaucoer took a charge meant for Phra and was speared. It was revealed that Flamaucoer was Isobel in disguise. Once again Phra had lost his love. He pledged to recount the tale of her demise to her family. King Edward allowed him to leave but charged him to also take a note to the queen. His ship tossed in storm, and he was thrown overboard. By coincidence he landed at the spot where he had first landed a thousand years before. Phra states he was "weary and tired" as he climbed into a burial crypt to sleep. The crypt's massive stone door had been propped open by small keystone. The intensity of the storm and Phra brushing against the keystone as he crawled inside the crypt were enough to loosen the doorstop. The massive crypt door closed and sealed Phra inside.

Phra was awakened and freed of his confinement by two grave robbers. Despite exhibiting the usual symptom of a long sleep—extremely stiff muscles—he seemed unaware that a great deal of time had passed. He made his way to London and managed to see the queen, who was amused to see him. This was Queen Elizabeth, who took his message from King Edward III as great wit. He soon discovered it was the year 1586.

Upon the road to London, Phra had met an old fellow and had enjoyed his company. After his audience with the Queen, Phra sought out his travelling companion, and the older man invited him to be his guest. The elderly man was Adam Faulkner, a great scholar. His estate had become rundown as he devoted all of his energies towards his great work, the creation of a mechanical marvel.

Adam Faulkner had a young daughter whom Phra promptly fell in love with, provoking the great jealousy of the Faulkners' Spanish servitor, Emmanuel Marcena. Adam Faulkner's great work was a mechanical marvel that turned out to be monstrosity. It was a steam driven automation that nearly killed Phra and Faulkner before Phra destroyed it. Faulkner attacked Phra, but regained his senses and agreed to the courtship of Phra and Elizabeth.

Phra began to write his memoirs. At their wedding feast, Phra and Elizabeth drank poisoned wine served to them by the jealous Marcena. Elizabeth perished. Phra was affected but was still strong enough to kill the Spanish servant. He was certain he would die from this poison, despite having survived near-decapitation and drowning twice.

Feeling the growing blackness upon him, Phra hid himself and his manuscript in a secret den in the thickness of the great walls of Faulkner Manor. He continued to write as his eyesight grew blurry and as visions of his lost loves swam before his eyes. Blodwen appeared before him: staring directly into his eyes, she took his hand and, as his last words state, "At that touch the mantle of life falls from me! Blodwen! Blodwen! I come, I come!" (p. 328).

Section 2: Examining Phra as Norman of Torn and John Carter

The story of Phra is a memoir written in his own hand and edited by Edwin Arnold. Although an interesting story in itself, a careful reading of the narrative raises many questions. The narrative as it stands was either drastically altered, with entire sections being excised by Edwin Arnold to fit his motif of Phra awakening whenever England was threatened by a new invasion, or else Phra wrote only what he knew, what he remembered.

Half of the recorded times after Phra entered hibernation he awoke in a different location than he had laid down to rest. Although Arnold states that the body had been moved about by clerics of one type or another, this could merely be Phra's explanation of why he awoke in a different place than he went to sleep, creating a logical explanation for the inexplicable. Although we do not doubt that the sleeping body was moved, we will dispute that it was done so in the ways Phra claimed.

Each time he awoke from a protracted sleep Phra exhibited great muscular stiffness that took a few hours to alleviate, yet each time he seemed unaware that a great deal of time had passed. He should have noted that the language and speech patterns had changed, but he did not.

For his final recorded hibernation, he probably did not enter the tomb in 1346 but much later.

Despite having a recorded "waking" life of approximately fifteen years, Phra continually seems about thirty, the age when he was first "killed." There are constant references to his youthfulness. He may have been a young looking thirty who could appear more mature or more youthful when he wished.

Although we cannot know exactly what caused his immortality, we can make a few speculations: a druidic elixir slipped to him by his wife Blodwen prior to his sacrifice, or that it was the interrupted sacrificial ceremony that kept his soul in limbo, as it were, or perhaps he had an innate immortality through inheritance.

While Phra experienced muscle "stiffness and soreness" after his extended periods of sleep, he did not appear at first glance to experience anything like the muscular atrophy that occurs in patients who suffer from comas of only months. This may be a sign that his body was kept in a sort of peak condition by his regenerative ability. His muscles atrophied to some extent, but once he was conscious and mobile and all of his bodily functions had ceased their hibernative mode, the regenerative nature of his immorality became fully active and quickly repaired the damage to his muscles. This rapid healing, though, did cause him a great deal of discomfort. It is this regenerative factor that plays a factor in explaining one of the main discrepancies that would seem to preclude Phra the Phoenician from having been John Carter, from Phra having been Norman of Torn, or Norman of Torn from having been John Carter.

First let us deal with Phra as Norman of Torn. There are at least three main points that would seem to preclude this theory.

(1) Norman of Torn's career takes place during one of Phra's extended sleeps.

(2) Norman of Torn was "proven" to be Richard Plantagenet by means of a distinctive birthmark.

(3) Phra had darker hair than Norman did, and he also bore a large tattoo that covered his back and chest.

The career of Norman of Torn took place between 1240 and 1280, although the main activity of Burroughs' novel occurs during 1243-1267. According to Burroughs, Norman was Richard Plantagenet, the son of Henry III and Eleanor of Provence. He was kidnapped at the age of three by Sir Jules de Vac, although according to historical records Richard Plantagenet was born about 1247, died at the age of nine, and was interred in Westminster Abbey in 1256. Burroughs has his birth placed at about 1240. Was this merely a mistake? According to Burroughs in the prologue to *The Outlaw of Torn*, the true story of Richard had been covered up.

The Richard Plantagenet of *The Outlaw of Torn* then seems to be a Richard who disappeared from the historical record. Henry III and Eleanor did have a child born in 1240; this was Margaret, who would become the Queen of Scotland. Burroughs' Richard seems to have been a twin of hers, who—as recorded in *Outlaw of Torn*—was assassinated at the age of three and thrown into the Thames.

In 1247 when Henry and Eleanor had another boy, they named him Richard, perhaps in honor of their missing babe. Yet this was not an auspicious name, for this child also died at an early age, and was interred in Westminster Abbey. That Burroughs' Richard was a different Richard from the known historical Richard can be deduced from this phrase in *The Outlaw of Torn*, "but nowhere was there a sign or trace of Prince Richard, *second* son of Henry III of England" (p. 25) [emphasis added].

According to historical records, the Princes born to Henry III were, in order, Edward b. 1239, Edmund b. 1245, Richard b. 1247, John, b. 1250, William b. 1252 and Henry b. 1256. As can be seen, the historical Richard was the third rather than the second son of Henry III. However Burroughs' Richard, who was born in 1240, would indeed have been the second son and the youngest prince in 1243, having predated and seemingly pre-deceased Edmund. It is odd that this earlier Richard did not make it into the historical record, but as Burroughs has stated the incident was covered up. Possibly all scant records of the Richard Plantagenet born in 1240 were expunged by order of his devious older brother Edward.

But a Richard Plantagenet, born to Henry III and Elanor of Provence in 1240, was indeed stolen away by Jules de Vac, raised speaking French, tutored in arms, and taught to hate the English, with the Plantagenet royalty held as especially vile. Norman was launched upon a career as an outlaw baron in an unlicensed, ruined castle.[313] By the time Norman was fifteen he was indeed a great fighter, having once slain three men in single combat. Yet in the early days of his outlawry he met someone who was destined to be the greatest swordsman of two worlds.

As de Vac and Norman traversed the woods one morning in Norman's eighteenth year, they found a knight in rusted armor and tattered clothing sleeping in a covered bower. Norman prodded him at swordpoint, which proved to be a fatal mistake. The knight lurched to his feet with a scream of fury and launched himself at Norman, who soon faltered under the onslaught.[314] De Vac joined in and was astounded that the man was able to defend against two great swordsmen. De Vac landed a blow against the head of the strange knight, throwing him off balance, and by happenstance driving the point of the stranger's broadsword through Norman's gorget and into his throat.

Seeing his work of years ended in one single blow, de Vac spun around to decapitate the senseless stranger lying on the ground. He was forced to turn aside his blade at the last second as he glimpsed the downed knight's face, so that the blade plunged into the dirt next to the man. What he had seen astounded him beyond belief. The stranger knight looked like Richard Plantagenet, Norman of Torn, enough so that they could be brothers. De Vac wondered if this knight was one of Henry III's by-blows or, more fantastically, some type of changeling. His initial scheme ruined de Vac thought of several more, all dependent on the stranger's cooperation. De Vac bound the unconscious stranger tightly. He stripped Norman's body of its armor, leaving it in the grove of trees where the strange knight had lain.

The strange knight awoke in a peculiar state. He claimed to remember nothing of himself—not his name, identity, or past. De Vac wondered if it were the clout on the head or just Providence smiling upon him. De Vac fixed the man a draught of herbal tea, which was supposed to aid in healing his head wound but actually kept the man in a stupor. De Vac thought of a bold plan, one bolder than his previous plan of vengeance. He took the unconscious man to a witch woman of the woods, one who knew the old arts of the druids. He paid the old woman for a supply of a potion to keep the stranger in a confused state, but the key to his plan was to have her tattoo a birthmark on the stranger's chest. After she had finished this task, he rewarded her with a swift and painless death.

Using the potion, de Vac convinced the amnesiac that he was Norman of Torn and provided him with Norman's history. Even after the stranger's head wound healed, the brainwashing held up. To his relief, de Vac discovered that the man was either a fast learner or remembering skills and knowledge previously acquired, such as French and skill at arms. The man appeared to be in his middle twenties, although at times he seemed older and at other times even younger.

After a sojourn of six months, de Vac and "Norman" returned to

Torn Castle. De Vac explained the changes in Norman's behavior and personality as the result of the head wound he had sustained.

The mysterious man that de Vac had found in the woods was, of course, Phra the Phoenician. It might be best to explain how he happened to be there, how he happened to look like Norman of Torn, aka Richard Plantagenet, and to clear up the main difference in his appearance and Norman of Torn, or for that matter John Carter.

According to the account written by Phra and edited by Arnold, Phra had four major periods of sleep, most of which corresponded to times of a change of government or of a threat against England. These sleep periods were 43 BCE to 408 AD—corresponding to the change from Celtic Britain to Romano-Britain; 410 to 1066—corresponding with the change from Saxon to Norman Britain; 1084 to1346—corresponding with the loss of the French territories; and 1346 to 1586.[315] These sleep periods were 451, 656, 262, and 240 years respectively. Except for the first one, every time that Phra went to sleep it was after suffering a tragic loss. The 1084 sleep seems inexplicable, since according to his narrative he and his family were given shelter in the nick of time. Yet given his later discovery of a marble replica of his wife and his two children, it may be that he remembered the incident as he wished to remember it, not as it actually happened. It may be that Phra was unable to save his wife and children and saw them cut down before his eyes just as the monks relented and allowed them inside. Phra was saved, but his family was not. Unable to accept this reality, Phra went to sleep.

We believe that Phra and Arnold were correct and that Phra awoke whenever he somehow became aware of danger to England, his adopted homeland. But we also believe that Phra did not sleep for hundreds of years each time. His hibernations were much shorter, although he remained unaware of many of his periods of wakefulness. The first long sleep placed his body in a state of torpor, a hibernative healing trace in which he recovered from his near decapitation. His regeneration was probably delayed by the ministrations of his wife Blodwen, who moved his body and over the course of twenty years tattooed it with an elaborate and intricate depiction of her life.

As for the theory that Norman of Torn was John Carter, it should also be mentioned that according to Burroughs Norman had an odd-colored lily-shaped birthmark, which identified him as Richard Plantagenet.

But Burroughs never described Carter has having a birthmark such as this. No Barsoomians ever remarked on Carter having any such tattoos, despite his nakedness and odd combination, for Barsoom, of skin, eye, and hair color. One could state that it was not germane to the stories and so Burroughs never mentioned it or that Burroughs never knew about it. Yet according to written record, the narrator "Burroughs" was related to John Carter and had known him for years.[316] The most likely explanation is that John Carter did not have this birthmark so this would seem to preclude John Carter from having been Norman of Torn.

Yet such a thing would equally preclude John Carter from having been Phra the Phoenician since in all the published accounts no mention is made of either a lily-shaped birthmark or a multicolored tattoo covering much of his upper torso. Such a large tattoo would have made Carter's appearance even more remarkable to the Barsoomians, and it certainly would have been remarked upon. Therefore we must speculate that John Carter never had the lily shaped birthmark or the all-encompassing tattoo so far as Edgar Rice Burroughs or even John Carter himself knew.

Tattooing is an ancient art. The recently discovered Alpine "ice man" may have been tattooed. How it is done, the inks that are used, and a variety of other factors will determine how long a tattoo will remain. Modern tattoos are done with inks that require laser treatments to remove. Some cultures used a combination of scarification and dyeing that also left rather permanent pictures. One may guess that the tattoo that was given to Phra by Blodwen, which lasted over four hundred years, was one that would have required the most modern techniques of laser surgery to remove. When Phra was being bathed after his resurrection in AD 408, a scrubber rubbed him raw trying to remove the dirt, which was in fact a tattoo. This factor and the fact that the tattooing was done over a twenty-year period demonstrate that these markings were true tattooing and not just epidermal staining.

Yet Phra's huge tattoo is never mentioned again after first time he awoke, nor is the ghastly scar on the back of his neck.

What happened to them? The best explanation is that they simply faded away as many scars and some tattoos do over time.

This tattoo is one of the factors that give credence to the idea that there may have been periods when Phra was active and did not know about it. Exposure to sunlight over the course of many years is one of the methods by which a tattoo may fade, and Phra's regenerative factor, which kept him young for centuries, may have speeded the fading as his skin cells were replaced over the centuries. His initial long hibernation in the dark, airless cave would have preserved the tattoo, which argues for few—or more likely no—periods of waking between 48 BC and AD 408.

Phra's seeming facility with language and uncanny acculturation may be another clue to his experiencing periods of wakefulness of which he was not aware. When he awoke the first time, Rome was still in power in Britain and Latin was still the main language. While there may have been some cultural and technological changes, likely there were not so many as to prevent him from adjusting to the new era within a few hours or days at the most.

However, in the period between 410 and 1066, there had been great changes in culture and language. When Phra awoke he was able to speak with his clerical host immediately, although it may very well have been that they spoke in Latin since that was still the language of the church. However, two days later Phra was able to overhear a conversation between Harold the Great and Editha and understand it. Although they could have been speaking Latin, it is more likely that they were speaking in the vernacular Old English of their day. Even if Phra had been familiar with the Saxon tongue from his days of defending Roman Britain against their incursions, this was an entirely new language. Granted, Phra and Arnold could have exaggerated either Phra's ability to understand and be understood or may have compressed the time frame, but a similar situation would occur twice more.

In 1346 when Phra awoke he was able to understand the conversations among the clerics at the church. Again they may have been speaking Latin, but since they were not on duty they were most likely speaking in their vernacular, Middle English. This is especially true when the clerics received a noble visitor, Lord Codrington, who would have definitely spoken to them in Middle English. The differences between Anglo-Saxon Old English and Middle English are quite pronounced, comparable to those between German and one of the Scandinavian tongues. Further, awakening and wandering the countryside as a near mad man grieving for Editha and his two children, Phra had very little trouble understanding or being understood by the common folk.

There is also the clue that in his aimless wandering he managed to find a fortune in gems just lying on the ground near a stream. Considering the likelihood of this, one has to wonder if he actually found these gems or was unconsciously remembering where he had stashed a fortune in jewels.

Having found the jewels, he was able to buy his way into society, purchasing clothes, arms, and armor, which seemed to make him a wandering knight. All of this happened in the space of a few months. Without having to be taught it, he was intimately familiar with the ritualized and often complicated culture of medieval knighthood. Again it may not be so much that he learned rapidly but that he unconsciously remembered learned behaviors and knowledge from periods when he had been awake without knowledge of the those events.

Another great leap in Phra's life occurred from 1356 to 1586. Although it was a lesser period of hibernation, it was a large leap in terms of language and culture. The Dark Ages had gone and the Renaissance had come. Middle English had transformed into Modern English, albeit of the Elizabethan Age. Once again Phra found himself able to freely converse and be understood; he was able to speak with ease to the graverobbers who freed him from the tomb in which he had accidentally sealed himself. Phra befriended Adam Faulkner on the road and the older gentleman accepted him as a learned man of about his own station, which could only mean that Phra was able to intelligently converse with this scholar. Although Adam Faulkner would prove to be a bit absent-minded, there was no indication that he found Phra's mannerisms or patterns of speech dated. Phra was also able to make his way to the court of the queen and freely converse there. Although he was thought to be either a madman or a fool because of the message he carried and his misunderstanding of royal politics, his speech was understood and his mannerisms seem acculturated to the time period.

We believe that Phra unconsciously used knowledge and mannerisms he acquired while being awake without his being aware of it. On the face of it this seems a bit ludicrous, but the explanation of how Phra could be awake and not remember having been so lies in Phra's psychological state.

Phra's first hibernation happened after he had received a near-decapitating stroke. As stated earlier, we cannot be certain if his immortality was the result of some elixir he had ingested prior to taking part in the sacrificial rite, the interruption of the rite, something about the environment of his burial cave, an innate immortality, or a combination of all of these factors. Although this hibernation saved his life, it cost him his family. Upon waking and realizing that Blodwen and his children were long dead, Phra's loss and grief manifested themselves in an abrupt personality change. For a time he became a libertine, drinking and wenching until his money was depleted.

Forced to find employment, he became a guardsman for a wealthy

Roman noblewoman, Lady Electra. Lady Electra was enamored of Phra, but Phra had come to love Numidea, a slave girl. Despite Phra's rejection of Electra's advances, there seems to have been some attraction towards and admiration of her. Had Numidea not been in the picture, things might have turned out quite differently. As it was however, his rejection of Lady Electra had tragic consequences. As they were fleeing from Saxon warriors, Lady Electra's party made their way across a swift and dangerous stream by use of a rope guide. Numidea fell into the river and Phra jumped into rescue her, although Lady Electra had forbade him to do so. As Phra and Numidea were making their way out the raging stream, Lady Electra cut the rope, sending the struggling pair downstream, tumbling out of control. Phra managed to pull Numidea and himself to shore, but she had drowned in their passage through the waters. They were approached by some fisher folk; upon seeing his love had perished Phra fell into a dark and dreamless slumber.

There is a slight discrepancy in his account of falling asleep on shore after having swum there under his own power and the account of the hermit cleric, who met the revived Phra in 1066, namely that the fisher folk had dragged him from the river in their nets already slumbering. Although these could be merely two versions of the same story, it is also possible that they describe two different events. There was no mention of Phra's rather remarkable tattoo by the cleric who claimed to have scrubbed Phra's body clean of dirt and grime. Nor was there ever any mention of it by Editha, Phra's wife for twelve years. We speculate that the tattoo had disappeared by this time. As stated earlier, this would mean that Phra had spent a considerable period of time awake, probably decades, for his body to have sloughed off enough skin cells for the tattoo to have disappeared. There is also Phra's "instinctive" knowledge of Old English, seen in his understanding the speech between Harold and Editha and Phra's own conversation with Harold.

Phra also recorded his entry to a centuries-long hibernation starting in 1084, although apparently the danger to his family had passed. As argued earlier, perhaps his family had not been unscathed and this tragedy propelled him into another sleep period. Once again in 1346 Phra fell in love with a woman only to have her tragically die in his arms. He found himself once again sleeping for centuries. In 1586, he once again loved a young woman, Elizabeth Faulkner, and she was killed before his eyes. This death was the last straw, and although Phra had survived near-decapitation, drowning, and possible suffocation, the poison administered by Emmanuel Marcena finished him off. Phra the Phoenician died in 1586, or at least his personality went permanently to sleep.

We believe that these periods of hibernation are a combination of true physical hibernation and also psychological hibernation. Phra seems to have suffered from a dissociative disorder that manifested itself in at least two, possibly three ways: dissociative amnesia, dissociative fugue, and possibly dissociative identity disorder (once called multiple personality disorder).

Dissociative amnesia may be present when a person is unable to remember important personal information that is usually associated with a traumatic event in their life. The loss of memory creates gaps in the individual's personal history.

Dissociative fugue may be present when a person impulsively wanders or travels away from home and upon arrival in a new location is unable to remember their past. The individual's personal identity is lost because they are confused about who they are. The travel from home generally occurs following a stressful event. The person in the fugue appears to be functioning normally to other people. However, after the fugue experience, the individual may not be able to recall what happened during their dissociative state. The condition is usually diagnosed when relatives find their lost family member living in another community with a new identity.

Dissociative identity disorder (DID) was formerly called "multiple personality disorder." When a person intermittently experiences two or more identities, they may have a dissociative identity disorder. While experiencing a new identity, a separate personality takes control, and the person is unable to remember important and personal information about him or herself. Each personality has its own personal history and identity and takes on a totally separate name.

The physical injuries that Phra sustained in addition to the great trauma of seeing his loved ones killed before his eyes caused him repeatedly to go into a hibernative sleep. The severity of the physical injury determined how long he slept. His psyche, however, was not as resilient as his physical body and the so the inner man slept much, much longer than the body.

Depending on Phra's physical state, a hibernation lasted anywhere from months to decades. The first hibernation was the longest because of the time needed to heal injuries to the spinal column and to regenerate brain tissue, which in normal human beings does not repair itself.

After Phra's body had healed, he awoke in a dissociative fugue with dissociative amnesia. He could not remember his identity or how he had come to his resting place; however, he could remember other learned skills such as language. In this state he would assume a new name or identity, but in most cases the basic personality of Phra would remain intact, albeit without the burden of his personal history. He might also have retained a general understanding of recent events, but his personal memories remained locked away. The names he used were either given to him by persons he met, or were adopted for various reasons. At times Phra would awaken with a form of dissociative identity disorder in which he self-created an identity composed of various components of his personality. Although this is not a classic form of the DID, recent studies have found that the disorder has many variant manifestations. Phra's repeated dissociative episodes are all traceable to his unwillingness to deal with the trauma of losing his loved ones.

It is important to remember that the story of Phra, as edited by Edwin Arnold, was taken from Phra's manuscript, written in his own words as he remembered the events that had transpired. For the most part the events detailed in Phra's alert phases are quite accurate. Others, however, seem to be altered. This is not to say that Phra was deliberately deceptive but rather was being self-deceptive and in doing so unwittingly deceived his audience.

The first such episode of self-deception occurred when he awakened in 1066. Phra found himself inside a hermit's hut. The hermit explained that Phra had been pulled from a river in fishermen's nets, and had remained in a state of senselessness for six hundred years. He had lain on a shelf in the fisherman's hut from 410 to about 875 when Alfred the Great had him transferred to Canterbury. Phra then lay in Canterbury until 1066, when King Harold had him transferred to the hermit's hut for safekeeping.

Besides the discrepancy between the hermit's story of the fisher folk pulling the already sleeping Phra out of the river in their nets and Phra's version in which he swam to shore under his own power, the story of his being stuck on a fisherman's shelf for over four hundred years just does not ring true. Given human nature, at the very least he would have become an object of great curiosity. Moreover one wonders why the fisher folk would show him such great disrespect, keeping him stuffed away like an old heirloom. It may be that this was not the case, that this ignominious state can be traced to Phra's mental state at the time he began his hibernation in 410. Having failed to save Numidea, he was filled with despair and felt worthless, a person to be shunned. So in his recounting of these events, his memories were colored by his depressive state.

At the time of his supposed long hibernation, Britain was a mixture of faiths—the old Celtic faiths, the incursions of the Saxon Nordic mythos, and Christianity. Given Phra's handsome features, his eternal youth, and his uninterrupted slumber, it seems more likely that Phra would have been an object of veneration, regarded as a god, a demigod, a mythic hero, an angel, or perhaps even a Prince of Faery.

In his narrative Phra drops two hints that refer to events that occurred during his waking periods. In many cases persons suffering from dissociative amnesia are totally unaware of gaps in their personal histories, as Phra seems to be. To Phra, he goes to sleep and each time wakes up centuries later. But, as demonstrated, the evidence of the faded tattoos and Phra's instantaneous facility with languages and culture shows this uninterrupted hibernation is doubtful. People suffering from dissociative disorders will recognize inconsistencies in their memories or in other aspects of their lives and will create plausible scenarios to ease the trauma that such memories cause. Phra did so when relating the story of being found in a fisherman's hut by King Alfred and his subsequent transferals to Canterbury and the hermit's hut. While it is true that Phra eventually recovered from the trauma of losing his loved ones, there remained the hidden trauma of his inability to process these traumas at the time, which was destructive of his self-image. It was far better for Phra to imagine that, instead of wandering about literally out of his mind, he had slept for centuries, as he had done right after losing Blodwen.

It is important to remember that when we are talking about personalities and different identities, at the core they are all Phra.

As a mental defense mechanism, Phra self-induced amnesia and created a role for his conscious mind to assume. While the core Phra persona was buried in the subconscious providing necessary memories and knowledge for the new persona to survive and adapt to his new surroundings, the new surface identity was also absorbing new knowledge and experiences, although he prevented himself from consciously acknowledging that this process occurred. Gaps in Phra's memory are due to the psychological problem of disassociative personality. He could not overcomeloving and losing mortal friends and family while he lived on. Phra relates two conversations with the spirit of his dead wife Blodwen. While we will not dispute the possibility that these might be actual spiritual manifestations, we will however state that they could also be signs of deeper psychological problems than Phra exhibits in his narrative. Such hallucinations can also occur with a disassociative disorder.

We can reconstruct the series of events provided to us by Phra's own account, although they are a bit out of sequence from his recorded version and have at least two periods when he was awake and living as other personalities.

After spending some time among the fishermen in suspended animation, Phra awoke. Eventually he wound up with King Alfred, probably fought alongside him at the Battle of Edington and may have taken part in the Battle of London. At some point, he fell in combat, believed to be dead and interred in Canterbury. He probably had received a serious wound that took decades to heal. Waking again, he became involved with King Harold as one of his confidants and fighting men. He may have been with the king when Harold and his brother conquered Wales. Phra was most probably with him when Harold was shipwrecked on the coast of Normandy. Phra was lost overboard in this shipwreck. It was there that Phra was pulled to shore in a sleeping state. Harold had been forced to swear fealty to William of Normandy but received the news that his friend lived, although in a coma. Returning to England, Harold had the sleeping Phra placed in the care of the hermit.

In the conversation between the old cleric and Phra, the older man is astonished that Phra does not know who Harold is and the recent history of the kingdom. If the hermit had been aware of Phra's centuries-long sleep, then his astonishment at Phra's ignorance is quite puzzling. However if the history of Phra sleeping on a shelf of a fisherman's hut for centuries was a fabrication, then this conversation makes a bit more sense. Phra created this tale to smooth over the inconsistencies in his memory. The hermit had likely told Phra how he had been found by fishermen and brought to this hut on the order of Harold. Phra eventually fleshed out the tale. Another telling point is that after Phra had awakened supposedly after centuries, the hermit made no effort to introduce Harold to this rather miraculous phenomenon. It is possible that the hermit knew that Harold was in the midst of a serious battle for his kingdom and for the sovereignty of Britain and did not wish to distract him the news that his friend had awakened but had become a raving madman. The hermit in fact made a concerted effort to keep Phra away from the king by sending him on an errand to find another army.

Purportedly after losing his wife and children in 1084, Phra slept until 1346. Again Phra's persona slept, but he likely went through another period of dissociative amnesia and fugue. It was during one of these periods that Jules de Vac convinced him that he was Norman of Torn. As we speculated, de Vac used a potion to keep the amnesiac Phra in a state of confusion. De Vac's rather crude methods of brainwashing probably would not have been successful had not Phra's need for an identity to fill the void of his amnesia also played a role. Even so, "Norman" began doubting many aspects of de Vac's story; primarily that de Vac was his father.

De Vac also had Phra tattooed once more, a tattoo that was supposed to be the birthmark of Richard Plantagenet. Again, although Philip José Farmer speculated that Norman was John Carter, John Carter so far as we know never had such a birthmark. Nor did he ever have a great tattoo such as Blodwen had given Phra. Clearly, the large tattoo had faded over the centuries of exposure to sunlight, which would be one of the reasons that John Carter was so bronzed. Therefore it would be very easy for a relatively smaller tattoo to have faded by the time Phra became John Carter.

De Vac's ploy of the tattooed birthmark would not have worked unless there had been a marked physical resemblance between Phra, Norman, and the Plantagenets. In fact, Phra was Norman's ancestor and the ancestor of all of the Plantagenet Kings.[317] De Vac was not as confident of this ploy as he let on. De Vac only disclosed the information that Norman of Torn was in fact Richard Plantagenet when he was dying and it appeared as though Norman was dying as well. This was a last ditch ploy to inflict a wound on the Plantagenets.

Despite the relatively happy ending at the end of *The Outlaw of Torn* wherein the Outlaw lives, marries the woman he loves, and is acknowledged by the King and Queen as their son; the true story of the Outlaw of Torn did not end altogether happily. Despite the private acknowledgement of Richard/Norman as their son, a public acknowledgment was not politically feasible. So far as the world knew, the only child of Henry III and Eleanor of Provence named Richard Plantagenet was born in 1247 and died in 1256. As Burroughs said, the story was suppressed by a Plantagenet king. Norman had caused too much strife and had led a rebellion against the crown. Too much blood had been shed for all to be forgiven.

A compromise was reached, in which Norman ended his career as the Lord of Torn and was in turn removed from the list of outlaws. He married Bertholde de Monfort, but she died within a year in childbirth. After Bertholde died, Norman adopted the name John Caldwell.[318]

Edward Longshanks, Henry III's eldest son, had never truly believed that Norman of Torn was his lost brother; it was he who had convinced his father that granting Norman amnesty and full acknowledgement as a prince would be unwise and he is the Plantagenet king to whom Burroughs refers. However, Henry and his queen were overjoyed to have their lost son returned to them, so Edward kept silent and bided his time. So long as the upstart knight kept to his place and demanded nothing from the royal family, he was content to let him live. Shortly after Henry III died in 1272 and Edward Longshanks became Edward I of England, John Caldwell found himself outlawed once again.

Although outlawed, Norman of Torn—now John Caldwell—continued to have loyal friends. One of these was the second Baron of Grebson. John Caldwell married Alicia, the daughter of the Baron Grebson. Since Alicia was his only child, Grebson allowed the marriage only if Caldwell would add the Grebson name to his own. Being a landless outlaw, Caldwell agreed. On his new coat of arms, he added a golden spinning wheel, which was also known as a torn. Hearing of this, Edward realized this was probably his putative brother and sent a team of knights to capture the outlaw.

In *Tarzan Alive*, Mr. Farmer asserted that Norman had died of wounds after defeating the five knights sent to kill him. A violet lily-shaped birthmark identified the corpse as the son of Henry III.

However in the "The Arms of Tarzan" Farmer made this speculation, "It is possible that John Caldwell was not killed, that he slew all of Edward's men, who actually numbered six, mangled the face of one tall corpse, and stained a violet lily mark on the corpse's left breast." He subsequently acquired both immortality and amnesia, and in 1866 "died" again only to awaken on Mars.

We argue that Mr. Farmer was in fact closer to the mark in his first speculation. Norman did die after defeating his attackers, which is to say he sustained some serious wounds and from all appearances was as dead. In reality Norman was Phra, and because of the severity of his wounds he fell into one of his comatose healing sleeps. As Mr. Farmer speculated, Norman did acquire amnesia, but it was the self-induced amnesia that Phra often used to maintain his own fragile sanity.

Though Phra's initial healing period lasted four hundred years, as his body became accustomed to frequent periods of healing, the time period needed for recovery was shortened as time went on. It could also be that the wounds Norman sustained were more severe than actually life threatening.

Despite his being outlawed, Norman's friends and family arranged for him to have a Christian funeral. This was done in secret so that

Edward would not go to the extreme of having Norman's corpse mutilated as a further sign of the royal displeasure, as he later did with William Wallace.[319]

Norman's body was hidden in St. Olaf's Abbey in the reliquary. He was hidden behind a relic, the mummified body of an unknown saint. He had been placed there because during his life Norman had been drawn to the abbey for reasons he could not explain and often prayed in the chapel. The actual relic, the unknown saint's body, had been placed there by St. Baldwin.

Sometime in the next few years, Phra's body was discovered and thought to be the body of the saint, miraculously preserved. When Phra awoke in 1326, not remembering his waking periods, he believed that he had been placed there shortly after going to sleep in 1084.

After nearly drowning once more, Phra went to sleep in 1346 and awoke in 1586. He met Adam Faulkner, fell in love with his daughter Elizabeth, and saw his love killed as he had so many times before. He withdrew to a secret den in the Faulkner manse with the narrative of his life, fully expecting to die. After this we know nothing more of Phra.

But, as Dr. Coogan speculates in "John Carter IS Phra the Phoenician":

> In *Gods of Mars* "Burroughs" notes that John Carter dandled his grandfather's great-grandfather on his knee (*Gods* v). The narrator "Burroughs" (as opposed to the historical Burroughs) was five years old just prior to the opening of the Civil War (1861), so he was born in 1855...John Carter [must have been] active at some point between 1705 and 1765 in order to have known Burroughs' grandfather's great-grandfather as a child. Phra "died" circa 1586, and he could have reawakened after about a century and emigrated to America at some point prior to the 18th century when he became associated with the "Burroughs" family, perhaps even fathering the boy he dandled on his knee.

Given the striking parallels between the texts of *Phra the Phoenician* and *A Princess of Mars* and the other evidence cited at length above, we can now state with certainty that Phra the Phoenician IS John Carter!

Bibliography

Arnold, Edwin. *The Wondrous Adventures of Phra the Phoenician*. New York: A.L. Burt, 1890.

Burroughs, Edgar Rice. *The Gods of Mars*. 1913. New York: Ballantine, 1963.

---. *The Outlaw of Torn*. 1914. New York: Ace Books, 1968.

---. *A Princess of Mars*. 1912. New York: Ballantine, 1963.

Coogan, Peter. "John Carter IS Phra the Phoenician!" *An Expansion of Philip José Farmer's Wold Newton Universe*. Win Scott Eckert, ed., 2001. <http://www.pjfarmer.com/woldnewton/Articles5.htm#PHRA>.

---. and Dennis E. Power. "Burroughing Beneath the Page: The Life of Matthew Nicholas Carter." *The Secret History of the Wold Newton Universe*. Dennis E. Power, ed., 2003. <http://www.pjfarmer.com/secret/Immortal/Burroughing.htm>.

---. and Dennis E. Power. "John Carter: Torn from Phoenician Dreams Part Two: The Lives and Times of John Carter." *The Secret History of the Wold Newton Universe*. Dennis E. Power, ed., 2002. <http://www.pjfarmer.com/secret/Immortal/phra2.htm>

Farmer, Philip José. "The Arms of Tarzan." *Burroughs Bulletin*. 22 (1971). *The Wold Newton Universe*. Win Scott Eckert, ed., 2001. <http://www.pjfarmer.com/woldnewton/Farmer_articles.htm#ARMS>.

---. *Tarzan Alive*: A Definitive Biography of Lord Greystoke. Garden City, NY: Doubleday & Co., 1972.

Geoffrey of Monmouth. *History of the Kings of Britain*. Trans. Sebastian Evans. Revised by Charles W. Dunn. New York: Dutton, 1958.

Lupoff, Richard. *Edgar Rice Burroughs: Master of Adventure*. Revised ed. New York: Ace Books, 1968.

Miller, John L. "Disassociative disorders." AtHealth. Jul. 2000. <http://www.athealth.com/Consumer/disorders/Dissociative.html>.

"Monarchs of Britain." Britannia. 2000. <http://www.britannia.com/history/h6f.html>.

Roy, John Flint. *A Guide to Barsoom: The Mars of Edgar Rice Burroughs*. New York: Ballantine, 1976.

Rutt, Todd & McConnell, Arn. "The Mysterious Case of the Carters Or How Hirohito Became Nick Carter's Aide." *TheWold Atlas*v1, n2, Spring 1977. *The Wold Newton Chronicles*. Mark K. Brown, ed., 2000. <http://www.pjfarmer.com/chronicles/Carters1.htm>.

---. "Caves, Gas & The Great Transfer Theory." *The Wold Atlas* v1, n2 Spring 1977. *The Wold Newton Chronicles*. Mark K. Brown,ed., 2000. <http://www.pjfarmer.com/chronicles/gas.htm>.

D is for Daughter, F is for Father

By Mark K. Brown

Kinsey Millhone is the detective whose highly entertaining memoirs are being presented to the world by Sue Grafton beginning with *"A" is for Alibi* (Henry Holt and Co., 1983). She lives in the southern California coastal community of Santa Teresa. Kinsey is both physically and mentally strong, key traits of Wold Newton Family members. She has excellent detective instincts and even a talent for disguise. She also possesses a strong urge to see justice done, even, in at least one case, if it requires her to take the law into her own hands and break it. She is a good candidate for Wold Newton Family membership.

Kinsey's parents, Randy Millhone and Rita Kinsey, met at Rita's debut in Lompoc, California, in 1935. She was eighteen. Randy was a waiter at the event. He was thirty-three. Despite a great deal of disapproval on the part of Rita's family, they were married in November. This caused Rita to become estranged from her wealthy parents. The Millhones settled in Santa Teresa, California, where both they and their daughter would live for the rest of their lives.

Kinsey was born on May 5, 1950, and apparently was an only child. This brings to mind two relevant facts. First, that Randy and Rita Millhone were married for fifteen years before they had a child, and, second, that by 1949 (the year Kinsey was conceived), Randy was forty-eight and Rita was thirty-three.

Lew Archer, whom Philip José Farmer has identified as a Wold Newton Family member, was born in either 1914 or 1918 (internal evidence is a little contradictory). This would make him either thirty-one or thirty-five in 1949. He was much closer to Rita Millhone's age than her husband's. We know from the books which Ross MacDonald edited from of his memoirs that Lew was not unattractive to the opposite sex, although not nearly as much of a womanizer as, say, James Bond or Travis McGee. Lew was married at this time, although, as we shall see, this was not to last.

My theory is this: Randy Millhone was sterile. Although Rita loved him very much, this caused a certain amount of tension and dissatisfaction in their marriage. In 1948 or early 1949, Lew Archer was brought to Santa Teresa for the first time on business of some sort. He met the lovely Rita Millhone, and the two had an affair. Neither was by nature very promiscuous, nor were they entirely comfortable with the relationship, but Rita was unhappy in her marriage and very attracted to Lew. Lew fell rather hard for Rita. Somewhere along the line, Lew's wife found out about the affair, and Rita became pregnant.[320]

Randy Millhone, although not happy with the situation, tried hard to understand his wife's position. The effort he made reminded Rita of the reasons she was in love with him and she broke off the relationship with Lew. After all, the main thing missing in her life with Randy was a child. Lew didn't take it quite as well, and had a much harder time returning to life with his wife. Things did not work out, and Lew was served with divorce papers in late 1949. Kinsey was born in May of 1950. Her parents were killed in a car crash in 1955, when she was only five years old. She had no clue that Randy was not her father.

We imagine that the cases Lew decided to write up would not only be the ones he thought would be interesting to an audience, but also the ones that he had an emotional connection to. The case of the wealthy family with scandal in its past; the case of the child who turns out to be the illegitimate result of an extramarital relationship; these would be the archetypal Lew Archer cases. And Lew was drawn back to Santa Teresa again and again over the years. Obviously, the events of 1949 left deep marks in his heart and mind.

So far, Kinsey Millhone and Sue Grafton have made little effort to explore the early days of Kinsey's life. The events described in this article may indicate why.

The Monster on Hold

a chapter from a projected novel in the Lord Grandrith/Doc Caliban series

By Philip José Farmer

World Fantasy Convention Program, 1983

The story following this introduction is a chapter in a projected novel originally titled *The Unspeakable Threshold* (now titled *The Monster on Hold*). This will be a "Doc Caliban" story and the latest in the series beginning with *A Feast Unknown* and continued in the *Lord of the Trees* and *The Mad Goblin. Feast* started in east Africa and is told in first person by James Cloamby, Viscount Grandrith (pronounced Grunith), an Englishman raised by a subhuman species (a variant of Australopithecus) in West Africa. Grandrith, while still a youth, became one of the high-echelon agents of the Council of Nine. The Nine are the secret rulers of earth, most of who were born circa 30,000-20,000 BC though they looked as if their age is only a hundred.

The Nine have considerably slowed their aging with a longevity "elixir" which they share with certain agents who have earned it. Grandrith is one of the very few so privileged. Though eighty-three he looks and feels like a twenty-five-year-old man.

In *A Feast Unknown,* Grandrith is suffering unforeseen side effects of the elixir. These make it impossible for him to get an erection unless, and to avoid one if, violence is involved. He finds this out when he is attacked by Jomo Kenyatta's forces. Then he discovers that an American agent for the Nine is out to kill him. Doc Caliban believes (wrongly) that Grandrith has killed Caliban's cousin, Patricia Wild, also an agent of the Nine. Caliban is suffering from the same side effects of the elixir.

Just as the two have what should be a final confrontation, they are summoned to a meeting of the Nine in a subterranean area in east Africa. The oldest man of the Council, XauXaz, has died, and Caliban and Grandrith are the top two candidates to replace him. One must kill the other to get a seat on the Council. In the end of *A Feast Unknown*, after many adventures, the two almost kill each other, but they then unite to fight against the Nine.

In *Lord of the Trees*, Grandrith manages to kill Mubaniga, the proto-Bantu member of the Nine. In *The Mad Goblin*, Jiinfan, a proto-

Mongolian member and Iwaldi, an ancient Germanic member, are killed during a night battle at Stonehenge. Four of the Nine are dead, leaving as head of the Council Anana, the withered hag born about thirty thousand years ago in the area which would become Sumeria. Other living members are Tilatoc (an ancient Amerindian), Ing (the patronymic leader of the early English tribes when they were living in Denmark), Yeshua (a Hebrew born circa 3 B.C.), and Shaumbim (a proto-Mongolian).

The three novels above took place in the late 1960s. The events of *The Monster on Hold* begin in the late 1970s when Doc Caliban penetrates Tilatoc's supposedly impregnable fortress hideout in northern Canada. I won't describe the result because I don't want to reveal too much about the novel. But Caliban goes into hiding again. He hears that Anana has decreed that whoever kills Grandrith and Caliban will become Council members even if they are not candidates. (Caliban almost loses his life when he gains this piece of information.) When the second section of the novel begins (in 1984), Caliban is in Los Angeles and disguised as an old wino. Tired of running, he's decided to attack, but, first, he needs a lead. One night, a juvenile gang jumps him, thinking he's easy prey. He disposes of them quite bloodily, but he spots a man observing the fight. Later, he sees the man shadowing him. After trapping him, Caliban questions him, using a truth drug he invented in the 1930s. As Caliban suspects, the man is an agent of the Nine. Caliban allows him to escape and then trails him. This leads to a series of adventures I'll omit in this outline.

During these, Caliban begins to suffer from a recurring nightmare and has dreams alternating with these in which he sees himself or somebody like himself. However, this man, whom he calls The Other, also at times in Caliban's dreams seems to be dreaming of Caliban.

Caliban thinks he has shaken himself loose of the Nine's agents, but then another appears. Caliban catches him and then recognizes him as a man he last saw in 1948.

He's shaken. The man, now calling himself Scott Free, figured prominently in an adventure which Caliban recalls with horror and much puzzlement. That is, when he does think about it, which is as seldom as he can help.

Caliban and his aides and some others had ventured deep into a labyrinthine cavern complex in New England. There they had encountered things which Mr. Free (one of the party) had said were the metamorphosed spirits of the dead. "Devils." Free claimed to be a lower-echelon devil who had escaped from Hades. Caliban, a rationalist and agnostic, did not believe Free's explanation. Yet, some of the events had no acceptable explanations. Whatever the truth, Caliban had escaped something very horrible. He had had no desire to explore the caverns again. At the same time his scientific curiosity about them had tormented him from time to time.

The adventure had been thirty-six years ago, and here is Mr. Free looking as young as then and trying to make him his prisoner. By whose order?

That of the thing which Free had implied was Satan? That of the Nine? Or was he trying to get Caliban on his own?

Doc gets into contact with his two aides, "Pauncho" Van Veelar and Barney Banks. They're living under assumed names in upper New York but come at once when Doc summons them.

The truth drug fails to work on Free, but Caliban forces a story out of him which seems to be true. At least, the instruments that Doc used indicate this. Free confesses that the story about the cavern being Hades and its inhabitants being doomed souls is false. But he was born in the middle of the eighteenth century, and he had worked for the Nine. Too ambitious, he doublecrossed the Nine to gain a vast fortune. Caught, he expected to be tortured and killed. Instead he was condemned to be one of the guards in the cavern complex in New England.

There he discovered that he was to help guard some thing that he could only describe as "the monster in abeyance" or "the monster on hold." But it did have a name, Shrassk, meaning "She-Who-Eats-Her-Children." Free has never seen the monster. He says that in the eighteenth century the Nine were faced with a situation similar to that of Grandrith's and Caliban's revolt. Then, three candidates had tried to overthrow the Nine. They had so disrupted the organization, slain so many agents and candidates, come so close to killing some of the Nine, that the Council, in desperation, had summoned a thing from another dimension or perhaps from a parallel universe.

(Not too parallel, Free says. Caliban says that things are either parallel or they're not. Free says that the other universe is, then, asymptotic. Which explains why the area in which the monster is contained in the cave is partly in this world, partly out of it. Or, from what he's heard, it may be suspended between two universes, acting as a sort of bridge.)

Shrassk, Free says, has the power, perhaps uncontrolled by it, a wild talent, to touch the subconscious of some sensitive human receptors and cause nightmares. God only knows what else.

Its touching may have been what caused Lovecraft to form his Cthulhu mythos, a dimly perceived and mostly fictional concept but based on the real horror.

In any event, Shrassk was not to be released directly upon the world in an effort to get the three rebels of the eighteenth century. While Shrassk was held in abeyance, it would reproduce after some mysterious mating and conception, and its "children" would be loosed to seek out and destroy the three without fail. Some children, that is.

Before that happened, the three rebels were caught, tortured, and then fed to Shrassk. It would not, however, go back to where it had come from. The Nine had to maintain the guards for the children and the forces that held it back from entering this world. Meanwhile, Shrassk was breeding, though very slowly, more of the children. Free says that Shrassk is imprisoned by geometry but, if it escapes, will do so by algebra. He is unable to clarify this enigmatic remark.

In 1948, Free had escaped from the cavern but had been forced to re-enter the cavern by Caliban and his aides. After they had gotten out of the cave, Free had teleported himself from jail. But teleportation is a power not always on tap. After a few "discharges," as Free puts it, the user has to recharge his battery.

Doc doesn't believe the story about TP. He thinks Free is lying and that he's just a superb escape artist.

Now, Free says, the Nine are so desperate that they are considering letting loose a "child" to destroy Grandrith, Caliban, Caliban's cousin, Pat Wilde, and Van Veelar and Banks. If that "child" doesn't succeed, another will be released.

Doc wonders if the truth drug isn't ineffective on Free and if Free hasn't been planted by the Nine to allure Caliban to go back to the cave. Nevertheless, he decides that he will attack. He gets into contact with Van Veelar and Banks and, after some difficulty, with his cousin, Pat. After taking the small stone fortress at the opening of the cave, the four descend into the many-leveled subterranean complex. This time, they penetrate much deeper than in 1948. They encounter a greater variety of denizens than the first time, including one which Doc thinks for a while is Shrassk. Doc becomes separated from his companions and has to go on alone.

The following is the first draft of a chapter of the proposed novel.

Free had said that the "children" were born out of flame by Shrassk.

Why then, as Caliban had proved so many times in the past twelve hours, were they terrified by fire? Was it fire itself, the reality, or the idea of fire that panicked them? Or both? Or something else?

He crouched behind the seven-foot-high cone of dark brown stuff oozing from the wide crack in the rock floor. Its rotten-onion stink and his knowledge of its origin sickened him. That the cone was building up at the rate of a quart every five minutes meant that monsters like the one he had just killed were in the neighborhood. Unless, that is, the dead thing was excreting after death and its wastes were flowing through the undersurface fissure complex. No. This cone was too far from the carcass.

Others of its kind must be nearby.

Soft noises came from the other side of the cone. Whisperings, chitterings. Nonhuman. He moved slowly along the edge of the cone. The gray-green light seemed to be dimming somewhat. Was the chocolate-brown goo absorbing the light? Nonsense. Or was it? He could not know here what was or was not nonsense. Anyway, calling something nonsense meant only that you did not understand it.

He looked around the cone. In the half-light he could see the rear of a creature he had not encountered so far. It had a tail two feet long, about an inch in diameter, hairless, studded with dark warts, and exuding slime. The tail was switching back and forth much like that of a cat thinking whatever sphinxlike thoughts a cat thought.

He moved slowly further around the edge of the cone, prepared to duck back if the thing should turn its eyes—if it had any—toward him. Then he saw that he had been wrong in assuming that the creature had a posterior part. It was two feet in diameter and a foot high. There was no head, hence, no rear, just an armored dome from which four tails—some kind of flexible members, anyway—extended. If the tail he had first seen came from the south of the round body, the others extended from the north, west, and east. The end of the west tail was stuck into the brown cone and was, since it was twice as large in diameter as the others, swollen with the sucking-in of the excrement.

Because the thing seemed to be eyeless, Caliban stepped forward two paces. Beyond the creature were four others, all feeding with the tail-like "west" organs.

Beyond them, its back to him—he supposed it was the back—was a bipedal creature. It was almost as tall as he and was unclothed. Though human in form, its skin was a dull blue. Black ridges ran both vertically and horizontally over its legs and body and hairless head. The ridges formed squares in the center of which was a livid red circle the size of a silver dollar. One hand, quite human, held a shepherd's staff.

The whisperings and chitterings came from the "shepherd."

The creature began to turn around. Caliban backed away around the cone. He looked around. No living thing in sight—as far as he knew. Here, he could not be sure what was or was not living. The rock floor slanted upwards at a ten-degree angle to the horizontal. At least, what he thought was the horizontal. The only relief to the smoothness and emptiness were some tall rock spirals, huge boulders, and brown cones here and there. The warm thick air passed slowly over his sweating skin.

He walked in the opposite direction so that he could watch the shepherd while it was facing the other way. And then the flickerings began again—flickerings he knew now were not phenomena outside him—and he saw The Other, his near-double.

For a moment he was frightened. Shrassk was touching his mind again. But, he reassured himself, that did not mean that Shrassk knew where he was. On the other hand…

He slid that possibility into a drawer in his mind and watched the vision with inner eyes while the outer watched the cone. If that shepherd strolled around the cone, it would have him at a disadvantage. He should go ahead with his plan. But he could not move.

The man who looked so much like him was walking through a rock tunnel filled with the same light as this cavern, the gray-green of an old bone spotted with lichen. He, too, wore a backpack and a harness to which was attached many containers for instruments and weapons. Suddenly, The Other stopped. His expression shifted from intense wariness to fright. That quickly passed and he stared straight ahead as if he were seeing something puzzling.

Caliban relaxed a trifle. The other man was probably also touched by Shrassk. He was seeing Caliban as Caliban was seeing him.

Caliban anticipated that they might soon do more than just see one another. It seemed to him that The Other was not perhaps in the same universe as Caliban's. Not yet. Perhaps never. But Shrassk was in the third universe which was a bridge between Caliban's and The Other's. A crossroads. And Caliban and The Other could leave their two worlds to meet in the third, Shrassk's.

This anticipation was based on Free's explanation, which meant that neither was grounded in reality.

Doc forced himself to move. With the first step, the little glowing stage and its single performer vanished. It was as if his connection with the vision had been switched off by muscular action. By the time that he came to the other side of the cone, he was running and his mind was completely wrapped around his intent. A big knife was in one hand and the gas-powered pistol was in the other.

The shepherd has his back to him. It was turning one of the round things with its staff so that the tail on the south side could be inserted into the cone. Caliban slowed down just a little because he was astonished. The crook at the end of the shepherd's staff was straight now. Its end had split into two, and these were clamped around the lower edge of the dome-shaped cone-eater. Using these, the shepherd was turning the thing so that it could insert another tail into the goo.

The checkerboard-skinned thing must have heard him or have felt the vibrations of Caliban's boots through the rock floor and its bare soles. It yanked the staff from the edge of the round tailed thing and whirled. The ends of the staff merged together.

Caliban noted this and also the sex of the shepherd. It had no testicles, but a thin orange-prepuced penis reached to its knees.

The shepherd grinned, exposing four beaverlike teeth. Its face was human except for the black squares and red spots. It raised the staff as if it were going to throw it at Doc. The end nearest Doc swelled, the shaft shrinking in length and diameter as substance flowed into the end, and the end became a thin pointed two-edged blade.

Doc raised the gas-pistol and squeezed the trigger. There was a hiss. The projectile appeared, its needle point buried in the blue chest. The thing staggered back two steps. It should have been unconscious in four seconds, but, screaming, it ran at Doc, the staff held as if it were a spear. Which it now was. The thing's arm came down; the spear flashed at Doc. He ducked. The spear missed, but the lower back end sagged, became supple, and whipped around Doc's arm.

Still holding the pistol, Doc sawed with his knife at the creature squeezing on his arm. Its body seemed to be as hard as hickory though it was as flexible as rubber.

By then the shepherd was upon him. Doc brought the knife up from the snake-shaft and down into the shepherd's thigh. The blade sank halfway into the flesh, but Doc was knocked down by the impact of its body. He rolled away and started to get up. The snake-shaft coiled the rest of its body around Doc's neck. He fell on his back, dropped the knife and pistol, and, while the thing cut his breath off, got his fingers between it and his neck, though not without cutting his skin with his fingernails, and, with a mighty yank, uncoiled it and cast it away.

Few men would have had the power to do that, but Doc had no time to congratulate himself on that. The shaft was writhing on the floor in an effort to reach him. Lacking the belly plates of the true snake, it was making little progress. The shepherd, however, screaming, blood gushing from its wound, was hobbling towards him. Doc rolled away until his right hand was within reach of the snake-shaft. His fingers closed around it just back of the head, which was swelling—toward what shape?—and he rose to his feet and threw the thing at the shepherd in one fluid movement. He had taken the chance that the staff might be so quick that it would whip itself around his wrist or even, perhaps, around his neck again. But, cracking it like a whip, he had avoided that. Now the shaft fell around the shepherd's head, chittered something, and the shaft fell off it.

Doc had hurled himself against the shepherd then, and he had knocked it down. It started to get up, but Doc's boot caught it under its rounded and cleft chin. It fell back, unconscious.

Panting, Doc bent over the shepherd. Since he wanted no witness left behind, no one to tell—whom?—that he had been this way, he intended to drag the shepherd to a nearby deep fissure and drop it in. He screamed and straightened up and grabbed at his crotch. Something had wrapped itself around his penis and was squeezing it. For a few seconds, he was so taken by shock and surprise that he did not recognize what it was that had seized him. Now he saw that the proboscislike sex organ of the shepherd—if it was a sex organ—had coiled itself around his penis. It was yanking at it as if it was trying to tear his organ off. Fortunately, the cloth of Doc's pants was interfering with the effort.

The shepherd seemed to be still knocked out. The drug from the hypodermic and its wound had surely done their work. But they should also have made its sex organ, or whatever it was, flaccid. Knocked it out, too. Unless it was partially independent of the blood supply of the main body.

No time to think. Gritting his teeth, Doc backed away, the shepherd's body dragging behind, pulled by the proboscis attached to Doc's penis. The pain became worse. He had a vision of his organ being torn out by the roots, but he kept backing until he was by the knife. He fell to his knees, grabbed it, and sliced away the blue length and orange prepuce with one motion. Blood, almost black in the dim light, geysered out from the shepherd.

"God Almighty!"

Doc staggered to the gas gun, picked it up, sheathed it and the knife, and ran. The pain faded away but not the memory. After a few yards, he slowed to a walk. A glance showed him the shepherd's still body, the shaft writhing, and the five round things. What next? When he reached the far wall of the cavern, he went along it for perhaps a quarter of a mile and found in the shadows the entrance of a smooth downslanting tunnel. With both arms outspread, he could touch its walls. The top was a foot higher than his six feet and seven inches.

The tunnel, after a half a mile, ended with a flaring out as if it were a trumpet. Before him was silence and the biggest cavern yet. The walls opposite him were draped in blackness which, for a second, he thought moved. The ceiling soared into darkness. The floor, far below, was bathed in a brighter light than that which he had gone through and was now green-yellow. Its source, however, was still unknown.

A ledge extended from the tunnel exit. Two feet wide, it ran more or less horizontally from both sides of the tunnel mouth as far as he could see. The straight drop from the ledge to the floor was, he estimated, about a mile. From here, the floor seemed to be smooth among the ridges, hillocks, and curious shapes, some of which looked human. Vaguely. They could not be, however. For one thing, they did not move. For another, they would have to be far larger than elephants for him to make out their shapes at this distance and in this twilight.

For the first time, he saw water in large quantity. A river wound through a rock channel, its surface dark, smooth, and oily. Perhaps it wasn't water.

Something darker than the river and the stone banks moved slowly on the surface. Doc removed his backpack and took out the night-vision subsonic-transmitter. He lay down on the ledge, his elbows propped near the edge, put the viewscreen to his eyes, swept the area that had attracted his attention, adjusted the dials, moved the instrument back and forth, and held it steady.

The slowly floating mass was a rowboat with an unmoving figure seated in it. The figure seemed to have its back to him. But something extended from its front out over the water. A fishing rod? What kind of creatures could live in the barren river? There was no food for them. Unless...there were cracks in the riverbottom and the chocolately onion-stinking stuff oozed up from them. Maybe the "fish" ate that stuff.

Doc moved the line of sight over the boat. It was white, though that may not have been its color. Objects on which the instrument focused looked white; objects near the edge of the screen and in the background were dark. He did not think that the boat was made of wood since wood was absent in this world. The boat had probably been carved from stone.

The fisherman could be of stone, too. He certainly had not moved any more than a granite statue would. If that were so, then the monk's cloak and hood on him were of stone, too.

Doc had to keep moving the instrument slowly because the boat, like the river, was moving sluggishly. Then he started, and he lost the boat for a moment. The fisherman had shifted. By the time that he was in the screen again, he was on his feet and holding the pole with both hands. The line from the pole was too thin for Doc's instrument to reflect, but Doc knew that there was a line. Proof of its existence was climbing out of the river on the line.

The thing ascending the line hand over hand had a ghostly-white face with enormous eyes. A snub human nose. Thick pale lips. A rounded chin. Under which hung a loose bladder of skin. The thing had a high and bulging forehead. If it had a head of hair, it was not visible. It had no ears or ear openings that Doc could see. The neck was fat, and the body was a baby's, the arms and legs very short. It stood swaying, its nonhuman round feet with long webbed toes spread out on the stone bottom of the boat. The fingers were also long and webbed.

Doc widened the field of vision. The fisherman was three times as tall as the catch. If the former was six feet high, then the catch was two feet tall.

Doc's muscles tightened, and the back of his neck chilled. The fisherman had turned so that Doc could see the profile under the hood. It was human and familiar. The big hooked nose could be Dante Alighieri's.

Stop thinking like this, Doc told himself. That is not the centuries-dead Florentine poet. He—or it—is probably, no, certainly, not even human. Free's claim that the dead were reincarnated here was ridiculous.

Now the fisherman had put the pole down in the boat. Now he was picking up the large but slim fishhook at the end of the line and was walking carefully—didn't want to rock the boat—toward the creature that looked like a hybrid of baby and frog. Now he had grabbed its neck—the creature was not struggling—and had savagely driven the end of the hook through one side of the bladder below the neck and out through the other side.

Even then the creature was passive. Perhaps it was in shock, though Doc did not think so. Something in its attitude indicated that it was fully cooperating. And now the fisherman had tossed the creature into the water. He walked back to the pole, lifted it, and sat down, becoming again a stone-still Izaak Walton. The pole did not move, which meant that the thing on the hook was not struggling.

What was the prey for which the baby-frog would be bait? Anything big enough to swallow it would be too big for the simple Tom-Sawyer fishing tackle to handle.

Getting answers here is secondary, Doc thought. I shouldn't be wasting time lying here and watching. I must be moving on. Besides, in this place, what I see from a distance, even with the viewer, may be quite different from what I'd see close up.

Nevertheless, he did not get up at once. The fisherman maintained his unhuman lack of movement, no wriggling, no looking around, no scratching of nose or hair. Only the boat and the river moved, and they did so very slowly. Nor had anything else moved except some shadows seen out of the corners of his eyes. When he looked directly at where the shadows had been, he saw only the pale dead-looking light.

Though he kept the viewer on the boat, with occasional sweeps across the floor, he could not help but think of other things. For instance, what was the ecosystem of this place? There had to be some kind of order here despite all the appearances of illogic and chaos. Everything he had seen had to be obeying or acting in accordance with a "law," a "principle." Everything had to be interconnected here as much as everything above it was. The "laws" of entropy, of energy input and output, conception, reproduction, growth, aging, and death had to operate in this deep underground. There had to be a system and an interdependent network.

What?

Doc vowed that, before he left here—if he did leave—he would at least have an inkling of the system. He would have some data on which he could theorize.

Finally he rose. He was ready to go on. But, lacking a parachute or enough rope, he could not get down or along the glass-smooth wall below the ledge. He could go to the right or the left on the ledge. One direction had to lead down to the cave floor. There was traffic from the lower levels to the upper, and, thus, this ledge was the highway. Perhaps both the left and right were used. He could not, however, afford the time to take one and find out that it petered out somewhere on the side of the immense bowl.

Take the left. Why? Because that was the sinister side. It seemed to him that the sinister would always be the right direction in this place. Chuckling feebly at his feeble pun, he began walking faster than caution recommended, his left shoulder brushing against the wall now and then.

After a quarter of a mile, the ledge began sloping gently downward. In an hour, he was halfway to the floor and above a roughly three-cornered opening in the wall into which the dark river flowed. By then the fisherman had inserted his pole into a socket in the corner of the boat and was rowing back up the river. Were his oars also made of stone?

The ledge took Caliban to the other side of the cavern before it reached the floor. He stood there for a while and listened to the total silence, which was a ringing in his ears. The fear bell ringing, he thought. Someone is at the front door and pressing on the button.

Though he had no reason to think so, he felt that he was getting close to his goal. Which perhaps explained why his fear had come back and was moving closer to that sheer hysterical horror he had suffered during an incident in his first venture into the cave so many years ago.

Caliban, your hindbrain is trying to take over, he told himself. Use your forebrain. Don't use it to rationalize and justify what your hindbrain is telling you. Don't turn and run away. Don't walk away, either. Push on ahead. If you flee now when you are so close, after you've gone through so much, you'll despise yourself forever afterwards. You might as well kill yourself. In which case, if you're going to die if you run away or die if you go ahead, you might as well, no, it'll be much better, if you die because you went ahead.

Despite this, the fire of panic was burning away his reason and courage. It might have caught hold of him and turned him around. He would never know because the vision of The Other sprang into light in some place in his mind. And, as fire lights fire, a cliché but sometimes true, the vision swept away the fear.

The Other was standing at the entrance to a cave. He was smiling and holding up one huge bronze-skinned hand, two fingers forming a V. Then the scene widened, and Doc saw that The Other was about three hundred feet from a great circle of stone symbols brightly lit by burning gas jets at their bases. There were nine: a Greek cross, a hexagon, a crescent, a five-pointed star, a triangle with an eye at its top, a Celtic cross, an O with an X inside it, a snake with its tail in its mouth, and a winged horseshoe. They enclosed a shallow bowl-shaped depression in the rock about three hundred feet in diameter. In the center was another circle of stone symbols, smaller than those that formed the outer circle and unfamiliar to Caliban. Inside the smaller circle was a platform shaped like an 8 on its side. The upper side of the 8 had holes which projected to the far ceiling bright violet-colored rays.

Where the two O's that formed the 8 met, a strip of stone about ten feet wide, was a highbacked chair cut from a bloodred stone. The chair was not empty.

Caliban felt as if every cell in his body had turned over.

The being on the chair, surely Shrassk, She-Who-Eats-Her-Young, was not at all whom or what he had expected.

The fear surged back in; the vision dimmed. But he forced himself to push it back down, though it was like pressing down on a lid over a kettle of cockroaches breeding so furiously that the lid kept rising. For a moment, the vision became brighter and clearer. Doc saw that his Other was making signs in deaf-and-dumb language, indicating that his *Other*, Caliban, must hasten to aid him. Alone, each would go down quickly. Together, they might have a chance.

Caliban began running in a land where it was not good to run.

* * * * *

Thus ends this chapter. Will Caliban and The Other kill Shrassk?

Or will they be lucky to get away with life and limb? Will both survive? Will Doc Caliban ever analyze the ecosystem of what might or might not be Hell?

You will find out when *The Monster on Hold* is published.[321]

Travels in Time
By Loki Carbis

The birth name of the man known to scholars of the Wold Newton Families as "The Time Traveller" was Bruce Clarke Wildman. He was the son of Sir Patrick Wildman and his wife, Mavice Blakeney Wildman, and the sibling of Alexander and Patricia Clarke Wildman. He was thus the descendent of such notables as Solomon Kane, Manuel of Poictesme, Raphael Hythloday, Micah Clarke, and Sir Percy Blakeney (the Scarlet Pimpernel). Although his siblings emigrated to the United States, Bruce was of a more solitary nature, and quite content to remain in England. His experiences during his school years, which earned him the much-detested nickname of "Moses," only confirmed these tendencies in him. He became ever more solitary and bookish, and had he been of a less boastful disposition, he might never have told anyone of his discoveries. Indeed, all records seem to indicate that he never so much as met his niece, Pat Savage.

Gottfried Plattner

In the mid-1870s, about two decades before his first travels through time, he purchased a house in Richmond, where he planned to pursue his studies. His explorations of science and chemistry took on a very different nature when he was given a sample of a mysterious metal by a man who identified himself as "Gottfried Plattner." This metal, which Wildman dubbed "Plattnerite" in honour of his mysterious benefactor, turned out to be the one thing that made time travel possible.

The source of this mysterious metal is unknown—Plattner himself had been given it by a student of his. His experiments with the substance created a sort of beacon in time that allowed another time traveler to home in on him, and displace him into another dimension. The identity of this time traveler would not be known for some years, but it was this impostor Plattner who passed the substance along to Wildman.

Wildman worked mostly alone at this time, although he did confide in two friends—Sir William Reynolds, a fellow inventor, and Herbert George Wells, a science journalist and author. All three lived in the vicinity of Richmond, and shared ideas and theories about time travel and the design of machines to traverse it. Wildman shared a small amount of his limited supply of Plattnerite with Reynolds and Wells.

The first time travel to be made by any of this circle was in fact using Reynolds' prototypical machine in 1888. Reynolds' assistant, Amelia Fitzgibbon, and her paramour, Edward Turnbull, took the machine for a joyride that went tragically wrong. They journeyed ten years forward in time, where they were vouchsafed a horrid vision of the War of the Worlds. Turnbull damaged the spatial controls of the machine, and inadvertently marooned himself and Fitzgibbon on Mars. Through luck and skill, the two succeeded in stowing away on the first of the Martian projectiles, and returned to Earth in time to help defeat the Martian invasion. Their report to Wells on the subject allowed him to get vital information to British Intelligence that contributed to the Martians' eventual defeat.

Reynolds deduced what the problem was, and advised Wildman to pay more attention to stabilizing the location of the time machine in space as it traveled through time. Wildman incorporated these improvements into his own machine, and finished its construction in 1892.

The Time Traveller

The initial voyage of the Time Traveller was related by him to a small circle of friends, but they were sworn to secrecy, and it was widely presumed that he had simply disappeared in some mysterious fashion. This case, the so-called "Richmond Enigma," was investigated by no less a detective than Sherlock Holmes himself, and solved only due to the intervention of Wildman, who assured Holmes that he would destroy the machine. It is an open question as to whether Holmes was truly deceived or simply allowed Wildman to believe that he was.

Wildman himself had set out to return to the future that he had discovered, only to find himself, again and again, blundering through the tangled web of alternate timelines. His companion in most of these journeys was an alternate future Morlock named Nebogipfel, whom he met on his second trip through time.

Eventually, with the aid of machine intelligences that had been built by his own descendents, he achieved a mastery over time travel, and discovered that it was his later self who had assumed the identity of Gottfried Plattner so many years earlier and set him upon his path. With newfound understanding of time, he was able to travel quickly and easily upon one determined timeline—that which led to the future of his beloved Weena and the other Eloi, as well as the despised Morlocks. Upon his return to the future, the Time Traveller set out to teach the Eloi and the Morlocks to live and work together, and trained them both in agriculture and the keeping of livestock

Eventually, the Morlocks rebelled, and the Time Traveller was forced to flee further into the future. The Morlocks perverted his lessons, and kept the Eloi as livestock thereafter. Moreover, they built themselves a time machine of their own and journeyed back to the past with it, seeking to destroy Wildman before he ever built the machine. Ironically, upon arriving in 1892, the Morlocks were defeated by another friend of the Time Traveller, a young man named Edwin Hocker. Hocker was recruited by a man calling himself Dr. Ambrose to assist him in a battle against the Morlocks. Dr. Ambrose, who claimed to be Merlin, told the young man that he was the reincarnation of King Arthur, although the truth of this claim is uncertain. Hocker rallied a small band of unlikely allies, and successfully defeated this invasion, although at the cost of his own life.

After fleeing from the Morlocks, Wildman established a base for himself in an even more distant future epoch, long after the extinction of both Morlock and Eloi. From here, he devoted himself to scholarly pursuits, chief among them the investigation of the time stream. On one such journey, he chanced to enter the realm known as "the Dreamlands," where he encountered and rescued Allan Quatermain, John Carter, and Randolph Carter, all of whom had arrived there from different time periods. He rescued them from an attack by Mi-Go, whom he had thought were Morlocks, and returned each of them to their appropriate points in time.

H.G. Wells

The story of Wildman's initial voyage was recorded by Wells, a noted writer of fiction and essays. Wells himself was no stranger to travels in time and space, having had a brief but memorable encounter with Doctor Who some years before the Time Traveller's journeys began. Wells would later publish an account of the Time Traveller's initial voyage, obscuring the identities of all involved. In the course of constructing his account, Wells took care to substitute scientific double-talk for the truth regarding the Machine's means of propulsion, corresponding with no less a scientist than Nikola Tesla to ensure that the secret of time travel would not fall into the wrong hands.

By 1893, his curiosity having gotten the better or him, Wells had constructed his own version of the Time Machine, using the notes that Wildman had left behind. When one of his friends, Dr. John Leslie Stephenson, used the machine to travel through time to 1979, Wells gave pursuit. Stephenson was at that time thought by the London police, and many others, to be Jack the Ripper himself, although it seems rather more likely that Stephenson was merely a copycat killer who sought to steal the evil glamour of the Ripper for his own. Wells pursued him into the future, although he initially overshot and arrived in the year 1984 at an inventor's convention. Correcting the oversight, Wells arrived in the year 1979, where he met Amy Catherine Robbins, his future wife, and defeated Stephenson, exiling him forever into the time-stream itself. He returned to 1893 with Amy, and married her soon after.

In 1896, Wells was forced to seek the assistance of Sherlock Holmes in solving the mystery of the death of a scientist friend. This incident was recorded by Dr. John Watson as "The Case of the Inertial Adjustor." Later that year, Wells encountered yet another time traveller, Jherek Carnelian. Carnelian had come to 1896 in his quest to reunite with his true love, Amelia Underwood. (Mrs. Underwood was the sister-in-law of Cecily Underwood, the woman whose jilted lover had become the vampire Spike in 1880.)

The following year, Tesla visited London and met with Wells in person. Although Tesla himself was skeptical as to the practicality of time travel, his assistant, Tatiana Cherenkova, was less so. She and Wells became lovers, and she remained in London with him. By 1899 she had succeeded in creating a Time Machine of her own (albeit, one that functioned on very different principles to that created by Wildman). She then took off into the time-stream, heading for 1999, and thence to further future. She seems to have made the voyage safely, but an auto-return function sent the machine racing back to 1999, where it was found by David Lambert, a scholar of Wells' work. He followed Tatiana into the future, although it remains unclear as to whether the two ever met, or what their final fates were. (Ironically, Tesla himself would later be recruited by a different group of Time Travellers, the so-called Harmonian Conspiracy of Mike and Lady Sally Callahan.)

As was previously mentioned, Wells encountered Fitzgibbon and Turnbull during the War of the Worlds. When the war was won, Wells would achieve fame for penning the definitive account of the Martian Invasion of the Earth, and his editing of a volume of accounts by others, some factual, some fanciful.

Wells was widely honoured as the inventor of the time travel story, and inspired many subsequent experiments with time travel, including those of Emmet Brown. In 2070 a group of four time travellers (one of them a distant cousin of Bruce Clarke Wildman) would christen their vehicle the *H.G. Wells I* in his honour.

It seems likely that either Wells or Wildman (the latter possibly using Quatermain as a courier), left his notes on Time Travel to those in authority. Certainly by 1999, British Intelligence was quite capable of building a greatly refined Time Machine in order to allow special agent Austin Powers to pursue his nemesis, Dr. Evil, into the past.

Alternate Time Travellers

Many alternate tales of the Time Traveller have been written, each depicting inconsistent futures. Modern chaos theory seems to hold the answers to this riddle, however. It is possible that each of the stories is in fact true, each future unfolding separately from the point in time at which the Time Traveller set out.

Certainly, the world in which Weena returned to 1892 and dramatically changed the face of world politics over the next fifty years is one such timeline, as are the tales of the Time Traveller's adventures in the 1930s.

Furthermore, the Time Traveller is reflected across otherwise unrelated universes. In one such, superhuman agents of British Intelligence were caught up in a battle between the Time Traveler's two sons.

But the most incredible example is that of Restin Dane, the Rook. He is the grandson of an alternate universe Time Traveller named Adam Dane, a Wild West gunslinger who became a British aristocrat upon inheriting a noble title. The Danes are explicitly from a different universe to Wildman—one in which Piccadilly Circus has a different name, and in which there never was an Invisible Man.

Adam Dane journeyed to the future in adventures that paralleled those of Wildman at first. However, on his second journey, he went further into the future, and fell in love with a woman he later discovered was a Morlock. Fleeing in disgust, he came to realize that there was nothing wrong with the Morlocks as a race, and that he truly did love her. His return was slightly delayed when he overshot, and found himself in our timeline, where he encountered Jherek Carnelian, Oswald Bastable, and Una Persson, among others. Eventually, he returned and married his Morlock lover. Although the couple was infertile with each other, they adopted a child, and it is his son that we know as the Rook.

The Rook had many adventures although on only one occasion did he cross timelines, when he sought the aid of Vampirella in a crisis that threatened both their universes.

Bibliography

Novels and Short Stories:
Anderson, Kevin J. (editor)
War of the Worlds - Global Dispatches
Baxter, Stephen
"The Case of the Inertial Adjustor"
The Time Ships
DeChancie, John
"The Richmond Enigma"
Farmer, Philip José
Doc Savage: His Apocalyptic Life
Tarzan Alive
Time's Last Gift
Friedell, Egon
The Return of the Time Machine
Jeter, K.W.
Morlock Night
Lake, David J.
The Man Who Loved Morlocks
"The Truth About Weena"
Moorcock, Michael
An Alien Heat
The End of All Songs
The Hollow Lands
Priest, Christopher
The Space Machine
Robinson, Spider
Lady Slings the Booze
Wells, Herbert George
"The Plattner Story"
The Time Machine
The War of the Worlds
Wright, Ronald
A Scientific Romance

Comics:
Chains of Chaos
Eerie
The Establishment
The League of Extraordinary Gentlemen
The Rook

Television:
"Fool for Love"—episode of *Buffy the Vampire Slayer*

"Lies My Parents Told Me"—episode of *Buffy the Vampire Slayer*
"Timelash"—episode of *Dr Who*

Movies:
Austin Powers: The Spy Who Shagged Me
Gremlins
Back to the Future III
Time After Time

A Review of *Final Menacing Glimpses*
By Art Bollmann

We are all familiar with Cordwainer Bird's landmark anthologies, *Menacing Glimpses* and *Wider Menacing Glimpses*. In the 1960s, these anthologies published some of the most controversial works by some of the biggest names in speculative fiction, permanently changing the contours of the field. With restrictions lifted, writers were able to explore forbidden themes, and able to use the narrative techniques of such mainstream giants as Nick Adams and Stephen Daedalus. The biggest and last volume in the series, *Final Menacing Glimpses*, has been delayed for decades. Many of us had given up hope of ever seeing it, and wished that Mr. Bird would spend less time feuding with the producers of *Galaxy Quest* and more time getting the volume to press.

But now, after several decades, Winton House has finally brought forth the final volume. FMG is, of necessity, something of a period piece, since most of the stories were written decades ago. We cannot help but be saddened by the fact that many of the writers in this volume are now dead, but we are glad to have this volume of stories, which, for the most part, put current literature to shame. In light of the fact that many of these authors are dead, it would be both depressing and repetitive to continually use the honorific "the late." We trust the reader to know who is alive and dead.

The volume begins with a personal introduction by Isaac Asimov. Asimov recounts his long running feud/friendship with Bird, and reveals that his novel, *Murder at the ABA*, was based on an actual murder case that Bird solved. (Bird is referred to as "Darius Just" in the novel.) We are perplexed, however, about a closing anecdote from Asimov regarding Bird and a talking dog. We suspect that Dr. A may be pulling our leg.

His own story in this volume, however, is an exercise in "documentary fiction," as Asimov recounts as actual mystery that he solved in the presence of a club called "the Black Widowers."

Pure fantasy follows, with the only known speculative fiction work by mainstream titan T.S. Garp. "The Bear Men of Ursus Five" deals with some ferocious looking but oddly domestic aliens. Or are they domestic…

Noted western writer Matt Helm also works outside his groove, in a story about a government spy. Frankly, this one lacks credibility, and we hope Mr. Helm sticks to horse operas. Write what you know, Matt.

Likewise, R. Questor, a writer unknown to me, has written a story from the POV of an android in "I, Robot." The story is unconvincing, and almost as bad as the title.

Things pick up as Peter J. Frigate offers up a story about the afterlife written in the style of *Finnegans Wake*. Highly entertaining, if a bit farfetched.

Mr. Bird's own story, "Redjac and Back," is a special treat, as he completes an unfinished fragment by Robert Blake, the horror writer who died under mysterious circumstances in the 1930s. The story concerns an alien entity that is responsible for the Jack the Ripper murders, and a number of others. This entity is almost captured by an undercover police officer with a cockatoo, but instead the alien frames the policeman for laundering money.

Simon Moon, the well-known Sixties activist, has supplied what may be his only short story. A broad sexual farce about a U.S. President who faces impeachment because of an affair with an intern, it is alternately hilarious and disgusting, yet compelling. We have a feeling that this will cause many raised eyebrows among Mr. Moon's current colleagues on the New York Stock Exchange.

Ellery Queen offers a classic whodunit set in space and burdened with an unreliable narrator. Mr. Bird affirms that this was actually written by Queen, and not by Kilgore Trout, his occasional ghostwriter.

There are other gems in this volume, including a humorous story of first contact by Luke Devereaux, and an early poem by Gallinger. Most interestingly, a short story by Brady X. Donaldson anticipates some of the themes he would later explore in his posthumous masterwork.

Two stories, however, stand out as the volume's major contributions. The first, of course, is a long novella by Alan Watts. Watts, of course, was the recipient of the first Grandmaster of Fantasy Award. An immigrant from England, he was familiar with the spiritualist scene of London, and drew upon it for a series of terrifyingly convincing stories for *Weird Tales* and Campbell's *Unknown*. For a while he even wrote the successful hero-pulp *The Green Lama*. Of course, he soon broke out of the pulps and attracted considerable attention for a series of historical novels set in the Far East.

The rise of the New Wave seemed to attract him back to science fiction, and during the Sixties his "Boddhisatva Trilogy" won the praise of figures as disparate as Pynchon, both Burroughs, and Timothy

Leary. His novella in this volume, "Stranger in a World I Never Made" offers a vision of a new society that may well be as relevant today as it was when originally written.

"Wolders Live in Vain" by Kilgore Trout closes the volume, and offers the most menacing glimpse of all. Trout imagines a parallel universe in which computers have linked every household, providing instant communication. In this world, such famous historical figures as Tarzan, Sherlock Holmes and Doc Savage are actually fictional characters. (In a sly in-joke, Trout actually postulates that Cordwainer Bird is a fictional character as well.) However, a group of fans on the "Internet" begin playing a game in which they pretend that these characters are real. Although we only know them through their computer messages, many of these characters are well drawn, and emerge as real people. (Fans of the "Masked Savage" will get a chuckle at the name of one of these "Wolders.")

This game hits a snagging point when the players cannot decide whether to pretend that comic book characters are real. Oddly enough, they have fierce, vicious arguments about this topic, on a weekly basis, for years and years. Trout is at his most Swiftian in describing these battles, creating characters that are at once incredibly thin-skinned and incredibly confrontational. One particular fight, between a stubborn English professor and an equally stubborn research scientist, is obviously intended to illustrate C.P. Snow's thesis about the two cultures.

This story, and the entire volume, is highly recommended.

Afterword:

This piece was written with the idea in mind that Cordwainer Bird, the WNU version of Harlan Ellison, must have edited an anthology in the WNU that resembles Ellison's landmark *Dangerous Visions* anthology.

On one hand, there is nothing more annoying than someone who feels compelled to explain all of his own jokes. On the other hand, it can be equally annoying to read a piece that contains nothing but obscure references. I'll split the difference, and explain some but not all of them.

In addition to Ellison, Robert Bloch and Theodore Sturgeon both contributed to *Dangerous Visions* and both have analogs in the WNU. Bloch and Ellison collaborated on two stories about Jack the Ripper, so it makes sense the Blake and Bird should collaborate on a story about the Redjac entity. Kilgore Trout was based partially on

Theodore Sturgeon. Since Sturgeon ghosted books for Frederic Danny and Manfred B. Lee (the creators of Ellery Queen) it makes sense to me that Trout must have written for the actual author Ellery Queen in the WNU.

Alan Watts was a figure in the 1960s counterculture. I speculate that his WNU counterpart might have used his knowledge of Eastern religion to become a popular author.

For my most obscure references, Luke Devereaux is from Fredric Brown's *Martians Go Home*. The poet Gallagher is from Zelazny's "A Rose for Ecclesiastes." Brady X. Donaldson is from Farmer's "Father's In the Basement." Simon Moon is not an author (insofar as we know) but is a recurring character in the work of Robert Anton Wilson.

Nobody knows the true identity of the Masked Savage.

This afterward is in the tradition of the numerous lengthy afterwards to every entry in *Dangerous Visions*.

Endnotes

[1] Examples abound. The WNU cannot take place in a truly "real" world, unless one strictly includes only classic literature or historical fiction without any fantastical elements whatsoever; that is to say, anything of the character of *Pride and Prejudice* to canonical Holmes, to Flashman, to Hornblower, to Sharpe. Once one begins to use elements of fantasy, such as Lovecraft's Cthulhu Mythos stories and Doyle's Challenger series (both of which were included in the WNU by Farmer himself), then one is no longer dealing with the real world.

[2] It is important to note that after he wrote *Tarzan Alive*, Farmer gave permission to Western and adventure writer J.T. Edson to use and refer to the Wold Newton concepts in his books. Several of Edson's books referred to Tarzan and family relocating to Pellucidar in the 1970s—a hollow-earth Pellucidar which Farmer had dismissed as "fictional" in *Tarzan Alive*! Farmer never objected to Edson's reintroduction of Pellucidar into the Wold Newton mythos. When, in the autumn of 2003, I discussed with Mr. Farmer that Edson had sent Tarzan looking for Pellucidar, Farmer's response was typically humorous: "Well, I hope he finds it."

[3] In addition to the above-mentioned Manuel of Poictesme and Robert Blake, Farmer included many other fantastical, non-real-world elements: an immortal Tarzan; an immortal Fu Manchu; the vampire Count Dracula (implied by a reference to a Van Helsing family member); Frankenstein and his Creature (via a reference to Victor Frankenstein's experiments); aliens as seen in Farmer's novel *The Other Log of Phileas Fogg*; a giant ape (Farmer's story "After King Kong Fell"); further weird horror through H. P. Lovecraft's Cthulhu Mythos (Farmer's story "The Freshman"); and a genius talking dog, Ralph von Wau Wau.

[4] As renowned pulp historian Robert Sampson noted in his *Spider* (Bowling Green University Popular Press, 1987), focusing on the 1934-1936 Spider novels: "Thirty novels in which more than 40,000 people die, and a dozen cities are mangled. Yet these cataclysms leave no trace. By the next novel, all is forgotten, as if last month's issue were written on self-erasing paper." (p. 75) Sampson notes that the 1935 novels are "heavily salted with science-fictional and fantastic elements." (p. 76) He describes the post-1936 novels as featuring "...large-scale social disintegration resulting from armed attacks that are as much political as criminal, if the two can be distinguished. In these novels, the Spider's role is modified from avenging mystery figure to resistance leader, often with strong religious overtones." (p. 76) Obviously Farmer knew all this, and nevertheless included The Spider in his Wold Newton mythology. A reasonable interpretation of this inclusion is that the Spider novels were fictionalized, but even so, The Spider must exist in a continuity which perhaps at first glance appears to be the real world, and yet

is not the real world.

[5] *A Feast* Unknown. N. Hollywood: Essex House, 1969. New York: Playboy Press, 1980. *Lord of the Trees*. New York: Ace Books, 1970. *The Mad Goblin*. New York: Ace Books, 1970.

[6] *Greatheart Silver*. New York: Tor Books, 1982.

[7] *A Barnstormer in Oz, or, A Rationalization and Extrapolation of the Split-Level Continuum*. Huntington Woods, MI: Phantasia Press, 1982. New York: Berkley Books, 1982.

[8] Fan fiction is not included. An exception to this policy is fiction that is written by professional authors, but which goes unpublished for some reason. This exception allows for the inclusion of:

- *The Final Affair* by David McDaniel (who has many other published *Man From U.N.C.L.E.* novels to his credit);
- *Tarzan on Mars* by "John Bloodstone" aka Stuart J. Byrne (not authorized by ERB, Inc. but Byrne is a professional science fiction author);
- *Farewell Pellucidar* by Allan Howard Gross (author of the ERB, Inc.-authorized Sunday *Tarzan* strip and several *Tarzan* comics published by Dark Horse); and
- *Red Axe of Pellucidar* by John Eric Holmes (author of the ERB, Inc.-authorized *Mahars of Pellucidar*, as well as *Mordred*, the authorized sequel to Philip Francis Nowlan's *Armageddon 2419 A.D.*).

[9] The Wold Newton Universe is not built solely through the use of crossovers. Crossovers are merely one vehicle by which I have expanded on Mr. Farmer's original work, which is based primarily on genealogical research. This volume incorporates many more characters that I and other Wold Newton researchers have added to the Wold Newton Family tree via the genealogical method.

[10] Regarding parodies, I am much more likely to include a parody that uses original characters to spoof a genre, such as the Austin Powers movies which spoof the genre of spy films, than I am to include parodies that substantially change existing WNU characters, such as those which cast Sherlock Holmes as an addlepated bumbler, or James Bond as a cross-dresser. Nevertheless, I have doubtless bent or broken this rule once or twice.

[11] It is undisputed that Farmer's line about Lois Lane and Clark kent can be characterized as a "throwaway line." In fact, when I spoke to him about in in July 2005, he characterized it as a "joke." Nonetheless, some Wold Newton scholarship regarding the inclusion of comic book superheroes has arisen as a result of his joke, and thus the discussion of how to handle the inclusion of superheroes in an expanded Wold Newton Universe is relevant.

[12] As an example, the inclusion of the character Clive Reston (*Master of Kung Fu* comic series) left open the question of his parentage. It was established

in the series that James Bond was Reston's father, and his great uncle was Sherlock Holmes. Wold Newton contributor Matthew Baugh postulated that Mycroft Holmes was Reston's grandfather, and that Mycroft Holmes had a daughter who had an affair with James Bond. I named the daughter "Shrinking" Violet Holmes, married her off to stuffy agent Charles Beauregard, Jr., and gave Violet and Bond's child his real name: Clive Reston Beauregard. Viola, we have a small bit of speculation, which fills in a hole in the Wold Newton Family tree.

[13] An example of reconciliation is my explanation in the *Crossover Chronology* of the history of Professor Moriarty and Captain Nemo, and the inclusion of Rick Lai's "The Secret History of Captain Nemo." Lai views some events as completely fictional, while Starr and Farmer believe other events to be fictional. My explanation views all the recorded events as having happened, and attempts to meld them together, thus rescuing the Prince Dakkar character and the events of Jules Verne's *The Mysterious Island* from the fictional oblivion to which Starr consigned them.

[14] An example here is my answer to the burning question raised by the inclusion of H.G. Wells' *The War of the Worlds* (through Sherlock Holmes and *League of Extraordinary Gentlemen* crossovers), Superman (through a 1942 Green Hornet crossover), and *The X-Files* (connected to the Cthulhu Mythos): if humanity has an established history of contact with extra-terrestrial beings, why is Dana Scully such a disbeliever in alien life? My answer is contained in the *Crossover Chronology*, and it is conjecture, but it is conjecture within the established facts and boundaries of the Wold Newton Universe.

[15] An example of this is Dennis Power's conjectural father-son relationship between evil genius Fu Manchu and master detective Charlie Chan. I have chosen to accept Power's theories, and thus have added Charlie Chan to Farmer's original Wold Newton Family tree; the addition of a viable Charlie Chan crossover bolsters Chan's presence in the WNU.

[16] Straight Dope Advisory Board.

[17] The Diogenes Club.

[18] Straight Dope.

[19] Quoted in Straight Dope.

[20] Loki Carbis suggested the Venn diagram metaphor.

[21] These examples are given for the sake of illustration. Some of them are contentious and not settled. For example, Win Eckert pointed out to me that Ian Fleming was strongly influenced by "clubland heroes" such as H.C. McNeile's Bulldog Drummond, and so he asserts that the Reilly connection may not be entirely valid.

[22] The name for this Woldview intentionally suggests Philip joSé Farmer.

[23] Many of the principles and concepts below were posted to the Wold Newton

discussion list on Yahoo Groups by members of the list. I have revised all of the posts that serve as the sources for these materials. I identify the poster in these footnotes, but for ease of reading I do not put their words into quotes. In many ways this article is a group effort. I wrote it in an attempt to elucidate the ideas that lie behind the Wold Newton articles, but I have drawn on a lot of discussion on the Yahoo Wold Newton group and private email with Wold Newton scholars.

[24] Chuck Loridans.

[25] Writer's fiat from Jean-Marc Lofficier and Win Eckert. Stewart's principle from Joe Littrell.

[26] Based upon posts by John W. Leys and Joe Littrell.

[27] Laura Brady, director of The Center for Writing Excellence at West Virginia University, offers this definition of discourse communities: "Most people, on any given day, move between and within several communities. They encounter their families, their neighborhood, their friends, their immediate colleagues, practitioners of their profession both local and national, people who share recreational or entertainment interests, and people who share their geographic area. In each community, there are conventions about what can be talked about, what gets assumed, and how one can talk about different things. These conventions shape a discourse community."

[28] Dennis Power.

[29] A much longer and fuller version of this article can be found on Win Eckert's *An Expansion of the Wold Newton Universe* website at www.pjfarmer.com/woldnewton/Woldnewtonry.pdf. Eckert's site forms the core around which the consensus WNU flourishes.

[30] The title of the book, when published, was *Tarzan Alive*.

[31] This lineage is no longer true, if it ever was.

[32] All quotes from *Twenty Thousand Leagues under the Sea* in this article are from the English translation by Walter James Miller and Frederick Paul Walter published in 1993 by the Naval Institute Press.

[33] Cyrus Smith was re-christened Cyrus Harding in the original English translations of Verne's novel. Other characters had their names altered as well. The 2001 Modern Library translation of *The Mysterious Island* by Jordan Stump restored Verne's original names.

[34] There were really many leaders of the Sepoy Mutiny. One of the best known was Nana Sahib, a man despised for being the author of the Cawnpore atrocities. After the failure of the Sepoy Revolt, Nana Sahib was believed to have fled to Nepal. His final fate remained a mystery. Jules Verne used Nana Sahib as the villain of *The Steam House* (1880) in which the notorious rebel died a violent death. Although Verne depicted Nana Sahib as evil, the author still demonstrated sympathy for the Sepoy rebels by noting the atrocities

committed by the British in their suppression of the insurrection.

[35] Perhaps this pale appearance resulted from Verne's original intent to portray Nemo as a Polish patriot rebelling against the Russians. Verne's publisher vetoed this idea since the author's works were selling well in Russia.

[36] In 1910, the United States and Chile agreed to have an economic dispute between them arbitrated by Great Britain. A final judgment was not rendered by the British until 1911. Since the impression is given in *The Power House* that the arbitration had just commenced, the events of the novel must have taken place in 1910.

[37] Florizel also appears in Stevenson's *The Dynamiter* (1885, also known as *More Arabian Nights*).

[38] I disagree with Mr. Smith's theory about the identity of the King of Bohemia. I believe the monarch from "Scandal in Bohemia" to be the same person as King Rudolf V of Ruritania (from Anthony Hope's *The Prisoner of Zenda* (1894) and *Rupert of Hentzau* (1898)). I also believe that Stevenson's Prince Florizel from *The New Arabian Nights* and *The Dynamiter* was really a previous ruler of Ruritania. My theory is that Florizel was forced to abdicate the throne as the result of his arrest by the French police in "The Rajah's Diamond" (from *The New Arabian Nights*), and the throne was then assumed by a puritanical cousin, the father of the future Rudolf V. In "The Rajah's Diamond," Stevenson claimed that Folrizel was deposed in a "revolution." Although Florizel's title is "Prince" rather than "King," the royal Bohemian was the reigning ruler of his country in Stevenson's stories. After his overthrow, Florizel ran a cigar store in London.

[39] Robert was the first name given to Professor Moriarty by William Gillette in his 1899 play, *Sherlock Holmes*. Gillette's play was written before Doyle revealed the Professor's first name to be James in "The Adventure of the Empty House."

[40] At the time of Stevenson's story, Bernard had been handling the funds of the Italian secret society for "six years" since "a period of great depression." The depression would seem to be the economic downturn that transpired in 1837 since the Carbornari's influence peaked in the 1830s.

[41] For details of the real Nine and its fraudulent counterpoint, consult Talbot Mundy's *The Nine Unknown* (1924).

[42] This Parker would later play a minor role in the events of Conan Doyle's "The Adventure of the Empty House".

[43] The liaison between John Clay and Urania Moriarty was postulated by Philip José Farmer in *Doc Savage: His Apocalyptic Life*.

[44] A minor character named Dr. Caber appeared in *The Other Log of Phileas Fogg*, but Philip José Farmer never explained the relationship between this Dr. Caber and Lord Dunsany's creation. Perhaps Mr. Farmer toyed with making

Dunsany's Caber an immortal before opting to portray him as Professor Moriarty's grandson.

[45] John Clay's trip to France is based on Philip José Farmer's theory in *Doc Savage: His Apocalyptic Life* that Holmes's adversary became Colonel Clay, the master of disguise from Grant Allen's *An African Millionaire* (1897). Colonel Clay had learned to construct wax masks by making figures at the Grevin Museum in Paris. The Grevin Museum opened in 1882.

[46] In "The Bloodhound" from *The Brotherhood of the Seven Kings,* Madame

was her exact double. When the woman died from natural causes, Koluchy's agents stole the body. Carefully preserved in a frozen chamber, Koluchy would use the corpse to create the illusion of her own death. Noel Moriarty (alias Andrew Lumley) could have employed a similar ruse with his brother's body.

[47] Medina's organization was never given a name in *The Three Hostages*, but its description is very similar to the earlier group led by Andrew Lumley. Subordinate to Medina in the Krafthaus was his cousin, the criminal known as Carl Peterson. In McNeile's *Bulldog Drummond* (1920), one of Peterson's henchmen called his leader's organization the Brotherhood. Since the Krafthaus resulted from a merger of the Brotherhood of Seven Kings with the Moriarty gang, some members referred to the syndicate led by Lumley and Medina as the Brotherhood.

[48] Sandy Arbuthnot, Richard Hannay's chief comrade in-arms, investigated Medina's background, and concluded "the man was one vast lie." However, Arbuthnot was convinced that Medina was Irish with some Latin ancestry.

[49] In *The Three Hostages*, Hannay overheard Dominick and the Blind Spinner talking in a strange foreign language. Hannay suspected that this was an ancient dialect of Ireland, but it was actually a secret language originally employed by the Brotherhood of the Seven Kings.

[50] The story of Yitzik Baline, aka Rick Blaine, is told in Michael Walsh's *As Time Goes By* (Warner Books, 1998), a companion novel to the feature film *Casablanca.*

[51] *The Private Life of Tarzan*, by Philip José Farmer, Doubleday, 1972.

[52] True, it was obviously not simple in 1969, but it probably would have been simple in 1912 when the story first appeared, and for the next few years, which is when ERB would have been concerned about someone trying to find out the true identity of the young nobleman. —ed.

[53] DPO is D. Peter Ogden, the editor of *ERBANIA*. Mr. Farmer's article is in reply to Mr. Ogden's article "The Red Herring."

[54] John Paul Clayton and John "Korak" Drummond.

[55] Quote from *The Avenger* n15, *House of Death*, CHAPTER XVII, "Hells

Host": "Carmella's screams kept sounding because she and Nellie had not plunged down with the rest of the stuff. And that was due to Nellie's almost super human agility. As had been demonstrated when she had outwitted the mastiff, she was trained in traveling high among branches of trees."

[56] The Avenger, leader of Justice, Inc, whose adventures were recorded in the pulp magazine *The Avenger* written by Paul Ernst under the house name Kenneth Robeson.

[57] The source is *The Yellow Hoard* by Kenneth Robeson, Chapter II, "Television Work-Out." Quote: "One, a little boy with black hair, came out with a girl of twenty-three or so… "

[58] Available on *The Wold Newton Universe* website.

[59] The Avenger n2, *The Yellow Hoard*, Chapter III, "Mexican Bricks and Murder."

[60] *Tarzan of the Apes*, Chapter XIII, "His Own Kind."

[61] In his insightful article "The Good Ship Orion," John L. Vellutini dismisses Farmer's statement that Aronnaxe Land is Doc's mother. He can see no reason to accept her as Doc's mother other than Farmer's unsupported statement. I think, however, that the present article explains Farmer's reasoning. As for those, like Vellutini, who note that Wolf Larsen appears to die at the end of *The Sea-Wolf*, recall Maud Brewster's words when his body is found: "But he still lives." Similarly, there is evidence that Professor Moriarty survived his terrible plunge from Reichenbach Falls when we remember Sherlock Holmes' contention that "I give you my word I seemed to hear Moriarty's voice screaming at me out of the abyss."

[62] Though Mr. Vellutini was wrong in his dismissal of Aronnaxe Larsen as the mother of Doc Savage, he was dead-on in connecting Doc with the Cthulhu Mythos. Some more details of this are provided in the introduction to Farmer's fragmentary Doc Caliban novel *The Monster on Hold.*

[63] There is an incongruity in Farmer's writings regarding Kickaha's relationship to Phileas Fogg. Chapter VIII in *The Lavalite World* reads: "Philea Jane's parents were of the English landed gentry, though his [Kickaha's] great-grandfather had married a Parsi woman." This is apparently a reference to Phileas Fogg, who married the Parsi Aouda Jejeebhoy in 1872. Thus, Farmer seems to be stating that Kickaha's great-grandfather is Phileas Fogg. However, according to the information in *Doc Savage: His Apocalyptic Life*, Phileas Fogg is Kickaha's grand*uncle*, not his great-grandfather. I had the opportunity to clear up this discrepancy in a conversation with Mr. Farmer, in which he stated that in the time between writing the biography and *The Lavalite World* he had forgotten the exact lineage. The correct relationship is as described in *Apocalyptic Life.*

[64] There was a typo in the original publication of this article, which has been

corrected here. Mr. Farmer wrote a letter about it, which appeared in the *Baker Street Journal*, March 1972:

The December issue was, as always, very entertaining and highly informative. I was pleased to find my article, "The Two Lord Ruftons," in it. However, there is an unfortunate typo which makes it appear that I said that Gerard's Lord Rufton was the ancestor of Watson's. But I am sure that the readers are perceptive enough to see that an apostrophe and an "s" were dropped. [On page 222, line 12, "If Gerard's Rufton was the ancestor of Watson…" should be "of Watson's."] Otherwise, I may have to write another article proving that Gerard's Rufton was indeed Watson's ancestor.

[65] The various names for the "female demon" given in this paragraph were derived from an excellent book by Dudley Wright entitled *The Book of Vampires*. Originally published in 1914, it is considered to have been the first serious study of vampirism in the English language; in it Wright assembled reports of vampires from all age and from all across the globe, and discussed various theories regarding vampirism. A revised and enlarged edition appeared in 1924, and this second edition was reissued in 1973 by Causeway Books; it is the Causeway edition which I have utilized in my researches for this article.

[66] The information regarding Kane's rebellion against Yog-Sothoth was originally set forth by writer Robert Tierney; I first became aware of it through reading an article regarding Wold Newton Pre-History, written by Chris Davies and posted in the "Wold Newton Articles" section of Win Eckert's *The Wold Newton Universe* website.

[67] Wold Newton scholar Dennis Power has suggested that the legend of Lilith's sojourn in this region near the Red Sea may have been the source of the following passage from the Bible: "Wildcats shall meet with desert beasts, satyrs shall call to one another: There shall the Lilith repose, and find for herself a place to rest" (Isaiah 34:14). This quote is from the New American Bible; the New International Version gives the following translation of the same verse: "Desert creatures will meet with hyenas, and wild goats will bleat to each other; there the night creatures will also repose and find for themselves places of rest." And the King James Version of Isaiah 34:14 reads as follows: "The wild beasts of the desert shall also meet with the wild beasts of the island, and the satyr shall cry to his fellow; the screech owl also shall rest there, and find for herself a place of rest."

[68] The concept of "soul clones" utilized here is based upon information which Wold Newton researcher Chuck Loridans has shared with fellow members of the New Wold Newton Meteoritics Society, and which is discussed at much greater length at Chuck's own *MONSTAAH* website.

[69] The story from Farnari's *History of Sorcerers* was quoted at length in Dudley Wright's *The Book of Vampires*, which is where I came across it. Although Lilith is not mentioned in the story, the behavior of the wife—Nadilla—as

described in this tale seemed far too consistent with other accounts concerning Lilith and her minions for there not to have been some connection.

[70] This is a variation of a theory advanced by Dennis Power.

[71] This is another legend mentioned in Wright's *The Book of Vampires*.

[72] The historical tales of Vlad Tepes have been the subject of several books in recent years, most notably Raymond T. McNally and Radu Florescu's superb 1972 volume *In Search of Dracula*.

[73] The reference to Dracula's "dealings with the Evil One" is taken directly from comments by Dr. Abraham Van Helsing, as recorded in Bram Stoker's *Dracula*.

[74] The facts surrounding this particular sequence of events is told in much greater detail in the Topps Comics mini-series *Zorro Vs. Dracula*; the reference to Lolita Pulido's illness and convalescence is derived from research by Matthew Baugh concerning the history of Zorro, detailed later in this work.

[75] This is taken from issue number 3 of Topps' monthly *Zorro* comic book series, a story entitled "Men Aren't The Only Ones With Dual Identities," by Don McGregor and Mike Mayhew. It was this issue that first introduced the heroine Lady Rawhide, who went on to individual adventures in two comic book mini-series of her own.

[76] The encounter between Lady Rawhide and Carmelita Rodriguez takes place in issue 4 of the second *Lady Rawhide* mini-series published by Topps Comics. Win Eckert notes that the mini-series suspended publication after issue 5 with the plot unresolved, and that no further adventures of Lady Rawhide have since appeared; this led Win to offer the original suggestion that led to the writing of this article. (Win also stated that *Zorro* and *Lady Rawhide* scribe Don McGregor attempted to convince Image Comics to publish the final issues of the second *Lady Rawhide* mini-series, but was unsuccessful. "Which means," Win wrote, "we're free to speculate on our own." And so here we are…)

[77] Wright's *The Book of Vampires* relates several legends from various countries in which suicide and vampirism are linked. Win Eckert has noted that the final published issues of the *Lady Rawhide* mini-series, issue numbers 4 and 5, are wrought with lesbian overtones, with Carmelita longing for more "kisses" and even Lady Rawhide feeling a twinge of longing. Win states: "So if Lady Rawhide truly appears to be lost to her (Carmelita), this might be an additional motive for her suicide."

[78] LeFanu's *Carmilla* was first published in a short story collection called *In A Glass Darkly* in 1872, although it is more of a novella than a short story. It was one of the very first English works concerning vampirism in literature to have featured a female vampire as protagonist. Carmilla has served as

inspiration for countless vampire films, particularly the Hammer Films trilogy *The Vampire Lovers*, *Lust of a Vampire*, and *Twins of Evil*. Years later, in 1998, Kyle Marffin wrote a sequel novel entitled *Carmilla: The Return*, which weaved flashbacks from Carmilla's past together with a contemporary storyline set in the 1990s; although to date I have not obtained a copy of the sequel, I remain intrigued by a review at Amazon.com which refers to the tale's "restrained and skillful writing, a complex and believable love story, gorgeous scenery, sudden jolts of violence, and a thought-provoking final sequence that will keep you reading until the sun comes up."

[79] The influence of LeFanu's *Carmilla* upon Stoker's *Dracula* is well documented. Both Wright's *The Book of Vampires* and McNally and Florescu's *In Search of Dracula* make mention of this fact, as do numerous books about the history of horror cinema including Ivan Butler's *Horror In The Cinema* (1971), Donald Reed's *The Vampire on the Screen* (1964), and Phil Hardy's excellent *The Encyclopedia of Horror Films* (1986).

[80] This account was later fictionalized in the form of a 1970 film entitled *Las Vampiras*—also known as *The Sign of the Vampire*—starring Soledad Miranda (aka. Susan Korda) as Nadina.

[81] This tale was fictionalized in the 1973 film *The Devil's Wedding Night*, aka. *Countess Dracula*. In the film the female vampire was referred to as "Countess de Vries." It should be noted that both *The Devil's Wedding Night* and *The Sign of The Vampire* were little more than "sexploitation" spoof films; having said this, however, it should also be noted that both films seemed to adhere more closely to certain established legends concerning vampires than many a great many "legitimate" horror films that have been produced over the years.

[82] A fictionalized account of this incident was told in the 1973 film *The Legendary Curse of Lemora*.

[83] Fictionalized in the 1966 film *Theatre of Blood*.

[84] Fictionalized in the 1970 film *The Terror of the Vampires*, which was of the same "sexploitation" genre as *The Devil's Wedding Night* and *The Sign of The Vampire*.

[85] This is based on information forwarded by Dennis Power theorizing that the planet Drakulon actually existed within one of the "pocket universes" referred to in the works of Philip José Farmer.

[86] This refers to the four-part *Doctor Who* story entitled "State of Decay," originally broadcast on the BBC between November 22 and December 13, 1980; the link between the *Doctor Who* tale and Drakulon was first suggested, as best as I can recall, by Matthew Baugh. It is possible that this world was also the setting for the 1965 Italian film *Terrore nello Spazio* (released in America as *Planet of the Vampires*), which tells of a group of space travelers victimized by a vampiric alien species.

[87] The account included here of Anita/Vampirella's encounter with Urthona, her arrival on Drakulon and her subsequent return to Earth is a somewhat altered variation of an account originally shared with the New Wold Newton Meteoritics Society by Dennis Power; I especially enjoyed the way Dennis worked in a reference to the *Planet of the Apes* films and retained it in my retelling.

[88] The notion of Vampirella as late night horror show host is my reworking of the first seven issues of Warren Magazines' *Vampirella* comics series. Like Warren's other title characters—Uncle Creepy and Cousin Eerie—and the characters of Cain and Abel in DC Comics' classic *House of Secrets* and *House of Mystery* titles, Vampirella originally served as story host, introducing a variety of short anthology horror tales. Unlike Creepy or Eerie, however, Vampirella also had her own series in her book—a series of comedic horror tales written by none other than Forrest J. Ackerman. My take on this particular series of stories is that the horror/comedy tales were in fact skits that Vampirella acted in during breaks from whatever movie was being shown on her program on any particular evening. I trust that anyone who grew up near Chicago in the 1970s watching the now-classic *Creature Features* or *Son of Svenghoolie* shows—or any one of hundreds of similar horror movie programs broadcast on local stations across the country—would appreciate the reference.

[89] The long-running storyline pitting Vampirella against Chaos and introducing Conrad and Adam Van Helsing and Pendragon, written by comics legend Archie Goodwin, began in Warren's *Vampirella* issue number 8 and was reprinted by Harris Comics in the 1990s as a trade paperback entitled *Vampirella Vs. The Cult of Chaos*.

[90] The storylines that sent Vampirella back and forth in time and introduced the Granville crime family began immediately following the wrap-up of the first "Chaos" story arc and culminated with issue number 27 of *Vampirella*.

[91] This series of adventures—written by an unknown writer using the pseudonym "Flaxman Loew"—began in *Vampirella* number 28 and lasted through number 42.

[92] The Spirit, whose adventures were for a brief time published in black-and-white magazine format by Warren, made a cameo appearance in *Vampirella* issue number 50, a single-issue anniversary "epic" which brought Vampirella and several back-up features running in Warren publications at the time together for a single adventure. Despite the Spirit's presence, however, this story marked the start of a downward spiral for the Vampirella series from which (at least in the minds of many fans) it never fully recovered.

[93] The "Blood Red Queen/Starpatch/Return To Drakulon" series of stories began in *Vampirella* number 60 and lasted through number 66; it is very rightly considered by many fans to be the nadir of the series, and how the series managed to continue beyond this point remains a constant source of

wonder and bewilderment to fans who have seen far superior series—such as the aforementioned *Lady Rawhide* mini-series and the more recent *Tarzan: Rivers of Blood*—cancelled without resolution.

[94] Vampirella's career as a Hollywood "scream queen" began in issue number 67 and lasted through about number 82.

[95] The adventures noted in this paragraph occurred between issue number 90 of Warren's *Vampirella* title and the final issue, number 112, dated February 1983. An all-reprint issue, number 113, was released in 1988.

[96] The full story of Vampirella's enslavement by Ethan Shroud, her rescue and the death of Conrad van Helsing at the hands of Chelesa was told in Harris Comics' 1992 mini-series *Vampirella: Morning in America*. The story of Chelsea's return was featured in the Harris 1992 one-shot special *Vampirella's Summer Nights*, which also included solo stories featuring Adam Van Helsing and Pendragon.

[97] The information concerning Vampirella's recruitment by Lilith was apparently a plot point in Harris Comics' ongoing *Vampirella* series that was launched following the success of *Morning in America* and *Vampirella's Summer Nights*. While I have not studied the sources personally, this plot device was alluded to in the 1997 DC-Harris crossover one-shot special *Catwoman/Vampirella: The Furies*.

[98] Regarding the aforementioned *Catwoman/Vampirella* crossover story, the theory that the Catwoman depicted here is someone other than Selena Kyle is my own, conceived to reconcile the Golden Age Catwoman's inclusion in the WNU (as shown in Win Eckert's *Wold Newton Universe Crossover Chronology*) with this particular contemporary-era adventure; the further suggestion that this Catwoman is in fact the descendent of Bruce Wayne and Princess Khefretari was originally put forth by Win Eckert and refers to the 1999 DC/Dark Horse Comics mini-series *Batman/Tarzan: Claws of The Cat-Woman*. The presence of The Penguin in the *Catwoman/Vampirella* tale must be regarded as fictional. In addition, although the were-cat creature in this story referred to herself as Pantha, this was not the same Pantha whom Vampirella had met on Drakulon so many years before; this Pantha's real identity was Shari Parker, a private investigator whose lycanthropic origins were not fully explained in this particular tale.

[99] I have since learned that subsequent comics stories have depicted Vampirella's apparent death and rebirth, her battles against such enemies as Mistress Nyx and the Black Pope, and a massive war in Heaven. These stories reportedly depict Drakulon as actually being a realm of Hell itself; given that the *Vampirella* series has developed in so many unexpected, convoluted directions over the years, it does not seem too much of a stretch to accept that this so-called "realm of Hell" may yet in fact be one of Farmer's "pocket universe" as discussed earlier.

[100] Recent translations have uncovered further generations of de Grandins, describing the adventures of two of Jules de Grandin's grandsons, cousins named Arnaud de Grandin (from *Artahe: The Legacy of Jules De Grandin* by Philippe Ward) and Gilles de Grandin (from *La Fontaine de Jouvence (The Fountain of Youth)* by Philippe Ward). I shall be conducting further research into the cousin's lives and parentage.

[101] Ultimately published as *The Other Log of Phileas Fogg* (Daw, 1973) – ed.

[102] This was this last of his cases recorded in novel form since Earl Derr Biggers died shortly after the novel's release in 1932.

[103] The events of this case were released in the film *The Shanghai Cobra.* Although the film was released in 1945, the events behind it actually occurred in late 1931. The other changes to the events of the film such as the use of Number Three Son Tommy and the comic relief chauffeur were fictional additions.

[104] In addition to being extraordinarily good-looking and possessed of considerable personal magnetism he had the "best legs in England," according to Nell Gwyn, companion to King Charles.

[105] According to hir biographer Orlando was, and remains, an immortal, still living and active today. (For obvious reasons I have used the name hir biographer bestowed upon hir, rather than hir real name). How Orlando might have existed for so long, unchanged and eternally youthful, and the cause of hir sex change, must remain a mystery, although it might be speculated that Orlando in some way was given the elixir of immortality by the Eridaneans or the Capelleans.

[106] One intriguing possibility exists, however. It is conceivable that the child of Ms. Hartopp and Orlando was the cousin of Sir John Hartopp (1637?-1722) . Sir John, a noted nonconformist and political figure in England in the 17th and 18th century, was born of obscure circumstances, and became the Third Baronet of Freeby, in Leicestershire, in 1658. His son, John (1680?-1762), died without issue, and the title became extinct with him. If the figures mentioned in this article could prove descent from Ms. Hartopp it might be that the title and lands could be revived.

[107] Arno by this time was acting under the name "Heinie Himmelstoss," and it was by this name that Smith knew him. However, "Heinie" is an anti-German slur, and "Himmelstoss" means "Heaven-struck." It is clear that Arno was using a pseudonym, though his reasons for doing so—not wishing to bring shame to the family name, perhaps?—remain unknown.

[108] The Zorro stories of Johnston McCulley and most other early versions used the simple "Vega" as Don Diego's family name. The 1925 movie, *Don Q, Son of Zorro* lengthened this to "de Vega." The Disney television series changed the name to the grander "de la Vega" and most subsequent versions

have followed this. For consistency's sake I have used "Vega" throughout this article.

[109] In the movie Isabella is Princess of Nogara and Ramon becomes King when he weds her. Since Nogara is fictitious it seems reasonable to assume Isabella is actually the titled lady of a region of Spain. If the hero of *Zorro e i Tre Moscheterri* really is Ramon and Isabella's son, then Isabella must be the Countess of Seville. Ramon's family name is not given but he does not seem to have been a Vega. Though the Vegas are proud of their *hidalgo* blood, they never allude to a title as lofty as "Count" in their heritage.

[110] There are a number of possible adventures in the many Italian Zorro movies produced in the 1960s and 1970s. As most of these are unavailable or very rare in English they could not be evaluated for this article.

[111] That the legend goes back farther than Don Diego is confirmed by the 1974 version of *The Mark of Zorro*. In that movie Zorro is mentioned before Diego ever assumes his identity. One of Diego's classmates in Madrid jokes that only Zorro makes the mark of the 'Z,' which suggests that Zorro is already a legendary character in Spain.

[112] The name of Diego's mother is never given in the McCulley stories. In the 1940 movie *The Mark of Zorro* she is Isabella; in the New World television series she is Elena; and in *Zorro and the Jaguar Warriors* she is Rosa. This article assumes that the first name given her, Isabella, is the correct one.

[113] A different version of the story is told in the Walt Disney television series. In the episode "Zorro's Secret Passage," Diego tells Bernardo that his grandfather built the passage. It is never made clear why Don Alejandro would have been unaware of it were this the case. The dates of this timeline make it impossible that there was an earlier generation of settlers before Don Alejandro's time.

[114] Isabella is alive and well in the 1940 version of *The Mark of Zorro*. Unfortunately, this must be discounted as fictional in this chronology. Every other account makes a point of the fact that Don Alejandro is a widower.

[115] There is a serious inconsistency regarding Bernardo in the McCulley stories. In *Zorro Rides Again* Bernardo finds a wounded Zorro and nurses him back to health. Eventually he becomes Don Diego's devoted servant. McCulley seems to have forgotten that Bernardo was already Diego's servant in the first novel, *The Curse of Capistrano*.

The best known version of Bernardo is the sprightly little character played by Gene Sheldon in the Disney series. McCulley's Bernardo was a huge, powerfully built man of mixed Indian and Spanish ancestry.

[116] The story of Diego's return from Spain was never told in the McCulley stories. It was first used in the 1940 film, *The Mark of Zorro*, and was most fully told in the Disney television series. The governor's name is another

detail that McCulley never supplies. For the purposes of the article I have used the name of the villainous *alcalde* from the 1940 film *The Mark of Zorro*. Luis Quintero is a curious blend of two of McCulley's characters, the unnamed governor and Don Carlos Pulido.

[117] In the earlier versions of the story Tornado is never named. The McCulley stories refer to him simply as "Zorro's black horse." The name Tornado originated with the Disney television series.

[118] In the novel Zorro kills Capitán Ramon in a duel. He then reveals that he is Don Diego for the entire *pueblo* to see. These are both very dramatic scenes, but they are negated in McCulley's sequels, in which Ramon is still alive and only a few people know Zorro's secret identity. For purposes of this article these details are considered fictional.

[119] Lolita's illness keeps her away from California for three years. The idea that Diego believes the illness to be fatal is never hinted at in the stories, but seems a logical way to explain his other romance in her absence.

[120] Sgt. Pedro Garcia is a huge man who ultimately becomes Zorro's friend, but he is not to be confused with the later Sgt. Demetrio Lopez Garcia. Pedro Garcia is a braggart, a bully and a good enough fighter to give even Zorro a hard time in their first encounter. Though Demetrio is patterned after the first Sgt. Garcia, he is kinder, rounder and a much less competent fighter.

[121] Capitán Monastario was not only the main villain in the first season of *Zorro*, he was also the villain in the Topps Comics series, the animated Warner Brothers series, the daily newspaper strip written by Don MacGregor and the Italian comic books collected as *Zorro in Old California*. He is easily the best known of all the villains Zorro has faced.

[122] Dennis Power speculated that Sgt. Garcia and his companion Corporal Reyes might actually be a pair of inept immortals whose comic misadventures span the millennia. For more information on this pair please refer to his online article "Immortals Befuddled" on *The Secret History of the Wold Newton Universe* website.

[123] The television episodes end with Don Estivan pledging to travel to Spain to fight for his king. The idea that he travels to Santa Fe is my own invention. I speculate that Don Estivan is the grandfather of Jeff Stewart, who took up the mantle of Zorro in *The Son of Zorro*. This movie serial is set in Utah and in 1807 Santa Fe had a thriving trade in animal pelts with the native nations of Utah. Santa Fe was also one of the great cities of Spanish North America and would have been a likely place for a man like Estivan to look for a wealthy señorita to marry.

[124] There is no mention of Monastario being reassigned in any Zorro story. Still, the adventures seen in *Zorro in Old California*, the Topps Comics series and the novels by Jerome Priesler and David Bergantino cannot be reconciled unless this is the case.

[125] It is difficult to discern what the original Spanish names for characters such as Lady Rawhide, Moonstalker and Quickblade would have been. Spanish names and titles require articles and prepositions to be translated properly.

[126] There is a pair of Murietta brothers in the story of Zorro. In the Disney television series two of the Eagle's agents were Carlos and Pietro Murietta. These brothers were mercenaries from Argentina and had mastered the use of several weapons from their homeland. Carlos first appeared in the episode "The Man with the Whip" and Pietro in "The Deadly Bolas." There does not seem to be any connection between these men and either the Mesones brothers or Joaquin Murietta.

[127] It says something about Cazador's mental powers that he is able to get away with his plans for any length of time at all. Though not as powerful as it once was, the Spanish Inquisition was still active in Zorro's time. Diego and Don Alejandro's relatively innocuous comments about religious tolerance in the novel would have been considered blasphemy and treason. Don Cazador's attempts to create an alternative religion would have been a capitol offense even if it had been as benign as he pretended.

[128] The names of the four riders are unusual and sound more like aliases than true names. *Miko* means "priestess" (which is appropriate since the character is a Shinto priestess.) *Washi* is a type of paper used in origami. *Tanuki* is usually translated as "badger" or "raccoon dog" and is a small animal which appears in folklore, sometimes as a rival of the fox. *Baku* is a spirit that feeds on dreams.

[129] It is possible that Don Diego could have obtained a manual from before the time the Portuguese were expelled from Japan. The novel is incorrect in assuming this could be a manual on karate. There was no such thing as Japanese karate until Funakoshi Gichin brought it to Japan from Okinawa in 1922. Even in Okinawa the use of the tern "karate" dates from the 20th century. Presumably the manual was actually on jujitsu and the author mistakenly applied a modern term. The novel also makes the claim that Diego was uncomfortable with the idea of the fighting stances in Japanese martial arts. This seems odd since Spanish fencing relies heavily on fighting stances.

[130] Yuri the Cossack and the Dragon Riders are even more unusual than the novel lets on. From the late 1600s to 1864 Japan had a "closed country" policy which forbade travel or commerce with other nations. The riders must have taken their lives in their hands to smuggle themselves out of the country. Yuri's risks would have been even greater. He would be subject to execution simply for being a foreigner living in Japan, and anyone who sheltered him would have also risked execution.

[131] Don Diego is married in *The Mask of Zorro* to a woman called Esperanza, who both he and Monastario have known for years. The relationship in the movie is very much like the relationship of Zorro, Lolita and Capitán Ramon, but the woman cannot be Lolita. The logical choices for Esperanza's true

identity are Arcadia Flores from the recent novels, Eulalia Bandini from *Zorro, the Dallies*, Lady Rawhide, and Isabella Torres from the Warner Brothers series. McCulley's Zorro was very concerned with his *caballero* lineage and it is unlikely he would marry a commoner like Arcadia or Eulalia, and Esperanza did not demonstrate the fighting skills of Lady Rawhide. Other possibilities such as Carmelita Ramon and Panchita Cancholes from the McCulley stories and Anna Maria Verdugo would probably have stopped waiting for Diego years earlier. By process of elimination "Esperanza" is probably Isabella.

[132] In the series the fifty-year-old Zorro was too decrepit to be very effective and was played for laughs. His son was named Carlos rather than Cesar and many of the other characters have joke names such as Comandante Pico Paco, Sgt. Sepulveda and Padre Napa.

[133] Nuova Aragon is a fictional location but the large number of African-descended peons and the mention of conflict with the English suggest that this may be Honduras.

[134] Many of the familiar names such as "Diego" and "Vega" are used in this movie, but not in their usual context. Diego's love interest is Ortenzia Pulido Dolvidades and Huerta's aide is Sgt. Garcia. This is clearly a different setting and different characters. The children in the marketplace talk about Zorro even before Diego first puts on his costume. It is reasonable to assume they are referring to the legends of Zorro that have come from California.

[135] This story is based on the novel *Don Q's Love Story* by K. and Hesketh Pritchard, but is altered in several important ways. The Pritchards' story is set in the 1840s with a different hero than Don Cesar Vega, and there is no character similar to Zorro. In the story the nobleman protagonist takes the name "Don Q" as an abbreviation of "Don Quebranta Huesos." Literally translated this name is "bone breaker" and it refers to a species of vulture. The film does not say how Don Cesar comes up with his alias. Possibly he is alluding to the literary hero Don Quixote de la Mancha.

There is another character that bears the name Don Q. In the 1946 serial *Daughter of Don Q*, Dolores Quantero is the daughter of a 20th century California landowner who still retains the traditional title of "Don." There is no connection between Don Quantero and his daughter and either of the other Don Qs.

[136] There is a poetic symmetry gained in making this change. Henry Darrow was the first Hispanic actor to play the lead in any American production of *Zorro*. He was the voice of Don Diego in the animated *The New Adventures of Zorro*, the older Don Diego in *Zorro and Son*, and in the New World series he replaced Effram Zimbalist Jr. as Don Alejandro after the first season. In this timeline he was actually Don Diego in all three versions. The main problem with assuming Darrow's character is actually Don Diego is that the timeline insists that Don Diego is married and has a baby daughter by this

time. Neither was evident in the series and we must assume their omission is a fictional detail.

[137] The idea in the series was that Diego (Cesar) had taken a vacation to France for several months. Given the slowness of sea travel in the early 1800s, it is virtually impossible that he could have completed the trip in so short a time. It also fits this timeline better for Cesar to travel to Europe at the close of the New World series.

[138] The evil governor in *The Mask of Zorro* is called Rafael Montero. He is described as a man who has been Zorro's enemy consistently for fifteen years. In reconciling the stories it becomes clear that Montero is patterned on Monastario. It makes a great deal of sense to assume they are one and the same.

[139] To try to separate fact from fiction in *Zorro, the Gay Blade* there are a number of things to remember:

The character called "Don Diego Vega" is actually Don Cesar Vega.

The character called "Bunny Wigglesworth" is actually Don Antonio de la Cruz.

The character called "Capitán Estiban" is actually Don Ignacio De Soto.

The character called "Florinda" is actually Señora De Soto.

The character called "Charlotte" is actually Victoria Escalante.

Nothing this silly ever really happened to Zorro.

[140] Fellow Wold Newton researcher Dennis Power theorizes that Don del Oro was actually the historical Augustin Cosme Damián de Iturbide y Arámburu. Both Don del Oro and Iturbide were enemies of Guadeloupe Victoria who planned to set themselves up as Emperor of Mexico. Iturbide was supposedly in exile during the events of *Zorro's Fighting Legion*, but both men died in 1824. For more on the Iturbide as Don del Oro theory, please see Dennis's Zorro article on *The Secret History of the Wold Newton Universe* website.

[141] A review of Yaqui myths and legends turns up no mention of Don del Oro. There is however a figure called Omteme, which means, "He is angry." Omteme was one of a number of semi-divine rulers over the Yaqui people. When Columbus came to Mexico Omteme stood on a great hill and challenged him. Columbus treacherously attempted to shoot Omteme down three times, but each time the bullets fell short. Finally Omteme fired an arrow into the ground at Columbus' feet. The ground split open and Columbus fell into the sea and drowned. Omteme told the Yaquis he was leaving and went deep into the earth.

Like Omteme, Don del Oro lived underground, using an old mine as his headquarters. His agents used a golden arrow to announce their presence. It seems likely that the Yaquis were told that Don del Oro was Omteme come back to lead them against the Spaniards.

[142] It is not clear why the story uses the name of Juarez. The background for the story is clearly the early Mexican government of 1824 so the character must be Guadalupe Victoria.

[143] In the first chapter of *Son of Zorro* Jeff says, "*Zorro was a relative on my mother's side*."

[144] The movie claims that 'Harry' is Captain Harry Love, an American and veteran of the Mexican War of 1846. Love founded the California Rangers and is credited with killing Joaquin Murietta and his partner Three Fingered Jack in 1853. Harry Love had come to Alta California in 1839 so he could have been involved in the events of *The Mask of Zorro*, but it is unlikely. Love died in 1868 when an employee of his estranged wife shot him.

Harry's name is one of many that have been changed in the film. The following list is designed to help keep the character's actual identities straight:

"Rafael Montero" is Enrique Monastario

"Alejandro and Joaquin Murietta" are Alejandro and Joaquin Mesones

"Esperanza" is Isabella Torres

"Harry Love" is an American named Harry but is not the famous Captain Love of California history.

[145] In the McCulley novels Fray Filipe was a small thin man with a quiet manner. The Fray Filipe of the Frank Lauria novels is a rotund, boisterous man who seems to be patterned on actor Eugene Pallette's portrayal of the friar in the 1940 version of *The Mark of Zorro*. Pallette patterned his Fray Filipe on Friar Tuck, who he played in the 1938 film *The Adventures of Robin Hood*.

[146] The movie never mentions the state Jeff is living in, only that he is in Box County, which borders on Jefferson County. The only state in the Union that has two counties with names like these is Utah. Box Elder County is on the northern edge of the state and borders Jefferson County.

[147] Two of the gangs mentioned as hiding in the area are the James Gang and the Dalton Gang. This cannot be accurate. The James brothers were still in Missouri in 1865, where Jesse was recovering from a war wound. The Dalton Gang did not form until 1890. Mention of Jesse James may shed light on the real identity of the fictional town of "Twin Buttes." Las Vegas, New Mexico was a stopping place for many of the famous badmen of the Old West. Doc Holliday, Belle Starr, Curly Bill Brocius, Johnny Ringo, Mysterious Dave Mather, the Clanton Brothers and Hoodoo Brown all passed through at one time or another. Jesse James is said to have passed through the Hot Springs (just outside of Las Vegas) in July1879. There is a persistent story that Jesse had dinner with Billy the Kid at the Old Adobe Hotel and invited the Kid to join his gang. Billy's friend, Dr. Henry Hoyt, claims that The Kid turned

Jesse down.

[148] The scene in the cave hideout is the only time in any of the serials that Don Diego Vega is mentioned by name. We are told that Diego is Ken's grandfather and Ken is thrilled to discover that Moccasin has even brought along Diego's sword. There is no swordplay in the serial but Ken brandishing the rapier creates a great connection with the original Zorro.

[149] Randolph Mason was an unscrupulous lawyer who cared more about manipulating the law for the benefit of his clients than about the abstract concepts of right and wrong. While this is nothing unusual today it seemed scandalous when the stories were written. Melville Davisson Post wrote Randolph's adventures. Perry Mason, of course, is the most famous of all the defense lawyers whose practice was located in the traditional Vega home of Los Angeles, California. Erle Stanley Gardner chronicled Perry's adventures. Buck Mason's story was recounted by Edgar Rice Burroughs in *The Deputy Sheriff of Comanche County.*

[150] The Ysabel Kid is one of the series characters of author J.T. Edson.

[151] Who is this Zorro? He does not come across as a terribly capable character. The Ysabel Kid guesses his identity because he is posing as a peon but carelessly uses the accents of a Spanish grandee. (Why the other Spanish-speaking characters in the story did not notice this is unclear.) It does not seem likely that he is Ken Mason or Jeff Stewart. I believe that he is either the son of Diego Guadalupe, or of Diego's sister Maria. This would make him a native of Mexico who could speak with a refined accent and who would have some claim to the name of Zorro.

[152] It is not at all clear why Randy chose to invent a new identity rather than to call himself Zorro as others had done. Nevertheless the connection to Zorro is established in the credits which read, "Character of 'Zorro' created by Johnston McCulley." This connection is the reason the Black Whip is counted as a member of the Zorro family tree while the Zorro-like heroes of the serials *Don Daredevil Rides Again* and *The Man with the Steel Whip* are not.

[153] Actor George J. Lewis played Gordon. Lewis eventually went on to play Don Alejandro in the Walt Disney television series.

[154] In our world there is not, and never has been, a railroad connecting California to Yucatan. There is no real commerce between the two regions.

[155] Actor Noah Beery who played Marsden had previously played Gonzales in the 1920 version of *The Mark of Zorro*.)

[156] The incident is seen in the 1979 movie *The In-Laws*. Zorro is never seen or even mentioned by name in the movie, but there is no mistaking his mark.

[157] Irwin Porges's biography was ultimately published as *Edgar Rice Burroughs: the man who created Tarzan* (Brigham Young UP, 1975) --ed.

[158] Old records often use a dash to indicate an unknown name.

[159] A term for children born out of wedlock. --ed.

[160] See Sir Arthur Conan Doyle's and Watson's Sherlock Holmes case "*The Adventure of the Empty House,*" collected in The Return of Sherlock Holmes.

[161] Fu Manchu briefly alludes to the impending war in Cay Van Ash's and Dr. Petrie's Ten Years Beyond Baker Street, which suggests that Fu Manchu had contact with German spies.

[162] For more information on Fo-Hi and his daughter Madame de Medici, see Rick Lai's "*The Brotherhood of the Lotus,*" published in Nemesis Incorporated, v4, n28, December 1988.

[163] I am indebted to Rick Lai for discovering Doctor No's lineage through Julius Von Herder and Dr. Noel.

[164] From the James Bond comic strip by James D. Lawrence and Yaroslav Horak in *The Daily Express*, January-June 1976.

[165] Dorus Noel's adventures were written by Arthur J. Burks and appeared in *All Detective Magazine* in the early 1930s. For more on Dorus Noel, see Jess Nevins's *The Encyclopedia of Pulp Fiction*, MonkeyBrain Books, 2007.

[166] See *Enter the Lion* by Mycroft Holmes, edited by Michael P. Hodel and Sean M. Wright, Playboy Paperbacks, 1980.

[167] See Philip José Farmer's *The Other Log of Phileas Fogg* and *The Wold Newton Universe Crossover Chronology* (available on the *An Expansion of Philip José Farmer's Wold Newton Universe* website).

[168] Collected in *The Memoirs of Sherlock Holmes*.

[169] While many researchers have commented on the possibility that the Moriarty from the film *Kelly's Heroes* and Dean Moriarty were a part of this infamous family, I am indebted to Brad Mengel for uncovering the true genealogical relationships.

[170] See Jack London's The Sea Wolf; Dennis E. Power's "Asian Detectives in the Wold Newton Family"; Farmer's *Escape from Loki*; Christoper Paul Carey's "The Green Eyes Have It - Or Are They Blue? or Another Case of Identity Recased," and the *WNU Crossover Chronology*.

[171] See Rick Lai's "*The Secret History of Captain Nemo.*"

[172] See *The Wold Newton Universe Crossover Chronology*.

[173] Doyle's and Watson's "*The Adventure of the Red-Headed League,*" collected in The Adventures of Sherlock Holmes; see also Rick Lai's "*The Secret History of Captain Nemo.*"

[174] For more information on Dr. Caber, please read Rick Lai's "*A Brief Biography of Dr. Caber (1883-1945?)*" on *The Wold Newton Universe* website. Lai has also identified the schoolboy Moriarty who appeared in P.G.

Wodehouse's novel *The Gold Bat*, which took place in 1901, as the same person later known as Dr. Caber; see the *Crossover Chronology* for more information.

[175] See *Tarzan's Quest* by Edgar Rice Burroughs and *Tarzan Alive* by Philip José Farmer.

[176] 1966 and 1969 feature films directed by Ralph Thomas, with accompanying novelizations by Henry Reymond.

[177] See *The Beekeeper's Apprentice, Or, On the Segregation of the Queen* by Mary Russell Holmes, edited by Laurie King, St. Martin's, 1994.

[178] See Christopher Paul Carey's "The Green Eyes Have It - Or Are They Blue? or Another Case of Identity Recased," wherein *he gathers a vast amount of evidence that Captain Nemo, Professor Moriarty, Wolf Larsen, Baron Karl von Hessel (Escape from Loki), Baron Karl (Fortress of Solitude), and Dr. Karl Linningen (Up From Earth's Center) are all the same person. However, Moriarty's career beyond Reichenbach in the WNU is well-documented, and argues against him being the same person as Wolf Larsen. (Interestingly, Wold Newton investigator Dennis Power independently discovered the Moriarty-Larsen connection in his "Asian Detectives in the Wold Newton Family," although he proposed the father-son relationship which is adopted here.) Nevertheless, there is nothing to argue against Wolf Larsen being the same person as Baron von Hessel and Baron Karl. In fact, von Hessel, when revealing his age-delaying elixir to young Doc Savage, states that he was born in 1858, which is close enough to the hypothesized time-frame for the birth of Larsen to be taken as accurate. That von Hessel is actually Doc's grandfather makes the battle of wills and testing of young Clark Savage in Escape from Loki all the more remarkable.*

[179] See Sax Rohmer's The Golden Scorpion.

[180] All of the material on Death Larsen's child and grandchildren is derived from, and explained in much greater detail in, Rick Lai's "*Sirens of the Si-Fan*," published in Nemesis Incorporated, v2, n20, August 1985.

[181] The *WNU Crossover Chronology*. However, there are many theories regarding Sunlight's parentage or identity. Christopher Paul Carey, in "The Green Eyes Have It - Or Are They Blue? or, Another Case of Identity Recased," asserts that Sunlight was Countess Lily Bugov after a sex-change operation, or perhaps just in disguise. Dafydd Neal Dyar's "Sunlight, Son Bright" from *The Doc Savage Club Reader* n8 postulates that Sunlight is the son of Fu Manchu. Rick Lai's article, "The Dark Ancestry of John Sunlight" in *The Shadow/Doc Savage Quest* n11 (December 1982), contends that his parents are Carl Peterson and a daughter of Fu Manchu (not Fah Lo Suee).

[182] See the *WNU Crossover Chronology*. However, there are many theories regarding Sunlight's parentage or identity. Christopher Carey, in "The Green Eyes Have It - Or Are They Blue? or Another Case of Identity Recased,"

asserts that Sunlight was Countess Lily Bugov after a sex-change, or perhaps just in disguise. Dafydd Neal Dyar's "*Sunlight, Son Bright*" from *The Doc Savage Club Reader* n8 postulates that Sunlight is the son of Fu Manchu. Rick Lai's article, "*The Dark Ancestry of John Sunlight*" in *The Shadow/ Doc Savage Quest* n11 (December 1982), contends that his parents are Carl Peterson and a daughter of Fu Manchu (not Fah Lo Suee).

[183] See Lester Dent's (aka Kenneth Robeson) Doc Savage novel *Fortress of Solitude.*

[184] "The Golden Ghost," James Bond newspaper comic strip in *The Daily Express*, August 1970-January 1971, and subsequent strips.

[185] See Doyle's and Holmes' "The Adventure of the Lion's Mane," collected in *The Case-Book of Sherlock Holmes.*

[186] James Ian Moriarty/Murdock/Murtagh also battled Jim Brandon (of *The Avenger* radio series; not to be confused with Richard Benson of *The Avenger* pulp novel series) under the alias "Professor Krueger." Perhaps he took the name Krueger out of admiration for the exploits of G-8's arch-nemesis, Herr Doktor Krueger. In any event, his death at the conclusion of his conflict with Brandon was greatly exaggerated, although he did confess that his real name was Moriarty. See Jim Harmon's short story "The Maker of Werewolves" in *It's That Time Again 2: More New Stories of Old-Time Radio*, Jim Harmon, ed., BearManor Media, 2004.

[187] See Brad Mengel's "Watching the Detectives, Or, The Sherlock Holmes Family Tree," addressing John "Hannibal" Smith's paternal descent. His maternal descent is addressed later in this article.

[188] Once again, I am indebted to Brad Mengel for revealing the descendants of James Murtagh.

[189] Rick Lai's "*The Secret History of Captain Nemo*."

[190] See John Buchan's *The Power-House*, 1916.

[191] See David McDaniel's The Man From U.N.C.L.E. novel *The Dagger Affair* (Ace Books, 1965) for more information on the evolution of THRUSH from the ashes of the Moriarty criminal organization. *The Dagger Affair* also reveals that THRUSH stands for the Technological Hierarchy for the Removal of Undesirables and the Subjugation of Humanity.

[192] See John Buchan's The Three Hostages, 1924.

[193] See David McDaniel's The Man From U.N.C.L.E. novel *The Rainbow Affair* (Ace Books, 1967).

[194] For complete information see Rick Lai's "*The Brotherhood of the Lotus*," in Nemesis Incorporated, v4, n28, December 1988.

[195] See John Buchan's The Three Hostages, 1924.

[196] For more information, see the December 1986 entry for "The Doomsday Book," listed on the *WNU Crossover Chronology*.

[197] See H. Rider Haggard's *Allan Quatermain* and Philip José Farmer's *The Adventure of Peerless Peer*. *Peerless Peer* states that Nylepthah was the granddaughter of both Curtis and Good. However, according to the chronological researches of Rick Lai, *Allan Quatermain* took place in 1885-1886. Lai continues: "Watson married the granddaughter of Curtis and Good in 1916. The Zu-Vendis brides of those two Englishmen could only have given birth to children no earlier than 1887. This means that the parents of Watson's wife had a child when they were both about fifteen years old, and Watson may have married a fourteen-year-old girl. Maybe the Zu-Vendis language was misunderstood by Tarzan and Holmes, and Watson's wife was only the daughter of Curtis or Good." Curtis is a more likely candidate since Haggard never mentioned Captain Good marrying.

[198] "Asian Detectives in the Wold Newton Family" by Dennis Power posits that Charlie Chan was a son of Fu Manchu. And as previously noted in this article, Myra Reldon was the daughter of Fah Lo Suee and Dominick Medina-Moriarty. It should also be noted that one prominent Wold Newton Family member, Shang Chi, the son of Fu Manchu, was also descended from Doc Savage. In the 1920s, Savage spent time adventuring in Asia under the name Doctor Francis Ardan. Shang Chi's mother was the clone of Ardan's daughter, Doctor Justine Ducharme, as told in my "The Vanishing Devil" (*Tales of the Shadowmen Volume 1: The Modern Babylon*, Jean-Marc and Randy Lofficier, eds., Black Coat Press, 2005). Justine's clone was also the mother of Fu Manchu's concubine, Ducharme. Ducharme's father was Pao Tcheou, Fu Manchu's cousin.

[199] First published in *The Cornhill Magazine*, 1890; reprinted in *The Captain of the Polestar, and Other Stories*.

[200] First printed as "*The Savage Reversion*" in Golden Perils, v1, n4, May 1986.

[201] For more on Victor Savage's relationship to the Savage/Wildman line of Doc Savage, please see Rick Lai's *Complete Chronology of Bronze;* see also Brad Mengel's "What's In a Name?" on *The Wold Newton Universe* website. Nayland Smith was four years old when the incident with Culverton Smith took place. Surely Culverton was hanged shortly thereafter. There was probably very little discussion of Culverton in young Nayland Smith's household. Many years later, in 1914, when Dr. Petrie teamed with Sherlock Holmes to rescue Holmes' nephew, Nayland Smith, from the clutches of Dr. Fu Manchu, there was no mention of the familial relationship between Holmes and Smith. Now we know why. Holmes had put away Smith's paternal grandfather, admittedly an evil man. Dr. Petrie, the soul of discretion, failed to mention their relationship in order to spare Smith and his family any embarrassment over his grandfather's misdeeds and capture by Holmes.

[202] *The Idler*, March 1892, collected in *Masterworks of Crime and Mystery* and *The Horror of the Heights and Other Tales of Suspense.*

[203] Published in *Harper's New Monthly Magazine*, October 1892; and in *The Great Keinplatz Experiment*, George H. Doran, New York.

[204] Henry Smith biographical background is derived from his "Detective's Who's Who" entry in the anthology *Four-&-Twenty Bloodhounds*, edited by Anthony Boucher, Mystery Writers of America, 1950.

[205] *The Strand Magazine*, December 1912; collected in *Smith and the Pharaohs and Other Tales*, 1920.

[206] Paul Ernst's (aka Kenneth Robeson) pulp novel *Justice, Inc.*, 1939.

[207] See Chuck Loridans's "The Daughters of Greystoke."

[208] Also released as *The Fighting Pimpernel*, directed by and starring Leslie Howard, who not coincidentally also played *The Scarlet Pimpernel* in the 1934 film version of Baroness Orczy's novel.

[209] For information on Joan Blakeney, Joan Fielding, and the three male Blakeneys described here, see my "'They Seek Him There...': The Demmed Fine Blakeney Family Tree" on *The Wold Newton Universe* website.

[210] Archie Goodwin was the grandson of Sherlock Holmes, as theorized by William S. Baring-Gould in his *Nero Wolfe of West Thirty-Fifth Street.*

[211] See Rick Lai's "*The Brotherhood of the Lotus*," published in Nemesis Incorporated, v4, n28, December 1988.

[212] The information on the Black Lotus is derived from Tom Johnson's article, "The Black Lotus," *Echoes* n32, August 1987. The three Black Lotus stories were written by James Reasoner under the pseudonym Brett Halliday.

[213] See Matthew Baugh's "Agent in the Shadows: The Life and Career of Cliff Marsland" on *The Wold Newton Universe* website. However, Mark Brown's "The Magnificent Gordons" posits a genealogy for John Gordon that is not compatible with that of Nayland Smith.

[214] See "The Adventure of the Camberwell Beauty" in *The Return of Solar Pons* by August Derleth. Also see Rick Lai's "The Brotherhood of the Lotus," in *Nemesis Incorporated*, v4, n28, December 1988.

[215] According to Brad Mengel's "The Land Family," on *The Wold Newton Chronicles* website, "the fifth child of Ned and Marie Land, Peter, married Belgian immigrant Yvette Poirot, who was the younger sister of famed Belgian detective Hercule Poirot. The pair had one daughter Erica, who married man by the last name of Shayne. They had a son and a daughter." The son was Mike Shayne, Sr. Further research reveals that Mike Shayne, Sr.'s father's name was Thomas Matthew Shayne, the same Thomas Shayne who was a friend of Hugo Danner, had been disinherited by his family for his wastrel ways, and was killed during the Great War, as seen in Philip Wylie's novel

Gladiator, Alfred A. Knopf, 1930.

[216] See Brad Mengel's "Watching the Detectives, Or, The Sherlock Holmes Family Tree."

[217] See Burl Barer's novelization of the 1997 motion picture *The Saint*, directed by Phillip Noyce; see also Mengel's "Watching the Detectives, Or, The Sherlock Holmes Family Tree."

[218] See Sax Rohmer's *The Daughter of Fu Manchu* and *The Mask of Fu Manchu*.

[219] Marvel Comics' *Master of Kung Fu*, n61 and 63.

[220] See *Ten Years Beyond Baker Street* and *The Fires of Fu Manchu* by Dr. Petrie, edited by Cay Van Ash.

[221] Dr. Petrie's full name was revealed in Evelyn A. Herzog's "*On Finding Petrie's Correct Name*," in *The Rohmer Review* n18, Spring/Summer 1981.

[222] 1940 feature film directed by Christy Cabanne.

[223] With thanks to the genealogical researchers at the *Company of Crimson* website.

[224] According to Jean-Marc Lofficier, the name Fantômas wasn't used for legal reasons, but it is a Fantômas serial. For more on Fantômas, see Jean-Marc and Randy Lofficier's *Shadowmen: Heroes and Villains of French Pulp Fiction*, Black Coat Press, 2003.

[225] Lin Carter's Prince Zarkon novel *Horror Wears Blue*. Besides Prince Zarkon and his Omega Crew, George Gideon of Scotland Yard, Sir Denis Nayland Smith, Bulldog Drummond, Doc Savage's aide Monk Mayfair, and Simon Templar (The Saint) all appeared in this case.

[226] See *Ten Years Beyond Baker Street* and *The Fires of Fu Manchu* by Dr. Petrie, edited by Cay Van Ash.

[227] *The Avengers* episode "Warlock," first broadcast January 26, 1963, provides Mrs. Cathy Gale's birth date and background.

[228] *The Avengers* novel *Too Many Targets*, by John Peel and Dave Rogers, St. Martin's Press, November 1990.

[229] Hugh Drummond was the hero of a series of post-WWI adventures written by H.C. McNeile.

[230] This of course was *Tarzan of the Apes*.

[231] This American ace with the hallucinogenic problems was the renowned G-8. How many of the fantastic elements contained in his chronicles are truly the product of madness and how many are true events remains undetermined.

[232] Kentov most likely did land safely because there is good reason to believe that he became the vigilante known as The Shadow, as chronicled by Walter

Gibson, aka Maxwell Grant.

[233] See the *London Times*, 6 January 1983. "Sherlock Holmes' Birthday Present… New adventures found!"

[234] As it would turn out, Tarzan was mistaken about Jane being killed. The Germans had substituted another woman's burnt corpse for Jane Clayton's body and placed upon it some jewelry that would identify the body as Jane's. They wished for Jane to take them to fabled Opar without Tarzan's interference.

[235] Although this may have nothing to do with it the lax record keeping, it is stated in *The Other Log of Phileas Fogg* that the Jejeebhoys were long-time Eridanean agents.

[236] John Clayton's stint in the Corps of Madras Sappers and Miners, and his mauling by a tiger in India was noted in *Tarzan Alive*, p. 283. The fact that John Clayton traveled with Colonel Moran and that his mauling was described in *Three Months in the Jungle* is stated in *Tarzan Alive*.

[237] The Jahangir meteorite of India was an iron meteorite that fell on April 10, 1621. Like its sister rock, the Wold Newton meteorite of 1795, its unique composition gave off an ionization that caused beneficial mutations in those people and animals who happened to be near the impact. Although many of the special traits remained unknown due to the isolation and then the dispersal of the descendents of those who had been exposed to the Jahangir meteorite, often, recessive genes will crop up among these descendents. Although the identities of those exposed to the Jahangir meteorite have been lost and so the exact family trees probably will not be revealed, sometimes certain people can be identified as probable descendents of those at the impact. It was realized that there was something special about this rock because the Emperor Jahangir, the fourth Mughal ruler of India, ordered that two swords, a dagger, and a knife be forged from the meteorite, which was believed to possess magical powers. Only the knife is still known to exist.

[238] According to Norse legend, Siegfried gained the ability to understand the songs of birds by ingesting Dragon's blood. *Teutonic Myth and Legend*, Chapter XXVII, by Donald A. Mackenzie.

[239] Of course Dr Siger Holmes was not the first remarkable Holmes.

[240] See The Childhood of Sherlock Holmes by Mona Morstein and The Strange Adventures of Sherlock Holmes by Hilary Bailey.

[241] See Baring Gould's *Sherlock Holmes of Baker Street* and Farmer's *Tarzan Alive*.

[242] *Game* magazine, July 1976.

[243] Thanks to the researches of Mike Winkle the following information is available. Fetlock Jones' father Charles was the brother of Andrew Jones. Andrew Jones was the father of Henry Jones, Sr. Andrew and Charles'

grandmother was Violet Yvonne Blakeney who married a descendant of Tom Jones. Andrew married Branwen Marias, the daughter of Allan Quatermain and his first wife Marie, and had two children, Henry and Marie Jones. Henry Jones married Caroline, the daughter of a wealthy Virginian family (it is still under investigation if this is the Carter family) and they had two children: Henry Jones, Jr. and Sara. Unfortunately, Sara passed away shortly after birth due to yellow fever (*The Young Indiana Jones Chronicles*, "China, March 1910"). At some point after 1950 Henry Jones, Jr., better known as Indiana Jones, married Dawn Sandberg and had at least two children, Henry III and a daughter. Henry III had two children, nuclear physicist Dr. Christmas Jones and Henry IV, or "Harry." The daughter had two children: "Spike" and Lucy. Dawn's sister Naomi Sandberg had a son, Blair, out of wedlock. Indy became a father figure to the boy and inspired him to an anthropologist. Blair's greatest work was the study of "The Sentinel," a phenomenon recorded by Richard Burton (a very distant relative). Blair was able to study the first urban sentinel, Det. James Ellison of the Cascade Police Department (*The Sentinel* television series).

[244] Challenger's experiment to prove, through drilling, that the Earth was a living organism was successful on that occasion, but like the cold fusion experiment of Dr. Emma Russell in 1996, it has never been able to be repeated.

[245] "When the World Screamed" by Sir Arthur Conan Doyle and *Tom Jones* by Jonathon Fielding.

[246] Scooby Doolittle, the grandson of Dr. John Dolittle, assisted Davy Jones. It appears that John Dolittle's son was constantly accused of being lazy and so he added an extra "o" to make the family name Doolittle.

[247] For more information, see Dennis Power's article "Mystery Inc." on *The Secret History of the WNU* website.

[248] *Tomb Raider* comics and films.

[249] *Palos of the Dog Star Pack*, *The Mouthpiece of Zitu*, and *Jason, Son of Jason* by J. U. Geisy.

[250] Sherrinford reportedly died in 1887 during the case recorded as *All-Consuming Fire* by John H. Watson and Prof. Bernice Summerfield, edited by Andy Lane. (In the book, Sherrinford, and the elder god he worshipped, Azathoth, were transported to the 1906 San Francisco Earthquake where they died, but as far we are concerned they effectively died in 1887.) But *All-Consuming Fire* in fact suggests this was not the case. After Watson's description of the death of Sherrinford we find this quote by Prof. Summerfield: "A lot of facts have been changed, mind you. I don't remember half of these things happening" (p. 302). This suggests that Sherrinford did not die, but was in fact saved. Baring-Gould reports that in 1896, Sherrinford was involved with black magic rituals and murder, from which his brother Sherlock had to

save him. Also, Anthony Boucher reported that it was not Sherlock Holmes but rather Sherrinford who solved the post-Hiatus cases (see "Was the Later Holmes an Impostor?" by Anthony Boucher in *Profile By Gaslight*).

The truth is Sherrinford did not die and after some recuperation began his own career as a detective, but not a consulting detective like Sherlock. He was an occult investigator. According to my research, his cousin Doctor Verner, who had bought Dr Watson's practice, aided him. (Verner had his own adventure recorded by Anthony Boucher: "The Adventure of the Empty Man.") It appears that when Dr. Verner's records of these cases were published, they were altered by their editors and sold as Sherlock Holmes stories written by Doctor Watson. So in any case involving Sherlock Holmes facing the occult it may in fact be one of Sherrinford's adventures.

[251] Julian Symons, *The Great Detectives*; Ellery Queen, *The Roman Hat Mystery*; Ellery Queen Jr. series; and the Gulliver Queen series.

[252] *The Lost World*, 1960 feature film.

[253] *Shirley Holmes* television program.

[254] *The Curse of the Nibelung* by Marcel D'Agneau and "The Affair of the Midnight Midget" by Ardath Mayhar.

[255] See the film *Spy Game*.

[256] *The Baker Street Mysteries* series by Thomas Brace Haughey.

[257] For more information see Matthew Baugh's "The Shang Chi Chronology" on *The Wold Newton Universe* website.

[258] See *X Esquire* by Leslie Charteris.

[259] The Baron was the hero of a series of novels by Anthony Morton, aka John Creasy.

[260] *The Saint*, 1997 feature film.

[261] *The Real McCoy*, 1993 feature film.

[262] See *The Strange Case of the End of Civilisation as We Know It*.

[263] See *The World Is Not Enough* and subsequent James Bond films and novels.

[264] Irene Adler also had two children with her husband Godfrey Norton: Christine Norton and Irene Norton. Irene Norton was also known as Nina Vassilievna.

[265] See *A Matter of Time* by James P. O'Neill.

[266] See *The Canary Trainer* by Nicholas Meyer and "Irene, Good Night" by D. R. Benson, *Ellery Queen's Mystery Magazine,* January 1984.

[267] See John T. Lescroart's *Son of Holmes* and *Rasputin's Revenge*.

[268] See the series by Rex Stout.

[269] See the series by Denny Martin Flinn.

[270] See *Sherlock Holmes in New York*, as well as *Sherlock Holmes and the Skull of Death* by Robert E. McClellan.

[271] See *The Adamantine Sherlock Holmes* by Alexander Jack, written under the pseudonym "Hapi."

[272] See *Law and Order: Criminal Intent.*

[273] *Cannon* television series.

[274] *Jake and the Fatman* television series.

[275] *Callan* television series.

[276] *The Equalizer* television series.

[277] *Now And Again* television series. For more information, see my article "Super-Soldiers" on *The Wold Newton Chronicles* website.

[278] See *Sherlock Holmes's War of the Worlds* by Manly W. Wellman and Wade Wellman.

[279] See the Philo Vance series by "S.S. Van Dine" (Willard Huntington Wright), *The Lusitania Murders* by Max Allan Collins and *The Last of Mr. Sherlock Holmes* by August Derleth.

[280] Sherlock Holmes II also appears in "The Curious Case of the Dead-Drunk Driver" by Richard Givan.

[281] See Basil Mitchell's *The Holmeses of Baker Street* stage play and Terrance Dicks' *Baker Street Irregulars* series.

[282] For more information on Sherlock III see *Sherlock's Logic* by William Neblett; for more on Richard Holmes see *Drop Dead* by George Bagby, aka Aaron Marc Stein.

[283] *Crossing Jordan* television series.

[284] See *The Adventures of Sherlock Holmes' Daughter* by Ian McTavish for more on Minerva Holmes; see *The Secret of Sherlock Holmes* by Gary F. Boothe for more on Alice La Graine.

[285] See *The Execution of Newcome Bowles* by Alan D. Mickle.

[286] See *Ms. Holmes of Baker Street* by C. Alan Bradley; "Sherlock Holmes' Daughter" by H. H. Ballard, *The Brown Book of Boston*, April 1905; and "Sherlock's Bastard Daughter" by David Maleh, *Adam* magazine, September 1976, respectively.

[287] An explanation of vampire "births" is in order here. According to Fred Saberhagen, when a vampire bites a woman, his/her DNA is integrated into the ova of the woman. When this ovum is fertilised it then splits into twins. One will be a normal human and the other will bear vampiric traits. In effect these twins have three parents.

[288] See Geoffrey Landis' "A Quiet Evening in the Gaslight" in *Alternate Outlaws*, edited by Mike Resnick.

[289] See the series of short stories by Jack Ritchie.

[290] See *Sophie of Kravonia* by Anthony Hope.

[291] See Hilary Bailey's *The Adventures of Charlotte Holmes*.

[292] See *The Wire in the Blood*, *The Mermaids Singing* and *The Last Temptation* by Val McDermid.

[293] See *The A-Team* television show.

[294] See "The Black Lotus", "Death from the Sky", and "Doomsday Island" short stories in *Mike Shayne Mystery Magazine*.

[295] See the Continental Op stories and *The Fat Man* radio series by Dashiell Hammett.

[296] See Marvel Comics' *Shang Chi: Master of Kung Fu*. For more information on the Smiths and some of their other relatives, please see "The Dynasty of Fu Manchu" section of Win Eckert's "Who's Going to Take Over the World When I'm Gone?"

[297] See the film *Legend of the Werewolf*.

[298] See *Columbo: Double Shock*.

[299] Reprinted in Peter Haining's *Sherlock Holmes Compendium*.

[300] From Carter Dickson's (aka John Dickson Carr) *Seeing Is Believing*.

[301] From John Dickson Carr's *The Plague Court Murders*.

[302] I should mention some other members of the Merrivale clan. Sir Henry's father had two younger brothers. The elder of these joined Scotland Yard and became a friend of Sherlock Holmes as seen in "The Adventure of the Shoscombe Old Place," although Watson spelled his name as Merivale. The other younger brother moved to America with his wife and had two sons, Richard and Francis. Unfortunately both he and his wife were killed and the boys, for some reason, were placed in separate orphanages. A clerical error recorded their last name as Merriwell. Frank Merriwell was later reunited with Dick. He married Inza Burrage and they had a son, Frank Jr., and a daughter.

[303] Indeed, some theorists have speculated that Solar Pons and Sir Denis Nayland Smith shared the same father. Both men share the habit of pulling on their ears while thinking. The truth is the Smiths and Pons families were quite close, and lived on neighbouring estates.

[304] *Legend* television series.

[305] See *MacGyver* television series. The other side of Mac's family is equally interesting. MacGyver's maternal grandmother was Celia Rush, sister of

Click Rush, "The Gadget Man." His maternal grandfather, Harry Jackson, was the middle child of three boys. Harry's older brother was Reginald Jackson, who assisted Richard Wentworth, "The Spider," in his battle against injustice. Harry's younger brother David was married to Marie Jones' daughter, Bronwyn (Marie Jones is the sister of Henry Jones, Sr.). David was the grandfather of SG1 team member and archaeologist Daniel Jackson.

[306] In Lin Carter's "The Descent into the Abyss: The History of the Sorcerer Haon-Dor," a Tcho-Tcho leader named E-poh lived in ancient Hyperborea. The story can be found in Robert M. Price's anthology, *The Book of Eibon* (Chaosium, 2002). This cannot be the same E-poh since Hyperborea existed anywhere from 10,000 to 750,000 years before Christ. The Hyperborean E-poh must be an earlier Tcho-Tcho leader with the same name as the ruler encountered by Eric Marsh.

[307] According to Philip José Farmer's *Doc Savage: His Apocalyptic Life* (1973, revised in 1975), Fu Manchu (born in 1840) was the illegitimate son of Sir William Clayton and Ling Ju Hai, the green-eyed daughter of a half-Chinese merchant and a Manchurian princess. William met Ling Ju Hai when he was sent to rescue her father from persecution by the ruler of Annam (modern Vietnam). My research has uncovered that Mr. Farmer was misled by Clayton's memoirs. In his rescue mission, Clayton enlisted the assistance of Dirk Struan (1798-1841), a Scottish merchant whose life was documented in James Clavell's *Tai-Pan* (1966). Ling Ju Hai slept with both Clayton and Struan, but the father of her son was the latter. From Struan, Fu Manchu not only inherited green eyes, but also a strong belief in keeping one's word and a vindictive disposition. Ling Ju Hai lied about the identity of her son's father in order to protect Struan from her father's retribution. Since Ling Ju Hai's father sent assassins after him, Clayton mistakenly believed that he had impregnated her. Since Struan also fathered a half-Chinese son, Gordon Chen, in *Tai-Pan*, the real Dr. Fo-Lan must also have been another of the merchant's illegitimate children. Fu Manchu, Gordon Chen and Fo-Lan shared the same father, but had different mothers.

[308] In Robert E. Howard's "The Black Bear Bites," a story included in *Nameless Cults* (Chaosium, 2001), the cult of Cthulhu were said to be major power in China. The priests of this cult, who were also identified as adherents of Lovecraft's Yog-Sothoth, were ruled by a Black Lama based in Mongolia. In "The Black Bear Bites," an unscrupulous Western adventurer impersonated the Black Lama for his own gain. The genuine Black Lama of Mongolia appeared in Howard's "The Return of the Sorcerer," an incomplete story first published in the *Bicentennial Tribute to Robert E. Howard* (George. T. Hamilton, 1976) and reprinted in the *New Howard Reader* n3 (November 1998). It was speculated by Daniel Harms in the first edition of *Encyclopedia Cthulhiana* (Chaosium, 1994) that the Chinese priests mentioned by Lovecraft could be the same group as the Kuen-Yuin, the Chinese sorcerers from Robert W. Chambers' "The Maker of Moons," a short story published in the 1896

book of the same name. However, the entry for "Kuen-Yuin" containing such speculation is missing from the second edition of *Encyclopedia Cthulhiana* (1998).

[309] Dr. Coogan's great-grandfather Francis Coogan, a famous vaudevillian in his day, served as an agent of The Shadow.

[310] Available online at <http://www.pjfarmer.com/woldnewton/Articles5.htm#PHRA>

[311] This statement by Phra that he does not remember much of his life before thirty years of age coincides with the statement of John Carter in *A Princess of Mars*, "I am a very old man; how old I do not know. Possibly I am a hundred, possibly more; but I cannot tell because I have never aged as other men, nor do I remember any childhood. So far as I can recollect I have always been a man, a man of about thirty. I appear today as I did forty years and more ago" (p.11).

[312]Wold Newton researchers Rutt and McConnell offer some interesting speculations concerning caverns and suspended animation in "Caves, Gas & The Great Transfer Theory."

[313] One can see here that the seeds of John Carter's personality are contained within Phra, but Phra was reactive rather than proactive in his personality. To Phra the idea of winning a kingdom by the power of his sword was mere fantasy; he did not yet have the force of personality to achieve this goal that he would as John Carter.

[314] Many such unlicensed castles were destroyed on the order of King Henry II, Richard Plantagenet's great-grandfather.

[315] This scream of fury may in fact been one of great pain as sleep-stiff muscles were suddenly forced into use.

[316] The last awakening in 1586 is a bit odd in that Phra usually awakens just as an invading force threatens England. Despite waking up close to the time of the Spanish Armada, the problems with the Spanish were not featured in this episode, except symbolically in that his main nemesis was a Spaniard. Also featured was Adam Faulkner's mechanical monstrosity gone awry, so perhaps the real villain in either Phra's or Arnold's eyes was the coming Industrial Revolution that would forever alter England.

[317] According to our researches, the editor of *A Princess of Mars* and the narrator of the various introductory frames of Burroughs' works was not Edgar Rice Burroughs but Matthew Nicholas Carter, John Carter's son. See Coogan and Power's "Burroughing Beneath the Page: The Life of Matthew Nicholas Carter."

[318] See Power and Coogan's "John Carter: Torn from Phoenician Dreams Part Two: The Lives and Times of John Carter."

[319] This change of names is documented by Farmer in "The Arms of Tarzan."

The adoption of this name may be significant considering Phra's recent loss. Caldwell means cold spring or stream, which he may have unconsciously adopted because somehow the death of Bertholde reminded him of the loss of Numidea, who had drowned in a cold stream so many centuries past.

[320] Phra's son John Caldwell continued the family tradition and became an outlaw. In explanation Farmer writes, "About all that remains to explain in the arms is the dexter supporter. Aside from its being green, it looks like the usual savage or woodman supporter. Actually, it represents the son of John Caldwell. After his father's supposed death, the son had to flee into the wilds of northern England to escape the King's officers. There he adopted a green costume and used a green-painted bow and green arrows. Because of these, he was known as The Green Archer or, sometimes, as The Green Baron. His legend was combined with that of Robert Fitzooth to create the Robin Hood legend."--from "The Arms of Tarzan."

[321] Interestingly, Wold Newton researcher Brad Mengel proposed the genealogical relationship between Kinsey Millhone and Lew Archer around the same time that I did, although his reasoning was slightly different.

[322] Unfortunately, *The Monster on Hold* was never published.

Contributors

Matthew Baugh has a B.A. in History and a Masters in Divinity. He has been a fan of pulp and heroic literature from Homer to Mallory to Edgar Rice Burroughs all his life and had worked out an early version of his Zorro article before he was aware of the Wold Newton Universe websites. Matthew is also an ordained minister who serves a church in Sedona, Arizona.

Art Bollmann has taught incarcerated juvenile delinquents in Riker's Island, done public relations for major tobacco companies, edited Victorian erotica, and spent entirely too much time in graduate school. He lives in Chicago.

Mark K. Brown discovered Edgar Rice Burroughs' Tarzan at the age of four and became a fan for life. He found Philip José Farmer's "Interview with Lord Greystoke" in a hospital waiting room nine years later and his subsequent encounter with Farmer's Wold Newton genealogies gave his life a new direction. His discovery of Win Eckert's *Wold Newton Universe* website and the realization that he was not the only lunatic out there provided him with a great deal of relief and an outlet for his speculations, as well as an inspiration for his own website. He has contributed a few articles to his and other WNU sites. His other interests include philosophy and the history of progressive rock. He is currently earning his teaching credential in high school mathematics and lives in the mountains of California with his beautiful and loving wife, Christine, three cats, and a huge quantity of books, comic books, and musical recordings.

Loki Carbis is would-be Renaissance man from Melbourne, Australia. Although he holds only one formal qualification (a Diploma of Multimedia), he has a wide-ranging knowledge of all manner of arcane and unusual subjects. (His application for a Ph.D. in Inter-Disciplinary Studies with the Banzai Institute is pending.) A particular fascination of his is the subject of time travel in popular entertainment. His other works include guides to online dating and digital music, a short story published in *The Other Side* and a recently completed novel for which he hopes to find a publisher. Loki shares his bedroom with a large and growing comic collection, and will soon be moving to another room to give the comics their space.

Christopher Paul Carey holds a B.A. in Anthropology and is currently pursuing an M.A. in Writing Popular Fiction. He has published a number of articles on the work of Hugo award-winning author and SFWA Grandmaster Philip José Farmer and contributed introductions to Farmer's latest anthology, *Pearls from Peoria*. He lives near Seattle with his wife Laura and their two cats and is at work on a science fiction novel.

Dr. Peter M. Coogan holds an M.A. in Popular Culture and a Ph.D. in American Studies. He earned his doctorate from Michigan State University in 2002 with his dissertation, "The Secret Origin of the Superhero: The Emergence of the Superhero Genre in America from Daniel Boone to Batman." He first became interested in Wold-Newtonry upon reading Philip José Farmer's *Tarzan Alive* at age thirteen and thinking, "It's all true, there is a Tarzan!" He became more interested when he learned that his great-grandfather Francis Alan Coogan, a vaudevillian and tavern owner, died in The Shadow's service. He published his first Wold Newton article, "John Carter IS Phra the Phoenician!," in 1999 and has chaired sessions on Wold-Newtonry at the Comics Arts Conference, held in conjunction with the San Diego Comic-Con International. He works as a writing specialist at Fontbonne University in St. Louis, Missouri.

Win Scott Eckert first read Philip José Farmer's *Doc Savage: His Apocalyptic Life* at the age of eight, and was instantly hooked. After graduating with a B.A. in Anthropology, and in preparation for law school, he served as a graduate assistant at the Savage Crime College in upstate New York. Thereafter, he received his Juris Doctorate. In 1997, he posted the first site on the Internet devoted to expanding Farmer's original premise of a Wold Newton Family to encompass a whole Wold Newton Universe (WNU). In addition to writing numerous articles and timelines for his and other WNU websites, Win has contributed a Wold Newton-related article to the popular graphic novel, *The Black Forest 2: Castle of Shadows*, and has penned a short story for the French pulp fiction anthology, *Tales of the Shadowmen Volume 1: The Modern Babylon*. He has also served as an expert consultant on crossovers involving characters from pulp fiction and Victorian literature for an intellectual property lawsuit concerning a major motion picture, and has participated in a panel session on Wold-Newtonry at the Comics Arts Conference at the San Diego Comic-Con

International. Win lives near Denver with his family and four felines, in a house crammed to the rafters with books, comic books, and *Star Trek* action figures.

Cheryl L. Huttner is a home-schooling mother who first discovered the Wold Newton Universe through an interest in genealogy. She served over twenty-six years in the Army, both active and reserve, and first found Mr. Farmer's biographies of Tarzan and Doc Savage in an army library. They inspired her to try to read all the books mentioned in both and to play this vast literary game of six degrees of separation. Her discovery of Win's site made her realize she was not alone in this minor obsession and she has never looked back. (Of course, her family thinks she's crazy…)

Rick Lai is a computer programmer living in Bethpage, New York. During the 1980s and 1990s, he wrote articles utilizing the Wold Newton Universe (WNU) concepts of Philip José Farmer for pulp magazine fanzines such as *Nemesis Inc.*, *Echoes*, *Golden Perils*, *Pulp Vault,* and *Pulp Collector*. Rick has also created detailed chronologies of such pulp heroes as Doc Savage and The Shadow. Recently many of these articles and chronologies have been revised and made available on Win Scott Eckert's *Wold Newton Universe* website.

Chuck "The Savage Chuck" Loridans has been participating in Wold Newton studies since 1999. "The Daughters of Greystoke" was the first article he submitted to Win Eckert. Since that time, Chuck has found his special niche, focusing his research on the classic horror icons which creep and stalk the dark, dank corners of the Wold Newton Universe (WNU). After studying art with the renowned artist Walter Paisley of the Pickman Correspondence School of Fine Arts, Chuck went on to show his art in several Louisiana galleries, illustrate for *Scary Monsters Magazine*, and write and produce several strange plays. He now teaches cartooning at the Renzi Education & Art Center in Shreveport, LA. Chuck is single, but really enjoys being the uncle of five great kids and a bunch of swell dogs and cats. Check out his WNU theories and webcomic at http://monstaah.org.

Brad Mengel lives in Australia, with his wife, daughter, dog, and cat. Over the years he has worked as a barman, teacher, and librarian. Currently, he is engaged in a study of the Aggressors, the often-violent action adventure series of the 70s, 80s, and 90s such as the

Executioner, the Destroyer and the Punisher, which he plans to turn into an encyclopaedia and one day publish. A long-time fan of the Wold Newton concept since reading about it in David Pringle's *Imaginary People* in 1987, he has been a frequent contributor to the various Wold Newton sites with articles, chronologies, and stories.

Jess Nevins was first exposed to the idea of great men and women meeting each other as a child, when his two uncles, the dwarf hunter and the albino thief, would regale him with stories of their exploits. Ever since then Jess has wanted to be one of those great men, but has instead settled for chronicling their lives. He is the author of *Heroes and Monsters: The Unofficial Companion to the League of Extraordinary Gentlemen* (2003), *A Blazing World: The Unofficial Companion to the League of Extraordinary Gentlemen, Volume Two* (2004), *The Encyclopedia of Fantastic Victoriana* (2005), *The Encyclopedia of Pulp Heroes* (2007), and *The Encyclopedia of Golden Age Superheroes* (2008). He has also served as an expert consultant on crossovers for an intellectual property lawsuit. He works in Texas as an academic librarian and lives with his wife Alicia, their menagerie (one dog, two cats, a dozen rats), and far, far too many books.

Dennis E. Power lives and works in St. Louis, Missouri. He first became aware of the Wold Newton Family when he read *Tarzan Alive* at the age of thirteen. Philip José Farmer convinced him that Tarzan was a real person. He has yet to shake that belief. These articles are his first published works. You can view his other research at *The Secret History of the Wold Newton Universe* at http://www.pjfarmer.com.

Having learned to read with the aid of his father's collection of Edgar Rice Burroughs books, **John A. Small** grew up to become an award-winning journalist, columnist and broadcaster whose work has been honored by the Oklahoma Press Association, the Society of Professional Journalists, the Associated Press, the National Newspaper Association, the Oklahoma Education Association, and the Veterans of Foreign Wars. A graduate of Olivet Nazarene University in Bourbonnais, Illinois, he has also served as project editor on a book entitled *The Men on the Sixth Floor*, concerning the assassination of President John F. Kennedy (http://home.earthlink.net/~sixthfloor/), and has worked as a freelance investigator for the Banzai Institute. A lifelong fan of the Kingston Trio and the Chieftains, he has been known to throw heavy objects at people who say they do not like the sound of the banjo or bagpipes. He and his family currently reside in Ravia, Oklahoma.

A Biographical Note about Philip José Farmer
Contributed by Mike Croteau
webmaster of the *Official Philip José Farmer Home Page*

In hindsight it is possible to look at Philip José Farmer's life and say that it was almost inevitable that he would create the Wold Newton Universe. Before laying eyes on a pulp magazine for the first time, at the tender age of eleven, he had already read the likes of Swift, Carroll, Baum, Doyle, Stevenson, Defoe, London, Burton, Twain and even Homer, among many others. Shortly before this he had discovered Edgar Rice Burroughs, arguably the center of his literary universe.

A young impressionable mind already saturated with the literature above, he was, fortunately, no snob. Entering his teenage years, with equal zeal he soaked up *Air Wonder Stories, Science Wonder Stories, The Shadow, Doc Savage, Weird Tales, Argosy, Blue Book,* and other pulps as well as the works of Dumas, Dickens, Haggard, Cooper, Cervantes, Chesterton, Shaw, Thackeray, Verne, Wells, and many, many others.

In Phil's world a great story was a great story, and a hero was a hero, no matter the source. It is the books, music, movies, and television that we are exposed to in our youth that leave the largest impressions on us. Phil was exposed to more literature and pop literature by the time he reached high school than a classroom full of college English majors. And did we mention his phenomenal ability to absorb and remember nearly everything he reads?

Not only did Phil read widely, but he also read deeply. When a subject sparked his interest he devoured it, from mythology (Greek, Norse and Amerindian), to religion and philosophy, to linguistics. Biographies of authors, and even "fan" speculations about his favorite characters in amateur publications were of keen interest to him. It was this last group, specifically articles about Sherlock Holmes, that finally led him to create the Wold Newton concept.

Well before he published his Wold Newton theory, Phil was often adding two plus two and coming up with something much more interesting than four. In the early 1950s he started with a standard science fiction tale of planetary exploration, threw in parasitology and sex and shook the sci-fi world to its core. And won a Hugo Award as the best new talent of the year for his troubles.

In the 1960s, prior to making Tarzan and Doc Savage the center pieces of his Wold Newton theory, he gave them libidos, and then a temporary sexual dysfunction, threw in Jack the Ripper for good measure and wrote a book that shocked, appalled and amazed aficionados of the two heroes (*A Feast Unknown*).

Written much earlier but finally published in the early 1970s, Farmer's Riverworld novels took real people (everyone who has ever lived in fact) and gave them fictional adventures in the afterlife. This is in part the antithesis of the Wold Newton concept where Phil postulated that Tarzan, Doc Savage, and everyone else in the Wold Newton family were real live people instead of just fictional characters as we had been led to believe. Another Hugo Award (his third) was the result.

In the world of science fiction writers, where having a more than ample imagination is the first requirement, Philip José Farmer's has long stood out as remarkable. It was the combination of this imagination, along with the recollection of the thousands of novels and stories he read, and loved, in his youth that led to the Wold Newton theory, one of his most intriguing concepts.

If Phil's development of the Wold Newton theory was not a certainty, it is certain that no one else could have done it. The chances of that are about the same as a radioactive meteorite flying over a horse-drawn carriage and causing mutations in its passengers that would, a few generations later, produce some of the most extraordinary people who ever "lived."